Praise for
Crampton of the Chr

A fun read with humour throughout … *Crime Thriller Hound*

An excellent novel, full of twists and turns, plenty of action scenes, crackling dialogue – and a great sense of fun. *Fully Booked 2016*

A highly enjoyable and well-crafted read, with a host of engaging characters. *Mrs Peabody Investigates*

An amiable romp through the shady backstreets of 1960s Brighton. *Simon Brett*

A highly entertaining, involving mystery, narrated in a charming voice, with winning characters. Highly recommended. *In Search of the Classic Mystery Novel*

A romp of a read! Very funny and very British. *The Book Trail*

Superbly crafted and breezy as a stroll along the pier, this Brighton-based murder mystery is a delight. Peter *Lovesey*

It read like a breath of fresh air and I can't wait for the next one. *Little Bookness Lane*

By the end of page one, I knew I liked Colin Crampton and author Peter Bartram's breezy writing style. *Over My Dead Body*

A little reminiscent of [Raymond] Chandler. *Bookwitch*

A rather fun and well-written cozy mystery set in 1960s Brighton. *Northern Crime*

Praise for earlier Crampton of the Chronicle mysteries …

The story is a real whodunnit in the classic mould. *M. J. Trow*

A fast-paced mystery, superbly plotted, and kept me guessing right until the end. *Don't Tell Me the Moon Is Shining*

Very highly recommended. *Midwest Book Review*

One night I stayed up until nearly 2.00 a.m. thinking: "I'll just read one more chapter". This is a huge recommendation from me. *Life of a Nerdish Mum*

Front Page Murder

A *Crampton of The Chronicle* Mystery

Front Page Murder

A *Crampton of The Chronicle* Mystery

Peter Bartram

Winchester, UK
Washington, USA

First published by Roundfire Books, 2017
Roundfire Books is an imprint of John Hunt Publishing Ltd., Laurel House, Station Approach,
Alresford, Hants, SO24 9JH, UK
office1@jhpbooks.net
www.johnhuntpublishing.com
www.roundfire-books.com

For distributor details and how to order please visit the 'Ordering' section on our website.

978 1 78535 648 3 (ebook)
ISBN: 978 1 78535 647 6

Library of Congress Control Number: 2016962423

A CIP catalogue record for this book is available from the British Library.

Design: Stuart Davies

Printed and bound by CPI Group (UK) Ltd, Croydon, CR0 4YY, UK

Also by Peter Bartram in the *Crampton of the Chronicle* series

Published by Roundfire Books:
Headline Murder
Stop Press Murder

Published online:
Murder from the Newsdesk
Murder in Capital Letters

Prologue

It always started with the same ritual.

Percy Despart opened the drawer in the small desk by the side of his artist's easel and took out his Swiss penknife. He held it for a moment and enjoyed the solid weight as it rested in his hand.

Then he pulled out the large blade and ran his finger ever so gently down the cutting edge. It was sharp but not keen enough for what he had in mind.

For Despart was planning an assassination.

He stood up from the stool on which he'd perched and crossed the room to a workbench. His whetstone was in the centre, always ready for use.

Despart looked closely at the knife's large blade. It had a pronounced curve in the centre where he'd repeatedly sharpened it. Briefly, he wondered whether he should invest in a new knife, but dismissed the idea. He'd used this knife since the day he'd first rented his studio on Brighton seafront. It was as much a valued part of the place as his easel, his palette and his tubes of oil paint.

Besides, all the other attachments on the knife were in perfect condition. Well, perhaps the bottle opener was a little worn. But the device for taking stones out of horses' hooves had never been used. Pity. He'd have liked to have been the Samaritan who came to the aid of a distressed donkey. But donkey rides had disappeared from Brighton beach years ago.

With a skill that came from long practice, he ran the blade smoothly along the whetstone. It made a pleasing humming sound. He could tell when the blade was sharp enough because the hum rose half an octave and then faded.

He raised the blade to his lips and blew gently on it.

Perfect.

He crossed back to his desk and surveyed his rack of pencils.

Years ago, he'd found an attractively weathered piece of driftwood on the beach. It must have floated in the sea for years. It was hard to say what wood. Possibly mahogany. Perhaps the jetsam from a shipwreck long ago. But he'd taken a fancy to its shape and its texture. He'd carried it back to his studio and fashioned it into a pencil holder. That's when the Swiss penknife's smaller blade had come in useful. And the little wood saw. And the marlinspike.

Now the pencil holder sat beside his drawing board with nineteen pencils standing proudly in a row, like guardsmen on parade. The pencils were graded from left to right – hard to soft: 9H hardest to the left, 9B softest to the right, the trusty standard HB in the centre.

Starting with the softest, he pressed his thumb gently against their points to test their sharpness. Most were perfect. But he used the large blade of the Swiss penknife to put an extra point on the 7B, 4B and 3B. He finished by pressing his thumb a little harder than usual on the 9H. He winced as the stiletto point drew a tiny drop of blood. He sucked his thumb to remove it.

He took a moment to glance out of the window. The Esplanade that ran alongside the beach was deserted. A cold January night was closing in. A few lazy snowflakes shone like floating nightlights as they drifted through the illuminations along the promenade. Despart drew the curtains to shut out the night and turned to his drawing board.

On the wall behind the board, he'd pinned up the ninety-nine comic picture postcards he'd drawn in earlier years. He surveyed them with pride. Perhaps they'd not sold as well as those by Donald McGill. Perhaps the critics didn't fawn over them as they did McGill's. But McGill had died last year, in 1962. If the world of comic seaside postcards needed a new star, Despart didn't see why he shouldn't pick up McGill's crown. But even if he couldn't win McGill's fame, he knew he could achieve something else.

Revenge.

Despart turned his attention back to his drawing board.

Now he was ready to draw his one hundredth comic postcard.

And this one, he'd decided, would be his most devastating assassination yet.

A character assassination.

His weapon would be his pencils.

Despart positioned a sheet of paper on his drawing board, selected a pencil and went to work. With a few deft strokes he sketched the outlines of a courtroom – the magistrate's bench, the lawyers' table, the dock in the background. He chose another pencil and drew the outline of a young woman with a voluptuous figure – bulging breasts, rounded buttocks. A lawyer. Dressed in wig and gown. Her wig was askew. She was flustered because her papers had fallen under the table. She had bent so far over to look for them her tight skirt had ridden up her legs to reveal her underwear. Despart chose a pencil with a harder lead to sketch in her lacy knickers.

Then he switched back to his original pencil to draw the other character in the scene. The magistrate. Despart's hand flew over the paper as it sketched the bald head, the pointy nose, the gawping eyes, the gaping mouth. The magistrate was leering at the barrister's behind. Despart enjoyed adding the final touches. A bead of sweat to the magistrate's brow. A dribble of saliva at the side of his mouth.

Despart sat back and admired his work. His lips twitched into a smile. He'd portrayed the cartoon magistrate as a repulsive lecher leering at the lady lawyer's underwear. But recognisable as the real-life beak he'd come to hate. The magistrate would come to regret the five-pound fine he'd imposed on Despart for being drunk and disorderly. When this postcard went on sale, it would be the magistrate's reputation that looked like the trash left behind by holidaymakers on the seafront after a hot summer's day.

And now he just needed to add the caption for the drawing:

Says the knicker-revealing barrister: "Have you seen my briefs, Your Honour?"

Replies the lecherous magistrate: "Cor! Wouldn't mind taking *them* down in evidence."

Despart shifted his Anglepoise lamp so that it shone more strongly on the sketch.

A gust of wind rattled the window.

Despart pulled the curtain to one side and looked out. The snow was falling more heavily now. It was time to leave. It would be cold walking up Edward Street to his flat. But he'd stop off for a glass or two of something warming at The Hangman's Noose.

He turned and gasped.

A figure had appeared silently in the doorway. He hadn't heard the usual creak on the stair. Or the rattle as the rickety old latch on the door had opened.

The figure frightened him because he couldn't tell whether it was a man or a woman. It was dressed in a long cloak with a large hood that threw the figure's face into deep shadow. The figure reminded him of a picture he'd once seen of the Ghost of Christmas Yet to Come in Charles Dickens's novel *A Christmas Carol*. The picture had showed a sinister shrouded figure with a black void for a face.

"Who are you?" Despart's voice quavered. "What are you?"

At least this ghost was real flesh and blood. The floorboards creaked as it moved towards him.

Silent. Purposeful.

"Keep away from me." Despart's voice rose in a shriek.

A stool toppled over as he scrambled away from his drawing board. He grabbed for his penknife. Fumbled as he pulled out the long blade. The sharp blade. Brought to an edge only minutes ago on his whetstone.

He lunged and thrust the knife viciously at the figure.

But the ghost evaded his attack. It glided to one side and seized a pencil from the rack. The pencil from the extreme left-hand side. The 9H with the hardest, sharpest point.

The ghost raised its arm. It grasped the pencil like a dagger. Despart rushed forward with another desperate thrust of the penknife. But the ghost sidestepped and the knife whistled through air.

The ghost's arm plunged in a blur of movement. The pencil flashed in the light. Despart shrieked with pain as the pencil punctured the skin in the soft part of his neck above the collarbone.

He heard a faint 'pop' as the 9H's stiletto point ruptured his windpipe. Warm, sticky blood welled in his throat.

Despart stumbled, fell to one knee. His eyes begged for mercy. He looked up at the ghost. But all he could see was a black shadow where the ghost's face should be.

And then the figure turned. Its cloak swirled around it as it retreated through the door. The ghost had disappeared before Despart, gasping helplessly for air, had fallen forward onto his face.

The last sound Despart heard was the air rushing from his lungs. Like the discordant wheeze of bagpipes when the piper has finished playing and the bag deflates.

For Percy Despart there would be no Christmases yet to come.

Chapter 1

My news editor, Frank Figgis, took a long drag on his Woodbine, blew a perfect smoke ring and said: "Have you ever attended a hanging before?"

"I once watched my mother put up some curtains in the outside lavvy," I said.

"The real thing is not so pretty."

"Neither were the curtains. She'd knocked them up out of old blackout material."

Figgis harrumphed. We were in the newsroom at the Brighton *Evening Chronicle*. It was a brisk December morning and only ten days until Christmas.

Figgis had stopped by my desk to let me know that it would be my byline – Colin Crampton, crime correspondent – on the story telling our readers that Archie Flowerdew had been hung by the neck until dead for the murder of Percy Despart.

"The whole business sounds a bit ghoulish to me," I said. "Especially as Archie is for the drop on Christmas Eve."

"At least you won't need to be in the room when the hangman pulls the lever and the poor sap falls through the trapdoor." Figgis stubbed out his ciggie and tossed the dog-end into my waste bin. "In the old days, reporters got to watch the show from a front-row seat."

"Instead, I'll be standing around outside the prison gates waiting for them to post the notice of execution," I said. "What's the point of that? We know in advance what the notice will say. It just feels like morbid curiosity."

"It's traditional. Hangings and notices of execution go together like Christmas pudding and heartburn," Figgis croaked. His sixty-a-day habit had left him with a voice that sounded like ancient bedsprings wheezing under the weight of a bouncing sumo wrestler.

"It's not traditional for Flowerdew," I said. "It's his first hanging. He doesn't get a dress rehearsal."

"The hangman does," Figgis said. "The day before, the hangman tests everything with a sack of sand about the same weight as the victim. He leaves the sack hanging overnight to stretch the rope. You could mention that when you come to write your piece."

"Any other gruesome titbits you'd like me to include?"

"Certainly not. This is a family newspaper. Just look on the hanging piece as the last chapter in a long-running story."

I nodded. It was certainly that. Since the day Despart's body had been discovered in his studio, the story had provided the paper with a string of headlines:

Police Probe Postcard Artist's Murder
Rival Artist Charged with Despart Killing
Flowerdew Remanded in Custody
Postcard Killing Trial Opens at Assizes
Jury Out in Postcard Murder
Flowerdew Guilty: Sentenced to Hang
Postcard Murder Appeal Fails

Figgis looked uncomfortably around the newsroom. The pre-deadline frenzy was building. Reporters pounded ancient typewriters like they wanted to beat them to death. Or stared at their shorthand notebooks like they were decoding an ancient codex. Or shouted down telephones at reluctant contacts who wouldn't give a straight answer to a leading question. A haze of cigarette smoke lingered under the fluorescent lights. The place smelt of tired bodies and paper dust.

Figgis's mouth twisted into the guilty smile he wore when he was about to say something truly disgraceful.

"Of course, there's one thing that could ruin our hanging headline."

"You mean if Flowerdew's plea for clemency is successful?"

Figgis nodded.

"Far be it for a man's life to deprive you of a front-page splash," I said.

"I didn't mean ..."

I held up my hand. "No need to make your excuses. The plea has been turned down."

Figgis had the grace to make an effort at looking shocked.

"That must be a big disappointment to Flowerdew's daughter."

"You're thinking of his niece, Tammy Flowerdew. Archie never married. He had no children of his own. But Tammy has run the campaign for clemency. And a one-woman campaign at that."

Figgis stroked his chin. "So that's the last we'll be hearing of Miss Flowerdew."

I leaned back in my old captain's chair. "I'm not so sure," I said.

Figgis gave his red braces a twang with his thumbs. It was a sure sign he was happy with the turn of events. Then he loped off to his office.

My telephone rang. I lifted the receiver and a voice said: "Thank heavens you're in the office, Colin. You could just be the person to save my life."

The voice belonged to Barry Hobhouse. He was a middle-aged bloke who worked as one of the subeditors on the paper. He lived with two cats in a one-roomed flat – or it may have been one cat in a two-roomed flat – in the Hanover part of town. Barry was one of life's worriers. Give him a million quid and he'd fret about what to spend it on. This morning, he sounded under more stress than usual.

"Don't worry about it, Barry," I said. "It may never happen."

He said: "It just has. I've put page nine together and the fourth column has come up fourteen slugs short."

In plain English, Barry was telling me the paper would appear with a blank space at the foot the page.

"And you'd like me to magic up some copy to fill it," I said.

"We've eight minutes to deadline."

"Leave it with me, Barry. I'll send the copy boy up with it in five minutes."

"Thanks, Colin. Terrible thing to happen on the last day before my holidays. I'm off tonight for an early Christmas break. Up to Scotland to stay with my aunt McConnachie."

"Don't pig out on haggis," I said.

He laughed and cut the connection.

I reached for my notebook and turned back a few pages. I'd been in Brighton magistrates' court the day before. There were always plenty of minor cases that were never written up for the paper. I just needed to find something long enough to fill the space.

I flipped a page. And there it was. A sorry tale with a seasonal touch. It would save Barry. And please Figgis. I reached for a couple of sheets of copy paper and rummaged in my drawer for a new piece of carbon to slip between them. Cursed that it had all gone. I crossed to fellow reporter Phil Bailey's desk – he was out of the office – and swiped a sheet from his top drawer. I put the carbon between the sheets of copy paper and rolled the set into the carriage of my old Remington. I typed:

> Harold Beecher, 26, a warehouse man from Station Road, Hove received an early Christmas present when he appeared before Brighton magistrates yesterday.
>
> The court heard that Beecher was arrested in West Street, Brighton after he had stripped to his underpants, climbed a lamp post and sung several verses of 'Rudolph, the Red-Nosed Reindeer'.
>
> Beecher told the court: "I don't know what got into me. But I think it may have been nine pints of Harvey's bitter with

whisky chasers. I realise it is wrong to sing Christmas songs in public in my underwear and I promise it will not happen again."

Chairman of the bench Sir Randolph Abercrombie told Beecher: "This is an outrage against public decency. Normally, I would send you to prison for seven days, but as it's the season of goodwill I will give you a caution. Consider it an early Christmas present."

I rolled the folios out of the typewriter, separated the two sheets from the carbon and spiked the copy. I called over to Cedric, the copy boy, and handed him the top folio.

"Take this up to Barry Hobhouse on the hurry-up," I said. "And then please bring me a new box of carbon paper. And while you're at it you'd better slip this sheet back in Phil's drawer. He's so mean he probably counts them!"

Cedric grinned. "Right you are, Mr Crampton."

He bustled off and I sat back with a nice warm feeling that I'd done Barry a good deed. But the trouble with good deeds I've often found is they come back to bite you on the bum.

Chapter 2

Freddie Barkworth downed half a pint of Harvey's best bitter at a swallow, wiped his mouth with the back of his hand and said: "I suppose Tammy Flowerdew has run out of options now the appeal for clemency has been turned down."

Freddie was the *Chronicle*'s chief photographer – a legendary lensman with a reputation for being on the spot to snap the shutter when the elements of a great picture came together in his patient viewfinder.

I sipped my gin and tonic in a manner expected of a responsible drinker and said: "She's exhausted legal options, but Tammy is not the kind of girl to accept defeat."

We were enjoying an after-work tipple in Prinny's Pleasure, a kind of drinkers' dosshouse that passed itself off as a pub. It occupied a corner site in a backstreet in the North Laine part of town. The place hadn't changed for years since the Prince Regent and Mrs Fitzherbert had reputedly held a love tryst in the rooms upstairs. To commemorate the unlikely event, a fading signboard hung from a rusting bracket above the front door. The board featured a portrait of Mrs Fitzherbert with pouting lips, a twinkle in her eye and a dead mouse hanging from her right ear. Or the latter may have been a large flake of peeling paint.

Freddie said: "So what do you suppose Tammy will do next? Anything with a good picture in it would suit me."

Freddie was a little imp of a man with big ears and a cheeky face. He reminded me of a hobbit. He'd been frustrated throughout the police investigation by the lack of picture opportunities. The cops wouldn't let him into the crime scene. And the courts barred him from the trial. Instead, he spent his time sprinting after the Black Maria that brought Flowerdew to court. He hoped to snap a picture of the poor bloke's miserable face peering through the van's window bars.

I said: "What will Tammy do next? I wish I knew."

"She's given no clues when you've spoken to her?"

"I've only interviewed her twice – once after the trial and once before the appeal court hearing. She wouldn't open up. I think she resented the coverage we gave the case. Took it as an attack on her uncle – especially when we reported the prosecution evidence. But we can only print what happens in court. I tried to explain that to her, but she won't have a word said against her uncle Archie."

"Loyal to the last, then."

"And the last is only days away now." I drained the dregs of my G&T.

Freddie nodded at my empty glass. "Another?"

I glanced towards the bar. Jeff, the landlord, was slumped on a bar stool with his head on the counter. We could hear his snores from where we sat.

A lank of his greasy hair flopped over a plate of pork pies. They'd end up stained white by his Brylcreem. But that wouldn't faze Jeff. He'd tell any finicky punter it was special Christmas mayonnaise.

"Seems a pity to wake Sleeping Beauty," I said. "Besides, I've got a better idea. Why don't we go and ask Tammy what her next move is going to be? There could be a story in it for tomorrow's paper. Maybe a picture, too."

Freddie shrugged. "Some chance. Anyway, from what you've said, she probably won't give us the time of day."

"We'll drive to her lodgings and find out."

But it looked as though we were going to be out of luck.

When we called at her lodgings – a small terraced house, a seagull's squawk from the harbour in Portslade – her landlady told us she wasn't in.

"Stomped out of the house not half an hour ago carrying a red holdall that looked as though it weighed a ton. I asked her what was in it, but she just gave me a sly grin and said, 'Just what an artist's niece needs.' She's a crafty one and no mistake; it looks like it runs in the family."

The landlady gave her name as Brenda Winklemann. "Don't forget to spell it with two Ns." She was a squat lady with a mountainous bosom that bizarrely reminded me of a holiday I'd once spent in the Peak District.

I said: "Does Tammy normally go out with the holdall?"

"Never seen it before – and you couldn't miss it in that colour. To tell you the truth, my first thought was that the girl was doing a runner to avoid paying the rent. But, to be fair to the lass, I've always found her as honest as the day is long. Twenty-three hours, isn't it?"

A droopy lid levitated briefly over her left eye like a moth in front of a flame. Brenda had winked at me.

"Did Tammy say where she was going?" I asked.

"The little madam said I'd find out soon enough."

"How?"

"She didn't say."

"Did she say what she was going to do?"

"She said, 'I'm going to do what Uncle Archie does best.' I hope she didn't mean knock off some poor bugger. Pardon my turn of phrase."

I grinned. "Don't mention it."

"As she stepped into the street, I wagged my finger at her and said, 'Don't do anything stupid.' And do you know what she turned round and said?"

"No."

" 'I won't do anything that hasn't been done before.' She had a really determined glint in her eye when she said it. That girl's going to end up in trouble."

I thanked Brenda for her help and turned to leave.

She tugged at my shoulder. "If you're writing an article about Tammy, I don't suppose you could mention I'll have a vacancy for a new lodger in a few days. Can't see the poor girl staying on after the … well, you know."

"I know," I said.

She shut the door.

Freddie and I climbed into my MGB.

"So that's got us nowhere," Freddie said. "Back to the pub?"

I thought about it for a bit. "I'm not so sure that we can't work out where Tammy's gone."

Freddie twisted in his seat and looked at me. "How so?"

"Well, Tammy told her landlady that she was going to do what her uncle Archie does best."

"Murder rival artists," Freddie said.

"Don't be flippant. What Archie indisputably did best was to draw and paint. In this case, I think it's the painting that's important."

"Why?"

"Because I've got a sneaking suspicion that red holdall was heavy because it contained paint and brushes. Remember, she told Mrs Winklemann the bag contained 'just what an artist's niece needs'."

"What would she be doing with that at this time of night?" Freddie asked.

"Think back to what Tammy said when Mrs Winklemann told her not to do anything foolish: 'I won't do anything that hasn't been done before.' But what has been done before – and only last Easter? I'll give you a clue: it used paint – lots of it."

Freddie's eyes widened. "So she's going to paint a slogan on the side of the Town Hall."

Months earlier, in April 1963, ban-the-bomb protesters on the way to their annual rally in Trafalgar Square had painted their peace symbol on the Town Hall. Council workmen had painted over it within hours. But not before Freddie had captured it for the *Chronicle*'s front page.

"If my reasoning is correct, that's where she's ultimately

heading with her holdall," I said.

"Ultimately?"

"She won't try now because there'll be too many people about. My guess is she's hiding up somewhere and will turn up at the Town Hall with her pot of paint between two and three in the morning. Nothing stirring then – not even the pigeons. The question is: can we find her?"

I looked at Freddie. He looked at me. The unspoken question that passed between us was: shall we put in the unpaid overtime for a good story?

We didn't even need to put the answer into words. We were both newspapermen.

But by two fifteen the following morning, we felt like we'd wasted the night.

"Can you think of anywhere else she might be?" Freddie asked.

I scratched my head. "We've looked in every pub in central Brighton. Every cafe, too. We searched the railway station and the bus terminus in Pool Valley. We've looked under both piers."

"So we're beaten?"

"Let's give it another half-hour," I said.

We were sitting in my MGB. I'd parked in West Street opposite the ice rink. The place looked dowdy and run down, and there were rumours it would close.

I pointed at the building site next door. A huge, new entertainment centre – a monster in concrete – was being built. "That's going to be the ugliest building in Brighton," I said to Freddie. "Even the artist's impression makes it look about as attractive as a glue factory."

"If he wasn't so fat, the old Prince Regent would be turning in his grave," Freddie said.

I slapped my hand to my forehead. "We're idiots!"

"We are?" Freddie sounded unsure.

"We've forgotten the most famous building in Brighton."

"The Royal Pavilion. Surely even Tammy wouldn't paint a slogan on that?"

I switched on the ignition, pressed the starter button and put the car into gear. I pulled out into the deserted road and raced towards the Royal Pavilion.

I aimed the MGB like an arrow through the triumphal arch into the Pavilion Gardens. I stamped on the brake. The car slid sideways and scuffed the gravel.

Tammy had been cleverer than we'd expected. She'd painted her slogan – Archie Flowerdew is Innocent – on the double doors of the main entrance in bright red paint. Then she'd chained herself to one of the pillars of the porte cochère. There was rarely anyone in the Royal Pavilion Gardens at this time of night. Tammy would have had plenty of time to go about her work unobserved.

Her chain rattled and she hugged closer to the pillar as we climbed out of the car and walked towards her. Her face looked pale in the light from the garden's sodium lamps. She was wearing a brown duffel coat over jeans and a pair of woolly mittens. She sported a bright red woollen hat with a pom-pom. Her light brown hair poked out from under the hat. She had sturdy shoes that looked as though they'd done a lot of walking. The red holdall was lying on the ground beside her.

"Keep away from me," she shouted as we approached. Then a kind of half-recognition crept into her eyes and she said to me: "Don't I know you?"

"Colin Crampton, from the *Evening Chronicle*," I said. "And this is Freddie Barkworth, a photographer with the paper."

By way of introduction, Freddie raised his camera and fired off three shots in quick succession.

Tammy scowled at Freddie. "Did I give you permission to take pictures?" she said.

I said: "I thought that's why you'd chained yourself up."

"This isn't about me. It's about justice for my uncle Archie. When people realise the lengths I'm prepared to go to, they'll think again about the verdict. This is an opportunity for me to keep on Archie's case."

I said: "This is an opportunity for you to get arrested and thrown in the can for a week. How much will you be able to help Archie, then?"

"Some old buffer in the magistrates' court will tick me off and let me out with a fine."

"After repainting the doors of the best-loved building in Brighton? I wouldn't bet on it."

"But I had to do something to attract attention." She shifted round the pillar.

"You've done that," I said. "This story will be on the front page of the *Evening Chronicle* later today. But if you stay here, the cops will pick you up and make sure you're out of circulation until your uncle Archie meets his fate."

Tammy snivelled. Rummaged in her coat pocket. "I've forgotten to bring a hanky."

I reached in my pocket and handed her mine. She blew her nose. Wiped her eyes. Looked uncertainly around her.

"How long will it take the police to come?" she said.

"Knowing the Brighton force, the night shift is probably playing poker in the canteen right now. But you won't last here for more than an hour or two. If you want to carry on the fight, you have to get away."

I squinted as Freddie fired off his flashgun and took some more shots. "Knock it off, Freddie. The flash could attract someone. If you've got enough shots, I suggest you head back to the office. You can walk it from here."

Freddie nodded. "See you later."

I turned back to Tammy. "Have you got the key to the padlock?"

She shook her head. "I threw it in the bushes."

I felt the chain. It wasn't thick – the kind used to keep bicycles safe. I hurried over to the car, opened the boot and took out a sturdy pair of pliers from my maintenance kit.

I looked towards North Street. A young bloke was staggering along towards us. He looked drunk. But he could cause trouble if he saw what we were doing. I trotted over to Tammy and applied the pliers to the chain.

It was tougher than I'd imagined. But with a lot of sweat and a bruised hand I managed to cut through one link. It was enough.

Tammy shook off the chain. "I better get back to my lodgings," she said. She grabbed her holdall.

I pointed to the slogan on the doors. "The police will have their suspicions you painted that," I said. "You need to keep out of their way."

Besides, I sensed Tammy had more to tell about her uncle Archie than she was letting on. If I could keep her away from the cops for a few days, she could provide me with a string of scoops that would boost our circulation and frustrate rival papers. And that would delight Figgis.

I said: "If we're to hide you from the cops, you need a safe house."

"Like the kind spies use?" Tammy asked.

"No, like the kind justice campaigners for uncles need."

"But I don't know anywhere like that."

"I do," I said. "And I'm going to take you there now."

Tammy looked suspicious. "Where is this safe house?"

"It's actually a safe basement flat. And it's where my Australian girlfriend, Shirley, lives. So we'll be going down under in more ways than one."

Chapter 3

I had to knock three times on the door of Shirley's basement flat before a light appeared in the hall.

I peered through the door's frosted glass window. The blurred outline of something that looked like the creature from the swamp emerged from Shirley's bedroom and made its way down the hall.

The chain rattled and the hinges squealed as the door opened.

Shirley was backlit by the hall light. She'd wrapped a thick woollen blanket around her shoulders and over her head. The blanket hung loose around her body and trailed along the ground. Did I say a creature from the swamp? She looked like a medieval nun on her way to vespers. And even with sleepy blue eyes and mussed blonde hair much too beautiful to be wearing a wimple.

"Jeez, Colin," she said. "If this is your idea of a good time to make a social call, you're as dumb as a box of rocks."

"Can we come in?"

"We?"

I stood to one side. Tammy peered nervously around my right shoulder.

Shirley's eyes widened suspiciously. "Who's the sheila?" she said.

"This is Tammy Flowerdew," I said.

Shirley moved closer. Her eyes no longer looked sleepy. They focused on Tammy in that appraising way she had when she was making up her mind about someone.

"Jeez, you're the daughter of that –" she began.

"Niece," Tammy interrupted.

"Well, don't hang around on the doorstep."

Beside me, I sensed Tammy stiffen.

Shirley grinned apologetically. "Sorry, kiddo. Hang around –

not a good choice of words. The brainbox isn't too sharp at three in the morning."

We stepped inside and closed the door behind us.

"Tammy needs somewhere to stay for a few days," I said. "A safe house."

Shirley rolled her eyes. "The window frame leaks, the back door is swinging on one hinge and the lights flicker every time you touch the switch. But I guess you could call this a safe house. Just."

Tammy cradled a mug of steaming cocoa in her hands.

She took a sip and said: "I didn't know what to do next."

"So you splashed paint on Brighton's best-loved building," Shirley said. "How not to win friends and influence people. That's dumb, kid."

We were sitting in Shirley's pint-sized sitting room – Tammy on the sofa, Shirley on a stool and me in the chair with the broken springs that twanged like a discordant harp every time I moved. Tammy's face was wreathed in steam from the cocoa.

"They're hanging my uncle Archie ... and for something he didn't do. What's a splash of paint compared with a man's life? I'd cover the whole town with the stuff if I thought it would save him."

"Getting up people's noses isn't a great way to make people root for you," Shirley said.

Tammy frowned. Stared into the cocoa while she thought about saying something. Changed her mind. Took a sip from the mug.

I said: "The important thing is to decide what you want to do next."

"I want to go back to my own lodgings," Tammy said defiantly.

"Where the police will track you down, arrest you and charge you with criminal damage to the Royal Pavilion."

"At least they'll have to take me to court. I'll get a chance to tell the whole rotten bunch of them – the coppers, the lawyers, the judges – what I think of them."

I shook my head. "That's not how it will happen. For a start, they don't have to bring your case before magistrates right away. You could just be remanded in custody. You'd get no chance to speak in a custody hearing except to confirm your name and address. Then, when you're finally tried, they'll prevent you from talking about anything not relevant to the case. They won't let you make impassioned speeches from the dock. They'll rule you in contempt of court if you persist. That means they'll stop you talking about Archie. And if you carry on, they'll take you back to the cells and hear the rest of the case in your absence. You can take it from me that the courts know how to deal with trouble-making defendants. You won't stand a chance."

The fire in Tammy's eyes dimmed while I spoke. Now she put down her cocoa. She rummaged in a pocket for my hanky and snivelled into it. "I don't mind being a martyr if it saves Uncle Archie."

I glanced at Shirley.

She said: "Tell her the truth, Colin."

The broken springs twanged a chord that sounded like the opening bar of 'Cwm Rhondda' as I leant forward. "Let me tell you something about martyrs. When they're performing their brave deeds, nobody stands up and cheers. Remember, martyrs only become martyrs because other people thought they were nuts. It's only years afterwards people realise the poor dead martyr may have had a point. By then, it's too late. Martyrs all have one thing in common: they failed to get what they wanted."

Tammy said: "So you're saying I hide away here and count down the hours until they fix the noose around Uncle Archie's neck?"

"No. I don't believe that. For a start, I'm going to write a front-page splash for the *Chronicle* today about your protest at the

Royal Pavilion. Freddie Barkworth has some great pictures that will grab attention. The story will be picked up by the nationals. It'll remind people of Archie's case. Perhaps get people thinking again."

"And perhaps not," Tammy said.

"Yes," I said. "Perhaps not. That's why I want you to tell me everything you know about the case. I want to examine every aspect of it again. See if we can find something that's been overlooked. Something that points to Archie's innocence."

I glanced at Shirley. She shrugged.

"You wrote enough about it at the time of the trial," Tammy said.

"I know. I was in court for each of the six days of the trial. I listened to the evidence just like the jurors."

"And would you have found Archie guilty had you been one of those jurors?" Tammy asked.

I paused. Thought about that for a moment.

"Yes," I said.

"I thought so." Tammy shot up, grabbed her holdall and moved towards the door.

"Wait," I said. "Let me explain what I think now. The evidence against Archie was largely circumstantial. But it was convincing. At least, it was strong enough to convince the jury. But that doesn't mean that there isn't evidence that was overlooked at the time – evidence that would throw a new light on the case. It sometimes happens. Recently, I read Ludovic Kennedy's book *10 Rillington Place*. It describes a miscarriage of justice in 1950. An illiterate man – Timothy John Evans – was hanged for murdering his wife, Beryl.

"In fact, the pair had the misfortune to live upstairs from a serial killer called John Christie. It later turned out he'd killed Beryl. Christie's specialism was gassing his victims. It was years before his killing spree was uncovered and by then it was too late to save poor Evans. The book convinced me that Evans was wrongly hanged. Kennedy showed that evidence that pointed to Evans's innocence wasn't even considered by the court."

"But it didn't prevent the hangman stringing up the poor bozo," Shirley chipped in.

"No, it didn't. Which is why if there is any other evidence that proves Archie is innocent, we have to find it in the next nine days."

Tammy moved back to her seat. She sat down heavily. "Uncle Archie told the court everything he knew. He was cross-examined on it."

"Yes, he gave evidence in his own defence," I said. "I sat on the reporter's bench and heard it."

And I'd not forgotten …

It was the fourth day of the trial on a sultry September afternoon when Archie's counsel, Peregrine Collingwood QC, stood up and faced the jury.

On the press bench, I took off my jacket and hung it over the back of my chair. The judge, Mr Justice Templeworth, gave me a look like he wanted to see me transported to Australia. I responded by loosening my tie. Templeworth puffed out his cheeks in annoyance and turned to Collingwood.

"You may open the case for the defence," he growled.

Collingwood was a tall man with an aquiline face and hooded eyes. He had a sharp brain and a tidy turn of phrase, but if I'd been Flowerdew I'd have chosen another brief. Collingwood had a kind of predatory look, like a hungry eagle in search of a small rodent for dinner. He exuded the kind of boundless confidence that comes across to more humble souls as bumptiousness. I sensed the jurors didn't like him. But Collingwood didn't look like a man who expected to lose his case when he began his speech to the jury.

"Members of the jury, we've heard a great deal over the past three days from my learned friend." He waved a hand in a dismissive gesture towards prosecuting counsel, Truscott Bonner QC. "We've heard a number of witnesses provide evidence that suggests my client, Archibald Flowerdew, killed the deceased, Percy Despart. But all that evidence – all of it, members of the jury – is what we lawyers call circumstantial. It does not provide a direct link between Mr Flowerdew and the crime. In each case, you must take that piece of evidence and make your own judgement as to whether or not it could provide a link.

"And, members of the jury, mark that word 'could'. Because each piece of circumstantial evidence involves you making an inference it cannot provide certain proof. And it matters not that there may be several pieces of circumstantial evidence. For the inference you make with every individual piece of evidence involves doubt. And no matter how many pieces of doubt you pile up, they cannot make a certainty. But there is one certainty that you can weigh with confidence – the trusted evidence of an honest man who knows the truth. And there is just one such man who can provide it. I call my client, Archibald Flowerdew."

It was a fine speech. I'd watched the jurors' faces as they'd listened to it. They didn't like Collingwood, but they'd been convinced by his words. If they'd been asked to reach their verdict there and then, I believe they'd have acquitted Archie.

But it didn't happen like that.

Collingwood spent most of the morning taking Archie through his evidence-in-chief.

"You knew Percy Despart for a good many years, Mr Flowerdew?"

"Yes. We first met at art school in London. The Slade. That would have been in 1931."

"And how would you describe your relationship with Mr Despart in those days?"

"Initially friendly. But we fell out."

"Why was that?"

"There was a prize at the end of the first academic year for the most original approach to a portrait. We both planned to enter. My subject was a Covent Garden flower seller. I pictured her at the end of a dark rainy day. She was huddled for shelter in a shop doorway with just one bloom. I introduced a chiaroscuro effect ..."

"Explain that for the jury, if you please."

"It's a way of creating the sense that light is coming from a source within the painting. In this case, my flower seller was left with a single red rose, which I painted as the source of light that illuminated her wrinkled old face against the gloom."

"And did you know what Mr Despart's painting was going to be?"

"No. He kept it secret. But, then, he kept most things secret. He was that kind of person."

"But Mr Despart never entered his painting for the competition?"

"No, it was disqualified by the judges."

"Why was that?"

"It turned out that he'd befriended a visiting Italian artist – a man of great talent. Percy paid the man to paint the picture for him."

"And the judges discovered this deception?"

"Yes. Percy blamed me for informing on him. But I didn't know about it. I explained that it couldn't have been me. But he didn't believe me. I think he was just thrashing around for someone to blame and I was a convenient whipping boy. I thought it would be possible to rebuild our friendship when Percy had calmed down. But it didn't work out like that."

"Why was that?"

"Because I won the competition. It just reinforced Percy's view that I'd told the judges about his deception."

"Was that the end of your friendship?"

"Yes."

"But not the end of your association?"

"No."

"When did you next become aware of Percy Despart in your life?"

"After art school, we went our separate ways. I settled in Brighton. I painted pictures of local landmarks, which I sold to tourists. But it wasn't enough to pay the bills. So I managed to get some work drawing picture puzzles for newspapers."

"What kind of puzzles?"

"Some were 'spot the difference' puzzles. There would be two pictures that looked exactly the same. In fact, there were a few small differences in the second from the first. Readers had to find them. Then there were 'spot the odd object' puzzles. In those I drew a common scene – such as a kitchen – but I'd include a few items that shouldn't really be there, such as a spanner hanging on a hook instead of a ladle. Readers had to spot the odd objects."

"But you also drew seaside postcards?"

"Yes. I landed a contract with a company that published them."

"That would be Seaside Smiles Limited."

"Yes. They have their offices in Saltdean. I was hired to draw picture postcards of local scenes. They proved to be very popular. Their sales gave us a comfortable living."

"You mentioned 'us'."

"My sister, Marjorie, had come to live with me. Her husband had been killed in the Korean War and she couldn't afford to keep up the rent on the house they'd had in Streatham. I had a spare room at my place, so it seemed the sensible solution."

"And that arrangement worked well?"

"Oh, yes. I'd always got on famously with Marje. She settled in well. She'd been an army nurse during the war and she found a job at the Royal Sussex County Hospital. Did well at it, too. Was a senior sister within three years. We were happy living together – as brother and sister, you understand. But it didn't last."

"Why was that?"

"Percy Despart came to live in Brighton. He took a flat just off Edward Street and set himself up in a small studio on the seafront."

"How did this affect you?"

"For a few months, I thought Percy's presence in town was something that I would be able to tolerate. Brighton is a large place and there was no reason why I shouldn't be able to avoid him. But it didn't work out like that. Percy also won a contract from Seaside Smiles to draw picture postcards."

"Like yours?"

"No, not like mine. Percy's were so-called comic postcards, but not the jolly broad humour of Donald McGill. You must remember the best known: 'I Can't See My Little Willie!' or 'A Stick of Rock, Cock?' "

There was laughter in court.

Templeworth gave Archie a filthy look. "That will be enough vulgarity in my court," he snapped.

Collingwood did his best to retrieve the situation. "But Despart's postcards did not feature good old British vulgarity, such as that which has come down to us from masters like Chaucer and Shakespeare?"

"No, Percy's postcards were like the man, crude and vicious," Archie said. "Worse than that, he took to caricaturing local people in some of the cards in tasteless jokes. It made him very unpopular in some quarters. He didn't seem to care. But then he went too far."

"How did he go too far?"

"He killed my sister, Marjorie."

Archie's statement caused a collective intake of breath around the court. There was shouting in the public gallery from two of Despart's relatives. The court usher called three times for silence.

When order had been restored, Templeworth leant forward towards the witness box.

"Flowerdew, are you telling this court that Mr Despart deliberately killed your sister, Marjorie?"

"As good as, My Lord."

"As good as is not good enough," Templeworth growled. He had beetling eyebrows that drew together in a single line across his forehead when he was frowning. He turned to Collingwood. "I think your client had better tell us exactly what happened."

"I think so, indeed, My Lord." Collingwood executed an obsequious little bow. "Mr Flowerdew, how did your sister, Marjorie, come to die?"

"She saw a postcard." Archie's face visibly sagged. His eyes shone with unshed tears.

"You will have to tell us more than that," Collingwood said gently.

"I've said that Despart drew cruel caricatures of local people he didn't like in his postcards. He drew one of Marje."

"And she saw it?"

"Yes. It was in one of the rotary wire stands outside a shop in Grand Junction Road. She was on her way to meet me at the entrance to Palace Pier. Apparently, she took the card and just seemed to go into a trance. She stepped into the road staring at it. A bus hit her. It sent her eight feet into the air. She was dead before she hit the ground."

"But you didn't see this?"

"I was waiting outside the pier about a hundred yards away. But it was soon clear that there'd been a terrible accident. It felt like an icicle had pierced my heart. I knew it was Marjorie. I just ran … I found her in the road. She was still holding that filthy card."

It was as though Archie had cast a spell over the court. His face crumpled in misery.

Collingwood said: "I have to ask you this question, Mr Flowerdew. What did the postcard show?"

Archie visibly braced himself in the witness box. "The

postcard pictured a scene in hospital. It showed a patient wearing horn-rimmed glasses lying in a hospital bed. His body is covered by a sheet. A nurse who looked like my Marje had her hands under the sheet. She was removing something from the patient's crotch. A doctor is shouting at Marje: 'No, nurse, I said remove the patient's *spectacles*!'

"I can just imagine the awful effect this must've had on my dear sister. She was so proud of her skills as a nurse. To see them demeaned in this crude way would have mortified her."

"And why do you think Despart chose your sister as a victim for one of his cards?" Collingwood asked.

"It was to get back at me. He knew I'd be hurt by it. It was a cowardly thing to do."

Collingwood leaned towards him. "Mr Flowerdew, I have one final question to ask you. We have heard during the prosecution case from four witnesses that, as you knelt in the road beside Marjorie's body, you shouted in rage."

"Yes."

"Did you shout, 'This is Percy Despart's doing. I'll kill Despart no matter how long it takes'?"

In a whisper, Archie replied: "Yes."

Collingwood tugged on the lapels of his gown. "And did you kill Percy Despart?"

Archie stood up straighter. Looked around the court. Cleared his throat. And spoke with a strong voice. "No. I would never kill anyone."

"Would you like more cocoa, Colin?"

Shirley's voice sounded miles away. But she was sitting opposite me in her flat. It was me who was miles away – thinking about that day in court when Archie Flowerdew had given his evidence.

I turned to Tammy. She was sipping cocoa.

I said: "I heard Archie give his evidence in court. He made a good first impression when his own counsel questioned him. I think the jury liked him. But he shouldn't have agreed to step into the witness box. The accused never has to give evidence. It's for the prosecution to prove his guilt. And, as it turned out when he was cross-examined, there was a fatal flaw in his defence."

It was a flaw I still believed would send Archie Flowerdew to the gallows.

The atmosphere in the courtroom was stifling when Truscott Bonner QC rose to cross-examine Archie Flowerdew for the prosecution.

On the press bench, I rolled up my shirtsleeves. Templeworth gave me a dirty look and angrily shuffled his notes.

Bonner was a short, heavy man with pouched cheeks and a whisky nose. His ample belly was encased in a dark waistcoat hung with a gold watch chain.

"Flowerdew, you're a man who shapes the truth to suit your own purposes, aren't you?" he asked briskly.

Archie's eyes glazed with confusion. He looked anxiously around the courtroom as though seeking help.

"I don't know what you mean," he said.

"I mean that as an artist what you paint is the truth as you see it, rather than as others may see it."

Collingwood rose: "My Lord, I can't see the point of this question. It seems more appropriate to a seminar on art."

Templeworth wiped sweat from his forehead with a spotted handkerchief. "Let us see whether or not it is also relevant in court. You may answer the question, Flowerdew."

"I suppose so," Archie said. "I always try to tell the truth whether in art or in life."

Bonner harrumphed. It hadn't been the answer he was expecting. "Well, let us put that admirable sentiment to the test. You told us in your evidence that you had never visited Mr Despart's art studio."

"Yes."

"Is that the case?"

"Yes."

"So it would be impossible for your fingerprints to be found on any objects in that studio?"

"I suppose so."

"But fingerprints were found, were they not? As we heard in police evidence at the start of the trial, your fingerprints were discovered on a catalogue of seaside postcards found next to Mr Despart's drawing board."

"I can explain that."

"Is that so?"

"The catalogue came from Seaside Smiles – the company that publishes Mr Despart's postcards as well as my own. I'd been at Seaside Smiles' office a few days earlier, browsing a catalogue while waiting for an appointment. It could have been the same one."

"And how many copies of this catalogue are there?"

"I don't know. Hundreds, perhaps thousands."

"So it would have been an extraordinary coincidence for the very same catalogue to have found its way to Mr Despart's studio."

"It must be the truth."

"That will be for the jury to decide. Let me turn to another matter. In your evidence, you said that you would never, ever want to murder anyone. And, yet, we have heard from witnesses that when your sister was killed in the unfortunate road accident, you shouted: 'I'll kill Despart no matter how long it takes'."

"But I'd just seen my sister's dead body, with that filthy postcard."

"Yes, a filthy postcard that could make a loving brother seek lifelong revenge."

"No."

"But you told us earlier that, 'I always try to tell the truth whether in art or in life'."

"Yes."

"But you are now telling us that when you said you wanted to kill Percy Despart – no matter how long it took – that was not the truth."

"Yes."

Bonner pushed his glasses to the end of his nose and looked over them at the jury. "The truth is, Flowerdew, we don't know when to believe you."

"But I am telling the truth."

"In that case, perhaps you will tell us where you were on the evening that Percy Despart was killed."

Archie's gaze flicked around the court like a hunted animal desperate to escape.

"I wasn't at Percy's studio."

"Are you telling us you have an alibi?"

"Yes."

Bonner grinned benevolently. "Then, pray, tell us what it is so that we may bring these dolorous proceedings to a speedy end."

"I can't."

"You can't?"

"I've already told the police that what I was doing that evening was private."

"Yes, I imagine you hoped to keep the fact that you were killing Mr Despart private."

Archie gripped the edge of the witness box so tightly his knuckles looked like pieces of chalk. "I didn't kill Percy," he screamed. "I was with a lady."

A shocked murmur ran around the court. This was new. There'd been no hint in earlier evidence that Archie had been with a woman when Despart was murdered.

Bonner's eyes widened in surprise. He straightened his wig. Fumbled with his brief. Looked to his junior counsel for assistance – but got only a shake of the head.

"And who is this lady?"

"I can't say."

"Can't or won't?"

Archie stiffened. Swallowed hard. Looked anxiously at Collingwood. "Won't," he said.

The judge turned towards the witness box. "Flowerdew, if you are now telling the court that you have an alibi for the time of the attack on Mr Despart, I must earnestly urge you to reveal it." He paused. Leaned forward. "Your failure to do so could have grave consequences. Who is the lady?"

"I promised not to reveal her name."

"Perhaps you can't reveal her name because she doesn't exist," Bonner said.

"She does exist," Archie screamed.

"Or perhaps she is a figment of truth as an artist sees it," Bonner said. "No further questions, My Lord."

Tammy's shoulders slumped. Her eyelids drooped.

The night's action – and the cocoa – had taken their toll. She needed to sleep. But, first, I needed an answer to one more question.

"At the trial, Archie said a lady could alibi him but he refused to give her name. Do you know who she is?"

Tammy shrugged wearily. "I've asked Uncle Archie a thousand times. He says that a point of honour is at stake. That if he reveals the lady's name her own life may be in danger."

"And he's given no hint about who she is or where she can be found?"

"None."

I leaned back feeling weary myself. But a black thought had formed in my mind. If this lady's life really were in danger – as Archie had said – could it be that, for some reason, he was protecting her?

Because she was Despart's killer.

Chapter 4

I arrived at the *Chronicle* later that morning bleary-eyed after three hours' sleep.

It had been a busy night. After I'd left Tammy in Shirley's safe care, I'd hurried back to the newsroom and batted out six hundred words for the Midday Special edition. I'd left a copy on Figgis's desk so he'd see it as soon as he arrived. Then I'd made it back to my lodgings for what proved to be a restless kip.

My mind was whirling like a spinning top. I'd spirited Tammy away from the Royal Pavilion before the cops could arrest her. Now they'd be hunting for her. And I wondered whether Shirley and I could be arrested as accomplices. We hadn't wielded the paintbrush, but we were keeping the miscreant from justice. Perhaps we would both end up in the slammer.

But a spell in clink could be worth it if I landed a scoop. And I was getting that twitching feeling between the shoulder blades that suggested one was heading my way. The fact Tammy believed her uncle Archie's mysterious alibi lady really existed was big news. When Archie had blurted out the tale about the lady in court I'd been sceptical. The judge and jury plainly felt he was lying. But why would he lie to Tammy? She was a wild card – there was no doubt about that – but I sensed she'd be able to tell truth from lies when it came to her uncle Archie.

Besides, Archie had given Tammy information that had never come out in court. That the lady's life would be in danger if her name became public. I wondered why.

My first thought had been that she'd murdered Despart. But was Archie the kind of man to shield a woman he knew to be a killer? A man with a passionate love for a woman might do that. But Tammy hadn't given a hint that there was such a femme fatale in Archie's life. And when it comes to lofty affairs of the heart – or even low tumbles in the bedroom – it takes a woman to know.

So could it be that the lady knew Despart's killer and was now hiding from him in fear of her life? If so, surely she should have told the cops and sought protection. But perhaps the woman didn't trust the boys in blue to keep her safe. Brighton police didn't have the wit to keep a fly off a jam tart. The poor woman would have been safer to stand in the middle of the promenade shouting: "Come and get me."

Last night, Tammy had been angry and upset – a combination that doesn't produce straight thinking. But I sensed she knew a lot more about what Archie had done than she was telling. It would be worth the risks to keep her safe for a few days and see what more she could tell. Besides, it would give the *Chronicle* a lead on the story the nationals couldn't match. But I'd need to move carefully and plan ahead.

So, although I'd had little sleep, I breezed into the newsroom feeling like a man who'd landed a great scoop – and expected more to come.

That nice warm feeling didn't last for long.

"Hollis is not happy," said Frank Figgis.

"Hollis is never happy," I said. "The last time I saw Hollis happy was when he got fitted with his new false teeth. And that only lasted half an hour."

"Didn't fit?"

"No. The little sugar balls off a blue Liquorice Allsorts got stuck under his plate."

We were sitting in Figgis's office. It was less than ten minutes after my triumphal entry to the newsroom. And already my trouble-seeking antennae were twitching.

"Hollis thinks there could be serious legal trouble," Figgis said.

"Hollis always thinks there'll be trouble," I said.

Reginald Hollis, barrister-at-law, was the paper's night lawyer

– a title only fifty per cent accurate. Hollis did most of his work during the day. But on newspapers the term 'night lawyer' was as traditional as misprints and inky fingers. On morning papers, lawyers cast most of their legal spells at night when the papers were being written. Because we were an evening rag, Hollis sat through a day shift and left punctually at half past four, driving his vintage Bentley back to a gloomy Victorian mausoleum of a house in Small Dole.

I said: "Every day Hollis predicts our stories will produce an avalanche of writs … and worse. They never do."

Figgis picked up a proof of the Midday edition's front page from his desk. The headline on my story screamed: A Right Royal Protest. Underneath, Freddie's picture of Tammy chained to a pillar of the Royal Pavilion's porte cochère was cut across six columns. My story described how Tammy had made a final dramatic plea to save her uncle Archie before going into hiding.

"This beats anything the nationals have on the story," I said.

Figgis cleared his throat. It sounded like a cement mixer churning ball bearings. He reached for his Woodbines. "Hollis tells me that if the paper knows where Miss Flowerdew is hiding, we should pass the information to the police. As she admits having painted the slogan on the Pavilion, she's guilty of criminal damage, says Hollis. It's better that the paper doesn't know where she is. That's why I'm not going to ask you to tell me."

"I wasn't going to tell you, anyway."

"That's as maybe. When I get the inevitable call from the chief constable, I'll be able to tell him I know nothing."

"And a truer word will never have passed your lips."

Figgis grinned, displaying a row of yellow teeth. For a moment, I thought he'd winked. But it may have been a speck of dust in his eye.

Anyway, I'd taken on board his meaning. He wanted the stories that exclusive contact with Tammy could provide, but none of the hassle that might go with them. A good deal from his point of view. Potential trouble for me.

"I'm assuming that should the Old Bill ask me if I know where Miss Flowerdew is hiding, you'll leave me to answer the question in my own way," I said.

"I trust your judgement on that." Figgis lit his ciggie.

"And what if the boys in blue sling me in jail?"

"You can rely on me to chair your escape committee. I may even get Mrs Figgis to bake a cake with the traditional file inside. The file won't be much use. But you can use the cake to batter the cell door down."

"Anyway, the police don't know what we know until the Midday Special hits the streets," I said. "At the moment, I imagine they're running around the town looking for Tammy in all her usual haunts."

Figgis put his finger to his lips. "Careful. I sensed you were about to tell me something I shouldn't hear. And then I'd have to mention it to that old worry-guts Hollis."

"And we wouldn't want that, would we?"

I left Figgis's office feeling a bit like a Monopoly player who's had his get-out-of-jail-free card confiscated.

I had an uncomfortable feeling I was going to need it before this story finally left the front pages. Archie Flowerdew was going to hang. And when that happened Tammy would have to give up her fight and face the consequences of her campaign. The police would haul her before the magistrates for defacing the Royal Pavilion. And because Shirley and I had given her sanctuary, we could also find ourselves standing in the dock.

Figgis had made it clear that he didn't want the paper linked with any deal I'd cooked up with Tammy. So where did that leave me? Would the paper stand by me if I had my wrist slapped by the beak? Or would they take the view their crime correspondent should be reporting on crimes, not committing them? I knew Figgis well enough to realise that he'd grumble a bit and leave it at that.

But he wouldn't make the final decision. Gerald Pope, the paper's editor, had the last word. His Holiness – as he was known behind his back – penned worthy editorials about high moral purpose. He was a regular at Brighton Methodist Church. Only a couple of weeks ago, I'd heard, he'd read the lesson: Matthew chapter five verse six, "Blessed are those who hunger and thirst for righteousness, for they will be filled."

And buggered are those who don't find it, for they will be fired. His Holiness would have me out of the door before you could say Amen.

I wouldn't be the only one deep in legal doo-doo. Tammy was hiding out at Shirley's flat. Shirl could find herself deported. The courts no longer sentenced convicts to transportation to Australia. But Shirley would soon find herself dumped on a steamer heading home on the six-week voyage. I couldn't let that happen.

If I could find evidence that proved Archie innocent all that would change. But it wouldn't be easy if Archie stayed shtum about his alibi. So, I reasoned, perhaps the best place to start was at the other end of the mystery. If Archie didn't murder Percy Despart, someone else did. And clues to that person might lie in Despart's own background. The court case had revealed him as a nasty piece of work who'd made enemies.

I hurried down the corridor from Figgis's office to the morgue – the paper's library that stored nearly two million press cuttings. I needed some help from Henrietta Houndstooth, who ran the place.

But when I walked into the morgue, Henrietta wasn't at her desk.

The Clipping Cousins – the three ladies who clipped the cuttings from the newspapers and filed them – were grouped around the large table in the middle of the room. They were related more by a love of gossip and squabbling than blood ties.

They reminded me of the three witches from *Macbeth*. Not much toil but plenty of trouble.

I said: "Where's Henrietta?"

Mabel, a sturdy lady with a homely smile and a tightly permed head of auburn hair, said: "The poor lamb's got a heavy cold. She's staying at home today in the warm. We've just been discussing the competition."

"Which competition is that?"

"The mince pie bake-off. We're all entering."

I'd forgotten. By tradition, the Mayor of Brighton organised an annual Christmas competition for the best mince pie made by a local resident. The prize was presented at the Corn Exchange two days before Christmas. If the Clipping Cousins were competing against one another there would be trouble ahead.

Mabel said: "Mr Crampton, here's a teaser for you. What's the most important thing you need when you're making pastry?"

"Flour, I suppose."

The Cousins dissolved into giggles.

"He got that wrong," Elsie said. She was the oldest among them. She was a small woman with a pointed nose. She looked like a bird pecking for worms when she bent over a newspaper. "He doesn't know," she chuckled.

"Could be butter," I said.

More laughter.

"You're nowhere close," Freda said. She was tall and thin enough to double up as a beanpole if she ever lost her job at the *Chronicle*.

"What's the answer?" I said.

"Cold hands," Mabel said.

"And what's the second most important thing?" Freda said.

"Hot feet," I said.

"He's nearly right," Elsie said.

"No he's not," Freda said.

"But it's a body part."

"No, it's an organ."

"An organ is a body part," Elsie said.

This was getting out of hand. So I said: "You'll have to enlighten me."

"It's a warm heart," Elsie said. "To make the best pastry you need cold hands and a warm heart. Like mine."

The other two glared at her.

"I'm just collecting a folder from the filing stacks," I said. "I don't have time for a cookery lesson. But let me leave you with a question. What's the best pastry for putting on your feet?"

The three raised their eyebrows and shook their heads.

"Choux pastry," I said.

I legged it into the filing stacks before one of them inevitably asked me to explain it.

Back at my desk in the newsroom, I realised I'd never looked in the Percy Despart file before.

During the trial my focus had been on the killer – or alleged killer, if Tammy was right – rather than the victim. But from the bulging file on my desk, it looked as though Despart had lived an active life. And not a saintly one.

There were about sixty cuttings in the file. I spent a few minutes sorting through them. About half of the cuttings mentioned Despart only briefly. He'd attended a meeting for a visiting painter at the municipal art gallery. He'd been profiled as a comic postcard artist in a puff piece that filled up empty columns during the silly season. There was a piece from the business pages about Despart signing a new contract with Neville Croaker, the proprietor of Seaside Smiles.

Most of the other cuttings I sorted into three main groups. At his trial, there'd been some brief references to Despart upsetting more than a few local people. But the prosecution certainly didn't want to chase that hare. And the defence didn't raise it in case it made Archie look as though he was speaking ill of the dead. The cuttings filled in the background. Percy plainly had a talent for climbing up the noses of important people.

First, there was retired Major Toby Kingswell. The first cutting I looked at didn't mention whether he was a galloping major. A second contained a recent picture. The good major must have put on a bit of weight since he resigned his commission. Or he'd ridden a carthorse. In any event, the cutting revealed he'd served in the Royal Marine Commandos – so no horses – and he'd seen action in Korea. Most of it with a knife and fork if his weight was anything to go by. Kingswell was pictured wearing a loud checked suit, which reminded me of a racecourse bookie, and a paisley kipper tie. I shuffled the cuttings into date order and followed the story from the start.

Kingswell had opened an art gallery in Ditchling, a village a few miles north of Brighton, after he'd left the army. He'd put himself about a bit in the art world. He was chairman of the hanging committee of the Brighton Masters' Art Show, the biggest painting exhibition in town. Eighteen months earlier, Kingswell had enraged Despart by rejecting his entry for the show. One cutting had a photograph of Despart's painting. It looked like a child's picture of a house sinking into the sea. Despart had called it *West Pier in a Storm*. He told the paper's arts reporter: "I see it as an experiment in primitivism, but drawing on influence from the cubist school and with a nod towards surrealism."

But Kingswell had a different view. He dismissed the artwork as "childish rubbish" and accused Despart of "flinging a pot of paint in the public's face". (Kingswell didn't sound like a man who could think up his own insults. John Ruskin had said exactly the same thing about one of James Whistler's paintings.) The story didn't end there.

It took three months for Despart to wreak his revenge. He drew a comic postcard that was printed by Seaside Smiles and sold through most of the souvenir shops on the seafront. The postcard depicted an obviously fat man with a striking resemblance to Kingswell hanging a painting on the wall of an art gallery. He'd been drawn in a knock-kneed stance – the artist's way of suggesting that Kingswell didn't have much to boast about inside his trousers. In the postcard's foreground, two curvy young women – a blonde and a brunette – are showing their stockings and suspenders. They are pointing at him and giggling.

Says the blonde: "That painting is well hung."

Replies the brunette: "About the only thing around here that is."

Further cuttings mentioned Kingswell threatening Despart and Seaside Smiles with a writ for libel. But I expect Kingswell's lawyer advised him that it's very difficult to prove a joke is defamatory. If the matter had come to court, the jury would have had a good laugh – but Kingswell would have lost his case. Not to mention what remained of his dignity.

He didn't sound like the kind of man to accept defeat with good grace. Despart had humiliated him. And Kingswell had been a commando. He had been trained to kill.

I turned to the second group of cuttings. The headline on the first story read: Sin is No Joke, Says Vicar.

Canon Gideon Burke, vicar of St Rita's, a church in the West Hill part of town, had delivered a sermon condemning "those blessed with hands of artistry that create salacious images to inflame untutored passions". If the good cleric had confined himself to more windy waffle, he'd not have run into trouble. But he'd taken a bunch of saucy postcards into the pulpit with him. He'd waved them around saying that a "thunderbolt of righteousness" would strike down their creator. It just happened to be Despart.

Perhaps Despart might have brushed that off as the wittering of a sanctimonious canon. But Burke had lived up to his name. He'd gone on to organise a series of prayer vigils to "save the soul of this son of Satan". And Despart drew the line at being compared with the Prince of Darkness.

Burke would have done better to find a less contentious campaign for his energy. Like raising a fund to fix the church roof.

Before arriving at St Rita's he'd been priest in residence at the Convent of the Five Foolish Virgins out Hailsham way. The whisper was that by the time he'd left there were only four. I'd remembered sharing a pint in Prinny's Pleasure with Simon Mackenzie, the paper's religion correspondent, who'd picked up the rumours about the randy canon.

It appeared that Despart had heard them, too. A couple of months later another of his comic postcards went on sale.

Two nuns are sitting in the choir stalls of a church whispering to one another. In the background, the head of a priest, looking rather like Burke, is peering guiltily around the church door.

Says the first nun: "When the Queen has a baby they fire a twenty-one gun salute."

Says the second nun: "When a nun has a baby, they fire a dirty old cannon."

Burke had delivered another of his fire-and-brimstone sermons the following Sunday. He'd called for a further prayer vigil, but not many wanted to spend more time on their knees. The thunderbolts from Heaven also seemed to be in short supply. But could Burke, I wondered, have decided to unleash his own divine retribution on Despart ...

I reached for the third pile of clippings.

The top one contained a large picture of Florian Le Grande RA, the artist. Le Grande was a painter whom time had passed by. He specialised in the kind of twee pictures of rural England that would look effete on a chocolate box. He was also a dab hand at turning out flattering portraits in which the tubby would lose a stone or two. Or a prominent pimple would disappear. Even so, he had the kind of driving ambition that made the most of what talent he had. I'd only met him once – at some official reception that Figgis had forced me to attend – and he was clearly a man who was difficult to ignore.

He was tall with a spindly body and a long face with thick lips. He'd had the misfortune to go bald at a young age and covered his head with a luxurious, curly blonde wig that made him look like a cherub from a medieval fresco. The syrup could have looked out of place, except that Le Grande dressed like a dandy who turned heads – usually to snigger – when he went walking.

He'd been Despart's tutor at the Slade and the two had evidently struck up some kind of friendship. Despart struggled to make a living from his painting for several years after leaving college. But then a big break came his way. Brighton Borough Council approached him to paint a portrait of a retiring mayor. The Council wanted a reference for Despart's ability as a portraitist. He gave his old tutor Le Grande.

But Le Grande evidently had less confidence in his former pupil's ability than Despart imagined. He didn't land the lucrative job. Worse, Le Grande ended up painting the portrait himself. (Several of the wrinkles around the mayor's scrawny neck disappeared.) Despart quietly fumed.

And last year, the clippings reminded me, he finally wreaked his revenge.

There were rumours that Le Grande, who'd wheedled his way into the post of vice-president of the Royal Academy, was in line for a knighthood. He'd successfully completed a commission in which he'd painted the portrait of a distant cousin of the queen. The cousin's pronounced squint had miraculously become a benevolent twinkle in her eye in the oil on canvas.

Despart went to work in his studio and a couple of weeks later a fresh Seaside Smiles postcard was on sale.

A drunken artist is in his studio surrounded by empty wine bottles. He bears a striking resemblance to Le Grande – except that the cherub wig is hanging from his easel. And the artist is leaning towards a mirror while he paints small rabbits on top of his bald head. A couple of courtier types are looking through a window.

Says the first courtier: "Why is that man painting rabbits on his head?"

Replies the second courtier: "Because from a distance they look like hares."

It was insulting certainly. But drunken vanity wasn't the worst slur Despart had ever tossed at someone. Even so, it was enough to frighten off whoever took the decision on handing out the gongs. And Le Grande never received his knighthood. In public, he'd borne the disappointment quietly. But I could imagine that, beneath the surface, an ambitious man like Le Grande would lust for revenge.

I sat back in my chair and surveyed the newsroom. The festive paper chains sagged like wet washing. Fallen pine needles from the Christmas tree in the corner formed a green carpet that crunched when anyone walked on it. The fairy lights had fused.

Cedric, the copy boy, bustled past my desk. "You going to save that poor guy from the gallows, Mr Crampton?"

I shrugged. "I don't know, Cedric."

My rummage through the files had revealed there were others who could have had a motive to kill Despart. None of this had come out in court. But there was a common thread that linked Kingswell, Burke and Le Grande.

They had all been pilloried in postcards drawn by Despart – and published by Seaside Smiles' proprietor, Neville Croaker.

Chapter 5

Seaside Smiles occupied a small lock-up shop a couple of hundred yards from Saltdean Lido.

I manoeuvred the MGB into a narrow parking slot between a baker's van and a grey Ford Zephyr with one windscreen wiper. (Perhaps the owner was only half expecting it to rain.)

I climbed out of the car and felt the first blast of an east wind whipping off the English Channel. Saltdean in the summer was full of pretty girls in new frocks. The Lido was packed with children frolicking in the water. But Saltdean in the winter might as well have been in Siberia. Beyond the cliff a gunmetal sea heaved in a heavy swell. A couple of lone seagulls rode the waves.

The headquarters of Seaside Smiles didn't look like a palace of unbounded merriment. A fascia board painted in fading red and yellow informed me that the firm had been 'raising a chuckle since 1936'. A small display window was crusted with dust. A broken drainpipe had left a slimy green stain down the wall. A typed notice on the door read: Knock and enter.

I obeyed.

I stepped into a room that had once been arranged as a pleasant reception. But that would have been about twenty years ago. The wallpaper – little groups of seashells – had faded. The paint on the skirting boards was chipped. A couple of cheap plastic chairs stood on one side of the room. A heap of cardboard boxes were piled up against the back wall. And on the other side was a wooden desk that held a typewriter, a telephone and an over-flowing in-tray.

A young woman with light brown hair in a beehive sat behind the desk. She had a pale face and the beginnings of crow's feet around the eyes. She looked up and frowned as I entered.

I said: "Is Mr Croaker in?"

"Who wants to know?"

"A simple seeker after truth."

"You won't find much of that here."

I grinned. "In that case, I'll take what I can get."

A door to one side of the desk led to a back room. From it a voice shouted: "Sandra, if that's the old git who's come about the rent, tell him I'm expecting a big cheque after Christmas."

Sandra muttered under her breath: "And I'm expecting a handsome prince to carry me off to fairyland."

I moved over to the door and poked my head into the room.

A broad-shouldered man with a large head, thin lips, a fleshy nose and crafty eyes was sitting behind a desk loaded with bulging files. His dark hair had receded and left him with a high, shiny forehead. Tiny tufts of hair sprouted from his ears. He was wearing a tweed hacking jacket that neatly complemented his hacked-off expression.

I said: "Good news, Mr Croaker. You can spend your rent money down the boozer."

"Some chance. I'll have to pay the old twister sooner or later. And, anyway, how do you know my name?"

I pointed. "It's on the nameplate on the front of your desk."

A small cloud of dust rose as he shifted a pile of files.

"Oh, yes. I'd forgotten that was there."

I moved into the room. The place was stacked with more of the cardboard boxes I'd seen in reception. I manoeuvred around a pile to reach the desk.

Croaker said: "Don't mind them. Just stock left over from the summer season. No chance of selling it now until Easter when the tourists return. Don't suppose you'd like to take a box or two off my hands? Give you a good price."

I perched on the edge of a pile of boxes and said: "I'm more of a country views type of person. You know, a green water meadow with a few ducks in the foreground and the spire of an ancient church in the distance."

Croaker grunted. "You won't find that here."

"I didn't think so."

Croaker shifted uncomfortably on his seat. He said: "Who are you, anyway?"

"Colin Crampton, *Evening Chronicle*. I don't want the rent but I would like some information."

"I haven't got much of either."

Sandra put her head around the door and said: "Would your visitor like a cup of tea, Mr Croaker?"

"No, he wants information instead. Saves on teabags."

I said: "Good choice."

Croaker grunted.

"How well did you know Percy Despart?" I asked.

"So that's what this is about. I thought it all came out in the trial."

"A lot of it did. But if Archie Flowerdew hangs next week the paper wants to run a background piece on the whole case. There could be some helpful mentions of Seaside Smiles."

Croaker straightened his tie as though he were about to go for a job interview. "Well, if you put it like that ..."

I said: "When did you first meet Percy Despart?"

"About fifteen years ago. I was at the official opening of some exhibition of seaside art that was on at the museum. Despart was there, too. He had a couple of pictures in the exhibition. Not the usual idealised images of seashores. His stuff had a bit of bite to it. But people who buy pictures to remind them of a holiday want a yacht sailing on a smooth sea, not a broken bottle down by a rotting groyne. Perhaps that's why Despart's work didn't sell."

"But you hired him anyway?"

"Yes. He pitched me the idea of giving a harder edge to the comic postcards by using a bit of contemporary humour rather than just going for the belly laugh. He was ahead of his time on that. In those days, most people were still listening to *Take It From Here* on the old steam radio."

"Did Despart's cards sell?"

"At first, sales were slow. But then he hit on the idea of including caricatures of local people in some of them. I was uneasy about it at first, but he produced a few that sold reasonably well. But then we had serious trouble with a couple of them and I decided to put a stop to it."

"One of those would've been the card making fun of Archie Flowerdew's sister, Marjorie. The one that led to her death."

"Yes. Percy wasn't entirely straight with me about that. I thought it was just a gag. I hadn't realised that it was based on a real nurse. And thc sister of one of my best artists, too."

"How did Archie react to that?"

"I've never seen a man so upset. I mean, I thought it was going to destroy him at one point. And I definitely didn't want that. The cards he drew were always some of our bestsellers."

"But I guess it changed his relationship with Despart?"

Croaker nodded vigorously. "You can say that again. The two had never been close. But from that day onwards, Archie treated Percy like a poisoned pariah. Not that Percy did anything to try to ease the situation. I don't think he ever apologised to Archie. Too much pride."

"But Archie carried on working?"

"Yes, I think he found some solace in it. But he never spoke to Percy again. I couldn't have them in the same office together."

I said: "You mentioned there'd been trouble with a couple of Despart's cards."

Croaker grimaced. "The second was more serious, if that's possible. It involved Lady Hilda Markham, the widow of a horse-race trainer, Sir Stamford Markham. He had his stables up at Plumpton. It all came to a head soon after Stamford died. Despart drew a postcard that showed a comely country woman – landed-gentry type – at a racecourse."

"And the comely type looked remarkably like Hilda Markham?"

Croaker nodded. "She'd always been a bit of a looker and had been years younger than Stamford when she married him. Well, when there's an old man with a younger wife there will always be rumours. Despart's card had a couple of racing tipsters leaning on the rails watching the Lady Hilda character lead a horse round the ring.

"Says the first tipster: 'That filly goes a bit.'

"Says the second tipster: 'And the horse is quite a runner, too.'"

I frowned: "And this went on sale just after Lady Hilda's husband had died?"

"Yes. Couldn't have been worse timing. It all came out at the inquest. She felt humiliated. She was already suffering from depression because of her husband's death. Now she believed the card implied she'd been unfaithful to her husband while he'd been alive. By all accounts, it seriously deepened her depression. She took an overdose and the maid found her dead in bed the following morning. Terrible. Had a young daughter just about to go off to London University, too. The coroner had some harsh words to say about it all. I told Percy to lay off real people in future."

"Why did he pick on Lady Hilda?"

Croaker looked embarrassed. "That was another reason I wanted no more of it. Turned out that a few months earlier Percy had met Sir Stamford at a race meeting. Stamford had given Percy a hot tip for one of his horses in the second race. Percy put a bundle on it, but the nag fell at the first fence."

"So why start publishing more caricature postcards again?" I asked.

"Percy came to me just over a year ago. As a matter of fact, it was shortly after *That Was The Week That Was* became a big hit."

"The BBC's late-night satire show with David Frost and Willie Rushton?"

"Yes. He suggested that we could both make some good

money by introducing satire into the cards. Ride the boom created by the TV show. He was very convincing about the commercial aspects of it all. It's a competitive business. If we don't make our money in the summer season … well, we're scratching around for the rent money by Christmas. Since sales hadn't been so hot, I agreed."

"And it's caused more trouble?"

"Controversy is the word I'd use. Trouble is bad for business – controversy ramps up sales. I made it clear to Percy that anyone he went after in his caricatures had to be a big enough person to stand up for themselves."

I thought about that for a moment. Kingswell, Burke and Le Grande all had a public standing. Satirists would argue they were legitimate targets. And perhaps they were. But none of them had enjoyed the way Despart had portrayed them.

I said: "When was the last time you saw Archie Flowerdew?"

"You mean in the flesh, rather than on the telly being led away in handcuffs?"

I nodded.

"It would have been three days before the event."

"You mean the murder?"

Now Croaker nodded.

"Where did you see him?"

"At the office here. I was planning a new catalogue for the next season and Archie said he'd drop by and discuss plans with me. We got out the previous year's catalogue and Archie flipped through the pages, pointing out how they could be improved. He jotted down some notes. He left them on top of the catalogue. He had some good ideas. Would have used them, too, but I lost the notes and the catalogue."

"How come?"

"If I knew I wouldn't have lost them." Croaker shrugged. "I thought I'd left them on my desk, but a couple of days later they weren't there. Looked through all the files. Sandra didn't know where they were, either. She wondered whether Percy might have taken the catalogue by mistake."

"Despart had been here?"

"Didn't I say? He dropped in unannounced the day after Archie. Had some new ideas he wanted to talk about. At least, that's what he claimed. Real reason was to touch me for an advance on his royalties. No chance. He didn't stay long."

That grabbed my attention. A key part of the prosecution's evidence was that a brochure with Archie's fingerprints had been found in Despart's studio. Archie swore he'd never been in the studio and had no explanation for the fingerprints. But what if Despart had noticed the catalogue with Archie's notes on Croaker's desk and pocketed it while Croaker was out of the room? Percy and Archie were bitter rivals. Percy might well leap at the opportunity to steal some of Archie's ideas.

I kept that to myself for the time being. Instead, I asked Croaker: "At the trial Archie said he had an alibi witness – a woman – but he refused to reveal her name. Do you have any idea who the woman might be?"

Croaker scratched behind his ear. "Archie kept himself to himself in that department. Of course, he was very close to his sister, Marjorie. And he's devoted to that niece of his – the one who still thinks he's innocent. But other women? I just don't know."

I thought Croaker was telling the truth. If Tammy had no idea who the woman was, it wasn't likely that Croaker would. Archie didn't strike me as the type to share bedroom tales with mates over a pint in the public bar.

I thanked Croaker for his help.

"Don't mention it." He pointed at a pile of invoices on his desk. "I don't suppose you'd like to give me a hand with this lot. Unpaid bills. Shops that have had their cards but haven't paid for them. Got to spend the next few days chasing them for the money. Not much of a way to get into the Christmas spirit, is it?"

I left Croaker collecting his debts and drove back to the *Chronicle*.

I planned to write a story that would explain how the catalogue with Archie's fingerprints had come to be in Despart's studio. I knew that the story would be speculative. I couldn't prove how it came to be there – and there were certainly other explanations. But it did raise reasonable doubt about one of the key pieces of prosecution evidence. I didn't think it would be enough by itself to overturn Archie's conviction. But it was a start.

So I strode into the newsroom with the confidence of a man who knows he has a front-page story to write. That confidence didn't last long. A note rolled into the carriage of my typewriter read: Put your head round my door when you're back – FF.

I walked round to Figgis's office, opened the door and stuck my head round.

I said: "Is this enough? Or would you like the rest of me?"

Figgis stubbed out his fag on the edge of his desk and said: "I'm in no mood for your cracks. And, just at the moment, I don't want any of you, but I've got no choice."

I entered the room and crossed to his desk.

Figgis handed me a copy of yesterday's Night Final edition. It was folded open at page nine.

"Look at the foot of column four," he said.

A headline read: Lamppost Singer Gets Early Christmas Gift. It was the story I'd belted out at supercharged speed the previous afternoon to oblige Barry Hobhouse.

"Have you read it?" Figgis asked.

"Been too busy. Besides, I know what it says. I wrote it."

"Read the last paragraph."

I picked up the paper and read: Chairman of the bench Sir Tobias Abercrombie told Beecher: "Normally, I would send you to prison for seven days, but as it's the season of goodwill I will give you a cushion."

I laughed. "Give you a *cushion*! I wrote: Give you a *caution*. Barry will be able to confirm that. He subbed the copy."

"Barry's disappeared. Apparently, he's left early for a long Christmas break in Scotland. Nobody knows where he is."

"His aunt McConnachie's, he told me."

Figgis shook the last Woodbine out of his packet, scrunched the packet and dropped it in his waste bin.

"Do you know how many McConnachies there are in Scotland?"

"Then surely the proofreader picked it up," I said.

"I've made enquiries," Figgis said ominously. "The galleys for page nine were proofed by Silas Burrage. He claims the word 'cushion' was in the original copy."

The fact Burrage had proofed the story was bad news. He had a reputation as a weasel who covered up his own mistakes by dropping some other poor sap in it.

I said: "Presumably, he still has the copy-edited folios to prove that."

"It seems not. Apparently, there was an unfortunate accident with a cup of coffee. They got soaked and he had to throw them out with last night's trash."

"Very convenient," I said.

"But you'll still have a black of the unsubbed copy on your spike," Figgis said.

I could feel the world falling away beneath my feet. If Burrage had conveniently removed his subbed folios, he'd already have made sure that my copy had been ripped off my spike.

I said: "Anyway, it doesn't make sense. Didn't Burrage question why the harshest magistrate in town was handing a cushion to a drunk who'd climbed a lamp post to sing 'Rudolph, the Red-Nosed Reindeer'.

"He says he took Abercrombie's words at face value – that he was giving the bloke a Christmas present."

"That's crazy."

Burrage had a talent for talking his way out of trouble. This time, he was talking me into it.

I said: "Presumably we'll run a correction in tonight's paper."

Figgis lit up his next fag, drew heavily and exhaled a long smoke stream. It drifted up to the nicotine-stained ceiling.

"We will, but it's not as simple as that. Abercrombie has been on the dog and bone bending His Holiness's ear. Abercrombie says the story makes him look like an idiot."

"He doesn't need our help."

"That's as maybe, but he's told Pope he's considering legal action. And His Holiness is getting twitchy – I can tell the signs. If you know what's good for you, you'll find a way to prove that you typed 'caution' and not 'cushion'."

I stood up. "I'll give it some thought," I said.

I was already doing so as I went through the door. Nobody was going to hang me for a misprint I hadn't written.

But now I had something in common with Archie Flowerdew. I knew what it felt like to be accused of something I didn't do.

Chapter 6

Needless to say, the black of my story had disappeared from the spike.

I asked around the newsroom if anyone had spotted Burrage skulking by my desk. Phil Bailey hadn't seen him for days. Sally Martin, who wrote the woman's page on the paper, said she'd noticed him late yesterday evening, but he'd been heading for the tearoom.

But Burrage was a master at covering his tracks. He'd have done the dirty deed when nobody was looking. Anyway, I couldn't afford to waste too much time on the weasel. The truth will out is my motto. And I was convinced Burrage would be undone by his own lies.

Back at my desk, I pulled the old Remington towards me and batted out a story on the new doubts about the catalogue fingerprint evidence. This time I made two blacks – one for my own spike. Then I crossed the newsroom to Susan Wheatcroft's desk.

I found her eating a giant mince pie.

"You've got a big one," I said.

Susan grinned. "All these years and you've only just noticed."

Susan was the paper's business reporter. She had a couple of chins that wobbled fetchingly when she laughed. And she was one of the nicest people in the newsroom.

She said: "Mabel gave me this on the QT."

"A practice bake for the mince-pie competition?" I asked.

"You've got it."

"And the verdict?"

"Pastry's a bit overcooked, but the filling's yummy. I could eat a whole plateful of these."

I said: "You may have to. If Elsie and Freda find out Mabel's using you as her personal taster, they may want in on the action."

Susan grinned: "The teeth and the taste buds are ready for

action."

"While you're waiting for the mince pies, I was wondering whether you could give me a hand."

"I could give you both hands." She held her arms outstretched. "And feel free to take the whole bod any time you like, honeybunch. It comes economy-sized."

I smiled. "I'll make a note in my diary. Meanwhile, how about impaling these folios on your spike?" I handed them to Susan.

She raised an eyebrow. "Your own spike full, then?"

"Not yet, but it soon will be."

The newsroom spike was the daftest filing system ever invented. The oldest stuff was always at the bottom of the spike. So when the cursed thing was full, you had to take everything off to chuck out the old stuff and then put the newer folios back.

I said: "My own spike is being targeted by a bandit." I told Susan about the misprint and my suspicions about Burrage.

"The man's a toad," Susan said. "He stitched me up last autumn. I wrote a story about a farm up near Horsted Keynes that was expecting a record harvest. I quoted the farmer saying, 'I'm expecting a big crop.' Anyway, the compositors introduced one of their accidentally-on-purpose typos and Burrage missed it. The piece went out with the farmer quoted as saying: 'I'm expecting a big crap.' Burrage conveniently 'lost' the carbon of my folios and it disappeared from my own spike. Frank Figgis gave me hell – after he'd finished laughing."

I smiled. "We need to fix Burrage for good. I'll give it some thought."

"Any fixing, count me in, honeybunch." And she sent me on my way with one of her saucy winks.

But Burrage's nemesis would have to wait.

Back at my desk, I called Shirley. Her voice was tense when she answered the phone.

"How's your visitor?" I said, taking care not to mention

Tammy's name.

"Climbing the walls. She wants to be doing something."

"She can't go out at the moment. She could become an involuntary guest you know where."

"I've tried to keep her amused. We've been listening to the radio – *Desert Island Discs*."

"Who was on?"

"Tallulah Bankhead, the actress."

"I know. The one who said, 'Only good girls keep diaries. Bad girls don't have time'."

"Yeah, she used that line with Roy Plomley."

I said: "I'm going to be another couple of hours. But I think I may have some positive news for your visitor this evening. I'll tell you more later. But don't build her hopes too high. We have a long way to go yet."

I rang off.

Just how long I realised when I reviewed my notes from the meeting with Croaker.

The story about how Despart had humiliated Marjorie in the nurse postcard strengthened Archie's motive for murder. All the while the authorities believed Archie wanted Despart dead they would look favourably on any piece of evidence that supported their view. If I was to shake their opinion, I'd need to point the finger of suspicion in other directions. And I'd have to show there was good reason for doing so. My visit to Seaside Smiles reinforced my view that Kingswell, Burke and Le Grande all had strong motives for seeing Despart in his coffin.

And art dealer Kingswell, the former commando who'd been trained to kill, was my top suspect.

A grey December twilight had settled on Ditchling by the time I reached the village. It was one of those places that had lots of quaint cottages with roses round the front door and septic tanks out the back.

I parked the MGB in a side road and hurried round to the High Street. A chill wind was blowing from the east and a few snowflakes flurried in the sodium glare of the street lights. I buttoned my jacket to pull it closer around me and wished I had a scarf.

The few village shops were still open for business. A brace of rabbits hung in the butcher's window. A basket of chestnuts stood outside the greengrocer's. A hand-written notice pasted outside the post office announced 'Last Posting Dates for Christmas'. A thin bloke wearing a trench coat and a brown trilby hat with a dark stain on the rim barged into me as he hurried out of the newsagent. He'd been studying my lead story in the afternoon's *Chronicle*. He mumbled an apology and scurried down the street.

Kingswell's art gallery was towards the north end of the High Street, between an olde tea shoppe and an ironmongers. I crossed the street and had a quick look in the window. Pride of place was devoted to a portrait of a wizened agricultural type with a forehead that had more furrows than a ploughed field. He had one of those long-handled sickles over his shoulder. The painting was entitled *Old Tom Goes Reaping*. It was just as well Burrage hadn't proofed the title card. I shudder to think what it would've ended up reading.

I opened the door and stepped into a long room hung with paintings, each tastefully illuminated by its own wall light. I glanced down. A letter in a Basildon Bond blue envelope lay on the doormat. I picked it up and looked at the front. The typewritten address read: Major Toby Kingswell. No street name or number, so it must have been delivered by hand.

The gallery was deserted. An elegant Georgian desk inlaid with hand-tooled green leather stood on the far side of the room. I crossed the room and put the envelope on the desk. The desk had the kind of old-fashioned bell that used to summon hotel porters. I was looking forward to giving the instrument a good *ting ting*, when a door at the back of the gallery opened and a woman appeared.

She looked about twenty-five but could've been older for life had treated her well. She had the kind of slender, well-shaped figure and blossoming complexion that comes from cycling to work and eating your greens. And let's not forget the contribution early nights make to the kind of beauty that's more than skin deep. I had time to think these thoughts because it took the woman a few seconds to walk the length of the gallery. She was wearing a green twinset and pearls with an ochre skirt. Her feet were shod in a pair of shoes that were so sensible they could've taken part in the *Brains Trust*.

She smiled revealing, inevitably, a row of perfect white teeth, and said: "I'm so sorry to have kept you. If it's a Christmas present for a loved one you're looking for, I can recommend *The Hay Barn in Moonlight*."

She gestured with a graceful flip of her hand at a painting on the wall behind me. I turned and gave the artwork the once-over.

"I think the artist has captured the pellucid quality of the light so beautifully," she said.

I smiled, hoping there were no fragments of my lunchtime sandwich stuck between my teeth.

I said: "I rather hoped to obtain some information with the same pellucid quality."

She frowned and a couple of wrinkles appeared one on each side of her forehead. They perfectly matched. They would do.

"I don't understand," she said.

"I'm Colin Crampton, a reporter with the *Evening Chronicle*."

"I'm Toby's – that's to say, Major Kingswell's – personal assistant, Camilla Fogg." She sat down behind the desk. Looked at the envelope, but didn't pick it up.

"I hoped to have a word with Major Kingswell, Miss Fogg."

"It's missus, but my husband is dead. Anyway, I'm afraid Toby isn't here this afternoon. He's attending a meeting of the hanging committee."

My eyes widened at that news.

"It's a hanging I wanted to talk to Major Kingswell about."

"Of a painting?"

"Of a man."

Camilla's finely fingered hand flew to her mouth. (Obviously, with the elegance of a swallow.)

"You're thinking of Archie Flowerdew who killed that dreadful Percy Despart," she said. "I'm sorry for the confusion. In fact, the hanging committee is for the Brighton Masters' Art Exhibition. The committee decides which paintings will be selected to be shown."

"The trial jury fixed it for Archie," I said.

"I'm sorry he will hang. But he is a murderer."

"That's what I'm looking into."

"You mean there's still some doubt? I thought Flowerdew's appeal had been rejected and the Home Secretary had turned down his plea for clemency."

"That's right, but where circumstantial evidence is concerned there's always some doubt. I'd like to know whether or not it's the kind of reasonable doubt that could make the Home Secretary think again."

"Never say die," said Camilla. "Oh dear, that sounded rather heartless. One is awfully sorry."

I moved closer and said: "I think we're beyond worrying about that kind of thing now. But perhaps you could tell me what Major Kingswell feels about the court case and the verdict. After all, he was the victim of one of Despart's so-called satirical comic postcards."

Camilla folded her arms angrily.

"I wish you hadn't reminded me of that," she said. "I've never seen anything quite so beastly. It made Toby fly into a rage. He called the man names I'd never heard of. Threatened to exact all manner of revenge. Said he wished the man would meet a painful and unexpected death. At one point, I thought he was going to kill him. It was weeks before he stopped raging about it. I advised Toby to remember the wise old Sicilian proverb: revenge is a dish best eaten cold."

"So Major Kingswell would not have wept buckets when he learnt of Despart's killing?"

"Cheered to the rafters, more like. Anyway, Toby wasn't the only one who'd been included in those disgusting postcards," she said.

"I know of at least four others," I said.

"There were more than that," Camilla said. "But I don't want to talk about them. They were all vile. Utterly foul. Despart was a beast."

"When will Major Kingswell be in the gallery again?" I asked.

"Not tonight. He'll go back to his flat in Sussex Square in Brighton after the hanging committee."

She rose from behind the desk. Her way of telling me she wasn't answering any more questions.

"Are you sure I can't interest you in *The Hay Barn in Moonlight*? It's by a local artist, Florian Le Grande."

"Not Florian Le Grande RA?"

"You know him?"

"Only by reputation," I said. "Did he also paint *Old Tom Goes Raping*?"

"I beg your pardon!"

"Sorry, I mean reaping. I've been having a lot of trouble with misprints."

"Yes, he painted *Old Tom*. In fact, Florian was here only yesterday to see if it'd been sold. He often drops by. But we've not had a lot of interest."

"Poor old Tom," I said. I turned at the door. "And poor old Florian," I added.

But Camilla had returned to her desk and was looking at the blue envelope.

Outside, the twilight had turned into night. Shops were shutting. The butcher had removed the rabbits from his window. He was swabbing down his cutting block. The greengrocer hefted the basket of chestnuts inside his shop.

I walked back to the car pondering the relationship between the good Major Kingswell and Mrs Fogg. She'd seemed more upset than I would have expected even from a loyal employee when I'd mentioned the postcard. Camilla had said her husband was dead. She was a young woman and I wondered how long she'd remain a widow. *Country Life* types like Camilla were as adept at hunting for husbands as for foxes. I wondered whether she had Toby in her sights. Whether she was in love with him. It would have explained her passion over the Kingswell postcard.

It all made for some idle speculation. But I couldn't see it got me anywhere in my quest to save Archie from the noose.

As I turned the corner, a full moon emerged from behind a dark cloud. It cast a soft glow over the street.

There were still too many unanswered questions. So the moonbeams looked like the only pellucid light I was going to see this night.

When I walked through the front door of Shirley's flat an hour later I was greeted with the rich aroma of a Bolognese sauce. Then I was greeted by Shirley's soft lips, which planted a long kiss on mine. I encircled my arms around her waist and returned the kiss with compound interest.

She said: "I'm going to be a Christmas fairy."

I said: "If you're planning to sit on the top of a Christmas tree you'd better buy a pair of those reinforced bloomers they sell in the ladies' department at Hanningtons. Those fir trees give an awful prickle in the sensitive areas."

She kicked me not so gently on the shin. "I'm going to be a model in a Christmas fairy-themed photo shoot."

In the summer, a scout – for a modelling agency, not the type with a woggle – had spotted Shirley sunbathing in her bikini at Saltdean Lido. He'd signed her up for the agency. Since then, she'd had half-a-dozen assignments. Not many, but they'd paid well.

Shirley said: "This could be my big break. It's for a magazine. They're paying one hundred and fifty pounds for a day's work."

I whistled. "Nice work if you can get it. When is the photo shoot?"

"In the next few days. Before Christmas. The agency will let me know."

"Do they provide the fairy costume?"

"I expect so. I wonder if they'll give me a wand to wave."

"You could sprinkle stardust just by smiling."

She kissed me again. "And you could spread bullshit just by talking. Anyway, I know what you want, but you'll have to have a gin and tonic instead. I've still got my house guest."

I said: "Not in front the children, eh?"

Tammy appeared from the sitting room and said: "What do you mean, children? I'm twenty-two."

I released Shirley from my arms. "It's been a long day. Let's eat – and I'll tell you what progress I've made."

We went into the living room and Shirley dished up the spag bol. We hunkered down around the small table and dug in. The spaghetti tasted as good as it had smelt.

I told Shirley and Tammy about my rummage in the morgue – and what I'd learnt about the pillorying of Toby Kingswell, Gideon Burke and Florian Le Grande.

Tammy said: "We already knew about them. Those postcards were sold all around town."

"That's true," I said. "But I sat through the whole court case and they were only mentioned briefly once. It's fair to assume the police never considered any of them real suspects, so they would never have investigated them thoroughly."

I described my visit to Seaside Smiles and how I'd discovered a possible explanation for Archie's fingerprints on the brochure found in Despart's studio. Tammy seemed excited by this news. But I warned her it wouldn't be enough to overturn the conviction or to win a plea for clemency. Finally, I spoke about my visit to Kingswell's art gallery, but tactfully avoided any mention of the hanging committee.

Tammy twizzled her fork around a stray strand of spaghetti. "I don't see where all this gets us," she said morosely. She put down her fork.

"It gives us hope," Shirley said.

"Does it?" Tammy slumped back on her chair. "I just feel so helpless. Uncle Archie saved my life – and now I can't save his."

Shirley and I exchanged glances.

"How did Archie save your life?" I asked.

"It's a long story."

"We've got all evening," Shirley said. "I'll make some coffee." She crossed to the gas ring, filled the kettle and put it on to boil.

Tammy shrugged. "None of this came out in court. I thought it should, but that snooty lawyer said it wouldn't help."

"Snooty lawyers don't know much about real life," I said.

"Same down under," Shirley said. "For all their gabbing, those bush lawyers might as well stick their heads up their arses."

For the first time, Tammy grinned. "It wasn't funny back then."

"In your childhood?" I asked.

"My father was a bastard. His name was Gilbert. But he had to be called Bert. And anyone who didn't would get the rough edge of his tongue or his fists. And it didn't matter if it was a man or a woman. Except I think he enjoyed it more if it was a woman."

Shirley said: "If he'd tried that with me, I'd have kicked him so hard his cobblers would have popped out of his ears."

"My mum weren't like that," Tammy said. "She were lovely. When I was frightened I would snuggle up to her. Even thinking about her now, I can smell the Otto of Roses she'd dab on herself after he'd hit her. I don't know why. Perhaps the aroma reminded her of something safe."

"Did your father ever hit you?"

"Yes. But mostly I learnt how to keep out of his way. But the slimeball was cruel. He knew how to hurt me in other ways. I remember once he wanted money to go to the pub. Jill, my mum, didn't have a penny. So he decided to raid my money box. But I didn't have any spare cash, either. He yelled at me saying I'd hidden the money, but I hadn't. He completely lost it. He stormed across the room, took my dolls, ripped off their arms and legs and tore all their clothes. Then he stamped on my doll's house and smashed it. I hid behind the settee. I was screaming. I usually did when he was like that. Then he stormed out of the house. I don't know where he went, but I guess he must have got some money from somewhere, because we didn't see him for three days."

Shirley moved back across the room and put her arm round Tammy's shoulder. "That's terrible, kiddo," she said.

"It was, but it was also the first time I realised what a good person my uncle Archie was. Archie was Gilbert's brother. But not a blood brother. Gilbert had been adopted as a baby by Archie's mum and dad."

"Your grandparents," I said.

"That's right. Gilbert was the child of friends of theirs who'd killed themselves in a motorcycle accident. They took Gilbert in out of the kindness of their hearts, gave him their family name and, from what I've heard, lived to regret it."

"He was a difficult child?" I asked.

"And a bastard of a father," Tammy said. "But Uncle Archie was quite different. He used to come round when Bert had hit Mum in one of his drunken rages. Sometimes, he could calm the brute down and sometimes, he'd take a hit himself."

"Sounds like a hero," I said.

"To me he was. And certainly that time. I remember he spent

hours repairing my broken doll's house. Then he glued together the dolls. We knew he was good at painting, but we never realised he was so good at that kind of stuff. He'd always said he was all thumbs when it came to using his hands. I remember we used to joke about his shoelaces always coming undone because he couldn't tie them properly. He was just bad at knots. It was a kind of blind spot. Anyway, he mended my doll's house."

"That's the kind of uncle I'd have liked," Shirley said.

Tammy smiled. "Uncle Archie even mended the dolls' clothes that Gilbert had ripped. I can still see Archie sitting there, with his glasses perched on the end of his nose, and a needle and thread in his right hand. He stitched up tears in the cloth and sewed on little pieces of lace where there were still holes. He even found some buttons to sew on where the others had been lost. He got real pleasure from it. I remember him helping me to re-dress the dolls when he'd finished and saying how nice they all looked."

"Sounds like a bonzer guy," Shirley said.

"Yes, he taught me to draw, as well. Told me I was good enough to become an artist myself if I wanted. I don't know whether or not I've got the dedication. But at least my drawing became a distraction from that brute of a father."

"But Archie wasn't able to stop Bert's violence?" I asked.

"No, more's the pity."

Shirley put a cup of steaming coffee in front of Tammy. "Knock that down your neck, kiddo."

Tammy sipped her coffee. Put down the cup and said: "Uncle Archie helped me so much – especially since that bastard father of mine was sent to prison."

Shirley and I exchanged worried glances. "When was that?" I asked.

"Eight years ago," Tammy said. "I was fourteen at the time. The brute went on a two-day bender, came home and knocked Mum about so badly she ended up in hospital on life support. A broken rib pierced her lung, her spleen was ruptured – and that was only the start of it. Bert was hauled up before the court and it all came out. I was the star witness and made sure it did. Ma was still in hospital and couldn't speak for herself. I cheered when the judge sent the bastard down for fifteen years."

"Did your ma recover?" Shirley said.

"She came back home, but was never the same. She died five years ago. Never recovered properly from her beating. I was seventeen at the time. I was devastated, but Uncle Archie helped me through that difficult time. He found me lodgings in Brighton and everything. And, eventually, as an independent girl, life seemed to get better. I even changed my name."

"What were you called before?"

"Thomasina. Apparently, it was Bert's idea. He wanted a boy but I didn't oblige. He used to call me Tommy, when it wasn't something worse. I hated it. It reminded me that I wasn't really wanted. So when I was independent and free of him I changed it to Tammy. And Tammy it is to this day."

"Tammy. I like it," Shirley said. "But, hey, you look flaked, kid. Why don't you turn in? Use my bedroom. I'll kip on the couch tonight."

Tammy yawned and stretched her arms. "You've both been very kind," she said. "Perhaps things will look better in the morning."

I smiled. "Perhaps."

Tammy stood up, shuffled into Shirley's bedroom and shut the door.

Shirley joined me at the table. She leaned towards me and whispered: "I feel sorry for the kid, but she can't stay here forever. Especially with the blue heelers on her tail."

I was worried about the cops catching up with Tammy, too. Especially if Shirley was implicated in hiding her.

I said: "We'll need to move Tammy elsewhere tomorrow. But I need to think about that overnight. Suppose we speak first thing in the morning?"

"Let's do that," Shirley said.

"In the meantime, I need to return to my own palatial residence."

Shirley leaned over and licked my ear. "Is there anything you need before you go?"

"Well," I said. "Seeing as the children have gone to bed …"

It was close to midnight when I stepped through the door of my lodgings in Regency Square.

I'd barely shut the front door before the Widow shot out of her parlour and cornered me by the hatstand. Mrs Gribble, my landlady – the Widow to her tenants – and I nurtured a healthy dislike for one another but found a way to rub along. Me because my rooms on the top floor of her house were convenient. She because she had a habit of getting herself into awkward scrapes and usually called on my help to extricate herself from them.

The Widow was dressed in a long flannelette dressing gown in shocking pink. She'd put her hair in curlers and fixed a net over it all.

She said: "I'd offer you a glass of cream sherry, but I've locked up the bottle for the night."

"Best place for it," I said. "Good night, Mrs Gribble."

A bony hand held me by the shoulder. "There was one other little matter."

I knew it. Otherwise, the Widow wouldn't have been lurking behind her parlour door waiting to pounce on me. It was usually quicker to hear her out.

So I said: "What's the problem?"

"It's to do with my Christmas cards. You see, my late husband's sister, Eunice, is coming to stay over Christmas, but she's let me know she won't be arriving until the late train on Christmas Eve. Anyway, I always get up early on Christmas morning on account of I have to get the turkey in the oven. So I'll have gone to bed by the time Eunice gets here. So I thought I'd leave her supper warming in the oven."

"What's all this got to do with Christmas cards?"

"Well, I was writing the cards today and I wrote one each for Eunice and Mr Evans, the butcher."

"I thought you'd fallen out with Evans."

"We sorted out that business about the faggots." The Widow shuffled uncomfortably in her fluffy slippers. "Anyway, the thing is this. I got the cards for Eunice and Mr Evans mixed up."

"You mean you sent Eunice's card to Mr Evans and his card to Eunice?"

The Widow nodded. She seemed close to tears.

"Does it matter?" I said.

"It's what I wrote inside them that's worrying me."

"Which was?"

"In Mr Evans's –"

"Which has gone to Eunice."

"I wrote, 'Seasons greetings. I won't be needing any of your tripe over Christmas.' And in Eunice's –"

"Which has gone to Mr Evans."

"I wrote, 'When you come on Christmas Eve, I'll be in bed but keeping something hot for you.' I'm worried that both of them may misinterpret the messages. What do you think I should do?"

I said: "It's late and I'm tired, Mrs Gribble. I'll see if I can think of an answer by the morning."

The Widow nodded as though it was only a matter of time before her world fell apart. She crept back into her parlour.

I raced upstairs to my room and buried my face in a pillow before I started laughing.

Chapter 7

My bedroom door flew open and two uniformed cops burst into the room.

I sat up in bed and glanced at the alarm clock: six thirty.

I said: "If you were planning an early call, at least you could've brought my morning tea."

One of the cops had a Hitler moustache. The other sported a bright red pimple on his nose.

Moustache said: "Where is she?"

I said: "If you mean Mrs Gribble, my landlady – also known as the Widow, but never in her hearing – she'll be in her parlour. Unless you trampled her into the hall carpet in your rush to get up here."

Pimple said: "We're not here for Mrs Gribble. We know she's a respectable landlady."

I said: "Everyone's entitled to their point of view."

"She let us in."

"I've warned her before not to admit undesirables."

"Don't get snarky with us," Moustache said. "We know you're hiding Tammy Flowerdew."

I simulated a puzzled frown and said: "Who?"

"You know who," Pimple said.

"Oh, that Tammy Flowerdew. The one who's campaigning to save her beloved uncle's neck from the noose."

"We don't want any of your newspaper sob stories," Moustache said.

I said: "If you want to look under the bed, be quick about it, as I'm planning to get up."

Pimple moved forward, but Moustache held him back. "She won't be under there. Check the bathroom."

"Yes, she might be crouched double behind the lavatory. And don't forget to look down the plughole while you're there."

Pimple said: "We're wasting our time here."

Moustache said: "We'll find her. Don't you doubt that."

The pair turned towards the door.

I said: "Just a friendly word of advice. That looks nasty. You ought to get something done about it."

Pimple turned. "Thanks for your concern, but I've already got some ointment."

I said: "I was talking about the moustache."

They stamped out and slammed the door.

I shot out of bed like it was on fire. Hurried into the bathroom. Rinsed myself in the shower. Ran the razor speedily over my chin. Gave my teeth a turbocharged brush. Huddled into my clothes and legged it down the stairs.

I'd been expecting the cops to pull a stunt like that, but not so soon. And as they'd raided me, perhaps they were planning to call on Shirley, too. Maybe they were already on their way.

I had to warn her. But not using the Widow's phone in the hall. The Widow had ears like radar antennae. Besides, if she was pally enough to admit the cops for a dawn raid, perhaps she wasn't averse to grassing up one of her tenants.

Namely me.

And after I'd offered to help her out of her Christmas card imbroglio.

I ran down the road to the telephone box on the corner. Shoved my four pence into the slot, dialled a number and listened to the ring tone. Shirley answered after seven rings. I pushed button A and said: "You have to get Tammy out now. The police may be on their way."

"The blue heelers?"

"The very same. But not in a healing spirit."

As I'd good reason to know in the past, Shirley was great in a crisis. So she didn't start shrieking. Or babbling nonsense. Or asking silly questions.

Instead, she said: "Where can I take her?"

I'd thought about that on the way to the phone box. The answer had come as a flash of inspiration.

"Take her to Henrietta Houndstooth's flat." Henrietta owed me a big favour – and now it was payback time.

Shirley said: "I met Henrietta once, but I don't know where she lives."

I gave the address and told Shirley the best way to get there. "I'll call Henrietta now, explain the situation and let her know you're on your way. And, Shirley, don't leave it a minute longer than you have to."

I waited for Shirley's reply but she'd already rung off.

When I arrived at Henrietta's flat, I found Shirley and Tammy sitting at the table stuffing their faces with toast and marmalade. Henrietta bustled in from the kitchen with a fresh pot of tea.

She said: "You look like a man who needs two spoons of sugar this morning."

I said: "I feel like a man who needs a strong sedative and a quiet lie-down. But I'm not going to get one."

I told the three about the dawn raid by Mr Plod. Tammy looked worried, but Shirley laughed and spooned a huge dollop of the Oxford Thick Cut onto her toast.

I joined the girls at the table while Henrietta poured the tea.

I said: "I'm sorry to spring this on you, Henrietta, especially when you're getting over a cold."

"Don't mention it. Since I was a girl, I've dreamed of taking part in a cloak-and-dagger operation. Besides, I'm feeling a bit better today."

Shirley munched her toast, had a slurp of tea and said: "I think we made it out of my flat just in time. After your call, I rang for a taxi. We had to keep our heads down as we drove away, because a cop car raced into the square with its blue light flashing."

I said: "If they spotted the taxi, they'll question the driver and trace you here."

"They won't," Tammy piped up. "Shirley was brilliant. She ordered the taxi to take us to Brighton station. Then she talked to me about how I should enjoy my stay in London. I nearly gave it away before I realised what she was doing."

"Misdirecting the driver," I said.

"It helped that Tammy had her red holdall with her." Shirley said. "She looked like she was going on a journey. We raced through the station like a streak of kangaroo pee and ran down the stairs to Trafalgar Street. Then we hustled down to the London Road and caught a bus over here."

"That's good," I said. "The police will make enquiries at the station and eventually realise you didn't buy tickets, but they'll be hard-pressed to trace you to the bus and here."

Henrietta grinned: "So I'm not getting a police raid. How disappointing!"

"Not yet," I said. "But we need to think of a plan to move Tammy in case the plods surprise everyone and manage to trace her."

"I have an idea about that. We can discuss it later," Henrietta said, with a conspiratorial wink.

I had an idea what that wink meant. Triple trouble.

Detective Chief Superintendent Alec Tomkins knocked a dottle out of his pipe and leaned menacingly towards me.

"You realise your presence here is purely voluntary," he said.

We were in interview room one at Brighton police station. The room normally reserved for hardened criminals. Murderers. Kidnappers. Rapists. Safe-crackers.

And journalists who've outsmarted the cops.

Tomkins's thick thatch of black hair looked less perfectly slicked back than normal. But his bushy eyebrows were drawn together in an angry frown.

I leaned forward and returned Tomkins's scowl. "Of course

I'm here voluntarily. It's only you who *has* to be here."

Tomkins harrumphed. The minute hand on the old clock on the wall ticked noisily to three minutes past nine. I lounged back as far as I could on the hard wooden chair and decided to enjoy myself. After all, I was helping the police with their enquiries. And when it comes to helpfulness, I just have that talent – I'm as helpful as a blind man in an archery contest.

An hour earlier, I'd left Tammy in Henrietta's care, looked in briefly at the office and then walked round to the cop shop for what I'd expected to be the routine morning press briefing. Instead, I'd been informed the briefing had been cancelled and a burly sergeant had invited me to step into the interview room.

Tomkins peered into the bowl of his pipe, seemed satisfied with what he saw and said: "You can leave at any time."

I said: "Why should I want to miss such pleasant company and commodious surroundings?"

Tomkins made a sound somewhere between a sigh and a snarl. He said: "You know that someone painted a slogan on the front doors of the Royal Pavilion two nights ago."

"Yes. It was Tammy Flowerdew. There was a picture of her with her paintbrush on the front page of yesterday's *Chronicle*."

"So you admit to aiding and abetting a criminal offence."

"I never admit to anything. It's a bad habit of mine. Tammy had already completed her artwork and chained herself to the porte cochère before the photographer and I turned up."

Tomkins scribbled a sentence in his notebook.

He said: "We can't have people running around town taking liberties with other people's property."

"Like the two plods who burst into my bedroom this morning before I was awake. Spoilt a perfectly good dream involving Brigitte Bardot and an ice-cream sundae."

"The two uniformed officers were making a routine search," Tomkins said stiffly.

"Without a warrant."

Tomkins fumbled with his pipe. "There may have been a technical delay with the paperwork."

While Tomkins was on the back foot, I said: "You were the arresting officer with Archie Flowerdew."

"Yes. I said so in court."

"When you interviewed him, did Archie claim to have been framed?"

Tomkins slapped his hand on the table. "That's enough of that. I'm not here to answer your questions. Where is Tammy Flowerdew?"

I grinned. "I really can't say."

"Can't or won't?" Tomkins said.

"A journalist is like a chef with a book of secret recipes," I said.

"What do you mean?"

"We never reveal our sources."

Tomkins and I fenced away for another ten minutes.

He finally realised he was getting nowhere. Besides, he plainly wanted to light his pipe and he couldn't fumble around with a tobacco pouch and matches while I was in the room taunting him.

I stepped out of the cop shop into Bartholomew Square planning to head straight back to the paper and write up the next instalment in the Tammy saga. But that was before I spotted a trilby hat with a dark stain on the rim moving behind the topside of a fishmonger's van on the other side of the road. I'd seen the same weather-beaten titfer the day before. The bloke who'd barged into me outside the newsagents in Ditchling.

The trilby moved a few feet to the right and the wearer emerged from behind the van. It was the same bloke. He headed towards The Lanes. I've mentioned before that I'm not a great believer in coincidence. I reckoned the odds of Trilby and I being in the same place at the same time on consecutive days must have been hundreds to one. I wasn't sure whether he'd been watching me. I hadn't noticed him when I'd breezed into the police station half an hour earlier. But I'd not been looking.

I was alert now.

If Trilby was keeping me under surveillance, he was a master of the craft. (And I know a thing or two about it.) One of the rules is to try to be in the place your target is heading for before he reaches it. Most people can't believe that somebody who is already on the scene is there to spy on you. It's not as difficult an art as it seems. You simply need to know your target's routine and you can be in position when they pitch up. The meeting in Ditchling probably happened by chance. But it wouldn't have been difficult for a watcher to know I attended the police press briefing at nine most mornings.

Trilby was a nippy walker. He set off at a punishing pace through the Lanes. Short people often seem to walk faster than tall. Presumably, shorter legs need more steps to cover the same distance. I had a good three inches in height over Trilby, but I struggled to keep up. Too little sleep the previous night had blunted my edge.

We headed into North Street, with me about twenty yards behind. Although early, the street was crowded with Christmas shoppers. They barged along with bulging bags and hefty parcels. Trilby was like a sprinter, weaving in and out of the crowds. I ploughed along in his wake. I could've run ahead and engineered a meeting. My usual ploy is to pretend we've met somewhere before. But Trilby looked like a professional in the surveillance business. So he'd be unlikely to fall for the obvious tricks. Besides, it's always best to garner as much information as you can before a confrontation.

Trilby marched down North Street and then surprised me by turning into Hanningtons department store. The place was a warren of different rooms, with at least four entrances. It would be packed just before Christmas. I could easily lose him in the crowds. I raced down the street and pushed through the doors.

There was a melee of shoppers around every counter. No sighting of Trilby. I moved further into the store. Clumped through the shoes department. Wafted into perfumes. No sign. I didn't think Trilby knew I was following him. But professionals don't make assumptions. They work on the safety-first principle. Which is always to throw off a tail – even if the tail is only in their imagination.

I asked myself the question: how would I throw off a follower in a department store? Answer: I'd head for the department I'd least be likely to visit. In my case – and, I suspected, Trilby's too – ladies' fashion. I shoved my way through a couple of rooms and made it. A row of mannequins wearing party dresses stood at the entrance. I went in. The place was heaving, with women rifling rails of skirts and blouses. I could see the trilby above the crowd. I pushed my way through the shoppers – and there it was.

Perched on the top of a mannequin. I thought Trilby had chosen well. He'd abandoned his hat on the head of a dummy wearing a pair of tailored slacks and a chunky-knit Fair Isle cardigan.

The man, himself, had vanished.

I arrived back at the *Chronicle* pondering the identity of Trilby – and wearing his hat.

I wouldn't put it past Tomkins to put a tail on me in the hope that I'd lead him to Tammy. But there were two objections to that theory. First, he'd already arrived in Ditchling before I'd turned up yesterday afternoon. My decision to visit the village was last-minute. I'd told no one where I was going. So I couldn't see how he'd figured out my destination.

And the second was his general appearance. I'd seen some shabbily dressed coppers in my time, especially among the plain-clothes mob. But Trilby looked like he'd picked up his outfit from the Sally Army.

So if Trilby wasn't the Old Bill, who was he? At the moment, I didn't have any other theories, but I would keep a close watch wherever I went in future. That wouldn't be so easy now, because Trilby would be wearing a different hat.

In the meantime, my long talk with Tammy the previous evening about her early life would give me some great copy. So I heaved the Remington towards me, rolled copy paper into the carriage and started typing. I'd just rolled the tenth folio out of the machine and called for Cedric to take the copy up to the subs, when Figgis appeared on the other side of the newsroom. He waved at me through the smoke haze and pointed at his office.

He was already sitting behind his desk and lighting a fag by the time I reached it.

"Close the door," he said.

"Feeling the draught?" I said.

"No," he said. "The heat. It's like a bonfire has been lit under my bum."

"Not the old trouble with your piles?"

"No, it's the old trouble with your misprints."

I sat down on his guest chair and said: "That caution to cushion business. I thought we were clearing that up with a correction in the paper."

"We're running a correction but, apparently, it's not clearing it up. It seems Abercrombie won't be satisfied. He claims the article as printed demeans his authority as chairman of the bench. He says it amounts to contempt of court."

"And he's told you this?"

Figgis puffed morosely on his Woodbine. His heart wasn't in it. "Not personally. He's been bending His Holiness's ear. And Pope has come down hard on me. He points out that if there's a contempt-of-court case he'll be standing in the dock as editor of the paper."

"No one better than a pope to call on divine intervention for an acquittal," I said.

Figgis waved his fag at me. "And you won't be so cocky, either.

You'll be standing right next to him as author."

I pursed my lips in annoyance. This trivial misprint was getting out of control. "But I typed caution. I'm absolutely certain of that. This is an issue between the comps and the proofreader Burrage."

"His Holiness doesn't see it that way. Burrage has covered his rear end with reinforced steel on this and you're in line for the slings and arrows of outrageous fortune."

"Then I shall have to take arms against a sea of trouble," I said.

Figgis stubbed out his ciggie and tossed it in his bin. "Then you'd better do it quickly. Pope says that unless you can prove you're the injured party in this, you're off the paper."

"How long have I got?" I asked.

"I suspect not long enough," Figgis said. "Even for you."

I walked back into the newsroom feeling like I'd just been slugged in the stomach.

By a heavyweight boxer.

I'd been set up as the fall guy for someone else's blunder.

It was sneaky. It was snide. It was unjust.

If I couldn't prove the truth of the matter in the next few days, I was going to lose my job. And perhaps my freedom, if Abercrombie went through with his contempt-of-court threat. The good magistrate was not renowned around town for his quality of mercy.

But I was not going to lose my neck.

Only Archie Flowerdew was going to do that. So I parked the problem of the misprint at the back of my mind.

I sat down at my desk and hauled the press-cuttings file towards me. Rifled again through the cuttings about Major Toby Kingswell, Canon Gideon Burke and Professor Florian Le Grande.

Le Grande, I remembered, had been Despart's tutor at art

school. One of the cuttings mentioned he now lived in Lewes, an arty town with a ruined castle, ten miles outside Brighton. Perhaps he'd have an insight into the relationship between the pair in those early days. Another cutting informed me that Le Grande was planning a controversial nude self-portrait of himself.

So, perhaps I would be able to catch him with his trousers down.

Chapter 8

Florian Le Grande's taste in fashion was for red velvet trousers.

And he had them on.

I said: "Painting a self-portrait of yourself in the nude must be one of the most difficult tasks since Van Gogh pictured himself with an ear missing."

Le Grande arched an eyebrow. "It's all a question of mirrors," he said. "You position them so you can get an all-round view of yourself."

We were sitting in Le Grande's studio, a cannonball's shot from Lewes's castle. It was late morning and the feeble rays of a winter sun filtered through the windows. Stacks of Le Grande's paintings leant against a wall. I spotted a landscape of the Seven Sisters, a pen-and-ink sketch of Brighton actress Dora Bryan, and a still life of cherries overflowing from a wicker basket. A long wooden workbench ran along another wall. It was loaded with half-used tubes of oils, brushes and old palettes encrusted with dried paint. An easel stood at a sideways angle to the window so that it caught the light. The easel held a large canvas – a work in progress of a scantily clad woman with a water pitcher on her right shoulder and a pained expression on her face.

Le Grande saw me studying the picture. "*A Maiden at the Village Well.* It's a commission from one of our grander stately homes."

He moved across the studio in a kind of glide and sat down on a wing chair covered with a paint-stained throw. Apart from the velvet trousers, he was wearing an artist's smock and a blue beret at a jaunty angle on top of his curly blonde wig.

He waved me to a basket chair. It creaked like a ship in a gale when I sat down.

I said: "As I mentioned on the phone, the news that you're painting the self-portrait is about to excite the art world. So we'd like to consider writing a profile of you for our Saturday supplement."

Back in the office, I'd thought up the ploy as a way of getting an early interview. Few people can resist the opportunity of a profile in a newspaper and, as I suspected, Le Grande was one of them.

He said: "The last time I was interviewed by your paper was in Brighton at my mother's funeral. She was well known for her charity work in the town, so naturally the press were in attendance."

"When was the funeral?"

"Just over a year ago. The service was at St Rita's, beautifully conducted by the vicar. I thanked him warmly afterwards. Anyway, one of your reporters recognised me. It was a sad occasion, but of course I was willing to answer some questions."

St Rita's – the church where Canon Gideon Burke was vicar.

So Le Grande and Burke had met. I filed the fact away in my memory. Le Grande also knew Kingswell. I wondered whether Kingswell knew Burke. If so, that would complete the triangle.

I pointed at the painting on the easel. "You mentioned just now that the *Maiden* is a commission, but are lucky members of the public ever able to purchase your fine paintings in galleries?" (When it comes to acting the crawler, even old Johnnie Gielgud couldn't ham it up like me.)

Le Grande preened himself by studying the fingernails on his left hand. "Much of my work is commissioned and there is such a heavy demand that only a few of my choicest works make it into the galleries."

I glanced at the rejects stacked along the wall. The truth was that Le Grande was turning out the kind of dated stuff you used to see hanging in minor municipal art galleries. Few big-time art lovers would fork out their hard-earned for it.

I said: "Your work is so eclectic, it must be hard to decide which paintings to offer the galleries."

"I paint where my muse takes me. When you're inspired to create great art, you can't be walled in by common public taste."

"So you don't do this for money?" I asked.

Le Grande's cheeks coloured slightly. "Of course, artists down the centuries have had to sell their work to eat."

"And drink," I added.

Le Grande frowned. "Yes, and drink. But it is the calling of the muse that is important."

"So where in Sussex may our readers view these wonderful paintings?"

"Well, I'm an international artist, not just limited to Sussex."

"But you wouldn't deprive local people of your genius?"

Le Grande gave a little wave as though the idea would never occur to him. "Of course not. I believe there may be one or two of my recent works in a gallery in Ditchling."

"Would that be the Kingswell Gallery?"

Le Grande scratched his head. "I don't immediately recall. It may be. One's paintings are in so many places, one simply can't remember everywhere."

But one should be able to remember the name of the place one pitched up at two days ago, I thought. I wondered why Le Grande seemed anxious to distance himself from a place Camilla had told me he visited regularly. Could it be professional vanity or was there more to it?

So I asked: "Do you visit galleries showing your works often – such as the Kingswell Gallery?"

"Not often. I think I may have visited the Kingswell Gallery a few years ago, when I permitted it to hang one of my works, but not lately."

That was an obvious lie. Le Grande couldn't possibly have forgotten he was at the gallery so recently. But why did he want to play down his connection to it? I wasn't getting anywhere with this line of questioning. So I switched tack.

"You used to be a professor at the Slade Art School," I said.

"That is correct. Professor of Painting. But now emeritus. And on an honorary basis."

"But you were at the Slade for many years?"

"Since the nineteen thirties."

"You must have taught many students in those days."

"Hundreds, if not thousands."

Underneath my notebook, I crossed my fingers before asking the next question.

"Are there any students who particularly stick in your memory?"

Le Grande gazed around the room as though seeking inspiration from his own work. "None that I recall. But, then, those of us who aspire to greatness rarely achieve public recognition in their own lifetime."

It wasn't the answer I'd been hoping for. But when that happens, a good reporter just asks the same question in a different way.

So I said: "I wasn't thinking only of students you remember for their artistic skill but for any reason."

"Some of my students lowered themselves in commercial art. I mean, what serious artist would design a cornflake packet?"

"What about students who lived and worked in Sussex?"

Le Grande shifted uncomfortably in his chair. "I don't keep tabs on where my former students live."

It was time to be blunt.

"Didn't you tutor Percy Despart?"

Le Grande banged his hand down on the arm of his chair. "His is a name I prefer to forget."

"I understand how sensitive you must be about Despart. Didn't he produce a comic postcard of you?"

Le Grande shot out of his seat. "This interview has gone far enough."

"I only want to build up a rounded picture of your life."

"The postcard had nothing to do with my life. It was defamatory."

"But you didn't sue."

"My lawyers advised against. Solely on the grounds of cost."

"And there were rumours that plans for a knighthood were dropped after the postcard appeared."

"I never comment on rumours. Or honours. And now I must ask you to leave."

I said: "One final question."

"If you must."

"The nude self-portrait – what style will it be painted in?"

"The naturalistic style."

"So everything where it should be. No eyes in the middle of the forehead, for example."

"Certainly not."

"And everything in proper proportion."

"What do you mean?"

"I wondered whether you planned to add a couple of extra brushstrokes down below. Just to interest the ladies."

Le Grande's face had turned as red as his trousers. He advanced towards me menacingly. His lips had curled into a vicious snarl. His hands were balled into fists.

"Get out!" he screamed. "You are an affront to art ... and to this palace of beauty."

I quoted some Keats at him: " 'Beauty is truth, truth beauty – that is all ye know on earth, and all ye need to know.' " I shoved through the door and headed out into the street. "But not here," I added.

I arrived back at the *Chronicle* shortly after four o'clock.

As I walked into the newsroom, Sally Martin hurried over to me.

She said: "I've just taken a call on your phone. It was Shirley. She needs to speak to you urgently."

"Did she say where she was calling from?"

Sally looked a bit sheepish. "Her flat. Actually, her exact words were 'what's left of my flat'."

I hurried across to my desk and grabbed the receiver. Dialled Shirley's number. She answered after two rings.

I said: "What's up?"

"I've been turned over."

"You mean burgled?"

"No. I don't think anything's been taken. But the place has been searched. Looks like a herd of wallabies have scampered through the place."

"Have you called the police?"

"After what happened to you this morning, I think it may have been the police."

Shirley had a point. Tomkins was the kind of officer who'd quote the rule book when it suited him. And ignore it when it didn't. He'd be well acquainted with the rougher element in the force – the officers who policed the late-night clubs and bars. They wouldn't be too fussy about helping out their guv if they thought there'd be something in it for them.

I said: "Are you OK?"

"Sure. I wasn't here when the hit squad burst in. Wish I had been. We'd have had some new nuts to stuff the Christmas turkey. And they wouldn't have been chestnuts."

I laughed. It would take more than a search of her flat to throw Shirley off her stride.

I said: "I want to make some calls about this. We need to find out what's happening. And we need to consider how this affects Tammy."

"Right. If the blue heelers are closing in, we should hide the sheila elsewhere. But don't ask me where."

"Leave that to me," I said. "I'll need to make a few calls and come round in about an hour."

I replaced the receiver.

Shirley's news was worrying on two counts. If the police had searched her flat, it meant they were more determined to track down Tammy than I thought. Even if her uncle Archie was a killer, Tammy had only committed a relatively minor crime. It didn't warrant the police effort Tomkins was mounting. But then Tomkins was a man who took every setback as a personal affront. He wouldn't be satisfied until he'd put Tammy behind bars, too. And if he could do it before Archie was strung up, that would give him a malicious pleasure.

But not if I could stop it.

I picked up the receiver and dialled Henrietta's home number.

Her voice sounded a little thick from her cold when she answered.

I said: "This is the removal man. I understand you have a package that needs to be shifted."

"The package is quite safe in my sitting room at the moment," Henrietta said. "But I'm concerned about the security of keeping it here for too long."

"Me, too. The trouble is I have nowhere to send my package at the moment."

"I may have an idea about that," Henrietta said.

"You do?"

"Yes. I'm thinking of three ladies who work in a *clip joint*." I could hear the grin on Henrietta's face as she said it.

I said: "You mean ladies who would be very *cut up* if they weren't invited to help. I'll tell them you're getting better but would welcome some company this evening. We'll get them to your flat and ask them to help."

"If I know my girls, they won't need much persuading," Henrietta said.

The line went dead.

I jiggled the receiver to get a new line and dialled a number at Brighton police station.

A rustic voice that reminded me of rooks cawing in an old elm tree said: "Ted Wilson."

Wilson was an honest copper in Brighton's police. He was one of the few who didn't spend Wednesday nights rolling up his left trouser leg. As a result, he'd not found promotion as fast as the funny handshake brigade. But he'd made detective inspector on merit and built a reputation for clearing up some big cases. He was my only reliable contact at the cop shop.

I said: "I hope you haven't been doing anything you oughtn't."

Wilson said: "I don't know what you're talking about. And, anyway, you're the number one naughty boy at the moment."

"I'm always the naughty boy. But I want to know which coppers broke into Shirley's flat this afternoon."

"What? That's the first I've heard of it."

"Tomkins would have been the brains behind the operation. I use the word 'brains' loosely."

"I think that would be a step too far even for Tomkins. If a scam like that backfired, he'd be back on the seafront asking buskers to 'move along'."

"I need a favour."

"You always need a favour. The question is, do you deserve one?"

I said: "Aren't we forgetting something?"

Ted sighed. "You're not going to bring that up again?"

Earlier in the year, I'd helped Ted arrest a member of the aristocracy on a murder charge. I reckoned in the currency of favours that left me in credit at the bank.

"I just want you to make a couple of discreet enquiries. If this is a stunt Tomkins didn't pull, perhaps the beat copper may have heard or seen something."

"Leave it with me."

"Thanks, Ted. I'll be in my usual haunt at ten this evening if you have anything for me."

I rang off.

Shirley and I reached Henrietta's flat shortly after six. I rang the bell and we waited.

Shirley said: "Do you think the Clipping Cousins will come?"

I said: "I'm certain of it. I told them Henrietta was in low spirits after her cold and needed some company to cheer her up. The three of them jumped at the idea of visiting her this evening."

The door opened. Henrietta stood in the dim light of the hallway. Her eyes were still watery from her cold and her nose was red. She'd wrapped a scarf around her neck.

She said: "Step into the sick house."

We marched in.

Tammy was sitting at the table holding a pencil with a few sheets of paper in front of her. She looked up as we came in. "I've been drawing to take my mind off things," she said.

Shirley and I crossed to the table to take a look. Tammy had drawn sketches of Henrietta, Shirley and me.

"These are really good," Shirley said.

"We hire artists on the paper who couldn't draw likenesses as accurate as this from memory," I said.

"Uncle Archie taught me well," Tammy said. "But now this is all I can do while he rots in prison."

I gave her shoulder a reassuring pat. "I think we've made some progress today."

She put down her pencil and said: "Tell me."

I described my visit to Florian Le Grande. "He had a motive to murder Despart," I said. "And, as I found out when I deliberately provoked him about his self-portrait, a temper that could goad him into doing it."

"Then why don't we get the police to arrest him?" Tammy asked.

"I don't have a shred of hard evidence to give them. They'll need more than a motive to reopen the enquiry."

Tammy slumped back in her chair. Tears pricked her eyes. "It's all hopeless," she said.

"No, it's not," I said. "Someone else is interested in this case, but I don't know who – or what – their interest is."

I told Tammy about my encounters with Trilby. "My first instinct was to think he was a cop trying to track you down. But even the plain-clothes boys who raid the brothels in Kemp Town don't dress that badly. I'm convinced he has another interest."

"What could that be?" Henrietta asked.

"I don't know," I said. "But I intend to find out."

The doorbell rang.

"That will be the Cousins," I said.

I turned to Tammy. "I think you should step into the bedroom for a moment. We need to explain to the ladies what's happening – and gauge their reaction before we introduce you."

"You think they'll turn me in?" Tammy asked.

"No. But let's take one step at a time."

Tammy stood up and shuffled off resentfully to the bedroom. Henrietta went downstairs to let the Cousins in.

Seconds later, they burst into the room. The next couple of minutes were taken up with introductions. None of the Cousins had ever met Shirley before. ("She's such a nice girl, for an Australian," Freda observed.) Then they fussed around Henrietta.

"The best cure for a cold is a hot toddy with lemon, and bed," Mabel said.

"I always recommend a mustard poultice wrapped in a towel and tied on the top of your head," Elsie said.

"My uncle Ethelbert once caught a cold that went right down onto his lungs," Freda said. "He rubbed his chest with grease made from the fin of a great white shark and never caught another cold in his life."

"Never?" asked Elsie.

"Never," Freda said. "He died three days later."

Henrietta held up her hand. "Ladies, please. My cold is getting better and I hope to be back in the office in a day or two

– without hot toddies, mustard poultices or shark grease. Now, sit down and listen, please. Colin has something very important to say."

I'd been wondering about how to approach this for the last hour. In the end, I decided I'd just lay the facts before them. So I told the story of the trial. I described why Tammy believed in her uncle Archie's innocence. I explained why it was important to keep her safe in the next few days so she could continue to campaign for her uncle's life.

"So, that's it," I concluded. "Tammy is staying here, but the police are on her trail."

"Hot on her trail?" Mabel asked.

"With Tomkins running the case, it'll be lukewarm," I said. "But they'll work it out in the end. Sooner or later, they'll come knocking on Henrietta's door. Just as they did with mine and, we think, with Shirley's. We need more houses where we can move Tammy. Places the plods won't think of searching."

I walked over to the fireplace and leant on the mantelpiece. Adopted a heroic pose. Delivered my peroration. "The question is, ladies, will any of you offer sanctuary to a fugitive who is fighting for justice?"

An uneasy silence settled over the room. It was like a scene in one of those films where the director is trying to wind up the tension by screening close-ups of all the characters looking uneasy. Where you're supposed to understand what's going through their minds by the looks on their faces.

Mabel looked at Elsie.

Elsie looked at Freda.

Freda looked at Mabel.

Shirley looked at me.

I looked at Shirley.

Then we all looked at Henrietta.

Henrietta pulled out a handkerchief and blew her nose.

Mabel stopped looking at Elsie. Instead, she looked at me.

And she said: "We've got a spare room Tammy could use. And if my Arnie asks who she is, I'll just say she's one of my sister's husband's cousins from the Wirral come down south for a couple of days. He's never taken any interest in my side of the family, anyway."

Elsie said: "I'd have to empty the box room, but I could put a camp bed in there. My Lennie spends so much time fancying those ferrets of his, I don't suppose he'd even notice there was someone else in the house."

Freda said: "My Bill is always moaning about unexpected visitors. But this time I'm going to tell him if he complains he can forget about his annual trip to my side of the bed on Christmas Eve."

I clapped my hands. The Cousins deserved a round of applause.

I said: "I think it's time you all met Tammy."

Shirley went to fetch her from the bedroom. Tammy came into the room and stood in the doorway.

I said: "With the help of the Cousins, we now have more safe houses than MI5."

Tammy grinned. "I don't know what to say."

Shirley said: "I think Tammy should move tonight. Especially after the break-in at my place."

I nodded. "If we keep Tammy moving from one house to another, we'll have the police chasing round in circles."

"Until they disappear up their own fundaments," Shirley added to general applause.

Tammy's shyness had melted away. She had the same fighting spirit as when I'd cut the chains holding her to the porte cochère at the Royal Pavilion.

"Don't think I'm not grateful for everything you're doing for me," she said. "But I don't want to be hiding away in safe houses – even in lots of them. I want to be fighting to save my uncle Archie. I can't do that when I can't meet people. I'm going out tomorrow."

I said: "You'll be arrested and up before the beak before you can say hangman's noose."

Tammy looked at me angrily.

"I'm sorry to be so blunt. But you placed yourself in an impossible position when you vandalised the Royal Pavilion. If you're in contact with us, at least we can work together. You can't do that if you're cooling your heels in a cell."

"But I feel so helpless."

"Let's give it one more night. See if we can make some real progress tomorrow."

Tammy shrugged. "I suppose so."

I didn't like it. Tammy was a natural fighter. We couldn't keep her holed up for more than a couple of days. I wondered whether I could cut a deal with the cops to lay off the vandalism charges until after the hanging. A touch of the Christmas spirit and all that. I didn't fancy my chances.

Henrietta said: "If Tammy's moving tonight, it's best if she goes to Mabel's. She lives closer than Elsie or Freda."

"That seems sound. But we need to be certain no one can see Tammy when we make the move. Remember that her picture has been plastered over the *Chronicl*e for the past two days. The *Evening Argus*, too." I turned to Henrietta. "Is there a back way out of your flat?"

She nodded.

"In that case, I think I have a plan. Do you mind if I use your phone?"

Half an hour later an *Evening Chronicle* delivery van reversed quietly into the mews at the rear of Henrietta's flat. Mabel and Tammy, clutching her precious red holdall, climbed into the back of the van. I walked round to the driver's window. Roy Carpenter wound it down.

"You caught me a couple of minutes before I was going off

duty," he said.

I reached into my wallet and handed Roy a ten-bob note.

"I guess a brown one is fair pay for a special delivery." He winked.

"But let's make sure this one doesn't hit the headlines," I said.

Roy wound up the window, put the van into gear and quietly drove out of the mews.

It had been a hectic day, but I had one other visit before I could return to my lodgings.

Ted Wilson had promised to call into Prinny's Pleasure if he could uncover any information about the break-in at Shirley's flat.

Shirley had headed back to her place to tidy up and try to get some sleep.

So I walked into Prinny's Pleasure on my tod.

Ted Wilson was sitting on a bar stool talking to Jeff.

As I walked up, I heard Jeff say: "Why do they always give those criminals a hearty breakfast before they hang them?"

Ted said: "Because it would be inhuman to hang them on an empty stomach."

"Waste of money, if you ask me," Jeff said. "Besides, I don't think I could manage more than a slice of toast if I were for the drop."

I said to Jeff: "Let's hope you never get to test that theory. In the meantime, a G & T for me and the usual for Ted."

We took our drinks to the corner table at the back of the bar.

Ted said: "I've asked around. But it wasn't easy. I don't want Tomkins finding out I'm taking an interest in this."

"I understand. So what's the score?"

"Well, the break-in at Shirley's flat definitely wasn't our lot."

"Security services?"

Ted gave me a withering look. "They're only interested in spooks. Not real criminals."

"So nothing," I said.

"Not entirely," Ted said. "I spoke to the copper who patrols the beat that includes Clarence Square. He noticed a bloke with a trilby hat sitting on one of the benches in the square earlier in the day eating a bag of chips. Lots of people eat chips in the square. It's a handy place to sit. But he also noticed the same fellow walking down Western Road later that afternoon. He seemed in a hurry. Knocked into a couple of old dears struggling with their shopping. It's what made the copper notice him. Could mean something." Ted raised an eyebrow. "Or it could mean nothing."

I knew what it meant. Trilby was taking an unhealthy interest in Tammy's campaign to reprieve her uncle Archie. I didn't know why.

But tomorrow I intended to find the answer to that question.

Chapter 9

I arrived in the newsroom at the *Chronicle* shortly before eight the following morning. The telephone was already ringing on my desk. I did a Roger Bannister sprint across the room and seized the receiver.

"Crampton," I panted.

A woman's voice, breathless with tension, said: "Thank heavens I've caught you. It's Mabel. Tammy's walked out."

"When?" I asked.

"Five minutes ago. Said she was tired of being cooped up like a prisoner. Said she was going to London to visit her uncle in Wandsworth Prison. Said she doesn't care what happens to her after. Said she wants to say one last goodbye."

"Crazy girl. The police will grab her before she gets within miles of the prison."

Mabel seemed close to hysteria. "What shall we do? I think I'm going to have one of my turns."

"Mabel, keep calm. Make yourself a cup of tea. I'm going to try to catch up with Tammy at the station. Hopefully, I can persuade her to come back to yours."

"And what if you can't?"

"I have to," I said. "For all our sakes."

Seven minutes later, I parked my MGB outside the Railway Bell pub opposite Brighton station.

I'd fumed at the rush-hour traffic, which had doubled my journey time. But at least it had given me the chance to think. If Tomkins caught Tammy, her campaign to reprieve Archie would be finished. He'd see to that. Worse, he'd break her in the interview room. He'd want to know where she'd been hiding. Tomkins would feed her false promises about release on bail if she answered his questions. She'd be desperate to get out of jail and carry on her campaign. So she'd tell him everything. But Tomkins would never keep his promise.

And what Tammy told Tomkins would give me some awkward questions to answer. Tomkins would see to that. I reckoned I could talk my way out of trouble with the police. After all, they'd conducted an illegal search of my rooms. But I had Shirley, Henrietta and the Cousins to think about. I'm no lawyer, but I wondered whether Tomkins could charge them with harbouring a fugitive. It would be a heavy-handed way of treating a natural human response to help another person in trouble. But Tomkins wasn't known for his delicate touch.

I also had to think what the repercussions would be at the paper if I ended up in the dock at the magistrates' court on one of Tomkins's trumped-up charges. Figgis would probably laugh it off, even though I'd be saddled with weeks of his creative revenge. But His Holiness wouldn't. He'd order Figgis to fire me. Or he might even indulge in the pleasure of doing it himself.

I clambered out of the car and headed over towards the station.

A couple of uniformed bobbies were patrolling the forecourt. They were stopping drivers parking on the taxi rank. And getting in the way of people late for their trains. Suited me. The last thing I wanted was eagle-eyed cops watching out for a young female law-breaker on the run.

I took a quick look at the crowds hurrying up Queens Road. But there was no sign of Tammy. I shoved through the crowds into the station. It was the busiest time of the morning. Trains arrived and disgorged hordes of travellers onto the platforms. Commuters hurried towards trains leaving for London. The station concourse rang with sounds. Feet tramped. Train brakes sighed. Doors slammed. Steam engines snorted. The station tannoy burbled.

I craned my neck in every direction, but I couldn't see Tammy. The place was so crowded she could pass within five yards of me and I'd miss her. I didn't think she'd had time to walk from Mabel's house and catch a train to London. So she must be somewhere.

But where?

Of course! In the ticket hall.

I pushed my way through the swing doors. There were long queues at each of the six windows. I scanned the queues. Couldn't see Tammy. Then, in the queue for window four, a tall man in a pinstriped suit and bowler hat moved to one side. And there was Tammy, clutching her red holdall. There were three people in front of her.

This was going to be difficult. I didn't fancy butting into the queue. It would be a tough job to persuade Tammy to abandon her plan and return to Mabel's house. There'd be an argument. Raised voices. Not something I wanted in the middle of a crowded ticket office. Not with impatient passengers earwigging the drama.

I decided I'd let her buy her ticket and then intercept her as she left the hall.

I moved closer towards the door. As I did so, the two cops I'd seen outside ambled in. They strode towards the ticket windows scanning the faces of people in the queues.

They were halfway across the hall. In ten seconds they would spot Tammy. Were they looking for her? Or was this a routine check? If so, they might overlook her.

It wasn't a risk I could take.

I hustled towards Tammy. Brushed aside complaints about queue jumping. Grabbed her arm.

She swung round. Her defiant eyes flashed with recognition. She said: "Don't try to stop me."

I said: "If you really want to go, I won't. But there are two cops twenty feet away and they will. If you don't want to spend the next week in a cell, we leave now."

Tammy's jaw dropped. She glanced over her shoulder. Saw the

cops. Stepped out of the queue and said: "Come on."

"Move naturally," I whispered. "Look as though you've just changed your mind about buying a ticket."

We were halfway to the door, when one of the cops pointed at Tammy and nudged his mate. The first cop started to push through the queues towards us. The other moved to block the door.

I grabbed Tammy's arm. "If you can run fast, this is a great time to prove it," I said.

People swore at us as we pushed roughly through the queues.

"The way out is the other way," Tammy screamed.

"It's blocked," I said. "We'll use the tradesmen's exit."

I'd spotted a door on the far side of the hall. A notice on it said: Staff only.

I prayed it was unlocked.

There was now uproar in the ticket hall as we shoved our way through the crowds.

The first cop yelled: "Stop them."

A couple of office types obediently stuck out their hands. I brushed them aside.

We reached the staff door. I grabbed the handle. It was stiff but I turned it and the door opened. We bundled through. There was a bolt on the inside. I shot it seconds before a body crashed against the door and the handle rattled.

A harsh voice screamed: "Open this door."

I grabbed Tammy's arm and said: "This way."

We were in a long corridor painted in British Rail green. There were no windows. The place was lit by harsh bulbs hanging from fitments without light shades.

At the end of the corridor, I opened another door. We rushed into a sort of vestibule. There was a glass door that led out on to the station concourse and a wooden door with sign which said: Private.

Tammy pointed to the concourse. "Let's get out here and leg

it."

I said: "The cops will already be rushing round to get that covered. They'll spot us as soon as we pop out."

I opened the staff door and slammed it behind us. We were in another corridor that turned to the left after about fifteen feet. In front of us was a pair of swing doors. We pushed through them and found ourselves in a kitchen.

The room was brightly lit with fluorescent lights. A row of hobs ran along one wall. In the centre of the room a stainless steel preparation surface was loaded with loaves of bread, piles of cheese, tomatoes, slices of ham, pork pies and sausage rolls.

A chubby man with a red face, a thatch of unruly brown hair and a stubbly chin turned from the preparation area as we entered. He was wearing a chef's smock over black-and-white checkerboard trousers.

He scowled and said: "You must be the catering agency staff." He looked at his watch. "You're late. But let's not worry about that now. We've got a rush on. The railway buffet is selling sandwiches like they're going out of fashion."

"On British Rail, they usually are," I whispered to Tammy.

"We need you to make some more," he said.

He pointed across the room: "See those white coats and chef's skullcaps on the hangers. Put them on and come over here."

Tammy looked at me like she'd just stepped into a game of charades. "What shall we do?" she whispered.

"Let's do as he says," I said. "I've an idea."

We hustled across the room and climbed into our food-prep togs like we couldn't wait to start work.

Our new boss said: "Now we've got everything you need here. I want you to make fifty cheese sandwiches and fifty bloater paste. Remember, only one slice of processed cheese in each sandwich and make a small jar of paste last for at least six slices of bread. I'm going to see where that delivery of cucumbers has got to."

He wandered off across the room. I took a slice of bread, slapped five pieces of cheese into it and put another slice on top. Tammy had grabbed a jar of fish paste and emptied it on to another. She spread it around and slapped another slice on top so the paste oozed out of the sides.

Our boss ambled out of a door on the other side of the room.

"Time to leave," I said. "We can't follow him or we'll run into him coming back, so we'll return the way we came. If we keep our white coats and chef's caps on, we'll look like railway catering staff."

Tammy grabbed her red holdall. We hurried back to the hallway with the door onto the concourse and raced outside. I'd hoped we'd be able to sneak out of the back entrance to the station. But a cop already blocked the way out. And as I looked around, four more uniformed plods trotted onto the concourse.

Tammy's head twizzled back and forth in panic. "We're trapped," she said.

"Only on foot," I said. "This way. Keep your head down as you walk."

The station tannoy announced: "The haeght twuuty-phive brootin bill fur vitoor oon pleetfurm eat iz aboat toe leaf."

I translated for Tammy: "The eight twenty-five Brighton Belle for Victoria on platform eight is about to leave."

"We can't catch the train," she said. "Travelling without tickets is against the law."

I said: "Since when have you become so fussy about not breaking the law? And, anyway, we're not passengers. We're catering staff."

"But we'll end up in London."

"I thought that's where you wanted to go."

"Not now."

We reached the ticket barrier. The collector gave us a queer look as we approached in our white coats and jaunty skullcaps. He pointed at Tammy's holdall.

"What's in that?" he said.

"Fresh linen for the Brighton Belle," I said.

"You'd better move, then. The train's just leaving." He waved us through the barrier.

We hurried towards the first carriage. We opened the door and scrambled aboard just as the whistle blew and the train started to move.

"What now?" Tammy asked.

"We need to get out of these togs quickly," I said.

We were in that area at the end of the carriage where people store their luggage. We took off our white coats and hats, and shoved them behind a suitcase.

I said: "Let's move up the train. It will make it easier when we get off."

We pushed through a door into a first-class carriage. It was furnished with armchairs and tables covered with white napery. The tables were laid with silver-plated cutlery. Breakfast service had started. The aroma of grilled bacon made my stomach rumble. Several of the seats were taken as we moved forward. We passed a distinguished gentleman with dark hair fringed with grey. He was tucking into a kipper.

Tammy nudged me. "Was that who I think it was?" she asked.

"Yes. Laurence Olivier. He often breakfasts on the train."

"I saw him in that film *Spartacus*. He was some kind of Roman general."

"Crassus."

"I rooted for that Kirk Douglas."

"You won't be rooting for anyone if my plan doesn't work."

We'd reached the no man's land between two carriages. I lowered the window, disobeyed the instruction above the door and stuck my head out. About a quarter of a mile ahead I could see Preston Park station. The train had travelled slowly over the points outside Brighton and was only just picking up speed.

I watched … and waited. When the front end of the train

arrived at the start of the platform, I reached up and pulled the communication cord.

There was a loud hiss as the brake mechanism engaged. The locked wheels squealed like an off-key soprano as they slid to a stop on the rails. The couplings between the carriages crashed and rattled. Even though I expected a jolt, I lost my footing and slipped sideways. But I was up in a second. Tammy was already opening the door to scramble onto the platform.

"Not that way," I said. "That's where they'll be expecting us. Follow me – and don't tread on any rails. One of them is electrified and will kill you."

I opened the door opposite the platform side of the train and jumped down onto the track. I helped Tammy out and we scrambled across the rails and up onto the opposite platform. We hurried towards the exit.

I looked back briefly. Most of the passengers were staring out of the train on the platform side. But one face looked bemusedly at us from his first-class compartment.

He held a fork with a piece of kipper on it. And he had a smile on his face. Not his sinister smile like Maxim de Winter in *Rebecca*. More the moody, defiant smile like Heathcliff in *Wuthering Heights*.

He put down his fork and waved.

I punched the air with my fist and shouted: "I am Spartacus."

And, of course, we all know what happened to Spartacus in the end.

I was determined it wasn't going to happen to me. Or Tammy.

It took us nearly an hour to make our way back to Mabel's house. I hired a taxi outside Preston Park and asked it to take us to Hove station, two miles away. I paid off the taxi driver using a five-pound note, so he would remember me. Then we hurried into the station and I bought a single ticket for Portsmouth. I pointed at Tammy and asked if there were any ladies-only compartments on the train to make sure the booking clerk would remember her. I reckoned that if the cops thought Tammy was heading for Pompey, they might reason she was fleeing abroad. Channel ferries left from the harbour.

Then we snuck out of the station and caught a bus back into Brighton. We kept to the backstreets as we walked the final half-mile to Mabel's house.

Mabel fussed over Tammy when we arrived. "You're a silly girl," she said. "But you look all in. Leave your holdall in the hall and go and have a lie-down on the bed in the spare room."

I expected Tammy to put up a fight. But she'd been exhausted by our morning's adventure. She nodded and shuffled off to the bedroom.

Mabel and I sat on opposite sides of her dining room table.

I said: "I'm sorry this has caused you so much trouble."

"Not really. I blame myself. I should've kept a closer watch on the girl."

"I think she's learnt her lesson. There's no going back now."

"For better or worse," Mabel said.

"Do you think any neighbours may have recognised Tammy when she left the house this morning?"

"I don't know. Could that be a problem?"

"It could if some bounty hunter decided to call the sighting in to the cops."

I stood up and strolled over to the window.

"When will we know whether that's happened?" Mabel asked.

"Now," I said.

Not a hundred yards down the road two police cars were approaching slowly. I could see the lead driver looking at the numbers of the houses. I glanced the other way down the street. A shabby figure wearing a smart new trilby hat was leaning on a tree watching the cars approach.

"Tammy," I shouted. "The cops are coming. We've got to leave – and in double-quick time."

I raced into the bedroom. Tammy was already up and scrambling into her shoes.

"We haven't a minute to lose," I said.

We rushed to the back of the house. Mabel was ready with the backdoor unlocked.

"Ring Elsie and tell her we're on our way," I said. "When the cops arrive just act dumb."

Mabel grinned. "I'm good at that."

We reached Elsie's house in Maldon Road just before she left for work.

There'd been no cops at the back of Mabel's house. And, frankly, I don't know what I'd have done if there had been. I'd certainly done enough running around for one morning. I longed for the controlled frenzy of the newsroom.

But Tammy was in a bad way. She kept twisting her fingers together, shaking her head, wiping the odd tear from her eye. The poor girl didn't know what to do next. She hadn't known whether to continue the fight to reprieve her uncle Archie. Or whether to make one last effort to see him and say her final goodbye. Well, that plan had foundered. And Tammy had added guilt to a cauldron of emotions that were bubbling inside her.

Elsie settled her down with a cup of coffee and told her to relax. And I said I'd call her from a phone box after I'd attended the morning's press briefing at the police station. She'd cradled her coffee mug in both hands as though it were the last source of warmth in the world.

Tammy was in such a state, I daren't voice my true thoughts. It was looking an increasingly tough proposition to find the evidence to save Archie, when I also had to fight a rearguard action to keep Tammy out of jail. There were plenty of avenues of enquiry I could follow up. The problem wasn't that I was running out of ideas.

I was running out of time.

Chapter 10

I realised just how far time had become my enemy when I arrived at the morning police press conference.

I hustled into the briefing room ten minutes late. Tomkins was seated at the top table. He was already well into his stride.

"And, furthermore, we shall use all our considerable resources and the full weight of the law to apprehend the perpetrator of this act of desecration on one of our much-loved monuments," he was saying.

From the heavy-handed way he was laying it on, you'd have thought Tammy had knocked Nelson off the top of his column rather than dabbed a few words in paint on the Royal Pavilion.

Tomkins continued: "I am pleased that the slogan has now been washed from the doors of this beloved building. And I can confirm that, despite the misplaced pleas for clemency from certain quarters, the murderer of Percy Despart will hang."

He reached for a glass next to him and took a sip of water. "By the neck until dead," he added, as though he'd been trying to think of a worse way to do it.

I looked around the room. There was a bigger turnout of journos than usual. That was hardly surprising. The killing and its aftermath had become a national story. Reporters from Fleet Street had been sent to the town.

Tomkins called for questions. An arm in the sleeve of a moth-eaten grey suit rose into the air from the front row. I might have known that Jim Houghton, my opposite number on the *Evening Argus*, would have something to say about the matter. During the coverage of Archie's trial we'd traded scoop for scoop and honours were even. Jim would be irritated that my interviews with Tammy had left him stumbling along behind. No doubt he'd have had his editor on his back wanting a new line on the story.

Tomkins nodded at Houghton with a conspiratorial grin. He

knew what was coming. Houghton heaved himself to his feet. He half turned so that the hacks sitting behind could hear him clearly.

He said: "Chief Superintendent, do you have any comment on the suggestions being made in certain quarters that another newspaper may be conspiring to keep the perpetrator of the Royal Pavilion vandalism from the full force of the law?"

From the corner of his eye, Houghton spotted me at the back of the room. He bared his teeth in a leer that was intended to say "got you".

Houghton sat down and Tomkins lifted a sheet of paper that had been lying on the table in front of him.

He cleared his throat and said: "I shall read a statement issued this morning by Sir Stephen Harding, the chief constable of Brighton police."

We all sat expectantly with pencils poised over notebooks. Tomkins made a performance of fumbling with his spectacles case and putting on his glasses.

He read: "In recent days there has been some newspaper speculation that questions the reliability of the verdict in the case of the murderer Archie Flowerdew. No doubt there are some newspapers that will follow any rumour, no matter how irresponsible, in order to boost their circulation."

There were a few titters around the room at this. Tomkins glared over the top of his glasses, then resumed reading. "I must remind the press that they need to conduct their news-gathering within the strict confines of the law. If it transpires that a newspaper has been complicit in an illegal act, it should expect to feel the full force of the law used against its proprietor, its editor and any of its journalists involved."

Tomkins replaced the paper on the table. He sat back in his chair with a benevolent smirk on his face. As though he'd just delivered a soliloquy from *Hamlet* to thunderous applause. Everyone in the room knew that this set-up had been aimed at the

Chronicle.

So before Tomkins could take a bow, I was on my feet. "Have you even a shred of evidence that any newspaper in this town has broken the law?"

Tomkins blustered: "We are making certain enquiries."

I said: "The police are always making enquiries – and often they lead nowhere. You should know that better than most."

That raised a laugh from my fellow hacks.

Tomkins's cheeks coloured. He scowled at me. "Don't make accusations you can't back up."

"Exactly my point about the chief constable's statement. And why isn't he here to read it himself?"

"Sir Stephen is attending to other duties."

"Like Christmas shopping in Hanningtons?"

Tomkins shot to his feet. He pointed angrily at me. "That's not true."

"It's not true that *Chronicle* journalists have broken the law. Yet Harding is quite prepared to write a statement insinuating that it is. And get his hired help to read it out."

My fellow hacks were enjoying this. Pencils were flying across notebooks.

"And while we're at it, exactly what duty was more important than reading his own statement to the nation's press?" I asked.

Tomkins blustered. "I ... er ... believe it was a matter of importance."

"But obviously too important for you to know about."

"Nothing is too important for me to know about."

"Then you'll know that I've had enough of this charade of a press conference."

I slammed my notebook shut, stood up and stalked out.

Outside I felt like a challenger who'd just laid Henry Cooper on the canvas for a count of ten.

The adrenalin from my early morning adventures with

Tammy and my tussle with Tomkins was pumping through my veins like a magnum of champagne. I'd admit that my verbal fencing with Tomkins verged on the unprofessional. As a journalist, my role at a press briefing was to listen, report and ask the occasional pointed question. I'd certainly stepped over that line. But so had Tomkins and Harding with their trumped-up statement virtually accusing the *Chronicle* of breaking the law. There'd been no one else to defend the paper's honour.

But the other journalists present would report the statement word for word. When it comes to an opportunity to trash a rival newspaper, dog not only eats dog, but it also licks its lips hoping for a second bite. I'd do exactly the same if Jim Houghton were in my position – and he'd think no worse of me for it.

Figgis had been in the newspaper game long enough to understand all about the hard knocks a paper and its reporters had to take from time to time. But His Holiness was too much of a gentleman to brush off such slurs lightly. His skin was so thin it was practically transparent. He wouldn't feel comfortable until he'd done something about the trouble.

Such as sacking me.

But by the time I walked into the newsroom ten minutes later, I'd thought of a way to handle the press briefing in my report.

So I sat down at my desk, yanked the Remington towards me and typed:

> Brighton Chief Constable Sir Stephen Harding came under fire today for accusing unnamed newspapers of breaking the law.
>
> Sir Stephen sent Detective Chief Superintendent Alec Tomkins to the police's regular press briefing to read a statement that said offending papers would feel the full force of the law. But Mr Tomkins failed to name any newspaper that had broken the law or produce any evidence to suggest they had.

I rattled on for a few more pars describing how the row had

arisen from Tammy's protest at the Royal Pavilion. I concluded:

> Speaking from a safe house somewhere in Brighton, Miss Flowerdew told the *Chronicle* exclusively that she will fight for a reprieve for her uncle Archie until the very last minute.

I read through my story and felt I'd made the best of a difficult job. I'd given the piece a spin that put the *Chronicle* in a positive light. There was no doubt the other papers would spin the story to favour the police point of view. But they'd be limited by the fact that there was no evidence to support Harding's allegations. At least, not yet.

As I rolled the final folio out of the typewriter, Figgis bounced up to my desk. He didn't look like a man who planned to offer me a Christmas bonus.

He said: "The rumour mill has spun into overdrive this morning."

I gave him my innocent look and said: "Anything I should know about?"

"I've just been talking to Mabel from the morgue. Apparently, the cops tried to raid her house looking for that Tammy Flowerdew."

"If I know Mabel she wouldn't have taken kindly to that."

"Too right. She asked them for their search warrant."

"Did they have one?"

"Tried to palm her off by waving a random piece of paper in her face. She snatched it. Turned out to be an invitation to the cop shop's Christmas party."

"They left?"

"Only after she'd given them succinct marching orders. I believe her second word was off."

I grinned.

"But that's not the only event that has sent my rumour mill spinning. I hear that the Brighton Belle made an unscheduled stop at Preston Park this morning. My contact tells me a couple of catering staff dressed in white coats boarded the train at the last minute. Know anything about that?"

"I think that might be best saved for my memoirs," I said.

Figgis shook a Woodbine out of his packet and lit up. "I thought it might." He looked around the newsroom and leaned closer. "You're turning in some great copy, but you need to be careful. I always remember a piece of advice old Eddie Tassiker gave me."

"The editor back in the thirties?"

"Yes, when I joined the paper. Anyway, old Eddie said, 'Never become part of the story.' Can't say I always took his advice. But the couple of times I didn't, I came to regret it."

"I'm keeping this objective," I said. "But you have to get close to an informant in a situation like this. It's the only way."

"I know that. But there are other people – people upstairs – who don't."

I said: "Has His Holiness spoken to you about this?"

"No. At least, not yet. He's a weak man, but he's not stupid. He'll know we're operating at the edge of the law. If anything goes wrong, he'll want to be able to turn up at the cop shop with clean hands."

"I'll be careful … and I'll keep the carbolic soap close by."

Figgis took a drag on his fag and blew the smoke in a steady stream towards the ceiling.

"You do that. His Holiness is not the only one who keeps his hands clean. As a boy, I won a Life buoy clean hands medal, too."

Figgis turned and bounced back to his office.

His timely warning reminded me that when it comes to a dangerous story, a journalist is on his own.

But there was no point sitting around worrying about that. I had to find a lead that would cast some doubt on Archie's conviction. I reckoned that even a decent-sized piece of doubt should be enough to persuade the Home Secretary to delay the execution until the police had evaluated the new evidence.

Of the possible suspects, Kingswell seemed the most promising. As a former commando he'd been trained in the noble art of killing with his bare hands. A pencil as a weapon would have been a luxury to a man like Kingswell.

Camilla had told me that he'd taken to spending more time at his flat in Sussex Square. I found that suspicious. Perhaps if another man was about to be hanged for a crime he'd committed himself he was feeling remorse. Perhaps he was worried about his moods being picked up by people around him.

I decided to telephone Kingswell and invite myself over.

Major Toby Kingswell answered the door of his flat wearing a blue blazer with regimental badge on the breast pocket.

He had a Royal Marines Commandos' cravat tied around his neck. He had run to fat, but it was still possible to see he'd once had a handsome face with even features. His brown hair was neatly barbered in a short back and sides. He wore a well-trimmed moustache that covered most of his upper lip. He stood as ramrod straight as a dumpling can, as though he were on a parade ground. I put his age at somewhere between forty-five and fifty.

He extended his hand and said: "Kingswell, Major. Formerly of Her Majesty's Royal Marines."

I felt a muscular grip as we shook. Perhaps intended to remind me who had the military training around here.

I said: "Crampton, Mr. Currently of the *Evening Chronicle* and journalist of this parish."

He ushered me inside and said: "Feet, wipe them. Floor tiles, Mrs Bludgen just washed them. Cleaner, absolute treasure. Without her, don't know what I'd do."

I guessed this backward way of talking came from a lifetime of giving orders on parade grounds.

As commanded, I gave my shoes a good rub on the mat. I

followed Kingswell down the passage, admiring the pristine floor tiles as I went.

He ushered me into a spacious sitting room furnished with the kind of stuff that looked as though it had been handed down the generations rather than bought in a Debenhams sale. There was one of those sofas with wooden handles in the top corners of the seats, held together with decorative ropes. There was an antique writing bureau with lots of little drawers so that you'd constantly be looking for the one that held your postage stamps. There was a multi-tiered whatnot displaying an impressive army of model soldiers. A couple of oriental rugs filled up the acres between assorted chairs. The walls were closely hung with paintings in several styles ranging from Vermeer to Salvador Dali. None of them looked like originals. But all had been carefully chosen.

Kingswell said: "Drink, can I offer?"

I said: "Gin and tonic, thank you."

Kingswell crossed to the table and poured the drinks. He handed me mine in a crystal tumbler.

He said: "Interviews, never liked them."

I said: "Questions, only a few to ask."

This way of talking was becoming infectious. I needed to take control.

So I looked admiringly around the room and said: "You have a magnificent collection of paintings."

Kingswell relaxed a bit. Sat down opposite me. "Built it over the years. Owning a gallery, great way to become a collector."

"Presumably you started the gallery after you left the Marines?"

He nodded. "Gratuity, not much but enough to get started in a small way."

"Big change – from being a soldier to running a gallery. What made you do it?"

"Saw plenty of action in the Marines. Some pretty ugly things over the years. Beauty, decided I needed to redress the balance with some of it."

"I visited the gallery the other day and met Mrs Fogg. The place seems to have prospered."

"Success, I've had a fair share. Worked for it, mind."

I said: "I'm writing a piece about the life of Percy Despart as his killer is being hanged. You knew him, I believe."

Kingswell stroked his moustache hard on both sides. "Rather I hadn't."

"Why was that?"

"Talent, Despart always overestimated his own, if you ask me. Sincerity. You can always tell whether or not an artist has it in his work. Is that sincerity really there? Or is he faking it? Great artists, there is never any doubt about that. Others, you're not sure. Sometimes they're sincere, sometimes not. Subject, depends what it is and how they feel towards it. Despart, I always felt that he was faking it. Sincerity, just not there."

"Is that why you turned down his submission for the Brighton Masters' Art Exhibition?"

"Hanging committee, they took the decision. Not me alone."

"But I understand the committee was evenly split. It was your casting vote that rejected Despart's painting."

"Even splits, we often had them. Only five on the committee – two vote one way, two the other. Up to me as chairman. Carry the can, never been afraid to."

"But it had unpleasant consequences in the case of Despart."

"The postcard, you mean that?"

"Yes. It must have deeply angered you."

"Distasteful, yes. But anger, no."

"You just let it pass?" I asked.

"Best way. Johnny Foreigner, when you've had him loosing off live rounds in your direction, meaning you ill, you know how to put these things into perspective."

"So you let the matter drop?"

"Damned thing, no point drawing attention to it."

Kingswell's version was so different to Camilla's that one of them had to be lying.

She'd told me Kingswell had exploded with fury. Threatened all kinds of revenge on Despart. That at one point she'd feared he would carry out his threats. And that it was weeks before he'd calmed down. Only after she'd reminded him that revenge was a dish best eaten cold. And here was Kingswell laughing the matter off. Telling me it hadn't bothered him.

I didn't know which story to believe.

I said: "Is there any doubt in your mind that Archie Flowerdew killed Percy Despart?"

Kingswell did that nervous stroking thing with his moustache again.

"Trial, never attended it personally. Newspapers, read about it in them. My view, probably yes. Evidence, it pointed that way."

I said: "Time, thank you for it. Interview, got everything I need."

We stood up and headed for the door along the passage with the spotless floor tiles.

I walked ahead of Kingswell to the front door. I opened the door to leave. Turned to shake hands before I did so.

But he was stroking his moustache. As though it gave him comfort.

Chapter 11

I was still thinking about Kingswell's moustache when I arrived back in the *Chronicle*'s newsroom.

But not for long.

Freda bustled into the room looking like she'd just escaped a firing squad. She hurried over to my desk. Glanced around nervously.

She leaned towards me and whispered: "Can you come to the morgue, Mr Crampton? Mabel's just had some bad news."

"What kind of bad news?" I asked.

"The kind that needs your help."

I stepped into the morgue twenty seconds later with Freda hard on my heels.

Mabel was sitting at the clippings table in the middle of the room. She was dabbing her eyes with a lace-fringed handkerchief.

She stuffed the handkerchief up the sleeve of her cardigan as I walked over to the table.

"I think I've been burgled," she said.

"How do you know?" I asked.

"Muriel from two doors down always picks up my weekly greengrocery order and leaves it outside the back door. When she went round about half an hour ago, she found the glass in the back door was broken."

"Smashed?"

"No, she said it looked like a circle of glass had been cut out, near the door handle."

This was an old housebreaker's trick. Too many people lock the back door on the inside but leave the key in the lock. So all the crook has to do is cut a hole in the glass big enough to stick his arm through and turn the key.

I said: "Did Muriel go inside the house?"

"No. She was too scared."

"Did she call the police?"

"No. She thought she'd better tell me first. What do you think I should do?"

I said: "I think we should go over to your house immediately and take a look for ourselves."

Mabel nodded. She managed a thin smile. "I'll get my coat on. But I'm so nervous I don't know whether I'll be able to do up the buttons."

We arrived at Mabel's house in my MGB ten minutes later.

At my suggestion, she gave me her keys and I let myself in the front door. I thought I was about as likely to run into the house-breaker as Sir Alec Douglas-Home, the Prime Minister. But it was safer to check. I did a quick tour of the place, looking in all the rooms and not forgetting to check in the cupboard underneath the stairs. Then I went to the front door and called Mabel.

We inspected the back door, which was in a utility room with a large sink and a mangle. Whoever had cut out the glass had made a neat job of it. Either he'd practised beforehand or it was part of his regular line of work.

Mabel was busy looking round the house. After a few minutes, she came into the utility room.

"I don't think anything's been taken," she said. "I've checked my few bits of jewellery and the tin where I keep my holiday savings and they're both there."

I said: "The thief wasn't after anything of yours."

"How do you know?"

"Because he came to steal Tammy's red holdall."

"My God!" Mabel exclaimed. She slumped down on a chair by the mangle.

"If you remember, when I hustled Tammy out of the back door this morning, seconds before the cops arrived at the front, she left her holdall behind. In the rush, I didn't think about it. She was in no position to retrieve it from the hall with the cops already outside the front door. It's not there now. I checked when I let myself in."

"But who'd want to steal it?" Mabel said. "Especially if it meant breaking into a house to do so."

"I don't know," I lied.

In fact, I knew exactly who'd stolen the holdall, but I didn't want Mabel worrying about the character I'd christened as Trilby. I'd caught a glimpse of him just before the cops pitched up. He was a man who was adept at sneaking around and spying on others. It was possible he'd seen Tammy and me legging it down the twitten after we'd bundled out of the house. If so, he'd have realised Tammy didn't have the holdall with her. Perhaps he'd hung around while the cops chased their tails and Mabel finally left for work. Then he'd seized his chance.

Whatever was in the holdall must be important to him. But what was it? I'd had my suspicions that Tammy had been holding back information. But now I needed some answers from her.

I stayed with Mabel for another half-hour while she made a more thorough check. I knew nothing else would be missing. But she wanted to be certain. She'd had a shock and looking at familiar possessions would help her recover.

Meanwhile, I telephoned for a glazier to come and fix the back-door window.

When Mabel had completed her check, I said: "I'll let the office know you won't be back this afternoon."

She grinned. "I never thought it would turn out like this. But, you know, I wouldn't have missed it for anything. I spend my days reading about other people's adventures in the press cuttings I clip. And now I've had an adventure of my own."

"Why would someone enter a house just to steal your red holdall?" I asked Tammy.

"I don't know," she said. "I really don't know."

Her voice was confident but her gaze slid off to the left as she spoke. It's the sign that gives away the inexperienced liar.

We were in Elsie's sitting room, a cosy little place with floral wallpaper and a Wilton carpet. The mantelpiece was loaded with photographs of Elsie's many nieces and nephews. When I'd arrived, I'd whispered to Elsie that I needed to speak to Tammy alone. Elsie had tactfully retreated to the kitchen to make us both a cup of tea.

I gave Tammy the kind of look which says 'pull the other one' and said: "Let me rephrase the question. What was in your holdall?"

"Just my clothes."

"Such as?"

"T-shirts, vests, bras and knickers. Do you want me to describe my knickers one by one?"

"That won't be necessary. What I want to know is what was in your holdall apart from the clothes?"

"Just some personal items."

"What kind of personal items?"

"The kind a girl needs."

I said: "Don't take me for a fool. It beggars belief that a house-breaker would risk jail to steal a few personal items that a girl needs. Especially if he were a man."

"He might have been a woman."

"We'll work on the hypothesis that he was a he. So what other item was in the holdall?"

Tammy pouted. "I suppose you'll find out eventually with one of your tricks. So I might as well tell you. It was a book. Just a book."

"What kind of book?"

"A sketchbook."

"Your sketchbook?"

"It is now."

"What do you mean by that?"

"It originally belonged to Uncle Archie. He gave it to me."

I said: "But this wasn't a gift he'd given you a long time ago."

"How do you know that?"

"Because it must have something to do with his court case. Otherwise, you wouldn't have it with you."

Tammy shrugged. "He gave it to me in prison."

"While he was on remand awaiting trial?" I asked.

Prisoners on remand are allowed writing materials and it was possible Archie had been compiling notes that could be used in his case.

"No. It was just a couple of weeks ago. My last visit to him."

Tears were shining in Tammy's eyes.

I said: "I know this is difficult. I know you're at your wits' end. But in these final days, if we're to stand any chance of reprieving Archie, you must tell me the truth. I can't help if you only tell me half of what you know."

Tammy brushed away a tear with the back of her hand. The girl was tough but she was close to breaking point.

She said: "Uncle Archie told me the warders had allowed him to have a sketchbook and pencils to while away the time. Apparently, condemned prisoners are sometimes granted concessions. It keeps them sane until ..."

I said: "Take your time."

Tammy pulled out her handkerchief and blew her nose. "Anyway, Uncle Archie had been drawing a series of pictures of that Christmas song. You know, the one that begins: 'On the first day of Christmas, my true love sent to me: a partridge in a pear tree.' "

"I know it. It goes through to twelve drummers drumming."

Tammy nodded. "I knew he was doing this because he'd told me on some earlier visits. But two weeks ago, he told me he'd finished it. He'd asked the prison governor if he could send it to me. But the governor told him that would be against regulations.

Uncle Archie said it would come to me as he'd left me everything in his will. Apparently, the governor had witnessed the will."

"So how did you end up with it now?" I asked.

"During all of my visits to Uncle Archie, there was a warder present. But at the last one, Uncle Archie feigned a choking attack. The warder hurried off to call for the prison doctor and Uncle Archie slipped me the book while he was out of the room. I hid it in a place where the warders wouldn't pat me down when I was searched at the end of the visit."

"Why was Uncle Archie so keen for you have to have the book now?"

"He didn't trust the prison governor to pass it on to me."

"But it was just a book of pictures?"

"It was more than that," Tammy said. "Uncle Archie said I needed to know the whole truth when he was gone – and the book would show me who to ask to find it."

"What did he mean by 'the whole truth'?" I asked.

Tammy shook her head. "I'm not sure. He wouldn't say. But I think it's something about his alibi and the woman he's protecting."

"And this book just contained pictures of the 'Twelve Days of Christmas', as in the song?"

"That's right."

"Not the name of the woman he's protecting?"

"No."

"Were there any clues in the book about the name of the person?"

"I couldn't see any. They were just pictures of the two turtle doves, three French hens, four calling birds and so on. Just like the picture puzzles Uncle Archie used to draw for newspapers. Perhaps a bit weirder, but just pictures."

"Did it look like he'd included puzzles in the pictures?"

"I couldn't see any. And I probably knew his work better than anyone. But Uncle Archie set some cunning puzzles."

I was about to ask Tammy whether she could think of anyone who might also want the book, when Elsie came into the room with a tray of tea and some hot buttered scones.

I took my tea and munched on a scone. Tammy fell silent. And Elsie picked up the mood and decided she had some things to do upstairs.

If Tammy had told me about the book when we'd first met, we might have been able to unlock the mystery. Perhaps it would have led us to the truth that would keep Archie from the gallows. But if Archie had information that would save his life, why hadn't he mentioned it in his trial? Why hadn't he told his lawyers, so that it could be used in an appeal? None of this made sense.

Archie was facing certain death. Perhaps his mind was in such turmoil he'd imagined that there was someone who could save his life. Psychologists say that people under extreme pressure invent fantasies to help them avoid the awful reality they face. Perhaps that is what Archie had been doing with his Christmas drawings.

Yet, someone else thought it was worth nicking the drawings. If Wandsworth Prison's governor and warders knew about them, it would be common knowledge among the old lags doing their time. Whether or not the drawings held secret messages, they could be worth big money. Newspapers would pay handsomely to publish them on the day Archie was hanged. There were hard cases in Wandsworth who'd fancy their chances of making some illgotten out of that. They'd think nothing of organising a heist from their cell. All they'd need to do was to pass information on visiting day. Or, more likely, get a bent screw to hand on the word. Then they'd need a trusted outside man to retrieve the drawings and handle the sale.

Could that man be Trilby?

If we were to stand any chance of keeping Archie from the gallows, I needed to find the sketchbook.

I took a swig of my tea. Tammy chewed her second scone.

I asked: "What does the sketchbook look like?"

Tammy swallowed hard and said: "It's about so big." With her hands, she shaped a size about twice that of an ordinary postcard. "It's got brown board covers and thick art paper pages, but no more than about twenty. Archie had only drawn on twelve of them."

So I would recognise the book if I saw it.

And I knew what the man I believed had stolen it looked like.

Now, all I had to do was find him.

But that wasn't going to be easy, I realised, as I headed back to the office.

For all I knew, Trilby could have been on the first train back to the Big Smoke after he'd nabbed the sketchbook. That would be the logical conclusion if he were the surrogate of a Mr Big inside Wandsworth. Even now, Trilby could be touting the book around the grubbier end of Fleet Street to find a buyer.

The man who would know whether Trilby was doing the rounds of the national papers was Albert Petrie, news editor of the *Daily Mirror*. A year earlier, Petrie had come close to offering me a job. I'd helped him with a big story that made the *Mirror*'s front page. He'd said I could call him if I ever needed help.

But when I reached the newsroom, I realised it wouldn't be easy to do this without giving Petrie a lead into my story. Petrie was as honest a news editor as you'd find anywhere in Fleet Street. But he wasn't going to turn up the chance of a scoop this big.

I lifted the receiver and dialled Petrie's number.

"Albert Petrie."

"Colin Crampton."

"Bold Colin. Well met. So are you working on another scoop from breezy Brighton? More important, are you going to share it with us?"

"No scoop, Albert," I lied. "Just wondered whether you could help me on some deep background."

Petrie chuckled. "Depends on how deep, young Colin."

"It's about the hanging of Archie Flowerdew."

"Bad business. We'll have our man outside the prison gates on the morning. Guess you'll be there, too."

"Afraid so. You get a lot of ghouls at something like this. And not only outside the gates."

"Too true."

"Have you heard of any of them trailing stuff about Flowerdew around the Fleet Street papers?"

"Think you're missing out down there on the coast, do you?"

"No, I just felt that if people are seeking to make money out of Flowerdew's hanging, there could be a story in it," I said.

There was a brief silence at Petrie's end of the line. I imagined I could hear him thinking. Then he said: "We've had the usual chancers. The kind who pretend they were the condemned man's deepest confidante on the basis of once sharing a pint with him in a pub. But nothing substantial."

"Nobody with stuff that would back up their claims?"

"What sort of stuff?" Petrie sounded interested. A little too interested for my liking.

"Nothing in particular. Just the usual things. Fading photos of Flowerdew as a nipper. Letters from his mum. Old school reports. That sort of thing."

"There's been a bit of that about, but not worth paying good money for. At least, not by us. The *Sketch* may fork out for some rubbish. They usually do."

"Thanks for your help, Albert. Looks like I've drawn a blank."

"Don't mention it, Colin. And when you want to tell me what you know is really out there, perhaps we can do another story together."

The line went dead.

I grinned. I was never going to fool Petrie completely. But, at least I'd left the matter vague enough so that he wouldn't know where to start looking.

In any event, Petrie had answered my question. If Trilby had the sketchbook, he wasn't trying to sell it in Fleet Street. At least, not yet.

So, perhaps he was still in Brighton. It would make sense to lie low for a day or two after making the snatch. And if he was in Brighton, he'd have to stay somewhere.

Trilby didn't look like the type who splashed out on five-star hotels. Or four-, three-, two- or one-star. He'd look for bed-and-breakfast lodgings. And the cheaper the better. There were hundreds of B & Bs in the town. Checking every one would be impossible. But I had Trilby's old hat. It was sitting on top of the stack of wire baskets on my desk like some bizarre trophy. If I were Sherlock Holmes, I'd be able to take that hat and deduce the wearer's age, occupation, height and weight, whether he had false teeth, what he'd eaten for breakfast, where he last went on holiday and whether he wore pink underpants.

But I wasn't Holmes. And I didn't need to analyse the hat. Because I'd seen Trilby wearing another hat. A spanking new one. Without the stain on the rim that his old one sported.

I would bet a penny to a Christmas pudding that Trilby had bought his second hat in Brighton. And I'd bet a further penny to a stuffed turkey I knew which shop.

I grabbed the trilby and headed for the door.

Hardcastle Hinchcliffe Hatters was a tiny lock-up squeezed between a cheese shop and a religious bookstore that sold dirty magazines under the counter.

It was in Kensington Gardens, a place ambitiously named as there wasn't a tree, bush, shrub or potted geranium in sight. It was a pedestrian thoroughfare, with shops that catered for people who couldn't find what they wanted elsewhere.

The lamps were on by the time I arrived. The street was

crowded with shoppers shuffling along, hugging themselves from the cold.

A bell tinkled as I pushed open the door of the hatters and stepped inside. I took a quick look around. The walls were lined with shelves filled with hats. I spotted bowlers, homburgs, panamas, deerstalkers, yachting caps and others I couldn't name. There was a shelf devoted to trilbies. On the far side of the room, a fat man with a barrel chest stood behind a glass counter. He was wearing a jacket in blue velvet, with a smoking cap elaborately embroidered in gold braid. The cap had a long tassel, which hung down over the man's left ear.

He nodded his head as I approached and said: "Humphrey Hinchcliffe at your service."

I said: "I'm sure you've heard of the old saying 'if you want to get ahead, get a hat'."

Hinchcliffe's eyes shone with pleasure. "Wise words."

"Well, I have a hat and want to get a head."

"I don't understand."

I placed the trilby with the stain on the counter.

Hinchcliffe took a horrified step back. From the look on his face, you'd have thought I'd just slapped a dead badger on the counter.

He said: "That is not a hat, sir. It is … It is, at best, a head covering."

"It's not covering anybody's head just now, but I'd like to find its owner."

"If I may venture an opinion, sir. The owner and the hat are well parted."

I nodded sagely. "I agree it's not the finest example of the milliner's art. But you add together a cold night and a bald head – well, you could be looking at pneumonia."

"I'm not sure …"

"The point is this. The fellow I'm talking about left his hat in the pub the other night. I'm just trying to do a good deed to reunite head and hat."

"But I don't see where we come in."

"I thought the old boy might have come in to buy a replacement. Have you sold any trilbies lately?"

"The trilby is one of our most popular lines, sir."

"The owner of this hat, as you can see, had a small head. Have you sold a small trilby in the last couple of days?"

Hinchcliffe picked up a pencil and turned the trilby over. Put on his glasses and peered inside the rim. "Six and three quarters. The smallest size. We don't sell many of those. Allow me to consult the day journal."

He rummaged under the counter and pulled out a large book bound in green cloth. He peered myopically at the pages through his glasses.

"We do seem to have sold such a hat yesterday, sir. It appears we did not have the size in stock and had to have one delivered from another supplier. We telephoned the gentleman when the hat arrived and it appears he called to collect."

"Did he leave an address?"

"I'm afraid not, sir."

"But you have the telephone number you called?"

"It was written on a scrap of paper and thrown out with last night's rubbish."

I felt my shoulders sag.

Hinchcliffe adjusted his smoking cap so that the tassel jiggled from side to side.

"I recall it was a Hove number. By a curious coincidence the telephone number was the same as my birthday – twenty-third of October."

"Twenty-three ten; two three one zero."

"I hope the owner is pleased to be reunited with his hat, sir."

I picked it up, nodded a thank you and made for the door.

Outside, I searched for a phone box and dialled the number.

A grumpy woman's voice answered: "Belvedere Guest

House."

I said: "Is that the Belvedere Guest House in Kingsway?"

The Grump said: "There isn't a Belvedere in Kingsway. This is the Belvedere in Arthur Street, opposite Hove station."

The Grump turned out to be Evangeline Turnbull.

She was a middle-aged woman with bleached blonde hair and too much lipstick.

She stood backlit by the light of her hall and said: "If you want a room, they're all taken."

There would be no danger of me booking in here. The stench of boiled cabbage wafted down the hall and out into the street. And the view promised in the place's name turned out to be the down-line railway tracks. The house stood between an ill-lit alley that ran up the right side and a transport caff on the left.

I said: "I've come to return some property. The gentleman who wears the trilby hats. He left this one with me the other night." I held up exhibit A.

Evangeline sniffed. "That'll be Mr Stubbs. Room four. First floor. Stairs at the end of the passage. Let yourself out of the back door into the alley at the side of the house when you leave."

She stood aside and I entered. Held my breath as I walked down the passage. At the end, another passage turned off to the right with a further door that led out to the alley at the side of the house.

I pounded up the stairs and arrived on a small landing lit by a dim bulb. I stepped around the mouse droppings on the threadbare carpet.

I found room four and knocked gently on the door. No answer.

I rapped more loudly.

Nothing.

I opened the door. The smell of human waste overwhelmed the cabbage. I retched loudly.

Stubbs was lying on his bed.
He wouldn't be needing his trilby any more.
He was dead.

Chapter 12

I took a deep breath before I stepped into the room.

The place had hardly been fragrant beforehand. But now the fetid stench of a man who'd fouled himself as he died hung like an evil presence in the air.

The room was a box hardly large enough to contain the iron bedstead, small wardrobe, bedside table and upright chair, which were its only furniture. Long ago, the walls had been covered with cheap regency-stripe wallpaper. Now they were spotted with black mould. Moth-eaten curtains hung over a window so tiny it hardly mattered what view it looked out on.

It was the kind of room you booked into if you were skint or desperate.

Which category did Stubbs fall into? I wondered. But only briefly. Because the next thought that hit me was that this set-up could be awkward. I knew Stubbs had been following me. If others knew that – and had even approved it – there could be trouble. Especially if those others were officials. Like the police.

But I put that thought to the back of my mind. I turned round and quietly closed the door behind me. I needed to find out more before I reported this, but I had to do it quickly. The landlady would know how long I'd been up here before I passed the hard word that she had a stiff as a lodger. She'd be questioned by the cops. If she told them I'd been poking around, that could put me on the receiving end of some pointed questions.

So I reckoned I had no more than five minutes to reconnoitre. I could tell the gorgon downstairs that it had taken me time to find the room and that I'd become faint when I happened upon the body. And if I remained in this stench for much longer I probably would.

I reached into my pocket and pulled out my handkerchief. I wrapped it around my right hand to act as a glove. I didn't want to leave my prints all over the place. It would be hard enough to persuade the cops I hadn't had a good shufti, anyway.

I approached the body, held my nose and leant over it. Alive, Stubbs had had a face like a frustrated ferret – small, pointy features permanently set in a moue of disappointment. In death, the features had become accentuated. The eyes bulged, so they looked like they wanted to leap from their sockets. The jaw had dropped and thin mucous had run from the left side of his mouth.

It wasn't hard to see the cause of this. A red welt around Stubbs's neck had broken the skin in two or three places. Blood had run from the cuts before drying after his heart packed up. Stubbs had been strangled. And from the lack of other injuries to his body, it looked as though it had been a professional job by a man, I assumed, who was much stronger and knew what he was doing. The fact that none of the contents of the room had been disturbed suggested that Stubbs had been overpowered before he could fight back.

But who would want to kill Stubbs – and why? I moved around to the far side of the bed and found the answer.

Tammy's red holdall.

So, as I suspected, Stubbs had been the sneak thief who'd lifted it from Mabel's house. The zip that closed the holdall had been opened and some of the contents spilt out onto the floor. I knelt down, lifted the side of the bag and peered in. There was a tangle of Tammy's clothes and a few personal items.

But the sketchbook had gone.

That posed a couple of questions. Had Stubbs's killer murdered him because he knew he'd stolen the sketchbook and wanted it for himself? Or had Stubbs been killed for some other reason, with his killer finding the sketchbook as a chance bonus? I thought the first was more likely. If Stubbs were murdered for some other reason, there would have been no reason for the killer to take the sketchbook.

I moved back to my original side of the bed.

The bedside table held a small pile of newspapers. Yesterday's *Daily Mirror*. The Afternoon Extra edition of today's *Evening Chronicle*. And a girly magazine called *Wild and Wobbly*.

A packet of blue Basildon Bond envelopes rested on top of the papers. I peered closely at it. The packet had been opened, but it looked as though only one had been used. Could that have been the same envelope I'd found on the floor at Kingswell's art gallery? I'd seen Stubbs in the village minutes before I'd discovered it. But why was Stubbs writing to Kingswell? And what was so important about the letter that it had to be hand-delivered?

Carefully, I moved the envelopes to one side and lifted up the pile of papers. And found that Stubbs had copies of the three postcards that Despart had drawn of Kingswell, Le Grande and Burke. The postcards lay on the top of a thick book – old with a brown cloth cover and faded title on the spine. It was called *The Art of Sussex Churches*.

I puzzled about that for a moment. It seemed strange companion reading matter for a *Wild and Wobbly* fan.

But who was Stubbs? I moved over to the wardrobe and opened the door with my handkerchief-covered right hand. Only one item hung inside: Stubbs's jacket. I reached into the inside pocket and took out a worn leather wallet. It had once been an expensive item tooled out of Moroccan leather with gold corner pieces – one of which was now missing. So Stubbs had once had the cash to treat himself to the best. But – I surveyed the room again – no longer.

Carefully, I opened the wallet and took a look-see. There was a ten-bob note, a driver's licence and a return train ticket to London. And a press card issued by the National Union of Journalists.

I carefully removed the card and looked at the picture on the front. It had been taken a good many years ago, before Stubbs's face had become so emaciated. Stubbs had never been handsome, but the picture suggested he'd once been presentable. I opened the card. It told me his full name was Richard Stubbs. The card had been issued seven years ago and identified him as a reporter with the *Daily Mirror*. The subscription record showed he'd not paid his dues for the past four years. As far as the NUJ was concerned, the Labour Party-supporting *Mirror* was a closed shop. So the fact Stubbs had not paid meant he hadn't worked for the paper for at least three years, when his last annual payment expired.

So was Stubbs now working as a freelancer? His fascination with me kind of began to make sense. If he knew that I was on to a big story, it would be in his interest to swim along in my wake, hoping to catch up with the action when it happened. But he'd have had to know what I was working on. So, perhaps, he'd only been following me because he knew I was in touch with someone else.

There was only one person that someone else could be. He'd have seen my pieces in the *Chronicle*.

Tammy.

Perhaps Tammy hadn't realised that Stubbs had her under surveillance. Or, perhaps, she did. I still wasn't convinced she'd told me everything she knew. There were urgent questions I needed to ask her. Such as why Stubbs had been so keen to steal Archie's sketchbook. And who else could have wanted it enough to throttle Stubbs.

But, more urgently, I needed to tell the landlady the good tidings.

It was more than an hour before I made it back to the newsroom.

When I'd passed the news to the Grump that she had a guest who wouldn't be paying his rent, she'd collapsed in a fit. I had to lay her on the sofa and cover her with a blanket before calling the cops.

Before they arrived, I'd had time to call the *Chronicle* and dictate a story to a copytaker in time to make the Night Final stop press. I'd gone out on a limb and linked Stubbs's death to the campaign to reprieve Archie Flowerdew. I'd not mentioned the sketchbook in my piece, because I didn't want Stubbs's killer to know I knew about it. But I'd hinted in the copy that there were dark forces at work – and they were trying to stop the truth about Percy Despart's murder coming out. Of course, I didn't have that from Stubbs himself. Dead men tell no tales. But they can't sue for libel, either.

I urgently wanted to talk to Tammy about the latest developments. But on the way back to the office, I'd been thinking about another aspect of the killing I couldn't understand. Subscribers to *Wild and Wobbly* magazine don't normally also show an interest in religious paintings. So was there something in *The Art of Sussex Churches* that would provide a clue?

When I reached the *Chronicle*, I went straight into the morgue. Henrietta was putting on her coat as I walked in.

"Pleased to see you back in harness," I said.

"My cold's feeling a bit better, but I've had enough for today," Henrietta said.

"Quick question before you go. Have you ever heard of a book called *The Art of Sussex Churches*?"

"No."

"So we won't have a copy here?"

"No. You could ask the paper's religious correspondent if he knows the book," Henrietta said.

"I don't want to do that."

Henrietta smiled. "Possible exclusive, is it?"

"Something like that."

Henrietta buttoned up her coat. "Leave it with me," she said. "I'll call into Brighton Reference Library on the way home. If Miss Fox hasn't heard of it, it can't be found. Anything else?"

I didn't mention *Wild and Wobbly*. Henrietta wouldn't have

understood.

"It's not my fault. I didn't kill him."

Tammy flounced across the room and threw herself onto the sofa.

"I know you didn't kill Stubbs yourself. But if you'd told me about the sketchbook before, we could have kept it safe." I strode across the room and stood facing Tammy with my back to the fireplace.

We were in Elsie's sitting room. It was the kind of room where I imagined a happily married couple might settle to listen to *Friday Night is Music Night* on the Light Programme. There were a couple of easy chairs on either side of the fireplace. One had a knitting bag overflowing with something in royal blue. The other had an antimacassar with a Brylcreem stain like an oil slick.

I said: "What I'd like to understand is how Stubbs came to know about the sketchbook."

Tammy looked away. Fiddled with a loose thread in her jumper. "I told him."

"You told him! When?"

Tammy shrugged. "You might as well know it all. He came to see me about ten days ago. Said he was writing a book about Uncle Archie's trial. Wanted to help me prove him innocent. He asked me some questions about Uncle Archie. I told him about the time we'd spent together. How Uncle Archie had helped me. I think I might have mentioned the sketchbook."

"You might have mentioned it. Did you or didn't you?"

"I did."

Tammy pouted. "It just slipped out. He was asking me all these questions. He said he was sure, like me, that Uncle Archie was innocent. Did I have anything that could prove it? I just mentioned the book."

"Did you show Stubbs the book?"

"No. He wanted to see it, though. He became a bit pushy

about it."

"Did he attack you?"

"A weed like that? That's a laugh. He wouldn't have dared."

"Did you describe the contents to him?"

"I just told him it contained Christmas drawings."

"Not that they held a clue to Archie's innocence?"

"No."

But she wouldn't have had to. Stubbs would have discovered that Archie drew puzzle pictures. He might have guessed that the sketchbook held clues about the mystery.

I said: "Well, whatever Stubbs learnt from the sketchbook died with him. What we don't know now is who has it and what they may learn."

"It breaks my heart, but I can't see how we can save Uncle Archie now," Tammy said.

Elsie came in from the kitchen. She was wearing one of those full-on aprons that cover the bodice as well as the skirt. Her face was red and strands of hair had fallen in front of her eyes.

"Sorry to appear like this, Mr Crampton. I've just had trouble getting a cobbler into the oven."

For a second or two the image of Elsie shoving a shoe mender into her Aga flashed before my eyes.

I said: "That must have been painful."

Elsie grinned. "Not a cobbler, Mr Crampton. I'm talking about a cobbler."

"That's all clear, then."

"A meat pie with suet dumplings on the top of it. Will you stay for some?"

"No thank you. I'm due to meet Shirley."

"Will you eat with her?"

"I'm certainly hoping for a nibble," I said.

Elsie giggled, but Tammy frowned.

I turned to Tammy. "I need to think what we can do now. I'll come back later with a new plan."

But, at the moment, I had no idea what it would be.

"I'm running out of rope," I said.

"Better not let Tammy hear you say that," Shirley said.

I gave a rueful grin. "It wasn't the best way of putting it, I'll admit. The one poor bloke not running out of rope next Wednesday will be Archie Flowerdew. What I meant to say was that I'm running out of ideas for proving his innocence."

We were having a quick supper in Prompt Corner, a restaurant in Montpelier Road much favoured by actors.

I said: "My interviews with Toby Kingswell and Florian Le Grande have raised suspicions but not produced the kind of hard evidence we'd need to win Archie a reprieve, let alone overturn his conviction."

"What about that third guy you mentioned? The sky pilot."

"Canon Gideon Burke. Over the years, the Church has been a cover for all kinds of dirty deeds, but I can't see Burke murdering Despart because he was humiliated in a postcard."

"Turn the other cheek and all that."

"Something along those lines. Even so, I shall find a way to interview him."

The waiter appeared with our meals – lemon sole for Shirley, lamb casserole for me. We picked up our knives and forks and began to eat.

Between mouthfuls of tasty casserole I said: "The killing of Stubbs throws a new light on the case. According to Tammy, he'd been researching a book about it. If Archie hangs, it could've become a bestseller. But if Archie is reprieved, the book might not even find a publisher. I wonder whether Stubbs discovered something we don't know about. Something about the sketchbook."

"But that's disappeared."

"Which is another puzzle. It suggests there is somebody else out there who knows the book is significant. Whether or not he can tease out its meaning is another matter."

"And it may not be helpful to Archie, anyway," Shirley said.

I scooped up the last of the casserole. "Too true." I said. I shovelled the casserole into my mouth and put my knife and fork at order arms on my plate. "Picking the bones out of that lemon sole is easier than this case."

"The fish is delicious – and it's good for my figure."

I grinned. "I may need to check the last part of that statement personally later."

Shirley kicked my leg under the table. "Focus on this case."

"It's not easy."

"Is there anybody you've not yet thought of who might know something?"

I cast my mind back to the summer and that hot courtroom. The trial had been dragging on for days. The evidence had run strongly against Archie, especially after he'd refused to give his alibi.

Peregrine Collingwood, Archie's brief, was struggling to build a defence. Part of it was to suggest there may have been other people close to Despart's studio at the time of the killing. He'd produced a Stella Maplethorpe who'd been walking her Yorkshire terrier along the front around that time. She'd given a statement to police that she'd seen a tall woman hanging around near the Fortune of War pub. On her way home, Stella had seen the woman again crossing Marine Parade and turning into New Steine. Collingwood tried to suggest the woman could have been an agent in the crime. He'd argued the police had failed to put in the footwork to trace her. It was a spirited effort to throw suspicion onto an unknown person, but nobody was convinced by it.

I explained what had happened in the courtroom.

"But the woman probably didn't kill Archie, anyway," Shirley said.

"That may be true, but misses the point. If, as Stella

Maplethorpe suggested, this woman was seen in the area, she may have spotted the killer entering Despart's studio."

Shirley nodded. "But you don't know who she is because the police never traced her."

"Tomkins had already arrested Archie and, as far as he was concerned, the case was closed."

"You'll never trace her now," Shirley said.

"I think there may be a way," I said.

"I'm not sure I can do it," Tammy said.

"I know you can," I said with a wide, encouraging smile. "This is a practical way you can help Archie. And we've seen how good you are at drawing. Those sketches of Shirley and me – and Henrietta – were excellent."

We were back in Elsie's sitting room. Shirley and I were perched on the edge of the sofa. Elsie was in her chair by the fire. Tammy was curled up, her legs underneath her, in the chair opposite. Elsie's husband, Len, had used our appearance as an excuse to retreat to the shed where he kept his ferrets.

Shirley and I had driven back from the restaurant via the *Chronicle*'s offices. I'd made a telephone call and picked up some papers from the newsroom. Then we'd hustled on to Elsie's house.

"I'd be too worried I'd get it all wrong," Tammy said.

"But think of the triumph if you get it right. After all, it was art that got Archie into this trouble. Why shouldn't it get him out of it, too?"

Tammy bit at her thumb anxiously. "I don't know. Describe the plan to me again."

I told Tammy about the mystery woman who'd been spotted near Despart's studio on the night of the murder. "If we could find that woman she might be able to provide new evidence that would make the authorities review the case."

"But we've got to find her," Tammy said. "The police never

did."

"The police never tried," I said. "We will. We'll publish a drawing of the woman in tomorrow's paper and offer a reward for the first person to identify her successfully. You've inherited your uncle Archie's talent for drawing. I'm sure you can produce a picture from a description."

"It's not as easy as it looks," Tammy said. "When I drew you, I did it from memory. I've never seen this mystery woman."

"Have you heard of the Identi-Kit system?" I said.

Tammy shook her head.

"It's a way of creating pictures of people. It was invented by a police officer in Los Angeles four years ago. It was used the first time in Britain a couple of years ago to convict a killer who'd murdered a lady from a London antique shop. The system works because it takes one part of the face at a time. So, for example, you start with the nose – the Identi-Kit system has thirty-three different kinds – and choose the one that fits the description. Then you move on to the chin – fifty-two of those. Then you choose from the forty lips and the one hundred and two eyes and so on until you have a true likeness of the whole face."

"We don't actually have an Identi-Kit set," Shirley said.

"But the principle works if you draw each feature of the face separately from the description," I said. "You can modify the drawing each time until the witness thinks you've got it right. Then just put all the different features together in one sketch."

Tammy shifted in her chair. "I suppose we could try it."

I heaved a sigh of relief. "That's great," I said. "Because I called Stella Maplethorpe from the *Chronicle*'s newsroom before we came here. She's agreed to see us this evening."

Chapter 13

Frank Figgis picked up the drawing I'd placed on his desk.

His eyes widened with astonishment. "By the sacred spike of Gerald Pope, who's this supposed to be? She looks like Princess Margaret after a heavy night."

"I'm told it's a very good likeness," I said.

"By whom? The blind man or his guide dog?"

"Actually, it was a woman – and apart from glasses for reading she assures me she has very good eyesight."

It was the morning after I'd taken Tammy to visit Stella Maplethorpe. Figgis and I were sitting in his office. His fag was sending up smoke signals from the ashtray on his desk. He picked it up and took a long drag.

"And you want me to print this on the front page?"

"We can run it as a missing witness story," I said. "I can see the headline now: Have you seen this woman? Her evidence could save a man's life."

"Not mine," Figgis said. "His Holiness will sack me if he sees this dominating the front page. Bejeezus, she looks like the queen of the harpies."

The picture showed a tall woman with dark hair styled in a beehive and covered with a tied scarf. She had a thin face, with rouged cheeks and lips coloured a deep maroon. She wore glasses with elaborate blue winged frames. Behind the glasses, her eyes looked hard and dark. She was wearing a thick, fake fox fur coat pulled tightly around her neck and chin.

"We'd explain it's a rough likeness," I said.

"Rough? It couldn't be rougher if it had been drawn on sandpaper."

I reached over Figgis's desk, picked up the picture and had another look.

"You must remember that when Stella saw this woman it was

night. But she was lit by the lamps on the promenade and she passed right by her. I agree the woman in the drawing looks unusual, but that's just the reason someone might come forward if they recognise her."

"She looks like the kind of woman you'd cross the road to avoid."

"Stella didn't think so."

"She had a dog to protect her."

I said: "Take the glasses, for example. They're unusual."

"They're grotesque," Figgis said.

"They're like the kind Edna Everage wears."

"Who's she?"

"She's a fictional character, a housewife from Australia's Moonee Ponds, actually. She does this stand-up comedy routine in clubs. Shirley told me about her. Or, actually, I should say him. Edna is played by an actor called Barry Humphries."

"And he – or her – has glasses like our unknown woman."

"Not exactly the same, but equally flamboyant. At least, they were when we saw her at Peter Cook's club in London last month."

Figgis slumped back on his chair and folded his arms in a listen-to-me-or-else posture.

"Let's get this straight. You're suggesting I go upstairs to His Holiness and say that we're publishing a picture of an unknown female who could be recognised because she has glasses that are similar to those of an Australian man who dresses up as a woman. He'll tell me to my face that I'm taking the pistachio."

"Why not just run the picture and deal with the fallout afterwards?"

"That's fine for you. It won't be your job on the line. Or, perhaps, it will be."

"It's Archie's neck on the line if we can't raise doubts about his conviction," I said.

Figgis stood up. Walked over to the window. Rubbed a hole in the condensation and peered out.

He turned back towards me. "I know. I'd like to see the old boy spared the noose as much as you. But will this make any difference?"

"I don't know. But it gives us a great exclusive."

"I don't deny you've scooped the competition. But this is something else."

Figgis was working himself up to spike my idea. I had to apply some more pressure.

"If we don't run the picture, I think Tammy could walk out on us."

"Where would she go?"

"The *Argus*. Or, more likely, one of the nationals. They'd jump at the chance of getting the access to Archie's nearest relative that we've enjoyed. Especially when the dark day dawns."

Figgis shrugged. Went back to his chair and flopped into it. He ran a weary hand over his forehead. He looked tired.

"Perhaps it wouldn't be so bad if Pope sacked me, after all. It's about time I had a pension book and a pair of slippers."

"You'll run it?" I asked.

"Yes. But let's leave it until the Afternoon Extra. I happen to know that His Holiness has a Christmas lunch with the Rotary Club today. He'll see the Midday Special before he leaves the office. By the time the Afternoon Extra hits the streets, he'll be half-cut at the Norfolk Hotel passing the port and swapping dirty jokes with his fellow Rotarians."

I grinned. "Now I know where I get my devious streak from."

"And speaking of devious streaks, what progress have you made on proving your innocence of that cushion misprint?"

I wished Figgis hadn't brought that up, because I hadn't had time to mount a proper investigation.

"I'm looking into it vigorously," I lied.

An hour later, I was sitting in the briefing room at Brighton Police

Station with a dozen other hacks.

The room hummed with raised voices and raucous laughter. There's nothing like a grisly murder to put crime correspondents in a good mood. We were waiting to be told how the cops had failed to make any progress in solving the murder of Richard Stubbs, who turned out to be better known as Dirty Dick Stubbs, the freelance journalist I'd found dead in his lodgings the previous evening.

Jim Houghton made his way over to me. Jim was wearing his old grey suit but a new tie. At least, I assumed it was, as it hadn't yet picked up any gravy stains. He slumped down in the seat next to me.

"I'd like a quiet word," he said.

"How about 'silence'? That's a quiet word," I said.

Jim harrumphed. "You won't be feeling so clever when you hear what I've got to say."

"In that case, you'd better make it a very quiet word. With a bit of luck, I might not hear it at all."

"It concerns Sir Randolph Abercrombie and that little matter of your misprint."

So Jim Houghton had heard about the imbroglio over the caution-to-cushion misprint. That didn't surprise me. Jim had excellent sources – and, in the past, they'd included the odd snitch on the *Chronicle*.

I said: "It's not my misprint, Jim. And Abercrombie has already had his correction."

"Yesterday I had a quick word with Randy."

"A quick word like 'rapid'?" I said.

"No, like trouble. Apparently, he's not satisfied with the correction and apology. Something may be heading your way."

"Not a bouquet of roses, I assume."

"More like a summons." Jim brushed back a lank of greasy hair that had flopped over his forehead. "For contempt of court."

It was time to show some bravado. "We've already heard

about that empty threat. The only contempt in Abercrombie's court is for the principles of justice. And, anyway, what were you doing having a quick word with Randy? Rolling up each other's left trouser legs?"

Jim didn't like the fact I knew he was a Mason.

"Just a friendly word," Jim said.

"Like 'amicable'?" I said.

Jim frowned. He heaved himself off his chair and loped down to a fresh seat in the front row.

It would've made Jim's day to pass on some bad news to me. Especially as I'd been scooping him all week with exclusive interviews with Tammy. And it would be topped off in today's Midday *Chronicle* with a front-page splash over my byline headed: I Find the Body of Murder Case Author. And then there'd be the follow-up in the Afternoon Extra with the picture of the mystery woman.

Even so, Jim's news needed a bit of thinking about. If there's one thing a journalist fears more than a writ for libel, it's a summons for contempt of court. True, the libel case can empty your bank account – although on the *Chronicle* we were all insured. But the contempt of court can land you in chokey. And when it comes to throwing journos in the slammer, the courts were no respecters of persons. Only a few years earlier, Silvester Bolam, the editor of the *Daily Mirror*, had spent three months in prison for contempt. So the judge wouldn't think twice about sending a humble crime reporter away for a holiday at Her Majesty's expense.

But I didn't have too long to ponder on that, because the door on the other side of the room opened and Ted Wilson slouched in. There were dark smudges under his eyes. His beard looked shaggier than usual. His tie was askew. His trousers had an extra crumple. And he'd done up his jacket on the wrong buttonhole. He didn't look like a man on top of his game.

He seated himself at the top table, slopped some water from a carafe into a tumbler and took a quick swig. He surveyed the room with the look of a big game hunter who's surrounded by a pride of hungry lions and realised he's just run out of ammunition.

He caught my eye at the back of the room and I winked. The shadow of a smile passed over his lips.

He picked up a sheet of paper and said: "I am going to read a prepared statement and will then take questions." Ted bent over the paper and started to read.

It was the usual guff the cops try to palm journos off with at the first press conference after a murder. "A body was found ..." (Well, we wouldn't be here if hadn't been.) "The police have identified the deceased as ..." (Actually, I did that, but thought it prudent to let the cops make their own discovery.) "Investigations are continuing into how the killer entered the premises unseen ..." (I'd worked that out in about five minutes the previous evening. It was through the back door that conveniently opened on to an alley.)

Ted finished his statement and asked for questions. In front of me, a bloke's hand shot up before I could get in.

"Did you find anything at the scene that might have given a clue as to why the dead man was there?" he asked.

Ted shuffled through his papers uncertainly. "We discovered what appears to be the manuscript of an unfinished book."

That must have been the book Stubbs had told Tammy he was writing. I hadn't seen the manuscript when I'd been in his room. But I hadn't had time to search thoroughly.

I made a quick note and asked before the bloke in front could barge in: "What's the book called?"

"*Anatomy of a Hanging,*" Ted said.

"The hanging being that of Archie Flowerdew, presumably?"

"That would be a reasonable conclusion, but we are keeping an open mind until we've had time to read it."

I nodded. The cops usually said they'd keep an open mind when what they meant was that they had an empty mind. I made a couple of notes.

"Where did you find the book?" I asked.

"It was in a small attaché case under the bed."

I made another note. And cursed myself under my breath. The only thing you normally find under beds in cheap guest houses are dust balls and old jerries. So I'd not looked under the bed. It would have been good to have had a peek at the manuscript before I raised the alarm. It could have yielded important clues.

I wondered whether the contents could have provided a clue as to why Stubbs had been murdered. It was a good question, but too good to ask in front of my fellow hacks. They could draw their own conclusions without help from me. If Stubbs had been poking around the case, could he have discovered information that pointed the finger at someone else? If so, that would give the new suspect a healthy reason for preventing Stubbs revealing his suspicions in print. But it would also undermine the book's theme – if Archie were reprieved, he would not play the lead role in an anatomy of a hanging. It was a tantalising puzzle. Perhaps when Ted had perused Stubbs's prose, I could finagle him over a scotch or two to give me a hint. There were a few more questions, which Ted batted away before the press briefing broke up.

I headed swiftly for the door before Jim could taunt me over my failure to find the book under the bed.

On the way back to the office, I put in a call to Tammy from a phone box.

She was still holed up at Elsie's house. And sounded as though she were climbing the walls with frustration. I told her the picture she'd drawn would appear on the front page of the Afternoon Extra and that I'd let her know as soon as we had a decent lead.

But back at the office, the hours ticked by as though each were a day. Shortly after two, Figgis stomped into the newsroom with a copy of the Afternoon Extra, which had just come up from the machine room.

He dropped it on my desk and said: "I hope you're right about this, or we'll all have some explaining to do."

Over the next couple of hours, we had a trickle of calls from the usual time-wasters. There was an old bloke who said the woman reminded him of a bridge partner he'd had before the war. A housewife who wondered whether she was the sister of a friend who worked in London Road market. And a fruity-voiced roué who wanted to know if the lady in the picture would like to join him for a quiet supper.

A couple of hours later, Figgis marched into the newsroom again – this time with the Night Final.

"I've kept it on the front page," he said. "But unless we get a positive lead today, I'm not running it any more. I've stuck my neck out once too often for you. This is the last time."

He pranced back to his office with that bouncy walk that always reminded me of a dressage horse doing the tango.

The call came at ten minutes to six.

It was a woman's voice. Educated but not posh. Nervous, even querulous. A good sign. It's the blaggers who come on all confident.

She said: "I'm ringing about the picture on the front page of tonight's *Chronicle*."

I said: "I'm Colin Crampton. Who am I talking to?"

"Veronica Rainsmith."

"Do you know the woman in the picture?"

"Well, I'm not sure I know the woman. But I certainly know that fox fur coat. I mean, how could you miss such a monstrosity?"

"You've seen a lady wearing it?"

"Only once or twice. But I have seen the same lady on other occasions."

"And does she look like the lady in the picture?" I asked.

"That's it. I'm not sure. There are some similarities, but your picture is not a convincing likeness. Not entirely. But, then, if she's the lady with the fox fur, it must be the same one, mustn't it?"

"Unless there are more of them."

"Ladies or fox furs?"

"Fox furs."

"Oh, I can tell you no self-respecting woman would be caught wearing something like that. Even the foxes would have been ashamed of it."

"Do you know where the owner of the shaming fox fur lives?" I asked.

"Well, that's it. I live in Picardy Villas in Kemp Town. It's not far from the seafront. I have the ground-floor flat in a house on the corner of a small mews."

"I know it."

"If this is the lady you're looking for, she lives in a cottage in the mews; converted stable block, I believe. It's quite private and not many people even know it's there."

"Do you know the lady's name?"

"No. I've only ever seen her on a handful of occasions – twice wearing the fox fur – and then usually at night."

"When did you last see her?"

"Not for months. I think it must have been back in February. In fact, I remember clearly that it was the day before I read about the murder of that postcard man – can't remember his name."

"Percy Despart."

"That's him. It was quite late. I was putting out the milk bottles and I saw her hurrying into the mews. Almost running, she was. But how she managed to in that fox fur, I'll never know."

"And you've not seen her since?"

"No."

"Could you give me your address and telephone number, and the address of the mews cottage?"

Veronica reeled them off. I thanked her, replaced the receiver and lounged back in my captain's chair thinking hard.

This was the best identification so far. Correction, it was the only identification. But it wasn't conclusive. Besides, it had been ten months since Veronica had last seen Madame Fox Fur. She could have moved on. In which case, the chances of tracing her would be slim.

But there was an obvious course of action. I had to call at the mews cottage and see whether the lady without any dress sense was at home.

"Ring again," Shirley said.

I pressed the bell a third time and listened to the chimes.

"Nobody at home," I said.

We were outside the mews cottage. It was a squat little place with knapped flint walls and a slate roof. It had a traditional stable door. The top and bottom halves opened independently. A layer of dust had settled around the window that was set into the top half of the door. Cobwebs dangled from the architrave above the door. No lights showed in any of the windows.

"Nobody has been at home for quite some time," I said.

Shirley nodded. "It reminds me of a haunted house," she said.

I'd picked up Shirley on the way. If the lady with the challenging dress sense was at home, I thought the presence of another woman might encourage her to talk more freely.

"Let's see if there are any ghosties or ghoulies inside," I said.

"Like we're going to turn into wraiths and materialise on the other side of the door?" Shirley said. "I don't think so."

I reached into my inside pocket and pulled out a thin metal strip.

"What's that?" Shirley asked.

"It's a printer's ruler. It measures points and ems in type. They make them thin but from very strong metal."

"And you just happened to have it on you."

"When Veronica said she hadn't seen the woman for several months, I thought we might need to invite ourselves in."

"By measuring the place?"

"Watch this," I said. "As you can see, it's the bottom half of the door that's locked with a conventional Yale. I expect the top half opens with a lever catch on the inside. Let's hope so."

I inserted the ruler carefully through the gap between the door and the jamb in the top half of the door. I moved it up until I felt it engage with the lever inside the door. Then I gave it a sharp upward jerk. The catch released and I pushed the top half of the door inwards. I reached inside, slipped the release button on the Yale and opened the bottom half of the door.

I stood back and grinned at Shirley. "After you, milady," I said.

Inside, the place smelt as though wet blankets had been hanging in the air.

Shirley sniffed. "You sure there are no horses still here?" she asked.

I ignored that and said: "We need some light. I'll pull down those blinds."

I switched the light on. We looked around. We were in a small room that served as a sitting room, dining room and galley kitchen. The place had bare flint walls painted white. There were a couple of cheap rugs on the floor. A worn easy chair had horsehair bursting from a couple of splits in the fabric. A small deal table had a single chair tucked up to it. There was a stove at the far end of the room, with a black chimney that rose into the air and disappeared through the ceiling. Everywhere was covered with a thin film of dust.

A steep set of wooden steps led to a kind of mezzanine floor, which stuck out over about half the width of the building. Looking up from the ground floor, I could see a single bed and a wardrobe.

"Nobody has been here for some time," I said.

"And they aren't coming back, if you ask me," Shirley said.

"But who lived here?"

There were few visible signs of the occupant. No pictures on the walls. No photos of family or friends. No letters in a rack. No ornaments or knick-knacks.

"I don't think anyone lived here," I said. "Unless they took a lot of personal stuff with them when they left. But it doesn't feel like that to me. It feels more like a pied-à-terre."

"A bolthole," Shirley said.

"Yes. But who would want a bolthole like this? Let's look upstairs."

We climbed the steps to the mezzanine floor. Shirley opened the wardrobe and looked in.

"Jeez. Whoever wears this clobber must think they're back in the fifties. Rock-around-the-clock skirts and button-up blouses. That stuff went out with Bill Haley."

I opened the top drawer in a small dressing table. "Hey, look at this." I rummaged around and pulled out a few items. "Stockings with seams. And a suspender belt. French knickers. And what are these?"

I held up a couple of conical pads.

Shirley giggled. "They're falsies."

"False what?"

"False titties, stupid. For the lady who's got a little but wants more."

"You could poke your eyes out with one of these," I said.

Shirley turned back to the wardrobe. "This is what you're looking for," she said. She unhooked a hanger and hefted out a coat. A huge fox fur.

"It must be the coat," I said. "It has to be the one Stella saw the woman wearing. But we still don't know who she is. There's nothing here that identifies her. I find that suspicious."

"But nothing we can do about it," Shirley said.

"Let's go," I said. "This is a secluded spot, but we don't want to push our luck."

Shirley started down the steps and I followed. Stopped halfway down.

"I made a mistake last night," I said. "When I stumbled on the dead Stubbs, I failed to look under his bed and missed a vital clue. The manuscript of the book he'd been writing."

I climbed back up the steps. Fell to my knees. Lifted the bedspread and peered under the bed.

"There's a box here," I said.

Shirley clattered back up the steps and joined me on the floor. We reached under the bed and heaved the box out.

It was a strong wooden item with a brass catch. I lifted it. Our heads banged together as we moved forward to look inside.

The first thing I saw was a photo of Archie Flowerdew.

He was wearing the fox fur over a pencil skirt. He had fishnet stockings and feet crammed into shoes with four-inch heels. He had a beehive wig. His cheeks were rouged, his lips richly painted and his eyelashes mascaraed. He was smiling. But, apart from the giveaway fox fur, he didn't bear much resemblance to the description Stella Maplethorpe had given us. Or the picture we'd published in the *Chronicle*.

Shirley and I looked at one another with open mouths and astonished eyes.

Finally, Shirley spoke. "He's a cross-dresser."

"A secret transvestite," I said. "You were right. This is a bolthole. It's the secret place where he becomes a woman."

"Became," Shirley corrected me.

"You realise this changes everything," I said.

"How?"

"We've been trying to prove that Archie was nowhere near Despart's studio on the night he was killed. Now we have a witness who says he was. Dressed as a woman."

"That's not a crime."

"No. If it were, Danny La Rue would have been in the jug years ago. But Archie's hobby was plainly something he wanted to keep secret. If Despart had found out – and he had a reputation for uncovering people's secrets – it would have given Archie a strong motive for killing him."

"So Archie could be the killer, after all?" Shirley said.

I nodded. "It's something we need to consider. But there's worse."

"What's that?"

"We have to tell Tammy."

Chapter 14

"That can't be true!" Tammy shrieked.

Her face was white, as though the blood had sunk down to her feet. Her eyes, wide and wild, stared at us.

"I'm afraid there's no doubt about it," I said. "Archie found personal fulfilment in dressing as a woman."

We were in Elsie's sitting room. Shirley and I perched awkwardly on the edge of the sofa. Tammy fidgeted in Len's chair. Elsie fiddled nervously with her knitting needles.

She said: "I'd better make us all a nice cup of tea." She stood up and headed towards the kitchen. Turned back at the door and said: "And perhaps I should bring some digestive biscuits, too."

"Uncle Archie never told me," Tammy said. "If he'd taken pride in dressing as a woman, I wouldn't have been prejudiced."

"It is a truth universally acknowledged that a man in want of a woman's wardrobe doesn't go around blabbing about it," I said.

"I can't understand how I drew his picture and didn't recognise him," Tammy said.

"That's because Stella Maplethorpe's description of Archie's features wasn't accurate. She was too fixated on the fox fur. But it was enough to identify him."

"I'm sure I'd have known if Uncle Archie liked dressing as a woman," Tammy said.

"Perhaps deep down you did, but didn't admit it to yourself. I remember you told me how Archie took great pleasure in repairing your dolls' clothes after your father had ripped them. He even redressed the dolls for you."

"I was a young girl then. Men dressed as men and women as women."

"Except when no one else was looking," I said.

"It's not unusual," Shirley chipped in. "Back in Oz, I once caught my uncle Bruce trying on one of my bras. He asked me not to tell Aunt Magnolia about it. Begged me for my support. I told the whacker he'd just been wearing it."

Tammy gave a thin smile. "What else did you find?" she asked me.

I told Tammy about how the picture she'd drawn of the mystery woman had led us to Veronica Rainsmith. About how Shirley and I had visited the mews cottage. Found a way to get inside. And what we'd discovered.

"The box under the bed contains more photos and letters. There are magazines and women's clothing catalogues, which make it clear that Archie had been using the cottage as a base for his female persona," I said.

"When he's a woman he calls himself Arabella. Or should that be she calls herself …" Shirley said.

"If only he'd told me," Tammy said.

"It's not so easy to explain that kind of thing, especially to someone you love," Shirley said. "Archie would've feared that you'd think less of him. He may even have worried that he'd lose your love forever."

"I'd never stop loving Uncle Archie," Tammy said. "Or Auntie Arabella. No matter what either of them did."

"Including murder?" I asked.

It was time for Tammy to face the implications of this discovery.

Tammy's eyes flashed angrily. "But we know Uncle Archie didn't kill the despicable Despart."

"Do we?" I said. "We believe he's innocent – and I assure you that I still think that's a possibility – but now we have a witness who puts Archie close to Despart's studio at the time we know he was killed. And dressed as a woman, too."

"But I know it couldn't have been him."

"Why?"

"Mistaken identity," Tammy said.

Shirley touched my arm. It was a sign she thought I was being too hard on Tammy.

"It's a possibility," Shirley said.

I shrugged. "Yes, it's a possibility."

"Besides, isn't the solution to this puzzle as bright as a kookaburra's bum?" Shirley said.

"That depends on the bum," I said. "But you mean Archie could be asked about it?"

Tammy's eyes shone with excitement. "I could ask for a last prison visit. I could tell him I know. That I don't mind and that I'll love him always."

I shook my head. "I'm not sure the Home Secretary would approve it. Besides, trying to arrange it would take up all the time we need to spend searching for the evidence that wins Archie a reprieve."

The door opened and Elsie came in with a tray of tea. She passed round the cups. Shirley handed out the biscuits. I helped myself to a digestive, dunked it in my tea, took a bite.

We all sat in silence while we sipped and chewed.

Elsie put down her cup. "Things always look brighter after a nice cup of tea," she said. She turned towards me. "By the way, I almost forgot. Henrietta phoned just before you arrived. She says she's got something for you. And she thinks it's important."

I met Henrietta in Prinny's Pleasure half an hour later.

I'd left Shirley with Tammy at Elsie's house. "Try to keep Tammy's spirits up," I'd said. "The news about Archie's cross-dressing will give her a lot to think about. But she needs to keep focused on the main problem – finding evidence to save him."

"Elsie can provide the tea and I'll dole out the sympathy," Shirley had said.

Henrietta and I took our drinks to the corner table at the back of the bar.

Henrietta sipped her Guinness and surveyed the place. She sniffed in that way she did when something wasn't quite right.

"This grey wallpaper doesn't do much for the room," she said.

"Actually, I believe it started life as green. But that was before my time, of course."

Henrietta took another sip of her Guinness and sighed appreciatively. "Anyway, I've got something for you to go with that gin and tonic," she said. "And it's not a packet of crisps."

She reached into a large bag she'd put on the seat beside her. Took out a book and handed it to me.

"*The Art of Sussex Churches* by the Reverend Horace Crockhurst, MA," she said.

"You found a copy."

"I borrowed a copy. From Miss Fox in Brighton's reference library. Normally, she wouldn't let one of her volumes cross the threshold. But I explained it might be a matter of life or death."

"It certainly seemed connected to Dirty Dick Stubbs's death. I couldn't understand why he had a copy in his room when his usual reading matter peaked at *Wild and Wobbly* magazine."

Henrietta sniffed again. "Anyway, you're to keep the book in perfect condition. Apparently, it's long been out of print."

"Makes it even more peculiar that Stubbs should have a copy, then."

"Perhaps he picked up one in Brighton. I bet you could still find copies in one of those second-hand bookshops in The Lanes."

"Maybe." I wasn't convinced.

Henrietta downed her Guinness in a couple of impressive swallows. She looked around again, had another sniff and said: "I'd love to stay but I've promised myself an early night."

I waved her off, then opened the book.

It was handsomely produced with two sets of colour plates. I turned to the verso page and found the book had originally been published in 1947, two years after the war. I sampled the text on a couple of random pages. The Reverend Crockhurst was no doubt a worthy cleric, but his writing was as dry as a Sunday sermon. It wasn't going to set the literary world on fire.

I wished I'd been able to take a closer look at the book in Stubbs's room. Perhaps a bookmark or turned-down page corner might have given a clue as to which section of the book had attracted his attention. Instead, I took a look at the contents page. Helpfully, the book was written as a kind of guide. So each chapter covered a different part of Sussex. There was a separate chapter on Brighton about halfway through. I turned to it straight away.

Most of the churches in Brighton were listed separately. There was a section on St Peter's, another on St Bartholomew's and a third on St Nicholas'. I flipped over the pages and found St Rita's. The church had a larger entry than some of the others. According to Crockhurst, this was because successive vicars had had a genuine interest in religious art. The church had also been blessed with a number of wealthy benefactors who'd made donations of paintings and sculptures over the years.

And, of course, I already knew that the vicar of St Rita's was none other than Canon Gideon Burke, the victim of one of Despart's nastier postcards. Was this, I wondered, why Stubbs had a copy of the book? Had he been researching Burke's background as part of his *Anatomy of a Hanging*? Or had he come upon this artistic background purely by chance? At the moment, I had no answers to any of those questions. So I read on.

Pride of place in the St Rita's collection, Crockhurst informed me, was a painting in the style of Raphael entitled *Avenging Angel*. The reverend art lover opined that the work had probably been painted by a pupil of Raphael, or perhaps one of the pupil's pupils. (Or, perhaps, the lodger of one of the pupil's pupil's sister's cousins – Colin Crampton, art critic.) Crockhurst praised the "thoughtful ingenuity of the composition" and the "vigorous energy of the brushwork". I could, Crockhurst helpfully mentioned, view a print of the painting on colour plate seven.

I flipped the pages immediately. Colour plate seven showed a buxom woman with blonde hair and a pair of wings emerging from a cloud. She had a look on her face like she'd been locked in the lavatory for a couple of hours – and didn't even want to go. Now she was determined to get her own back on anyone who happened to stumble into her view.

From her cloud she was slinging thunderbolts earthwards and a few hapless souls down below were catching the wrong end of her wrath. They were lying around nursing their injuries and generally feeling sorry for themselves. It looked a bit like West Street in Brighton just after the pubs have turned out on a Saturday night. Except that the poor saps in the painting were all dressed in medieval clobber. In West Street, the avenging angel usually turned out to be a uniformed plod with a truncheon rather than a thunderbolt.

I sat back and considered what I'd learnt. On the face of it, the only connection between Percy Despart and Gideon Burke was the postcard Despart had drawn. Yet, both had an interest in art – Despart professionally, Burke as a cleric with a prized collection of religious paintings at his church. I couldn't think how all this could save Archie Flowerdew's neck. But I'd not yet met Burke. I needed to take a closer look at him.

Besides, the campaign to save Archie badly needed a dose of divine intervention.

But the intervention awaiting me when I finally reached my lodgings that night was anything but divine.

Mrs Gribble was lurking behind her parlour door and shot out as soon as she heard my key in the lock. The flannelette dressing gown looked more creased than the previous night.

She pointed a bony finger at me and said: "I blame you."

"Most people do, Mrs Gribble. I bear it with fortitude." I made for the stairs.

"Don't think you can just brush this off. You were going to advise me what I should do about the Christmas cards."

I clapped my hand theatrically against my forehead like a bad actor in a provincial rep miming forgetfulness. In fact, I had forgotten. Mrs Gribble had sent the wrong Christmas cards to her sister-in-law, Eunice, and Mr Evans, the butcher. Instead of just calling them and laughing off the mistake, she'd turned it into a Cold War incident – and demanded I think of a way out of her predicament. But I'd just been too busy to bother about it.

I said: "I'm giving deep thought to the best damage-limitation strategy."

"So how are you going to damage limit this?" she said. She brandished a telegram in front of me. "It's from Eunice," she said. "Read it."

She handed the paper to me. I read:

DON'T NEED MY TRIPE OVER CHRISTMAS INDEED STOP SO THAT'S WHAT YOU REALLY THINK OF ME STOP WOULDN'T STAY WITH YOU IF YOU PAID ME STOP WILL BE PUTTING UP AT NORFOLK HOTEL ON SEAFRONT INSTEAD STOP GRIBBLE STOP

I handed the telegram back to the Widow.

She said: "At sixpence a word, that's one pound two shillings. That sister-in-law of mine always did have more money than sense."

"What are you going to do?"

"If she wants to stay at the Norfolk, it's no skin off my parson's nose."

"So why the worry?"

"Because I still haven't heard from Mr Evans."

"To whom you sent Eunice's message. I imagine he hasn't even read the card."

The Widow looked hopeful. "You think so?"

"Christmas is his busiest time of the year. I doubt he even opens his cards until Boxing Day."

"I hope you're right. But I'm double locking the front door on

Christmas Eve in case."

I was about to say something, but the Widow had stormed back into her parlour.

It was mid-morning the following day before I reached St Rita's.

It was a small brick-built church in the West Hill part of town. The sort of place a Victorian worthy would have endowed in the hope that his generosity would guarantee him a place in the Big House upstairs when his time came. I was no expert in church matters, but it seemed a modest berth for a cleric who'd been honoured with the rank of canon. But I was forgetting that Gideon Burke had a reputation – and perhaps the bishop had sent him to Brighton to keep him away from virgins.

Despite the modest size of the church, I could hear some lusty singing emerging from inside. A hymn from *Ancient & Modern*, I thought. The organ was growling with bass chords and the choir was trilling the descant parts.

I stepped into the church porch and tarried while the hymn continued. A noticeboard tacked up on the wall announced future activities. It held a photo of Canon Burke and a brief outline of his career. It carefully avoided mentioning virgins, but touched on his time as a wartime army chaplain, attached to the Royal Marines Commandos.

That had my attention. Kingswell had served as a commando. So it was possible – as I'd pondered when I'd met Le Grande – that Kingswell and Burke knew one another. I was wondering whether that could be significant, when some fortissimo chords from the organ signalled the last verse of the hymn.

While the congregation sang it, I picked up a leaflet about St Rita, to whom the church was dedicated. St Rita of Cascia, I learnt from the first page, was the patron saint of impossible causes. That figured. She'd find more than enough of them in Brighton.

Not least my campaign to win a reprieve for Archie.

But before I could take that line of thought any further, the hymn ended. I thrust the rest of the leaflet into my pocket and crept quietly into the church.

I took a seat in a pew at the back, while Gideon Burke ascended the steps to the pulpit. Burke laid down his notes on the lectern and surveyed the congregation. He was a sturdy man. Not fat but muscular. Or perhaps it was just his clerical vestments that made him seem larger. He had a fleshy face with pronounced jowls and a broad nose. His eyes, hooded by heavy lids, looked deep and searching. His mouth was set in a permanently condescending smile.

Burke grasped each side of the lectern and said: "My lesson today is taken from the Book of Revelations chapter twenty-one verse eight: "But for the cowardly and unbelieving and abominable and murderers and immoral persons and sorcerers and idolaters and all liars, their part will be in the lake that burns with fire and brimstone, which is the second death."

"And a merry Christmas to you, too," I murmured softly.

Not softly enough. A matron with a large hat, sitting in front, turned round and shushed me.

I guess most of the small congregation hoped that in the run-up to the festive season they could've enjoyed a few well-worn homilies about virgin births. But, perhaps, that was too sensitive a topic for Burke. Instead, he gave them a hell's-fire sermon on the evils that awaited the cowardly, unbelieving, abominable et al. When it came to hell fires, Burke could stoke for Satan. As they stood up and shuffled down the aisle after the service, most of the congregation had faces like troops retreating from heavily bombarded trenches.

I made my way to the back of the church and hung around for a bit. I wanted to have a nose about. I fancied a quick look-see at the painting of the *Avenging Angel* by a pupil of Raphael. During Burke's sermon I'd been looking around. Each of the church's transepts held a small chapel. Most of the artworks seemed to be hung in these chapels. The chapel off the right-hand side of the nave looked the most ornate. I guessed that's where the *Avenging Angel* would be slinging her thunderbolts.

I threaded my way through the pews and entered the chapel. I was right. The *Angel* hung on the end wall above a small altar. After viewing the colour plate in *The Art of Sussex Churches*, I'd been expecting a large canvas. But this was strangely unimpressive. An ornate, portrait-shaped frame about twenty-inches high by fifteen across held a picture that lacked the vibrant colours I'd seen in the book. Old paintings, I knew, gathered dirt over the years and were cleaned by specialists. The *Avenging Angel* looked as though she were long overdue a spruce up.

I was mulling this over when a voice behind me said: "Just because she's small, don't underestimate her power."

I turned. Burke was standing there in his canonical gear. He had the kind of grin gangsters use when they're collecting protection money but want to keep it friendly.

I said: "Size isn't everything – for women or men."

Burke took that in his stride. "I haven't seen you at divine service before."

"It's my first time. I just felt it might help me think out a worry on my mind."

I'd had an idea that might help me discover whether the rumours about Burke and the virgins were true.

"Would you like to talk about it, my son?"

"It's difficult. Very personal. And a bit embarrassing."

"Embarrassment is only your conscience talking to you. Listen to it."

"The thing is it involves a girl."

"Really?" Burke flicked a lizard-like tongue over his lips. He moved closer.

"Yes, it's my girlfriend, Shirley."

"Does it involve your feelings for Shirley?"

"In a way, but it's more her feelings for me."

"You are both wondering whether you should consummate

your love, perhaps? I have to tell you I do not believe in sex before marriage."

I grinned. "Especially if it delays the ceremony, vicar."

"This is not a matter for misplaced levity."

"I'm sorry. To come to the point, Shirley wants me to make love to her – and I'm not sure it's right for me to do the other thing she wants, either."

A fleck of spittle had appeared at the side of Burke's mouth. "And what does she want?"

"She wants me to dress as a vicar while I'm giving her the benefit. Well, actually, not the full gear. She wants me to skip the robes and all that, and just wear the main item."

"The main item? I don't understand."

"The dog collar."

Burke's Adam's apple bobbed as he swallowed hard. "Let me get this right. Your girlfriend wants you to make love to her wearing only a dog collar?"

"That's about the size of it. Of what she wants. Not the size of the dog collar. I expect they come in different sizes. Do they?"

Burke's jowly cheeks had become red. A bead of sweat trickled down his brow. "Yes, they do come. I mean in different sizes. But that's not the point."

"What is the point, vicar? That's what I want to know."

Burke took a guilty glance at the *Avenging Angel*. "I think you should bring your girlfriend, Shirley, to see me. It's clear the girl needs divine guidance."

"You really think that's the answer?"

Burke harrumphed. For the first time, he looked embarrassed. Perhaps his conscience was talking to him. Or, more likely, he'd just told it to shut up.

"I could manage a short interview with her at about half past seven this evening," he said. "After the evening service."

"That would be very helpful, vicar."

"I shall call upon the spirit of St Rita to guide me."

"I'll let Shirley know. I think she knew a Rita as well. I believe she was a hostess in a nightclub. More of a sinner than a saint."

I turned to leave. Looked back over my shoulder. Burke had taken a handkerchief from somewhere in his vestments and was wiping sweat from his brow.

Chapter 15

Shirley fixed her turquoise eyes on me in a death-ray stare.

"Let's get this straight, whacker," she said. "You want me to turn up at the holy house playing a saucy sheila so that a dirty old canon can crack a fat?"

"I wouldn't put it quite like that," I said.

We were sitting at a window table in the restaurant of the Royal Albion Hotel. I'd decided it might soften the blow if I broke the news about what I wanted Shirley to do over a good lunch.

Shirley glanced down at her plate of roast beef, Yorkshire pudding and all the trimmings. "So that's what this top tucker is all about. You want me to play a tasty tart with this root rat."

"It was an unexpected opportunity," I said. "Canon Burke took me for a parishioner in trouble. I had to think on my feet."

"Think with your feet, more like." Shirley cut into her beef, added a slice of Yorkshire pudding and conveyed the generous forkful to her mouth.

While she was chewing, I explained the evidence I had that linked Kingswell, Le Grande and Burke.

"I think Burke could be the weak link because of his fascination with the female form. I suspect he's already had his card marked after he left the Convent of the Five Foolish Virgins. Another black mark and he could find himself unfrocked."

"Sounds like he's no stranger to unfrocking when he puts his pecker on parade," Shirley said. "Well, I won't be saluting."

"Remember what's behind all this. In just four days from now Archie Flowerdew will hang, unless we can prevent it."

"Yeah, I know. That Tammy looked all in this morning when I saw her at Elsie's. I just don't understand how this can help."

"I think Dirty Dick Stubbs must have found some kind of link between Gideon Burke and the murder. It would explain why he had a copy of *The Art of Sussex Churches.*"

Shirley speared a broccoli floret with her fork. "You've got a theory, haven't you?"

"Try this. Stubbs knows like the rest of us that there is no love lost between Despart and Burke. Despart has already pilloried Burke in the postcard, but Burke has hit back in a way that only a sanctimonious humbug can. Despart wants more revenge. And, remember, he's an artist. Perhaps he discovered something about one of the paintings at St Rita's. Maybe one turns out to be a forgery. Or perhaps one was stolen. Despart is always short of money. So he puts the black on Burke. With a history already, Burke can't afford any more scandal, so he has to silence Despart."

"Got any evidence to support that?" Shirley asked.

"Only Stubbs's possession of the book – and his uncharacteristic interest in church art. He's more of a *Wild and Wobbly* man. That's why I need to take a good look around that church – preferably when no one's about. If you can distract Burke for half an hour, that should do it."

"So I go along and play the seductive strumpet while you rootle around in the church looking for clues?"

"You've got it. I've told Burke that you've always wanted me to make love to you pretending to be a vicar and wearing only a dog collar. He made out that was the greatest sin since Adam and Eve took a bite out of the Golden Delicious. But I could tell he was working out in his dirty little mind that he might be in with a chance by offering you the real McCoy."

Shirley scooped the last of her peas onto her fork. "If he tries anything, there'll be a couple of little offerings in the church's poor box."

I grinned. "You'll do it, then?"

"Only to help Tammy." Shirley parked her knife and fork on an empty plate. "So what's for dessert?" she asked.

"I think they've got spotted dick and custard on the menu," I said.

Shirley's eyes popped. "Don't get me started on dicks – even spotted ones."

I dropped Shirley off at the vicarage shortly after half past seven.

She had risen to the occasion. She'd dressed in a short denim skirt that only just covered the bare essentials and a tight-fitting T-shirt with the slogan 'Is That a Stick of Brighton Rock in Your Pocket – Or Are You Just Pleased to See Me?'

"I'll take just half an hour to look around the church," I said as Shirley climbed out of the MGB. "Then I'll come and rescue you from a fate worse than death."

Shirley grinned. "Let's hope the slimeball isn't down to his dog collar by then."

I watched as Shirley walked up the short path that led to the front door of the vicarage. Then I drove the car around the corner and parked behind the church.

Light still shone through the stained glass window depicting St Rita performing her impossible missions. But there were no parishioners about. I crunched up the gravel path that led to the door, turned a heavy ring handle and stepped inside.

A pungent musk hung in the air, as though incense had recently been burnt. The place had a silence that seemed heavier than just the absence of noise. As though the air itself refused to transmit sound waves. It had been cold in the street, but the church had an icier air. It felt like somewhere that never knew warmth. I shivered – and not just from the cold. The mewling of the wind through a loose window sounded like the ghostly cries of the long departed. Some of their tombs formed flagstones in the floor.

Over lunch, the idea of searching the church had seemed like a sound ploy. Now, I wondered exactly what I should do. The more I thought about it, the less likely it seemed that Burke would keep incriminating papers in the church. After all, it was a public place. There were sidesmen, choirboys, vergers, gravediggers, parochial church councillors and, for all I knew, the Ghost of Christmas Past, who could stumble upon a cache of secret evidence. Instead, the mystery seemed to focus on the painting of the *Avenging Angel*.

I threaded my way through the pews to the chapel and looked at the picture again. Did it really hold a secret that linked Burke, Kingswell and Le Grande? And, if so, what was the connection to Despart – and poor Archie Flowerdew? I stood staring up at the picture for two minutes while I vainly sought an answer to the questions.

"Have you seen enough of that picture? I'll be locking the church in five minutes."

I turned sharply. A woman holding a dustpan and broom was standing at the entrance to the chapel. She was little more than five-feet tall. She had a small face with large eyes and criss-crossed smile lines around the mouth. She was wearing a floral housecoat and a brown felt hat. I'd been so absorbed I'd not heard her approach. She stepped into the chapel.

"They all seem to get drawn to that picture," she said.

"All?" I asked.

"Visitors. Can't say I like it myself. *Avenging Angel* throwing those fireworks at people."

"They're thunderbolts."

"Don't care whether they're streaks of lightning. She shouldn't be doing it."

"You don't like the painting, then?"

"Not my cup of Typhoo. But what do I know? Avril, the cleaner, that's me. Not an art expert, like the others who come."

"Art experts come?" I asked. "Very often?"

"Sometimes. You can tell by the trousers they wear. Red velvet. I ask you! What kind of man wears red velvet trousers? I'll tell you. The kind that wouldn't dare show his face in the public bar of the Rat & Trumpet. Not while he was wearing them, at any rate."

"You don't happen to remember the name of the man with the red velvet trousers?" I asked.

"No. Something strange. Not English."

"French?" I suggested.

"Could be."

"Might it have been Le Grande?"

"It might. Anyway, he was definitely the one who did the cleaning."

Avril pulled out a duster that had been stuffed in the pocket of her housecoat and flicked it over the altar.

"He cleaned the church?"

Avril laughed. A high-pitched choking sound, like a corn crake.

"He weren't the type to sully his hands with hard work. No, he took her away to clean." She twitched her thumb towards the *Avenging Angel*.

My jaw dropped at that. "He took away the painting of the *Avenging Angel* to clean it?" I said.

"That's what I've just told you."

"When was this?"

"Months ago."

"Earlier this year?"

"It was a couple of weeks after Epiphany."

So that made it about the middle of January, I thought.

"And how long was the painting gone?" I asked.

"It didn't come back until after Easter," Avril said. "I remember there was a row about it in the Parochial Church Council. Edna Simpson – she's on the PCC – was quite angry about it. She said the painting should have been in the church for the Easter celebrations."

"But it came back, obviously."

"There were those on the PCC who said it should never have gone. Created a lot of bad feeling, it did."

"Why was that?"

"It was the vicar, Canon Burke, wanted the painting cleaned. Said it was a treasure of the church and it should be shown off at its finest. But the old dears on the PCC pointed out the weekly collections barely covered the cost of laundering the choir's vestments. So they voted down the plan. I remember the day after the vote the vicar was in a right grump about it."

"But the picture has been cleaned," I said.

"Yes. Well, the vicar wasn't going to have the PCC telling him what to do. So he went off and got a donor to pay for the cleaning. Even that caused a few raised eyebrows, because the bloke wasn't even a parishioner."

"No?"

"Apparently, he ran an art gallery. In Ditchling of all places."

"Did the donor ever visit the church to view the result of his generosity?" I asked.

Avril scratched her chin. "Don't know about that. He'd be disappointed if he did. I've been dusting that painting for years and it came back looking darker than when it went. Mind you, it still attracts the occasional visitor, like you."

"Anyone lately?" I asked.

"The regulars couldn't care less, but I saw another fellow here a few days ago taking a close look. Some people just don't know how to behave in church. I had to tell him sharply to take his hat off in the presence of God."

I didn't need to ask whether the hat was a trilby.

"Anyway, he asked a load of questions about the painting," Avril said. "I told him what I've told you about the row over the cleaning. He wrote some of it down in a notebook. I'd have kept me mouth shut if I'd have known he was a thief."

My eyes widened in surprise. "How did you know that?"

"I think he stole one of the books we keep on that shelf near the font before he left."

I didn't need to ask which book. So that was where Stubbs had acquired his copy of *The Art of Sussex Churches*.

I said: "I think the police may have that now. I'll let them know you want it back."

"How do you know that?"

"Your book thief is dead."

Avril looked up at the *Avenging Angel*. There was a sense of awe in her eyes.

"So she's felled another one," she said.

I had been longer than the half-hour I'd promised Shirley when I finally rang the doorbell at the vicarage.

But at least there was no sound of her yelling 'rape' from inside.

Burke answered the door after the second ring. He was panting slightly and his face glistened with sweat. Behind him, I could see Shirley smoothing down her skirt and straitening her mussed hair. She pushed past Burke on her way out.

He raised a hand in the sign of the cross. "Remember, my dear, the path to righteousness is strewn with many hard stones. Step carefully along it and you will find true happiness."

We hustled back to the car. "Jeez, that Burke is about as graceful as a dingo's dingle-dangle," Shirley said as she climbed into the MGB. "If you bottled Burke's body odour as a weapon you could conquer the world."

"So not God's gift to women, after all."

"The man's got a mind like the Sydney sewers – dirty and devious. At one point he said I looked flushed and suggested I take something off to cool down. Look at me. The girls at the Windmill theatre wear more than this."

"At least your virtue is intact," I said.

"Yeah – at the price of giving a horrible holy man a cheap thrill. I hope it was worth it."

I nodded. "It was. I think we need to get back to Elsie's house and tell Tammy what I've discovered."

I put the car into gear and pulled out into the traffic.

"The poor girl is turning into a shadow," Elsie said.

She'd greeted Shirley and me at the front door with a worried frown. We stepped inside and huddled together in the hall.

"She's in the sitting room now, poor love, just staring into the fire," Elsie whispered. "She won't eat anything and I don't think she sleeps. I hear her pacing around her room at night."

I said: "It's hardly surprising the strain is telling. But Shirley and I have uncovered another lead. I think it may help us."

We shuffled into the sitting room. Tammy was sitting in the chair by the fire. She looked up as we came in and nodded at us.

"I feel useless," she said. She turned back towards the fire.

"I know it's hard," I said. "But we've discovered new information. I need your help to understand what it means."

Shirley crossed the room and perched on the edge of Tammy's chair. She put her arm around Tammy's shoulders. "Don't give up yet, kiddo," she said. "Archie is relying on you."

Tammy looked up at Shirley. "It's so hard," she said simply.

For a moment, there was silence in the room. I think we were all feeling Tammy's pain.

Then Elsie said: "I'll make us all a nice of cup of tea. That should help." She bustled off to the kitchen.

Shirley and I sat down.

I leaned towards Tammy. "Did Archie ever mention a painting called the *Avenging Angel* to you?" I asked.

Tammy shook her head. "Uncle Archie was never much interested in religious art."

"Dick Stubbs, the man who was writing the book about the court case, has shown an unusual interest in it," I said. "I've just been round to the church where it's on display to take a closer look."

"And if you're wondering why I'm rigged out like a fairground floozy, I've been distracting the dirty old vicar while

Colin did it," Shirley said.

Elsie came in with a tray of tea. We passed the cups round while I told them what I'd learnt in the church.

"But how does that all help Uncle Archie?" Tammy asked.

"I think if we can prove who murdered Stubbs, it will raise enough doubts about who killed Despart to get Archie's case reviewed. It would certainly delay any action until the Home Secretary has taken a closer look at the evidence. No Home Secretary wants an innocent man's blood on his hands."

"The more time we can buy, the more we stand a chance of proving Archie is innocent," Shirley said.

"It seems hopeless," Tammy said.

"There are several links in the chain," I said. "The first is that Stubbs was researching the background to Despart's murder for his book. We know that he knew about the humiliating postcards of Kingswell, Le Grande and Burke, because he had copies of them in his room. The postcards provided a link between all three. And I suspect as a former tabloid newshound Stubbs would have tried to find if those links went any deeper.

"Avril, the church's cleaner, is a charming old gossip. Just the kind we journalists love. Stubbs discovered from her that the *Avenging Angel* painting had been cleaned by Le Grande, financed by Kingswell."

"But where does that get us?" Tammy asked.

"I hate to admit it, but Stubbs and I both think the same way. It's what we've been trained to do as reporters. When we see something that doesn't make sense, we look for an explanation. It seemed too much of a coincidence that the three men who were humiliated by Despart should have joined together to get a painting cleaned."

"So what were they up to?" Shirley asked.

"I think the plan wasn't to clean the painting," I said. "That was just a story to keep the parochial church council quiet. The real plan was to copy it. Then they'd display the copy and sell the original. Avril told me the regular churchgoers didn't take much notice of the painting. Why should they? It'd been there for years. Besides, the three had the perfect conspiracy – Burke was the current custodian of the painting, Le Grande was a painter with the skill to copy it and Kingswell was the art dealer with contacts to sell it; no doubt on the under-the-counter market."

"But the old thing was by some unknown artist. It wouldn't be worth much," Shirley said.

"It was by a pupil of Raphael," I said. "Years ago, it's true that paintings by a pupil of a great master wouldn't have been worth the canvas they were painted on. But times have changed in the art world. More people are shelling out big money for works by the top painters. If you can't pay top dollar, you can't get into that game. So you start collecting lesser works in the hope they might make more money in the future. And that's just what's been happening with works by pupils of some of the better-known painters."

"I still don't see the link between this and Uncle Archie," Tammy said.

I was pleased to see she'd shaken off her torpor. Her eyes were alive and her mind was working again.

"I think Stubbs found out about the scheme and tried to blackmail Kingswell."

"Why not the other two?" Shirley asked.

"Because he's the only one who seems to have any money."

"Can you prove it?"

"The evidence is circumstantial," I said. "But it's stronger than that which convicted Archie. When I visited Kingswell's gallery, I saw Stubbs in the village high street. At the time, I didn't know who he was, but I never forget a hat. Then, when I went into the gallery, I found an envelope addressed to Kingswell, which had just been pushed through the letterbox. It was one of those blue Basildon Bond jobs you see everywhere. I reckon Stubbs had pushed it through the door and then scarpered minutes earlier. I handed the envelope to Camilla Fogg, Kingswell's assistant. Then, when I found Stubbs's body in his lodgings, I noticed a new packet of Basildon Bond envelopes. Only one had been used."

"So you think the envelope contained the blackmail threat?" Shirley said.

"I'm certain of it," I said. "A couple of days after delivering his blackmail threat, Stubbs was dead."

"But how does all this help Uncle Archie?" Tammy asked.

"Because I believe something similar may have happened earlier this year, when Burke and his cronies cooked up this plot. Avril told me the painting went for cleaning two weeks before Despart was killed. There would have been no secret about the fact the painting wasn't in the church. Any parishioner would have noticed. And, perhaps, some started to talk about it. I think Despart heard the news. He'd already crossed swords with Burke. He'd be expected to take an interest. And, I imagine, when he discovered that Le Grande and Kingswell were also involved, he suspected more. If he tried to blackmail Kingswell, then he probably received the same treatment as Stubbs."

"But there's no proof," said Tammy.

"No, there isn't," I said. "Only suspicion. But I think we can panic the three into providing us with the proof we need."

"Which is to produce the original painting," Shirley said. "By a pupil of Raphael."

"Rather than a forger of a pupil," I added. "It looks as though tomorrow could be the make-or-break day."

And it looked as though the following day would also be important for Shirley.

When we arrived back at her flat, she found an envelope had been pushed through the door.

She ripped it open and said: "It's from the modelling agency with the details of the Christmas fairy photo shoot. Oh, it's tomorrow. Short notice."

"Photo shoots often are," I said. "Where is it?"

"Seems to be a studio in Carden Avenue. Gives the address."

I peered over her shoulder at the letter. "That's a new one on me."

"I've heard that fairies come out at night, but tonight this one is going to have a good kip," Shirley said.

She put her arms around my neck and kissed me. We held each other for a few moments and then broke apart.

Shirley gave me one of her penetrating stares. "Can we save Archie?" she asked.

"I don't know," I said. "By the end of tomorrow we'll have a better idea."

Chapter 16

"If this plan doesn't work, you'll be lucky to get a job carrying the bucket and shovel on *Horse & Hound*," Frank Figgis said.

"If this plan doesn't work, we'll need a bucket and shovel on the *Chronicle* – to clear up the carnage Tomkins and his plods leave after they've raided us," I said.

We were in the newsroom. It was just after nine o'clock the following morning. The fag fug under the fluorescent lights was thicker than I'd ever seen it. The fairy lights on the Christmas tree in the far corner blinked through the haze like demented fireflies. The tension in the room was palpable.

"I've thought this plan through in every detail," I said. "Nothing can go wrong."

"Every time anyone says that I find I need another fag," Figgis said. "Just run me through it again."

I gave the concise version of the thinking I'd described to Shirley and Tammy at Elsie's house the night before.

"The plan is to panic Kingswell, Le Grande and Burke. I'm going to do that by letting them know I've got suspicions about their painting scam. I think that will worry them enough to call a council of war to decide on their next move. Most important, I think that whoever has the real painting of the *Avenging Angel* will bring it to the meeting. They'll worry that their hiding place has been rumbled and want to move it elsewhere.

"If we catch them with the painting, I think we can use that to squeeze the true story out of them. Burke or Le Grande should crack under pressure. I'm less confident about breaking Kingswell. After all, if my theory is correct, he killed Stubbs. But once Le Grande or Burke has coughed, it's game over."

"Only if you catch them with the painting," Figgis said.

"Even without the real painting, I can challenge them to have the painting currently hung in the church authenticated by an independent expert. Le Grande will have done his best to make the forgery look like the original, but he'd never have thought it would be tested by an expert. Why should he? The only person who ever took any interest in it before was the bloke who wrote that obscure book on Sussex church paintings."

"So you make your calls – and that gets the three on the move?" Figgis said.

"Yes. And I've briefed three reliable colleagues to watch and follow."

I'd called round the newsroom to find volunteers for the job. Now, Susan Wheatcroft was parked in her Hillman Imp a few yards down the street from Le Grande's studio. Sally Martin had her Lambretta round the corner from St Rita's vicarage. And Phil Bailey was sitting in his Triumph Spitfire on the opposite side of Sussex Square to Kingswell's flat.

I said: "When any of the three move, our watcher will follow. We only need to hit lucky with one of them to discover the location of their council of war."

Figgis took a drag on his fag. He blew a contemplative smoke ring. It drifted up to the ceiling and merged into the fug.

"Better make the calls," he said. He turned and pranced back to his office.

I sat down at my desk and pulled the telephone towards me. Dialled a number in Sussex Square.

"Kingswell."

"Colin Crampton. I'm the journalist who interviewed you the other day."

"Yes. What do you want now?"

"Do you know another journalist called Richard Stubbs?"

"Journalist fellow? Never heard of him." A round denial. But Kingswell had missed a beat before he answered.

"You've never had a letter from him?"

"Why should I?"

"Perhaps Mr Stubbs had a business proposition to put to you."

"Just told you, I don't know the man."

"Did you know that he was murdered?"

"This is intolerable. I've had enough." The line went dead.

I grinned.

Score one to Crampton.

I dialled the number of St Rita's vicarage.

A young woman's voice answered the telephone.

"Could I speak to Canon Burke, please?"

"Who shall I say?"

"A friend of Shirley Goldsmith."

A minute's silence and then: "Gideon Burke here. Is that Shirley's friend?"

"Yes, Canon Burke. My name's Colin Crampton. We spoke in church and I brought Shirley to see you yesterday evening."

"I remember. A charming girl, with an interest in … Perhaps I should refrain from mentioning details."

"Very wise. What I failed to mention is that I'm a reporter with the *Evening Chronicle*. I've heard that the painting of the *Avenging Angel* hanging in St Rita's is not the original. Is there any truth in that?"

A sharp intake of breath. Words muttered in a whisper. Perhaps a prayer.

Then: "I don't know what you're implying, Mr Crampton. But I take accusations of this kind very seriously. Very seriously, indeed."

The line went dead.

Score two to Crampton.

I dialled the third number.

"Professor Florian Le Grande at your service."

"I'm delighted to hear it, Professor Le Grande. Colin Crampton following up on our interview at your studio the other day."

"I thought we'd said all we had to say to each other. At least, I hoped so."

"It's about your work. I wanted to ask you a further question."

"If you must."

"Did you paint the copy of the *Avenging Angel* by a pupil of Raphael that hangs in St Rita's church, Brighton?"

"I ... I ... I don't know what you mean."

The line went dead.

Score three to Crampton.

I leant back in my old captain's chair feeling a bit like the old *Avenging Angel* myself. I'd slung down three thunderbolts. Now I had to wait to find out whether they'd hit their marks.

"It's been nearly two hours," said Figgis.

"That's good news," I said. "I think."

"Why do you think?"

"Because it gives my brain something to do."

"I meant why is it good news?"

"Because if none of the three had moved, Susan, Sally or Phil would have checked in from a nearby phone box by now to let us know they were staying put. Silence means that our team are on the move – in hot pursuit."

Figgis had been prowling round the newsroom most of the morning. From the number of fags he'd smoked I reckoned his bloodstream must be fifty per cent nicotine.

"I hope you're right." Figgis lit a new Woodbine from the stub of another.

"After my calls, Kingswell and the others would've thought about it for a moment and then started to phone one another. When they compared notes, they'd come to the conclusion that we're on to them. They'd have to meet to decide what to do next. It's exactly what we'd do if we were pulling a scam like that and got rumbled."

"If we were pulling that scam we'd get away with it," Figgis said.

"Let's get away with this one first," I said.

Phones were ringing all around the newsroom. A typical morning. There'd be sad cases with real human dramas to tell. There'd be con artists with phoney tales hoping to spring some tip-off money. There'd be time-wasters with hobby horses to ride. There'd be public relations hustlers with promises of the story of the year.

But my phone was silent. Mute of malice. And it was the one phone I wanted to ring.

"If we don't hear anything by one o'clock, I'm going to call this off," Figgis said. "We'll move into a damage-limitation exercise."

"Meaning?" I asked.

"Meaning I'll have to disown what you've been doing and call Kingswell, Le Grande and Burke to apologise. I'll eat a triple helping of humble pie. No doubt I'll have to promise a reporter will write puff pieces about them."

"I pity the poor sap who'll have to do that," I said.

"That will be self-pity, no doubt."

I was about to reply when my telephone rang. For a second or two, I sat staring at the damned thing. I was transfixed by its insistent shrill. Then I seized the receiver.

Susan Wheatcroft sounded excited. "The seagull has landed," she said.

"What are you talking about?"

Susan chuckled. "I just followed Florian Le Grande to a pub called The Highwayman in Plumpton, not far from Lewes. He's sitting in the private bar waiting for the others. I decided to give him a code name."

"Why the seagull?"

"Because he's all show on the outside but full of shit on the inside."

I laughed.

"I'm in the phone box a hundred yards down the street from the pub," Susan said. "I haven't got a code name for it."

"We don't need code names, Susan. But well done. We now

know where they're meeting. The other two will be on their way. Try to keep out of sight until I arrive. I should be about twenty minutes."

I stood up and grabbed my notebook. I turned to Figgis. He was twitching from foot to foot.

"They're meeting at The Highwayman in Plumpton. Could you cover the calls from Phil and Sally when they come in? When I reach the village, I'll ring from the phone box with an update."

I hurried across the newsroom to a chorus of "good lucks". Now the plan was under way, I had a nagging suspicion I was going to need it.

Lots of it.

There's never any need to ask reporters where they'll be if you have to find them on a story. If they're not at the scene of the crime, they'll be huddled around the nearest telephone box.

So as I sped into Plumpton, I kept my eyes skinned for the familiar red. The phone box was just across the street from the village stores.

I left some rubber on the road as I brought the MGB to a halt and jumped out. Phil Bailey and Sally Martin had arrived. Which meant that Kingswell and Burke must have joined Le Grande in The Highwayman.

Phil and Susan were stamping their feet outside the box trying to keep warm. Sally was inside on the phone. She'd be speaking to the newsroom, probably Figgis. She'd stay in the box and keep the line free while the rest of us went to the pub. When the action started, we'd need an open line to phone through copy. There'd be a phone at the pub, but there was no guarantee the landlord would let us use it after what was going to happen.

Phil raised a gloved hand in greeting as I approached. "They're all in the pub's private bar," he said.

"And Kingswell was the last to arrive," said Susan. She was snuggled in an outsized duffel coat with the hood up.

"Burke and Le Grande had the worried looks of men on the run from the law," Phil said.

"They soon could be," I said. "Were any of them carrying packages?"

"Not that I saw," said Susan. "And I was first here."

That was disturbing news. I'd hoped to panic them into bringing the stolen painting to the meeting. But perhaps whoever was keeping the *Avenging Angel* had left it in his car.

I heaved open the phone-box door and we all huddled round to discuss our next move.

Sally stopped speaking on the phone. She turned to me and said: "I've got Mr Figgis on the line."

I said: "Tell him we're about to put the plan into operation. We should have some copy to dictate over for the next edition in about half an hour."

Sally nodded. I closed the phone-box door, looked at Phil and Susan, and said: "Let's go."

As we walked up the street to the pub, I said: "Susan, I want you to come in with me and wait just outside the door to the private bar. Keep out of sight, but see if you can hear what's being said and get every golden word down in shorthand."

"Sure thing, honeybunch."

"Phil, I'd like you to wait outside the pub in case anyone tries to leave. We can't stop them, but get the usual quote about what they've got to say. If they're running, they won't want to talk, but 'no comment' is always damning."

As we reached the pub, a motorcycle roared up and skidded to a halt. A small gnome-like man swung his leg over and jumped onto the road. He was wearing motorcycle leathers and a deerstalker hat. He retrieved a fancy-looking camera from a pannier on the side of the bike and ambled over to us. Freddie Barkworth, the *Chronicle*'s chief photographer, had arrived.

He treated us to his lopsided grin and said: "Frank Figgis decided he wanted some pictures of the showdown. I'm not sure whether he wants to print them in the paper or use them in evidence against you if this party goes belly-up."

I said: "Let's get the party under way and then we'll know. But, Freddie, I think you should keep your camera out of sight until the action hots up."

I opened the door to the pub and Susan and I stepped inside.

We were in the public bar, a long room with a large brick fireplace at one end. Logs were crackling merrily in the grate. A couple of agricultural types wearing thick guernseys and trousers stained with farmyard gunk were supping ale at the bar. The landlord looked up from a copy of the *Daily Sketch* as we came in. He eyed us suspiciously, then realised we could be paying customers and put on a fake smile.

I said: "Where's your private bar?"

He pointed left and said: "Through there, but it's taken."

I flashed my genuine fake smile and said: "We're expected."

"They didn't mention as they were ..."

But his words trailed off as Susan and I bustled through the door.

We were in a corridor leading to the back of the pub. A couple of doors on the left led to lavatories. There was only one door on the right. The words 'Private Bar' had been neatly lettered on the door's woodwork.

I nodded to Susan, opened the door and stepped inside. I left the door swinging on its hinges behind me – cover for Susan as she earwigged the events I hoped were about to unfold.

Kingswell, Le Grande and Burke were clustered round a table in the corner of the room, warming themselves on both bars of an electric fire.

There was a bottle of whisky on the table. If it had been unopened when they arrived, it had already taken a hammering. Le Grande had a glass to his lips as I stepped across the room. Burke was pouring another measure for Kingswell.

Their heads swivelled in my direction.

Kingswell started to say: "I said no interruptions …" But stopped himself when he realised who I was.

I halted a couple of feet from their table. As one, their mouths dropped open and their eyes goggled. If Freddie had been in the room he could have taken a snap and entitled it: Three Stupefied Drunks Await Their Comeuppance. Then Le Grande and Kingswell exchanged baffled looks. Burke's eyes looked upwards, but he wasn't going to find any help coming from that direction today.

I said: "I'm glad I've caught you all together. It'll save more irritating phone calls. I just hate it when people hang up on me as I'm about to ask awkward questions."

Kingswell gave me a nuclear-powered hate glare and said: "Journalist Johnny, nothing to say. Police, we'll complain to them about harassment."

"I thought the whole point of this meeting was to find a way to keep the Old Bill out of your affairs," I said.

Le Grande said: "What's going on here, Toby?" For an emeritus professor, he was remarkably slow on the uptake.

"Set-up, we're on the receiving end, Prof."

Burke swallowed a large gulp of his whisky and said: "Surely, at a time like this, we should all remember the words of Saint Paul to the Ephesians … Or was it the Romans …? No, I think it was the Corinthians …"

"Sanctimonious old windbag, shut up," Kingswell said.

I said: "I think we should bear in mind Saint Crampton's words to the Unholy Trinity."

"Unholy Trinity?" Burke seemed more baffled than ever. Or, perhaps, he was more drunk.

"You three."

"Which words?" Le Grande asked tartly.

"You're rumbled," I said. "I know all about your painting scam – and I know how you silenced Dirty Dick Stubbs."

"Silenced, what do you mean?" wailed Burke.

"I mean murdered, by one of you."

Le Grande stiffened. "I would never take a human life …"

Burke's hands came together in prayer. "My vocation holds the sanctity of life holy …"

But they were both cut off by Kingswell. "Wittering, stop it, both of you. Couple of old washerwomen, you sound like them. Can't you see he's trying to provoke us? Proof, he has nothing. Mouths shut, problem will go away."

"You wish," I said. "I'll be writing a story for this afternoon's *Chronicle* about your painting scam – no doubt the Old Bill will get round to reading the paper. After they've used it to wrap their chips. They might even get round to interviewing you. If you're still in the country by then."

"You'd give us time to get away?" Le Grande asked. He was obviously the first to conclude nothing about this was going to end well.

"Depends on whether you can tell me what I want to know," I said.

Kingswell slammed his fist on the table. "Nothing! We tell him nothing," he yelled. He pointed a threatening finger at Le Grande. "Same fate as Stubbs – you speak one word out of turn and you'll suffer it."

Le Grande's face turned as white as the chalk on Beachy Head. "So it was you," he said. He slumped back on his seat. He was trembling with fear.

Kingswell leapt up so fast, he upset his chair. It clattered to the floor. Burke let out a frightened squeak. Closed his eyes and started to pray.

Kingswell grabbed the whisky bottle and hurled it at me. I ducked. The bottle sailed over my head and crashed into a mirror hanging on the wall. The sound of splintering glass filled the air.

Kingswell charged towards me. He had a scowl on his face that would have got him a lead role in a Hammer horror movie.

I turned sideways to take the force of his charge on my shoulder. When it came it sent me spinning across the room. I regained my footing. Turned to face Kingswell's attack. But he was already racing for the door.

Susan's ample figure stepped into the door frame. But Kingswell had already built up speed. He cannoned into her and she crashed onto her back. He vaulted over her and raced down the corridor towards the bar.

"Hey, honeybunch," she called after him. "You're the first man to have me on my back for over a week. Must you leave so soon?"

I pointed at Burke and Le Grande, and yelled at Susan as I raced after Kingswell: "Keep those two jokers here until I get back."

I thundered down the corridor. Charged through the bar and out into the street. Kingswell had taken Phil and Freddie by surprise.

I shouted at Phil: "Join Susan in the private bar."

He took off.

Freddie pointed at Kingswell: "He's making for that car."

A sleek red Jaguar sat in pole position in the pub car park. As we watched, Kingswell hauled open the door and threw himself into the driver's seat. Within seconds, the engine roared and the car shot into the road.

"Your motorcycle," I shouted at Freddie. "We'll follow on that."

We ran across the pub forecourt and jumped on the bike. Freddie kicked the engine into life and we roared down the road.

I peered around Freddie's shoulder and shouted: "What's your top speed?"

"More than his," Freddie yelled back. "I can see him about a quarter of a mile ahead."

Freddie turned the accelerator and the speedo climbed past seventy.

"We're closing the distance," he shouted.

"But how can we stop him?"

"We'll need a stretch of straight road. Then, perhaps, I can force him to pull over."

But the road from Plumpton to Ditchling wound through narrow lanes with high hedges on each side.

"How long do you think he can keep this up?" I shouted.

"Not long, I hope," Freddie said. "I've just realised I'm nearly out of fuel."

As if to taunt us, Kingswell accelerated and opened up the gap.

"He's heading for his gallery," Freddie yelled over his shoulder.

"I don't think so. Not while we're on his tail. He can't let us catch him."

But two minutes later, the Jag passed the first houses on the outskirts of Ditchling. We raced in a hundred yards behind.

Kingswell approached the crossroads at the centre of the village without slowing. He swung a left so fast, the Jag fishtailed wildly. Over Freddie's shoulder I could see Kingswell fighting to control the steering. The bike tilted at a forty-five degree angle as we swerved after the Jag. It was just yards ahead.

"Overtake and cut him off," I shouted.

But as I said it, Kingswell accelerated and the Jag hurtled out of the village.

"He's making for Ditchling Beacon," I yelled. "It's the highest point in Sussex – and one of the steepest roads. He reckons he'll throw us off his tail."

"Then he's wrong," Freddie screamed.

But then the motorcycle's engine sputtered. It was soaking up the last drops of the fuel.

"Better slow down and conserve the juice," I said.

"Never," shouted Freddie.

As the Jag moved into the climb towards the top of the Beacon, Freddie stepped up the speed and closed the distance.

We swept around curve after curve as we ascended. But the Jag stayed resolutely ahead.

"There's a very sharp turn near the summit," I yelled. "He'll have to slow. We'll cut him off there."

But as the Jag approached the bend, Kingswell didn't slow. Instead, he floored the accelerator.

"He's taking that bend way too fast," screamed Freddie. "He'll not make it."

I watched over Freddie's shoulder. The Jag sped into the bend. It was as though Kingswell knew he couldn't make it – or didn't want to.

The Jag powered off the road towards the Beacon's steepest escarpment. Kingswell maintained his speed. He raced the car over the edge. Like a wingless plane, its speed propelled it into the air.

And then it lost its momentum, tilted forward and fell.

I could see Kingswell in the driver's seat. He turned his head towards me. His arm snapped up in a smart salute. And then he was gone.

Freddie brought the bike to a halt on the edge of escarpment. We scrambled off and looked down in horror.

The Jag smashed into the ground six hundred feet below. A sickening crunch and a piercing shriek of tearing metal shattered the silence. The car's doors flew off and the roof caved in. The bonnet burst open and a wheel bounced off. The windows shattered and a fountain of shimmering glass crystals sprayed into the air.

And then the car exploded into flames. High above, we felt the rush of heat race past us like a desert wind.

I watched the car burn for five minutes as Freddie scrambled to take pictures from every angle. Then we remounted the motorcycle and drove away.

I had copy to file.

Chapter 17

I dictated my story about Kingswell's death from a telephone box in Ditchling. After I'd finished with the copytaker, Figgis came on the line.

"This is great stuff," he said. "What about the other two?"

"If you mean Le Grande and Burke, they're still at The Highwayman with Susan and Phil. If Sally is still holding the line in the Plumpton call box, you can tell her to join them. Freddie is giving me a lift back there after he's filled up with fuel. Perhaps you can call in the crash details to the cops. Best if I don't speak to them until I've had time to interrogate the terrible two."

"I agree," Figgis said. "And after Freddie's returned you to The Highwayman, tell him to get himself back here pronto. I want pictures for the final edition."

The line went dead.

When I walked into the bar at The Highwayman, the landlord pointed at me angrily.

"I don't want no more trouble in here," he said. "You're barred."

I looked around the place. The agricultural types had gone.

"Don't be ridiculous," I said. "You're going to be the most famous pub in Britain. People will be flocking from miles around."

The bloke looked at his cash register. Decided it could do with more action. "You reckon?" he said.

"I reckon," I said.

I headed through to the private bar.

Le Grande and Burke hadn't moved since I'd left them.

Susan, Sally and Phil were sitting opposite them. Susan was eating a pork pie. She looked up when I walked in.

"You should get the old misery of a barman to give you one of these, honeybunch," she said.

"Later, perhaps."

Phil shifted round to make room as I pulled up a chair.

I looked at Le Grande and Burke. "Kingswell is dead," I said. "He drove his car off Ditchling Beacon. He saluted on the way down, but that won't get a mention in my dispatches."

"But he had the ..." Burke began.

But Le Grande put a restraining hand on his arm.

"You were going to say that Kingswell had the real painting," I said.

Burke shrugged. He looked like a man who expected a difficult time when he finally reached the Pearly Gates. "There's no point not telling the truth now," he said.

"Perhaps not for you," Le Grande spat. "I'm still a respected academic and artist. You'd already lost your reputation at that convent."

"I never trusted you," Burke said. "I hope you rot in hell."

"Whatever happened to love thy neighbour?" I said. "Now, I want some answers. If I like what I hear, I may write a story that suggests Kingswell was the prime mover in this conspiracy. You'll still face trouble with the law, but it may be easier. If you stonewall me, you can be sure my copy won't be helpful."

Le Grande and Burke swapped worried glances. They weren't sure whether I'd just looped a lifeline around their waist or a noose around their necks.

"Whose idea was it to copy the painting?" I asked.

Le Grande shot Burke a malevolent look and said: "I guess it was mine. I'd lived in Brighton years ago when my mother attended the church. I'd taken an interest in all the paintings in the chapel – the *Avenging Angel* was particularly fine. After we'd all been pilloried in Despart's foul postcards, I'd got to know Gideon and Toby – that is, Kingswell. Originally, we'd considered banding together to sue Despart. But a lawyer advised us that a legal action would be unlikely to succeed."

"Something to do with a joke not being libellous," Burke said.

"Anyway, my share of the lawyer's fees for that advice had left me rather more strapped than usual. I discovered that Gideon was also short of money. And although Kingswell seemed to be comfortably off, he was one of those men who can never have enough cash – and is not too fussy about how he makes it."

"That seems to apply to all of you," I said.

"Anyway, I suggested that a painting by a pupil of Raphael may well fetch several thousands in the right quarters such as New York. If I copied it, the original could be sold quietly abroad to a private collector who would obviously say nothing. Kingswell leapt at the idea. He said he knew several collectors in America who would be interested."

"But before we could sell the picture, Despart was murdered in his studio," Burke said. "Because we'd all been his victims, we knew we'd be suspects, so we agreed we'd lie low and not to sell the real *Avenging Angel* until the investigation, trial and its aftermath were over."

"So you'd planned to sell the painting after Archie had been hanged?" I asked.

"Yes," Burke said. "Kingswell intended to fly to America in the new year."

"But that plan was upset when Stubbs appeared on the scene researching his book," I said. "Stubbs stumbled on the truth about the painting."

"We were all worried at first. But Toby said he would be able to handle the matter," Le Grande said.

"By killing him," I said.

"I never condoned that," Le Grande said. "As an artist I revere the human form."

"And I am a man of God," Burke chipped in.

"Who also has more than a passing interest in Mammon," I said. "Had Despart also found out about your painting scam? Is that why one of you killed him?"

"No, that's not true," Le Grande said. He was agitated now and some of the colour had returned to his face. "How could he have known? I was briefly questioned by the police – routine, they said – and I satisfied them that I was in London the night Despart died. I attended a reception at the Royal Academy and stayed with … with a friend."

"And I was at an ecumenical conference at Chichester Cathedral," Burke said. "I spent the night at the Crown & Anchor. Without a friend."

"Do you know whether the police questioned Kingswell about Despart's murder?" I asked.

"He never mentioned it to me," Le Grande said. "But I suppose they must have done. And I suppose they were satisfied with whatever alibi he provided."

"Brighton police are too easily satisfied," I said. "Especially Tomkins."

Besides, there was no chance of getting the truth from Kingswell now.

I stood up.

"Is that it?" Burke said.

"For now," I said.

"What are you going to do?"

"I'm going to charm the landlord into letting me use his phone so I can call in my copy. Then I'm going to drive back to Brighton."

"What should we do?" Le Grande asked.

I looked at the pair. Their heads drooped forward and their shoulders slumped. Their worlds had collapsed. They looked like a couple of lost children.

I said: "You should hand yourselves in to the police. It will win you brownie points when your cases come to court. You can call the nearest cop shop from the telephone box opposite the village stores."

I rummaged in my trouser pocket. Found some coppers.

"Here's four pence," I said. "Have this call on me."

I suppose I should have been elated as I drove the MGB back to Brighton. I'd just exposed a forged painting racket involving an art gallery owner, a member of the Royal Academy and a randy old vicar. The story would certainly hit the nationals. But I'd landed the scoop. That would keep Figgis happy – and it might even earn a favourable nod from His Holiness next time I passed him on the stairs.

But I felt as deflated as the Christmas balloons that hung in the corner of the *Chronicle*'s newsroom.

And confused.

I'd been certain that one of the Unholy Trio had killed Despart. I still thought that was possible. My money would have been on Kingswell – trained to kill at Her Majesty's expense. But now he was dead – and I could think of no way of proving it. From the way Burke and Le Grande reacted I was convinced they'd had nothing to do with it. Burke was too sanctimonious and Le Grande too effete to get mixed up with any serious violence.

Which left the finger of guilt still pointing at Archie Flowerdew.

Worse, I would have to write the story as I saw it. And that would send Tammy into an even deeper depression.

The one small consolation was that, after a scoop this size, I'd be making a triumphal entry when I arrived back at the paper.

But even that was denied me when I walked into the newsroom.

Instead of Figgis's face cracked into a smile behind a haze of cigarette smoke, he stomped across the newsroom looking like the *Avenging Angel*'s grumpy uncle.

"Trouble must be your middle name," he said as he arrived at the side of my desk.

"Actually, it's Tottington," I said.

Figgis's eyebrows headed north. "That is trouble."

"Which is why I normally keep quiet about it."

"Very wise."

"And don't bother to thank me for the biggest scoop the paper has had for months. All part of the service."

The corners of Figgis's mouth turned down – the closest he ever came to looking embarrassed.

"Yes, well, I'll grant you that. Trouble is, it's not what His Holiness is worrying about right now. He's just received the summons for contempt of court from Abercrombie over the cushion story."

"It was a caution story when it left my typewriter," I said.

"So you claim, but if you want to keep out of trouble, you'd better lose no more time in proving it."

"How can I? The evidence has been destroyed."

"Then it looks as though you're deep in it."

"In what?"

"That stuff which is a four-letter word beginning with S. And I don't mean snow," Figgis added over his shoulder as he turned back to his office.

And that wasn't the only trouble.

After I'd filed my copy about Burke and Le Grande, I left the office and drove to Shirley's flat. I knew something was wrong as soon as she answered the door. She had a glum face with tear-streaked mascara.

I hurried inside and took her in my arms. "What's wrong?"

She clung to me. "It's the modelling. It all went wrong," she sobbed.

I guided her to a chair, sat her down and knelt by her side.

She sniffled, produced a handkerchief and blew her nose.

"I'm acting like a simpering sheila," she said. "Really, I'm angry. I just want to punch somebody."

"Tell me what happened and then we'll line up some candidates for the punchball."

Shirley managed a tiny smile. "Well, you know I was going to be photographed as the Christmas fairy for a magazine. It turned out to be a smutty little porn sheet called *Wild and Wobbly*. The greaseball of a photographer only expected me to pose in the nude."

My eyes widened. "With nothing on at all?"

"He wanted me to wear some tinsel threaded through my hair. 'To give a seasonal touch,' he said. I felt like giving him a seasonal touch – and it wouldn't have been in his hair."

"Who was this bloke?"

"Called himself Kristopher Pickles. A nasty little predator who preys on girls wanting an honest modelling career. I had a quick rootle in his reception area while I was waiting. Picked up this leaflet." Shirley rummaged in the pocket of her jeans and pulled out the crumpled item.

She handed it to me. It was headed: 'Girls: Earn ££££s as a Photographer's Model'. It went on to promise riches for 'young women with outgoing personalities'.

Shirley said: "When he told me what he wanted, I told him where he could stick his telephoto lens and then I went round to the modelling agency to complain. They didn't know about him. He'd never used the agency before. They said they were sorry for sending me there. They won't be sending any more girls. So I've got a bit of my own back. But it's not enough."

"What do you want?"

"I'd like to see him humiliated – like he does to the girls."

I thought about that for a moment. "Maybe we'll find a way," I said.

Shirley shrugged. "Maybe," she said. "But, hey, enough of my troubles. Hadn't we better check up on Tammy?"

It was gone seven by the time we reached Elsie's house, where there was even more bad news. Tammy and Elsie were sitting in the living room with faces like a wet weekend in Worthing.

"Tammy has been seen by a neighbour," Elsie said.

"It wasn't my fault," Tammy said. "The doorbell went and as Elsie was in the back scullery I just answered it without thinking. It turned out to be the woman from two doors down."

"Mrs Hampton," Elsie explained. "Hairnet Hampton we call her on account of she's always wearing one. She's a vicious old gossip, always poking her nose in."

"Do you think she recognised Tammy from the newspaper pictures?" I asked.

"I really couldn't say," Elsie said. "When I heard voices, I hurried to the front door. Hairnet was eyeing Tammy up and down like she was a pound of prime steak on a butcher's slab. I told the old bag Tammy was my cousin's niece from up Wivelsfield way. I don't know whether she believed me, but nothing's happened since then."

"No cops unexpectedly patrolling the street?" I asked.

"None when I went out earlier," Elsie said.

"No cars suspiciously parked?"

"A few, but none suspicious."

I ran my hands through my hair in frustration. This was the last thing we needed. I couldn't risk the nosy neighbour passing word to the Old Bill.

I said: "I think we'd better decamp to Freda's house. I'll call her now and make the arrangements."

But even that didn't work out as I wanted.

We boxed our brains trying to think of a way to smuggle Tammy out of the house unobserved.

"Disguise her as a clown on her way to a kiddie's party," Shirley said.

"Wrap her up in the middle of that old roll of linoleum we've stuffed in the loft," Elsie said.

"Don't mind me," Tammy said. "Cut me into pieces and feed me to the pigeons if you can't think of anything else." She folded her arms and turned away from us.

"We'll draw less attention if Tammy just travels as herself," I said. "I'll drive the MGB quietly up to the front of the house. We'll turn the hall light off, open the front door and Tammy can slide into the car without anyone seeing her. We simply reverse the process at Freda's."

And that's exactly as it worked at Elsie's.

But not at Freda's.

I drew the car into the kerb outside Freda's semi-detached house, not far from Preston Park, just as a dog walker came round the corner.

His mutt – a miniature schnauzer, I later discovered – looked like a feather duster on a lead. As soon as it saw the car, the beast started barking. Its high-pitched yelp echoed off the houses.

By now Tammy and I were standing on the street. I hustled her up the path towards Freda's front door. But, as I looked back, I could see curtains twitching on the other side of the road. The animal was still growling after Freda had closed the door.

It hadn't been the unobserved arrival I'd hoped for. But I thought the curtain-twitchers would be focused on the dog rather than Tammy.

I joined the curtain-twitchers' union and kept a close watch on the street for the next hour. But the schnauzer had moved on to yelp at others. The street was quiet.

Freda settled Tammy down with a mug of cocoa and soon she was asleep on the sofa.

"Poor girl," Freda said. "She's been through so much."

"Tomorrow will be important," I whispered so as not to wake Tammy. "I'll collect Shirley and we'll call round at about half past seven. Perhaps we'll have a sound night's sleep and have some good ideas by the morning."

But the way I felt, I wasn't confident of either.

My hope of getting a good night's sleep receded further when I arrived back in Regency Square after dropping Shirley at her flat.

I inserted my key silently into the lock and crept into the hall. But the chances of sneaking upstairs before the Widow caught me turned out to be zero.

Her parlour door was ajar. She shot out as soon she heard the creak when I stood on the first stair. She was brandishing a Christmas card. It had a picture of a snowman with a robin perched on his head.

She handed me the card and said: "I call this obscene."

I looked at the snowman. "That's not obscene. The carrot is supposed to be his nose," I said.

"I know the carrot's his nose. I was talking about the message inside. It's from Mr Evans, the butcher."

The very same who would have received the Christmas card intended for the Widow's sister-in-law. The card with the message: "When you come on Christmas Eve, I'll be in bed but keeping something hot for you."

The Widow wagged a bony finger in my face. "Just read what he's written."

I read: "As it's Christmas, you can rely on me for a good stuffing. Gwilym Evans."

"I don't think he means sage and onion," the Widow said.

I said: "Why don't you just speak to Mr Evans and explain the mix-up?"

"After receiving this? What sort of woman do you think I am?"

I said nothing, looked down and studied the stains on the carpet.

After an awkward silence, the Widow said: "I'll tell you. I'm nothing like my sister-in-law, Eunice, who'll chase after anything in trousers. Especially if there's a pair of hairy legs in them. You've got me into this mess. And I expect you to get me out of it."

The Widow turned on her heels, stomped back into her parlour and slammed the door.

They came the following morning just as the sixth pip of the Greenwich Time Signal on the radio announced it was eight o'clock.

Shirley and I had arrived at Freda's house five minutes earlier. Neither of us had had much rest. Tammy was curled in the chair by the fire staring vacant-eyed into the flames. Freda was in the kitchen boiling an egg for Tammy's breakfast.

I'd joined the curtain-twitchers and was peering out of the window, when I saw two cop cars and a Black Maria swing into the street. The Maria screeched to a halt outside the house. The cop cars took up positions blocking the road so no other traffic could pass.

Cops piled out of the cars and the Maria. They gathered in the street. Detective Chief Superintendent Alec Tomkins swaggered to the front of the group and surveyed the house. He was wearing a gaberdine raincoat belted at the waist and a slouch hat with a wide brim. He looked like Peter Lorre in a B-rated spy movie.

Freda called from the kitchen: "Tammy, how long would you like your egg boiled?"

"Three minutes."

"Better make that two," I said.

Seconds later, we heard the knock on the door.

I hurried into the hall. I opened the door. Tomkins was standing there. He had a smirk on his face as greasy as a bacon sarnie. The two uniformed plods behind him were the ones who'd burst into my bedroom: Moustache and Pimple.

I pointed at them and said to Tomkins: "If those two changed into drag they could play the Ugly Sisters in the Hippodrome's panto."

Tomkins frowned. "We're not here for light banter."

"And this time we have a warrant," Pimple piped up. "Signed by no less than Sir Randolph Abercrombie."

Tomkins gave him a look that could have bored a hole in a steel plate. "We're coming in," he said.

They barged down the hallway and burst into the living room. Tammy jumped to her feet with a little cry.

Shirley said: "Jeez, it's the blue heelers." She pointed at Pimple: "One look at that face counts as police harassment."

Freda came into the room with a boiled egg balanced in a spoon.

"What's this?" she cried.

"It's not second sitting for breakfast," I said.

"Give me that," Tomkins said, pointing at the egg.

Freda dropped the egg into his hand.

"*Yeeoouw*! The egg's still boiling," he yelled. He threw it on the floor. It smashed into a yellow splatter on the carpet. "I've burnt my hand. I'm arresting you for assaulting a police officer," he screamed.

"You asked for the egg," Freda shouted. "I'm suing you for ruining my carpet."

"Slap handcuffs on her," he commanded.

A plod seized Freda's arms.

"Police brutality," Freda screamed. "I know all about it. My mother was a suffragette."

Shirley barged in front of Tomkins to protect Freda. Another plod grabbed Shirley's arms. She stamped on his foot. He yelled in pain.

I shouted: "Let's all calm down."

But I was too late. Tomkins had lost his rag. He was yelling at officers to handcuff everyone. We were all pushing and shoving like shoppers in the January sales. But there was no doubt about the outcome. Within a couple of minutes Tomkins had handcuffed us all.

"Now we're taking you down to the station," he said.

One by one we were escorted out of the house. The back doors of the Black Maria were opened. Freda was first out, followed by Shirley, then Tammy. I was last.

On the other side of the road, Jim Houghton was scribbling in his notebook. By his side, an *Evening Argus* photographer raised his camera and a flashgun flared.

Jim called out: "This will make a great splash in today's *Argus*."

"Not as good as the story I'll write from the inside," I shouted before I was pushed into the back of the Black Maria.

Tomkins ordered Moustache and Pimple into the Maria to guard us on the journey.

I leaned towards Freda. "I'm desperately sorry this has happened," I said.

Freda's eyes were burning with excitement. "Haven't had so much fun since I knocked a copper's helmet off in Trafalgar Square on VE night," she said. "My old mum knew how to take on the rozzers. So I learnt from the best."

"Shut it!" Moustache said.

Freda stuck her tongue out at him. Then she started singing the suffragette song: "Shout, shout, up with your song! Cry with the wind, for the dawn is breaking."

"Shut it!" yelled Moustache.

Freda started on the second verse. And Tammy joined in.

Shirley turned to Pimple: "Do you know what a wallaby's arse looks like?"

Pimple shook his head.

"Take a look in your bathroom mirror," she said.

"Shut it!" Moustache screamed.

By the time we reached the cop shop, we'd sung two verses of the suffragette song and moved on to 'We Shall Overcome'.

As we were transferred from the vehicle to the cells, I whispered to Shirley: "I've got to get a story back to the paper. I can't let Jim Houghton scoop me on my own arrest. When we're in the custody suite, organise a distraction."

Shirley winked. "Leave it to me."

Moustache saw the two of us talking.

"Shut it," he yelled.

"Do you ever say anything other than 'shut it'?" I asked.

"Shut it," he said.

In the custody area, I demanded the right to a phone call. Tomkins reluctantly led me to the custody sergeant's desk and removed my handcuffs. He turned his back to admire Shirley, who'd adopted a sexy pose that would easily have got her onto the cover of *Wild and Wobbly*. I swiped a pencil from the desk. Shoved it inside my shirt.

Then I called Figgis. He enjoyed a throaty chuckle at the news. I could almost smell the Woodbines coming down the line.

He said: "I'll want the inside story, if you take my meaning."

"You'll need to organise a P U," I said.

Tomkins was hovering nearby but he wouldn't know I meant a pick-up. Figgis would have to arrange for someone to collect the copy if I was still in the cells.

"It'll be the lawyer. He'll be at the cop shop within an hour," Figgis said.

I replaced the receiver.

Tomkins sidled over. He said: "Don't think a clever lawyer will get you out of here easily. You're arrested and there's no reversing that. I'm CID."

I said: "Reversing CID would make you a DIC." Tomkins flushed angrily. Before he could reply, I said: "I'm making a formal request to visit the lavatory."

Tomkins shrugged. "I suppose I have to allow that." He gestured to Moustache. "Escort Mr Crampton to the toilets."

We marched down the corridor and shoved through a door marked Gents. I pushed into a cubicle and shut the door behind me. I quietly uncoiled a dozen sheets from the toilet roll and shoved it in my pocket. I was pleased to see it was the hard stuff rather than that soft, absorbent tissue. When you've got five hundred words to write, you don't want your pencil tearing the paper.

We were placed in separate cells all opening onto a long corridor.

For the next hour, the girls kept up a constant barrage of sound. They sang songs. They told insulting jokes about the police. They rattled the doors of their cells.

Every two minutes, like a programmed alarm, Moustache shouted: "Shut it!"

Reginald Hollis, the lawyer, arrived ninety minutes later. He looked more worried than us. We were taken in to see him one by one, me first. With the cops outside the room, I slipped the pages I'd written across to him.

He looked at the toilet paper and sniffed: "I've heard about the gutter press, but this tops it."

I said: "Don't knock it and remember that Frank Figgis wants it back before deadline."

He said: "I'm talking with the police about this, but I think it may not be until the afternoon that we can get you out of here."

"All of us?"

"The police may want to keep Miss Flowerdew. But I'll do what I can."

We finally walked out of the police station – all of us – at four o'clock that afternoon. There'd been no charges pending further investigations, Tomkins had gracelessly told us.

We stood shivering in an icy wind in Bartholomew Square. We all felt drained.

Shirley arranged to take Tammy back to her flat. I said I'd check in with the office, then come and see them later. Freda was planning to meet Henrietta and the Clipping Cousins for a jailbreak party.

There was plenty of backchat when I walked into the newsroom.

"Did you tunnel your way out like Dickie Attenborough in *The Great Escape*?" Sally Martin asked.

"Or perhaps you disguised yourself and bluffed your way

past the guards like those guys in *The Colditz Story*," said Phil Bailey.

"Or perhaps you talked your way out of trouble, as usual." Frank Figgis appeared behind me. He didn't look like he was about to hand me a medal. He said: "Come to my office."

We trooped across the newsroom.

I knew something was wrong as soon as we were inside his office. He invited me to sit down. And then he offered me a Woodbine. He'd never done that before. I waved it away.

He said: "I've just been to see His Holiness."

I said: "All that kneeling must make the knees on your trousers shiny."

"I'm in no mood for your cracks. And neither will you be when you've heard what I've got to say."

"So it's not seasonal good tidings of great joy."

"No. His Holiness isn't at all happy with Abercrombie's summons for contempt. Have you made any progress on that as yet?"

"From the inside of a cell?" I said.

Figgis nodded. "That's the other thing. His Holiness thinks your arrest and its coverage in the *Argus* is the last straw. He's ordered me to fire you."

I think my heart must have stopped for a moment. It certainly missed a beat. Then I felt blood pounding through my body. My vision went hazy.

"He can't mean that," I said.

"He does. He's firm about it."

"But I even turned the arrest around and gave us a great front page." I pointed to the *Chronicle* on Figgis's desk. The splash headline read: Arrest: The True Inside Story.

"I know that. Pope says that as you've turned in some great scoops, he'll delay the firing."

"It's not immediate?" I said hopefully.

"No."

"Then when?"

"Pope says you're fired from December the twenty-fifth."

"But," I said, "that's Christmas Day."

Chapter 18

I walked back into the newsroom feeling like my whole world had fallen apart.

The *Chronicle* was more than my job. It was my life. I'd always felt I'd been born to be a reporter. And I believed I'd been a good one. And now I was out. Out of the *Chronicle*. And, probably, out of newspapers. I couldn't think who would employ me – especially if Tomkins pressed ahead with a prosecution and Abercrombie delivered a conviction. The pair were malicious enough to do that. They'd look on it as an extra Christmas present.

News travels faster than the speed of light on a paper. So the newsroom fell silent as I pushed through the doors. They were all reporters – and good ones. They knew what had happened. Sad eyes watched me as I crossed the room to my desk. Eyes that said we know you're hurting and we know there is nothing we can say to make the hurt go away.

Susan Wheatcroft came up to me. Her eyes were shining with unshed tears. She tried to say something, but the words wouldn't come out. Instead, she threw her arms around me and gave me a bear-sized hug.

Someone started typing again. The insistent clack of the keys on the typewriter carriage broke the spell. This was a newsroom. There were newspapers to publish. A telephone rang. The door opened and Cedric bustled in. The newsroom had absorbed the news. They hadn't liked it. But there were events elsewhere to report.

I sat down at my desk. Ran my fingers lightly over the keys of my old Remington. I was thinking hard what to do next. It didn't take me long to decide. I was to be fired on the twenty-fifth of December. But today was the twenty-second – two days before Archie Flowerdew would hang. And I was still a reporter on the story. I wondered what I should write for tomorrow's paper.

I'd hoped my stories would create the momentum to persuade the Home Secretary to reprieve Archie. I'd even hoped I might find the evidence to clear him. But everything I'd done seemed to make the position worse. Chasing after the mystery woman on the seafront had only exposed Archie as a cross-dresser who'd been close to Despart's studio on the night he was killed. And Archie's sketchbook – which he'd told Tammy would provide the name of a woman who knew the truth about his alibi – had almost certainly gone up in flames, along with the painting of the *Avenging Angel*, when Kingswell crashed.

I'd let Tammy down.

But if I had only two more days to be a journalist, I decided I would not let myself down.

And my first task would be to piece together how a conspiracy to steal a painting had led Kingswell to murder. To do that, I'd need his file from the morgue. I stood up and headed across the newsroom.

This time, no one's gaze followed me.

I was back at my desk studying the clippings in the Kingswell file five minutes later.

As usual, they started with the most recent and worked backwards. Several clippings dealt with his work as chairman of the hanging committee of the Brighton Masters' Art Exhibition. There were duplicates of the clippings I'd originally seen in the Despart file about the row over the humiliating postcard of Kingswell.

There were other items about art shows in his gallery. There were pictures of Camilla Fogg posing with artists at a reception in the gallery. Diligently, I worked my way backwards – through 1963 … into 1962 … into 1961 …

There was a cutting that mentioned Kingswell delivering a valediction at the funeral service of Dominic Fogg, Camilla's late husband. The cutting said Dominic had been a pilot. He and Camilla had been married for just a year before he was killed. The cutting described Camilla as a history of art graduate from London University.

A tiny worm of memory wriggled in my mind.

Earlier in my investigation, someone had mentioned London University.

I cudgelled my memory.

I remembered. It had been Neville Croaker at Seaside Smiles.

I headed back into the morgue. A couple of minutes later, I'd returned to my desk with the file on Dominic Fogg. There were a dozen clippings. They told the story of how Fogg had left the Royal Air Force with the rank of squadron leader and established a small airfreight business at Shoreham Airport. There were pictures of him with planes. I rustled over the cuttings. If it existed, there was one I wanted to see. It was the last in the file.

The cutting was dominated by a photo. A happy couple standing in a church porch on their wedding day. He in top hat and a grey morning coat. She in a lustrous white gown and veil. The two were smiling and their eyes sparkled with love.

I read the caption below. I felt the gooseflesh rise on my back and arms. Enough to put Goosey Goosey Gander to shame.

The medical boys tell us that it's impossible for our blood to run cold. But had a doc been in the room at that moment, I'd have grabbed him by the lapels of his white coat and told him to feel my veins.

A series of short scenes flashed into my mind. Like you see in film trailers – incomplete but compelling.

Sometimes shocking.

Croaker at Seaside Smiles, with his shiny forehead and tufts of ear hair, recalling the suicide of Lady Hilda Markham after her humiliation in Despart's postcard. "She had a daughter about to go to London University."

Camilla Fogg in Kingswell's gallery, brushing her hair with a sly smile and commending the wise old Sicilian proverb: "Revenge is a dish best eaten cold."

I picked up the cutting again. Looked at it. Read the caption on the photo: "Squadron Leader Dominic Fogg marries Miss Camilla Markham."

Daughter of the late Lady Hilda Markham.

And the art graduate who believed revenge is a dish best eaten cold.

Could Camilla Markham have waited ten years for her dish of revenge to cool?

The thought pounded through my brain as I floored the accelerator of the MGB. The engine responded with a throaty roar. I swung the wheel and overtook a bus.

I was powering up the London Road towards Ditchling. I wanted to reach the art gallery before Camilla shut up shop and headed for home. She had some questions to answer.

Correction: she had one question to answer.

Did she kill Percy Despart?

She'd never appeared in the police investigation. But why should she? The death of her mother had been ten years earlier. There'd been a fuss at the time, but it had been long forgotten.

But not, I suspected, by Camilla Fogg née Markham.

Had she been waiting all these years for her moment? She would have required the patience of Saint Monica herself. But Camilla had struck me as a woman who could bide her time. Perhaps she'd been waiting for a moment when other events would throw suspicion elsewhere. The row over the Kingswell postcard would have diverted attention away from her. She'd been keen to emphasise Kingswell's fury at the card when I'd spoken to her at the gallery.

The MGB's wheels squealed as I slung a sharp right at Pyecombe and headed up the lane past the Jack and Jill windmills.

A woman whose dish of revenge had turned positively arctic would surely have no qualms about allowing someone else to take the punishment for her killing. Except that the cops had soon ruled out Kingswell. Poor Archie had turned out to be the sap who'd pay the ultimate price.

Unless I could prove Camilla was the real murderer.

Half a mile ahead the lights of Ditchling nestled in a fold of the Downs. I roared into the village. Squeezed into a parking place just outside The Bull pub. Climbed out of the car. The cold night air hit me. A keen wind was blowing from the east. I shivered convulsively.

The street was empty. The few shops had closed for the night, but the lights still burned in the art gallery.

I crossed the road and tried the door. Locked.

A blind had been drawn down over the window. I peered around the edge but couldn't see anything.

I rapped on the door. Hard, like a cop. Or a debt collector. The kind of rap that gets people inside wondering: who can that be?

The door was opened by a middle-aged woman wearing a button-up overall with a stripy pattern and headscarf tied with a front knot. She was holding a yellow duster in her left hand.

She said: "The gallery is closed. Don't know when it'll open again, what with all the trouble."

I said: "Camilla asked me to drop by."

A puzzled frown appeared on her brow. "She never mentioned someone dropping by to me."

"I expect she forgot," I said.

"Well, the girl was certainly in a rush, and no mistake."

"Can I come in?"

"Don't know about that."

"It's freezing out here. I can tell you what Camilla wanted."

"Can't see that she wanted anything, the snooty little cow. Waltzed out of here half an hour ago and said she wouldn't be back. And all this after Major Kingswell has died and been accused of murder. And him a man who polishes the back of his shoes, too. I don't know what to think." She started to snivel. "And me, poor old Doreen, Major Kingswell always called me, left to clean the place, not knowing whether or not I'll still have a job come the new year."

I pulled out the clean handkerchief I keep for tearful interviewees and handed it to her. She grabbed it and I took the opportunity to step inside and close the door behind me.

From what poor old Doreen had said, Camilla had scarpered.

So I said: "Yes, it's because Camilla had to leave so quickly that she's asked me to check a couple of points she overlooked."

"Never mentioned it to me." A couple of grey eyes gave me an uncomfortably penetrating look. "What did you say your name was?"

"I didn't. But I have suggestion, Doreen. Why don't you make us a cup of tea? Perhaps you could look out some of those nice biscuits Camilla was telling me about."

There was little risk in that lie. Cleaning ladies always have a stock of biscuits somewhere.

Doreen shook her head sadly, pocketed my handkerchief and bustled off towards the kitchen.

When she'd gone I hurried over to Camilla's desk. The one she'd sat at when I'd originally visited.

It was one of those desks with three drawers in a single pedestal to one side. I yanked open the top drawer. It contained three paperclips and some dust fluff. The second drawer yielded a small stack of compliments slips and a couple of rubber bands. This didn't look good. Camilla had cleared the place before she'd vamoosed.

The bottom drawer didn't look promising, either. It was filled with old memos, expense sheets, used envelopes and miscellaneous office detritus. I rummaged quickly through. First useful find was an envelope addressed to Camilla at what I assumed was her home address – a flat in Hove. Second was a letter, dated three months earlier, from the Civil Aviation Authority. It confirmed that she'd completed the requisite number of flying hours, had the appropriate medical check and that her licence to fly light aircraft was approved for a further year.

So Camilla was a daring young woman in her flying machine.

It was clear I wasn't going to find anything else. Especially as my charm had already worn thin on Doreen. If I started to rootle around the place any more there was a real danger she'd call the cops.

A high-pitched whistle told me the kettle was boiling. I pocketed the letter and the envelope, and tiptoed to the door.

I doubted that Camilla would be at her flat.

It turned out to be on the second floor of a handsome mansion block in Second Avenue, Hove. I rang the doorbell three times. No answer.

I checked a couple of neighbours. The first claimed no more than a nodding acquaintance with Camilla and had no idea where she'd be. The second, a dotty old bloke with a walrus moustache, said he didn't hold with carol singers, but if I sang the first two verses of 'Good King Wenceslas' he'd give me sixpence. I told him it was half a crown for the whole thing or nothing and he slammed the door.

I stepped out into the street wondering what my next move should be.

The night was closing in. The east wind cut through my tweed jacket and I wished I'd taken my old mum's advice always to wear a vest. Worse, it had started to snow. Fat, lazy flakes drifted down, translucent in the street lights.

In hundreds of homes excited children would have their noses pressed to their windowpanes. They'd be going to sleep dreaming of Father Christmas and Rudolph, the Red-Nosed Reindeer. If I hung around in the street any longer, I'd be able to compete with Rudolph in the red-nose department. So I bundled into the MGB. I sat with the heater blasting and thought about my next move.

There was no doubt in my mind. Camilla's hasty exit couldn't be explained simply by Kingswell's death. The gallery was still a going concern and would continue to pay the kind of salary a girl like Camilla expected. If she'd murdered Despart, she'd worry that Kingswell's link to Stubbs's killing would lead to unwelcome revelations about herself.

She'd managed to keep a low profile during the Despart enquiry – watching patiently as her revenge cooled. She might not be so lucky when the cops got to work on Kingswell. At the very least, they would want to interview her in depth about his activities in the period running up to Stubbs's killing. Perhaps her own link to another victim of Despart's postcards would come to light during that. Tomkins was too dim to remember that a Markham had featured in an earlier scandal. But Ted Wilson did his homework thoroughly. He read the files. He'd make the link, sooner or later.

Camilla would worry that it might be sooner. Hence her hasty flight. But where was she going? She'd sounded like a clever girl who'd sailed into university with ease. She'd be concerned that word on her was already out to ports and the main air terminals. Extra passport checks would be in place for escaping fugitives. Standard practice. She'd want a way to leave the country without the need to show a passport to a border official with eagle eyes and a suspicious mind.

And she had the perfect opportunity. Her own pilot's licence. Her husband had owned a small fleet of light aircraft. The Civil Aviation Authority letter, which showed she'd kept up her flying hours, suggested she might have retained one of her husband's planes. If so, I knew where she would be.

Shoreham Airport.

It was small enough to avoid a formal passport check. Besides, the place was on the coast. Once in the air, Camilla could be across the English Channel and in France in little more than an hour.

There was only one question left in my mind.

Could I reach the airport before she took off?

The airport terminal was in darkness when I arrived.

There would be no control tower telling Camilla she was cleared for take-off. But did a pilot in a small plane really need that? Especially when there were no other planes moving. I didn't think so.

I brought the MGB to a halt on the north side of the airfield. The snow was falling more heavily now. At least an inch covered the airfield like a lacy shroud. The art deco stucco of the terminal building glowed in the dark like a huge Christmas cake.

I turned off the car engine. I wound down the driver's window and listened to the night. The wind rustled the branches of the trees to the north of the airfield. But no aero engines revved into life.

Silence.

I sat and watched. A winter fox loped across the airfield and headed off in the direction of the River Adur. No cars moved on the airport's perimeter road.

I tried to think of something else to do if this plan failed. But my mind had become as cold as the snow.

I rubbed my eyes and peered harder through the darkness.

In the distance, something black showed against the whiteness of the air terminal's stucco. It moved slowly at first, then faster. I strained my eyes to see. It was a person. Possibly a woman. And she was running.

I started the car engine. Quietly on low revs. I let off the handbrake and drove the car slowly across the airfield. I kept the lights off.

Steadily, the car moved closer to the air terminal. The engine hummed like a child's lullaby. The tyres crunched through the snow.

I was fewer than fifty yards from the air terminal.

But the figure had vanished.

I stopped the car.

I listened.

Silence.

Then the grating sound of metal on metal. Heavy doors being dragged open. I looked in the direction of the noise. About a hundred yards to my right, a light came on in a small hangar.

I swung the car through a turn and drifted it quietly towards the hangar. Light flooded from the open doors. I pulled the car up in front so that it blocked the exit.

I stepped out of the car.

Inside the hangar, Camilla had a hatch open in the underside of a small plane. She was stacking some packages inside it.

She was dressed in a sheepskin jacket and jodhpurs. She wore a leather flying helmet with the buckle hanging loose.

Her eyes flared with anger when she saw me.

I stepped into the hangar. I gestured my thumb towards the MGB and said: "Don't try to take off with the car there. I'd hate you to put a dent in the roof."

Camilla picked up a large adjustable spanner from a bench at the side of the hangar. She hefted it in her hand. Then she moved towards me.

She said: "I'll put a dent in your head first."

I moved back a step and said: "I thought a sharpened 9H pencil was usually your weapon of choice. And you used it on the neck."

Camilla smiled. It was a smile as cold as an arctic night. She said: "I'd borrowed Toby's old service revolver and planned to shoot Despart. That way, Toby would have had to take the blame if the police investigation got anywhere. But Despart rushed at me with his penknife and I just grabbed the pencil instinctively. Didn't have time to reach for the gun in the folds of my cloak."

I said: "Seems strange that an artist's assassin wasn't quick on the draw."

"Despart deserved to die. No man more. After what he did to my mother. Have you ever watched someone eaten from the inside by humiliation? It's like watching a body being ravaged by cancer. That's what Despart did to my dear mama – and he thought it was a joke."

Camilla's arm, with the spanner still in her hand, dropped to her side.

I said: "But you expect someone else to pay the price."

"Someone has to."

"But not an innocent man."

"Life's not fair. It wasn't fair to Mama."

" 'The rain falls on the just and the unjust.' That's your philosophy, is it?"

"Something like that."

"I don't think Bertrand Russell would agree with you."

"He's not here."

"That's the trouble with philosophers. They're never around when you need them," I said.

Camilla raised the spanner and moved towards me. "I don't want to kill you, but if you try to stop me I will."

I said: "I don't need to stop you. Have you looked at the snow? General Winter has advanced. You can't take off in that."

"I can – and I will."

"And go where?"

"Somewhere the police and muckraking journalists like you can't touch me."

"Thanks for the compliment. But you need money to go into hiding. Lots of it. I doubt a personal assistant's savings will last more than a month or two, wherever you go."

Camilla's eyes lit up with the kind of triumph that happens when someone has a secret. It's always a dead giveaway. At least, it is if you spend your time interviewing the dodgy characters who inhabit my life. Camilla hadn't meant to signal she knew something I didn't. She just couldn't help herself. People like Camilla never can.

And now I knew it, too.

I said: "You've got the painting, haven't you?"

Camilla pursed her lips. She was angry. "I don't know what you mean."

"The *Avenging Angel*. By a pupil of Raphael."

Camilla's eyes lit up again. Like searchlights strobing a night sky. So there was another secret.

I said: "It wasn't by a pupil of Raphael, was it?"

Camilla looked at the plane's hold, back at me. "No."

"It was by Raphael. The golden lad himself. Pride of the Renaissance."

"If you must know, yes. That fool Toby Kingswell should have stuck to guns and crawling through mud. That's what commandos do, isn't it? He couldn't tell a Canaletto from a cornflake packet."

"But what about Le Grande? He was a professor of painting and he copied it."

"Le Grande was too wrapped up in his personal vanity to look beyond the end of his nose. He copied it faithfully and never realised he was copying the master."

"A real Raphael must be worth much more than a painting by a pupil," I said.

"A hundred times more. Enough to keep me in champagne until I'm in my dotage."

"And Kingswell consulted you about the painting? Even though it had been stolen from a church."

"Of course not. He hid it at the gallery. But nothing happens there I don't know about. Toby may have been a brave soldier, but he knew nothing about keeping secrets. Perhaps that was why he was so concerned about his own coming out."

"And why he killed Stubbs?"

"Stubbs was just another muckraker on the make."

"And you're a connoisseur of great art preserving the finest pieces for posterity, I suppose."

"I'll sell the picture to a private collector who will keep it safe for the next generation."

I folded my arms and tried to look defiant.

"No, you won't, because I'm not moving the car."

Camilla hefted the spanner again. "This says you will."

"Only if you can hit me with it."

"What makes you think I can't?"

"The fact that the spanner is too heavy for you. Your arm is already drooping again with its weight. You won't be able to swing it fast enough to hit me. I'll grab your arm before the spanner comes within a foot of my head."

Camilla thought about that for a moment. I could see the cogs turning in her mind.

"What if we could do a deal?" she said.

"What kind of deal?"

"What if I had something you wanted?"

"You've got nothing I want."

Camilla's eyes shone again. This time cold and hard. Like light arriving from a distant galaxy.

Of course! The sketchbook. The book Archie had drawn in prison. The one he'd told Tammy contained a clue to the person who knew the truth about his alibi.

When Kingswell killed Stubbs, he must have stolen the book. Perhaps he thought he could sell it under the counter like the painting.

I said: "You have Archie Flowerdew's sketchbook?"

"Yes."

"How did you get it?"

"Toby hid it at the gallery. In the same place as the painting. He really was hopeless about secrets. It was the first thing that raised my suspicions he'd killed Stubbs. Of course, the manner of

Toby's death proves he was the murderer."

I refrained from pointing out that she was also a fully paid-up member of the cold-blooded killers' club.

Instead, I asked: "But why keep the sketchbook as well as the painting?"

"If Toby thought there might be money in it, there was no point in ignoring it."

"What's the deal?" I asked.

"You let me take off with the painting, I give you the book."

It was cold in the hangar, but I felt a thin film of sweat form around my neck. My mind raced into overdrive. I could try to detain Camilla. If the cops interviewed her, they might break her and get a confession. But would a woman as hard as Camilla break easily? I didn't think so. In any event, I'd displayed some bravado over the spanner – but it was a formidable weapon in anyone's hands. Especially someone who'd previously killed with a pencil. So perhaps I should settle for the sketchbook and let Camilla fly to her fate. With the book, at least we'd have a chance of cracking Archie's alibi and winning a reprieve.

I said: "My mission is to stop Archie from hanging. If you can help me achieve that by handing over the sketchbook, I might find it impossible to stop you taking off."

Camilla looked hard at me. "We have an agreement?"

"We have an agreement," I said.

It took ten minutes of haggling to work out the handover arrangements. Camilla was suspicious that once I'd got the book, I'd stop her leaving. In the end, we agreed a complex set of actions. She'd sit in the cockpit of the plane, with the propellers turning ready to taxi out and take off. I'd sit next to the plane in the MGB with its engine fired up. She'd toss the package with the book down to me and immediately start to taxi. I'd have a few seconds to check whether it was the real book. If it wasn't, the acceleration of the MGB would get me in front of the plane before it could move out of the hangar.

And that's how it happened.

I sat in the MGB and watched as Camilla accelerated across the airfield and the plane's wheels left the ground. She made a looping pass to the north before turning south.

As the plane passed over the airfield she waggled the wings in the traditional victory salute.

I watched as the plane gained height and flew out to sea.

Then I put the MGB into gear and headed back to Brighton.

Chapter 19

Archie Flowerdew's sketchbook lay in front of me on my desk in the *Chronicle*'s newsroom. I stared at its brown board covers. They were scratched and stained. They had a hell of a tale to tell.

After all, the book had been drawn in jail.

Smuggled through a prison's gates.

Stolen in a housebreaking.

Taken as a trophy of murder.

Purloined by a false friend.

Bargained for a killer's freedom.

And now it was to help me save a man's life. I hoped.

I tore my eyes away from the book and glanced around the newsroom. Since I'd received my marching orders, I'd been looking at the room in a new light. I'd spent the best part of the last two years of my life in its scruffy heart. I was going to miss the fug that hung below the fluorescent lights. And the way the floor vibrated when the huge rotary presses in the basement began to roll off the papers. I was going to miss the machine-gun rattle of typewriters and the insistent shrill of a dozen telephones ringing at once.

But I still had two full days before I was out on the street. No doubt with a festive sprig of holly behind my ear.

I was going to use those days to save a man's life.

And win the greatest front-page splash I'd ever penned.

It was nearly ten o'clock and the day staff had long since quit. Jake Harrison and Chava Hoffman, the two night reporters, were over by the teleprinter. They were leafing through agency copy looking for local leads. They'd given me a sympathetic nod when I'd burst in. The kind that says we know you're on the way out, we'd help if we could, but what can we do?

I returned their nod with one of my own. The confident one that says I may have been sacked here but by the end of next week I'll be editing *The Times*.

I wrenched my mind back from my own predicament to Archie's. After all, his was more pressing.

I was itching to open the sketchbook, but I was waiting for Shirley and Tammy to arrive.

As soon as I'd got back to the newsroom, I'd called Shirley and told her what I'd found. I knew I would stand no chance of cracking any mystery in the book without Tammy's help. She knew how her uncle Archie's mind worked better than anyone.

A few minutes later, Shirley and Tammy pushed through the newsroom's swing doors. They were breathless and rosy-cheeked. The temperature had dropped outside and snow was still falling.

They hurried across to my desk and pulled up spare chairs.

"Jeez, it's cold enough out there to freeze the winkle off a wombat," Shirley said.

I ignored that and pointed at the sketchbook on the desk.

Tammy had already spotted it. Despite the cold, her eyes burnt like little furnaces.

"How did you get it?" she asked.

I told the tale in a few words: "I faced down a piece of posh dressed as Biggles. She was wielding a vicious adjustable spanner and planned to make a dent in my head with it. Her name was Camilla Fogg née Markham. She admitted that she'd stuck the 9H pencil into Percy Despart's neck. She was in the process of leaving the country in a hurry."

I described the deal I'd done with Camilla to gain the sketchbook.

Tammy's eyes popped. Her face turned a deeper shade of red. I thought she was going to explode.

"You're saying this Camilla bitch admitted to killing Despart and you let her get away?"

"It wasn't like that," I said.

"Sounds like it to me." She was on her feet and looked as

though she was planning to take a swing at me.

Shirley placed a restraining hand on her arm.

"For a start, if the cops were involved, Camilla would never admit to killing Despart," I said. "Tomkins wouldn't be interested in listening, either. As far as he's concerned, it's case closed. Given a choice between believing my version of the conversation and Camilla's, he'd take her side every time. Even if I'd been able to detain her physically, there was no way I could call the cops from a hangar on a deserted airfield. And even if I did, they'd only hold her on stealing a painting – and possibly not even that. I've a feeling that Camilla could talk her way out of most tight corners."

Tammy shrugged. "I'm not happy about it."

I said: "We're not here to be happy. We're here to save Archie – and, at last, we have the book that may help us do it." I picked up the sketchbook. I said to Tammy: "You've seen this before. Have you been able to make anything of it?"

Tammy shook her head. "I knew all about the picture puzzles Archie drew for newspapers and magazines. But this was like nothing I'd ever seen before. I couldn't understand it – apart from the first page."

I opened the book.

Archie had headed the first page with a quotation: 'Truth sits upon the lips of dying men – Matthew Arnold.'

I said: "Let's hope that, in this case, Arnold was wrong. If we can discover the secret in these pages, Archie may live."

Underneath the quotation, Archie had written several lines in his perfect copperplate lettering. I read it aloud: "To Tammy: My dearest girl, you should know the truth, but not yet. Of one thing I can say: I am not guilty of the murder of Percy Despart. But I cannot use my alibi to clear my name. The life of a lady who became my friend is at stake and I will not allow it to be forfeit by my hand. Therefore, seek in the puzzles in this book for the name of that lady. When it is safe for her, she will tell you what really happened. You will solve the puzzle in time. Of that I am as certain as that I go to a peaceful place. Love to you always, my dearest Tammy. Your Uncle Archie."

Tammy's eyes brimmed with tears. "Solve the puzzle in time … We have less than two days."

Shirley put her arm around Tammy's shoulders.

"But we have our first clue." I tried to sound confident. At least we knew what we were looking for. But even if we found the name of the woman, would we be able to find where she lived? But perhaps I was catching Tammy's pessimism. I worked for a newspaper – and reporters specialised in tracking down people who'd prefer not to be found.

I turned to the next page.

Archie had created a title page. It read: On the First Day of Christmas, My True Love Gave to Me …

It was the first words of the famous song.

I turned another page. It was headed: A Partridge in a Pear Tree.

Below the heading, Archie had drawn a healthy specimen of a tree laden with ripe pears. The partridge sat on one of the upper branches. It had the smug look of a bird that knew it would still be perched in the same tree for many Christmases to come.

Tammy and Shirley crowded round to look at the picture.

"Can you make anything of it?" I asked.

"At first I thought it might be a variation on the 'spot the difference' competitions Archie drew for newspapers," Tammy said.

"Spot the what?" said Shirley.

"You see two pictures that look the same but, in fact, there are a number of detailed differences between them. You have to find what they are," I explained.

"I thought there might be differences in the pears," Tammy said. "But I've looked and looked, and they're all exactly the same."

"And there's only one partridge, so no differences there," I said. "Let's see whether the next pages help."

But as we turned the pages we goggled in amazement. I'd seen this Christmas song illustrated many times before, but never in such a style. The pictures moved from the fanciful to the dark and, finally, the sinister.

Two turtle doves: the doves are portrayed as proud parents standing in a newly decorated nursery. There is a crib and in it an egg.

Three French hens: the hens are cancan dancers kicking up their legs and showing their frilly petticoats. Behind them is a windmill picked out in a red spotlight.

Four calling birds: the birds are dressed in jumpers with hooped stripes and berets like Parisian apaches. They are sitting in a cafe talking secretively to a flic – a French cop.

Five golden rings: only they are not rings at all but sets of handcuffs.

Six geese a-laying: the geese are dressed as prison warders. They are gathered around a table loaded with pills and a hypodermic needle.

Seven swans a-swimming: they are gliding up the River Thames with Tower Bridge opening majestically behind them.

Eight maids a-milking: the maids are dressed as landladies. One is on the doorstep of a tenement slum. She is taking a large handful of money from a young girl dressed in ragged clothes and carrying a small suitcase.

Nine ladies dancing: the ladies have voluptuous figures and bored faces. Some are naked. They are dancing on a small stage in a seedy nightclub.

Ten lords a-leaping: the lords wear coronets on their heads, but are dressed only in their underwear. They are taking turns to jump over a large four-poster bed.

Eleven pipers piping: the pipers are gas fitters. Their pipes are the pipes that carry the gas around a house. They have toolboxes and are repairing the pipes.

Twelve drummers drumming: the drummers line the road as a funeral cortège arrives outside a church. They are beating out a rhythm as the pall-bearers carry the coffin.

I closed the book and turned to the girls. They both looked baffled.

"Well, what do you make of that?" I said.

"Weird," Shirley said. "Unsettling, even. Never seen anything like it. Not even those boys' adventure comics they used to sell down at Old Dan's store near the Torrens river when I was a kid."

Tammy shook her head despairingly. "It's not like anything that Uncle Archie's drawn before," she said. "His work was always so bright and cheerful. But this …" She pointed at the book. "This is just so dark. I never realised prison could do that to a man."

"It's bad, kiddo." Shirley gave Tammy a hug. "But, worse, I don't see how it helps us identify the woman who knows the truth about the murder. Sorry, I'm usually as sunny as a daybreak on Bondi Beach, but this has blown in the thunderclouds."

I'd admit that when I closed the book I wondered whether it was the end of the road. Game over, for us. And for Archie.

But as I started to think about the pictures, I wondered whether they could help us identify the mystery woman.

"At first glance, the twelve pictures all seem to be unrelated scenes; although they all take the 'Twelve Days of Christmas' song as their inspiration," I said. "But the more I think about it, the more I believe they tell a story."

Shirley shifted on her chair. "What story?"

"The story of the mystery woman's life. I don't mean her whole lifestory. I think the pictures just pick out the key turning points."

"How do you mean?" Tammy said. "What kind of story starts with a partridge in a pear tree?"

"Yes, that's a problem. I don't think the first picture is part of the story. It may serve a purpose, but I'm not sure what that is yet. I think the real story starts with the two turtle doves. You notice how they're looking anxiously at that egg, which already has a crack in it. It's going to hatch. I think this is about the mystery woman's birth." I opened the book at the picture. "And look at the crib. That blanket with the blue background and yellow cross. It's the Swedish flag. I think this picture is telling us the woman was born in Sweden."

Shirley and Tammy shook off their tiredness and pulled their chairs closer to my desk. Now, their faces were intense with concentration.

"Then there's the three French hens – all dressed as cancan dancers in a setting that the red windmill clearly suggests is the Moulin Rouge. It's a nightclub in Paris. Perhaps this woman moved to Paris and worked as a dancer."

"That's a hell of a leap from a cracked egg to a cancan hen," Shirley said.

"Sure. But if I'm right, the pictures focus on just those points in the woman's life that shaped her and led her to the point where she knows the truth about Despart's murder. Look at the four calling birds all dressed as French lowlife in some backstreet cafe. And they're all talking to a flic. I think Archie's trying to tell us that the woman was shopped to the police for some reason."

"Grassed up by calling birds. Must be a first," Shirley said.

"And that theory is supported by the next picture – five golden rings portrayed as five sets of handcuffs," I said. "I suppose with artistic licence handcuffs are just a pair of large rings."

"Never gold, though," Tammy said.

"Archie was telling a story," I said. "He had to make compromises with the exact words of the song. Like the next picture – the geese a-laying. Prison warders who look like they're laying consists of selling the lags drugs on the side. I'll guess that our mystery woman spent time in a cell. And the screws turned her into an addict."

"Bastards," Shirley said. "I'd shove their filthy pills so far up them they'd have to blow them out of their Gallic noses just to breathe."

"I guess the mystery woman had had enough of France," I said. "The swans swim up the River Thames. She came to Britain. And then found herself paying hard-faced landladies to rent rooms like hovels. An inventive touch for Archie to realise that landladies milk rent out of tenants even faster than dairymaids squeeze the real stuff out of cows."

Shirley frowned. "But then her life gets worse."

"It rather looks like it," I said. "The ladies dancing are in a strip club."

"A skin joint," Shirley said.

"The way Archie's drawn it suggests it's several steps down from the Moulin Rouge," I said. "But she's not yet hit rock bottom. Those lords are leaping for a very good reason."

"They've been pumping their Percys," Shirley said.

"It looks as though our mystery woman ended up working as a prostitute in a brothel," I said. "But we don't know where. And we don't know when."

"But there are two more pictures," Tammy said.

I nodded. "But I don't understand them. Why the pipers should be portrayed as gas fitters I don't understand. The rest of the pictures fit into a sort of coherent story. But it just doesn't make sense that a woman who's been a stripper and a prostitute should end her career as a gas fitter."

"Except she doesn't end it there," Shirley said. "Doesn't that last picture – of the drummers at a funeral – mean she died?"

"That can't be right," I said. "Archie specifically tells us at the beginning of the book that she's alive. Perhaps the funeral is someone else's."

"Like Despart's?" Tammy said.

"Yes," I said. "That would make sense." I leant back in my

captain's chair and glanced at the clock on the newsroom wall. Half past one. "If our deductions are right, we know the kind of woman we're looking for," I said.

"But we don't know her name," Shirley said.

"Or where we can find her," Tammy added.

I rubbed my eyes. They felt as though they were filled with grit. I hadn't slept for hours. But the girls looked even more exhausted.

I said: "Somewhere in this book, Archie has hidden the woman's name. Possibly even her address. But we're too tired to find it tonight. Shirley, why don't you take Tammy back to your flat and both get some rest? I'll finish up here and we'll meet back at eight tomorrow morning – and crack this mystery once and for all."

Shirley managed a half-smile, Tammy barely a nod. The poor girl was all in. They stood up and shuffled out of the newsroom. I watched from the window as they trudged down the street through the snow. They stumbled along arm in arm like a couple of drunks who'd been thrown out of a pub.

I yawned and stretched my arms. Decided I'd take one final look at the book before getting some shut-eye back at my flat.

I sat down at my desk and opened the sketchbook at the first page.

Chapter 20

"Wake up, Colin. 'The morn, in russet mantle clad, Walks o'er the dew of yon high eastward hill'," a voice said.

I stirred painfully. Felt an ache in my shoulders. My eyes opened. My head was lying on my folded arms resting on my desk. I peered up. Chava Hoffman was smiling at me.

"What did you say?"

"I gave you a few words from the Bard. Did you know I'm writing a play?"

I said: "If it's called *The Knackered Man,* I could take the title role."

I shifted uncomfortably on the desk. I didn't know how long I'd been asleep. It felt like a hundred years. But it might only have been ninety-nine.

A cup of steaming coffee appeared in front of my face.

Chava said: "I don't normally do room service, but you look as though you need this."

I levered myself off the desk and sat upright.

She said: "I'm just going off-duty, but I thought I'd do my good deed for the night before I do."

"Is it still night?" I asked.

"Seven," she said. "In the morning, in case you were still wondering."

I picked up the cup and sipped at the coffee. It was as strong as a muscleman's biceps. I must have grimaced.

Chava smiled. "Sure, it's strong. I find only two things get a man moving in the morning. The other one's hot coffee."

I grinned. Raised the cup and sipped some more. Felt the caffeine surging through my tired veins like an electric shock.

"Cheers," I said. "A merry Christmas, Chava."

"Not for your prison man," she said. "Are you going to get him off?"

"I don't know. We've made some progress, but we're running out of time."

Chava shrugged. "That's the way it is sometimes. When your number's up …"

She turned and hurried across the newsroom.

She pushed through the swing doors. They fell back and waggled back and forth like they do when they're settling into the closed position.

I watched them.

Mesmerised.

What Chava had said was chasing around my mind like a terrier after a rat.

When your number's up …

There had to be a reason why Archie had chosen 'The Twelve Days of Christmas' as the theme of his puzzle. Because it had numbers. But what did the numbers mean? I drank some more coffee. I tried to put myself in Archie's place. He wanted his puzzle book to do two things – to tell us something about the woman he knew. Perhaps he felt we would need that information for a reason. Perhaps because without it, we might not take her seriously. If I'd interpreted her story correctly, the woman had fallen low in life. Perhaps Archie reasoned we'd dismiss whatever she had to say because of that. He wanted us to know that she could still be trusted. So he portrayed her life in pictures. And he'd succeeded.

But, secondly, he also needed to convey her name. The numbers had to be the key to that. But you can't write a name in numbers. You have to do it in letters. So the numbers must be a code for letters. Could each of the numbers one through to twelve represent a different letter of the alphabet? I wondered. It would be a very limiting way to work. It would only be possible to represent twelve letters of the alphabet. The other fourteen would be left out. If Archie was providing a first and second name, twelve different letters might not be enough. Besides, how would we know which number represented which letter?

I discarded that idea and had another gulp of coffee.

The numbers had to be related in some way. 'On the first day of Christmas, my true love sent to me: a partridge in a pear tree.' So did number one relate to the partridge or the pear tree? There was no way of knowing. And then there were the other numbers – two turtle doves and so on. What if Archie intended each number to represent a letter from the line of the song? If so, number one could be the first letter of partridge in a pear tree – the letter P.

I wrote it down.

Perhaps Archie intended us to take the first letter of each verse of the song. In which case, the next would be the T from turtle doves. I went through the whole song and produced a list of twelve letters: P T F C G G S M L L P D.

I looked at the list. That couldn't be right. For a start, there wasn't a single vowel among the letters. I couldn't see how it would be possible to make any words, let alone names, without a selection of vowels and consonants.

In any event, if Archie had only wanted us to choose the first letter of each line of the song – or each verse – he could have chosen any song. There must be a reason why he'd chosen a song that featured the numbers one to twelve. And I think I had it. It was because we had to choose the first letter from the first verse, the second letter from the second verse and so on.

First came the P from the partridge in a pear tree.

For turtle doves, we would choose the second letter. That was U.

And the third letter of French hens was E.

I carefully worked through every verse. When I'd finished I'd written down another row of twelve letters: P U E L E A S I N P N M.

I looked down at the letters. This was more promising. There was a mix of consonants and vowels. But was it what Archie intended? Was this, perhaps, an anagram with a woman's name as the answer? The only way to test this hypothesis was to try it. But that presented another problem. With these twelve letters there were thousands of possible combinations and I didn't know where to start.

I would never be able to do it.

But there was one man who could.

I reached for my telephone and dialled a Brighton number.

Bartholomew Augustus Digby Mann strode across the newsroom.

He walked up to my desk and said: "This had better be important. I hate leaving the house in the morning before I've trimmed my moustache, drunk my carrot juice and completed a successful bowel movement. This morning I've done none of them – and I hold you personally responsible for the consequences."

Bad Mann – as he was known because of his initials – had been the English master at a boys' public school in the Windsor area. He was a tall man of about fifty with a handsome lined face and a roguish eye. He had a head of luxuriant brown hair, which was permanently tousled.

The rumour mill had it that he'd been sacked after a liaison with the headmaster's wife. I once asked him about it.

"Was it true, Bad Mann, that you rogered her on the floor of the art room?"

"Complete fabrication, my dear fellow. Absolutely wrong. It was the chemistry lab."

Word got around and Mann found teaching jobs thin on the ground – especially from schools whose headmasters had wives. But Bad Mann wasn't going to allow his impressive command of the English language – not to mention his twisty mind – go to waste. He turned his hand to compiling crosswords. He produced the *Chronicle*'s daily cryptic puzzle, which had become a circulation builder for the paper.

Bad Mann adjusted his half-moon glasses and gave me a hard stare. "Personally responsible for the consequences," he repeated.

"I seem to be responsible for most things around here," I said. "At least for the next two days."

Bad Mann gave me a sympathetic nod. "Heard about that. You know what I think. I sum it up as a cryptic clue: 'External anger makes a passion.' Seven letters."

"Outrage," I said.

"Correct," he said.

"Perhaps it won't be if we can solve an anagram that's come my way." I avoided going into the background. Bad Mann would only want to discuss every detail.

His eyes sparked with interest. "Anagram, you say. Tricky blighters for the uninitiated but not the cognoscenti."

"In that case, what do you make of this?" I handed him the list with the letters: P U E L E A S I N P N M.

He glanced at it for ten seconds and said: "Enamel pin-ups."

"No."

"In that case, 'a nipple's menu'."

"It's definitely not that. Will you let me explain? The answer is a person's name. First name and second name."

"Man or woman?"

"Woman."

Bad Mann's tongue flicked over his top lip. "Interesting," he said. "But there are at least three problems solving the puzzle."

"Which are?"

"First, we have no idea which letters go into the first name and which into the second. Secondly, there are a huge number of girls' names that could be possibilities given the letters we have here – I can see Melanie, Elaine and Pauline at a cursory glance. And third, there are so many possible second names we simply wouldn't know where to start. So this anagram is, to coin another clue: 'French bone and girly suffix follow goblin type'. Ten letters."

"Imp-os-sible," I said.

"Exactly."

"The man who set the puzzle believes it isn't impossible," I said. I told Bad Mann about Flowerdew's sketchbook. "Archie was as much a master at setting visual puzzles as …"

"Spare my blushes." Bad Mann waved away the coming compliment.

"I was about to say as Frank Figgis is at writing headlines."

Bad Mann scowled. "And may one be given the privilege of seeing this book?"

"No offence, Bad Mann. I really appreciate you coming so early – and before you'd trimmed your moustache or drunk your carrot juice."

"It's the third of my morning routines that is currently giving me – and should, therefore, cause you – some concern."

"In that case, let's not delay."

I handed him the sketchbook. He beetled his heavy brow as he flipped through the pages.

"And you derived the letters for the anagram from the verses of the song?" he asked.

I explained how.

"It seems logical," he said. "But one of the pictures must provide a clue as to how to divide the letters between the first and second names. If we could do that, it would give us a start."

I took back the book and opened it at the first page. The partridge was still perched smugly at the top of his pear tree.

"I've wondered whether the clue lies in this picture," I said. "There are twelve pears on the tree – just as there are twelve verses in the song."

"With each pear representing a different verse?" Bad Mann said.

"Yes. Archie was an expert at drawing 'spot the difference'

competitions and I've tried to spot differences in the pears, but they all look the same."

Bad Mann stroked his chin meditatively. "Have you considered the exact words of the first verse?" he asked.

"A partridge in a pear tree," I said.

"Precisely. *In* a pear tree. Not *on* a pear tree. This partridge is perched on the pear tree. Suppose there is another that is in the pear tree."

I stared hard at the picture. "I can't see that."

"Not from this angle. Try turning the book upside down."

I swivelled it around. And gawped at the page.

I had to admire Archie's draughtsmanship. He'd drawn the picture in such a clever way that upside down some of the tree's branches and leaves transformed into the outline of a partridge.

Bad Mann pushed his glasses further up his nose. "I think we may be getting somewhere."

"And now I also see a small difference in the pears," I said.

There was a small blemish at the foot of each pear. It looked identical when the book was the right way up. With the book turned the other way, the blemish leaned to the left on six of the pears, to the right on the other six.

I said: "Look at this – two groups of pears. With the left leaning group being the first name."

"And the right leaning group the second."

"Do you agree it makes sense to count from left to right starting at the top and working down the tree?" I said.

Bad Mann nodded.

"So pear number three is the first left leaner. That must represent the French hens. And the third letter is E. The fourth pear represents the calling birds."

"Letter L," Bad Mann said.

When we'd decoded the pears we had two lists of letters.

First name: E L A S I N.

Second name: P U E P N M.

Bad Mann leaned forward and studied the lists. He muttered to himself as he did so.

He looked at me. "The first name is simple," he said. "The only woman's name that uses all of the letters is Selina."

"That's a great start," I said.

"But only a start. It's the second name that bothers me. I can't think of a common English name that uses all of them. I can't even think of an uncommon one. In fact, I don't think the name is English."

"I think the name may be Swedish," I said. I showed him the picture of the two turtle doves with the crib and its blanket in the colours of the Swedish flag.

"Then, as Shakespeare might have put it, 'our revels now are ended'," said Bad Mann.

"You mean you can't solve it?"

"Ask me to discover the most obscure noun or a little-used adjective and I will oblige. But to discover a family name in an unknown language when I don't know any names in that language – can't be done."

"What about Greta Garbo?" I said.

"What about her?"

"She's Swedish. That's one name you know. And then there's Anita Ekberg, Ingrid Bergman ..."

"All right. I accept my defeat gracefully. But you realise that six random letters can be arranged in seven hundred and twenty different combinations."

"But some of those combinations are non-starters. After all, what name would begin P P M N?"

"We have two vowels among the six letters," said Bad Mann. "Let's assume they both form the centre of three letter groups, with a consonant on each side."

"You mean like 'pum' and 'pen'?"

"Or 'pem' and 'pun'. I suggest we create as many of these three-letter groups as we can, then join them together and see which look as though they may sound like names."

We went to work. I scribbled away while Bad Mann printed his thoughts more ponderously in a notebook. Then we tried combining the three-letter groups into six-letter names. When we'd finished, we had a list of five possibilities:

Pumpen.

Meppum.

Neppum.

Muppen.

Nuppem.

"None of them sound like Swedish names to me," Bad Mann grumbled.

"There's a quick way to find out. I'll call the press attaché at the Swedish Embassy."

But that didn't prove as quick as I'd hoped. A helpful secretary told me the attaché had not yet arrived, but she'd pass on my message as soon as he did.

Bad Mann disappeared to trim his moustache, drink his carrot juice and complete a bowel movement, but not necessarily in that order.

And then Shirley and Tammy arrived.

They burst into the newsroom like a couple of tyro reporters on their first scoop. Shirley was wearing jeans and a denim jacket over a yellow sweater. Tammy was dressed in dark red slacks and a duffel coat. My fellow journos watched them as they crossed the newsroom towards my desk.

The tension in the room crackled like icicles breaking. Everyone knew what was at stake.

An eerie silence fell over the room as Shirley and Tammy reached me. Eyes in the newsroom turned to the wall clock. The minute hand showed one minute to nine. As though controlled by a weird invisible force, we all held our breath.

Clunk!

The minute hand moved. It pointed at nine o'clock. At

precisely this time tomorrow morning, a man would pull a lever. A trapdoor would open. And Archie Flowerdew – perhaps praying, perhaps shaking with fear – would drop through and his neck would snap. A doctor would step forward and pronounce him dead two minutes later.

We had just twenty-four hours to save Archie.

For a moment, the silence in the newsroom held. And then the energy, the noise, the controlled chaos that miraculously produced three editions of a newspaper six days a week returned.

Tammy turned towards me. Yesterday she had looked tearful. This morning her eyes glinted with determination.

In a few words, I told Shirley and Tammy about the progress Bad Mann and I had made.

"We're convinced our mystery lady is Swedish and her first name is Selina. I'm waiting for a call from the Swedish Embassy, which may give us a lead on her family name."

But for the next hour, the telephone stayed silent.

Shirley, Tammy and I looked at the sketchbook again. We went over all the clues trying to find out whether we'd missed anything vital. But we found nothing new.

Colleagues came over to talk. The best journalists have what someone once called a 'low-bred curiosity' and everyone wanted to know whether we'd crack the case. I took it in my stride. But after a dozen good wishes Tammy was feeling the strain. I suggested to Shirley that she take her down to Marcello's for coffee. I'd call the place as soon as there was a development.

They left and the minutes ticked by with no call from the Swedish Embassy. I was tired, but my nerves felt as tight as tent drawstrings.

Frank Figgis emerged from his office and made his way over to my desk. He looked weary, too.

He said: "Hollis has just told me we've received the formal paperwork on the contempt-of-court case that snob-nosed excuse for a magistrate Abercrombie is bringing."

I'd pushed it to the back of my mind. "So he's going ahead," I said. "At least I'll be gone, so it won't affect me."

Figgis scratched his chin – the sign that he was embarrassed. "From what I hear, it may not be quite as simple as that. As the author of the piece, you'll still be standing in the dock alongside His Holiness as editor. Only difference is that the paper won't be paying your legal fees."

"That's outrageous. I wrote the story on behalf of the paper."

"In his benevolent wisdom, Pope has decided that as you'll no longer be working for the paper, he sees no reason why it should pick up your bills – especially as he says you caused the problem."

"My copy was accurate."

"Prove it, then."

"I wish I knew how," I said.

Figgis patted my shoulder sympathetically. "Life is going to be that little bit duller without you around the place," he said. He loped off to his office.

I sat at my desk pondering the injustice of injustice. Decided I was just too tired to figure that out. It was one for the philosophers.

And then my telephone rang.

I seized the receiver and said: "Colin Crampton."

A lightly accented voice said: "This is Pers Johannson, the press attaché at the Swedish Embassy. I had a message to call you urgently."

"Thank you, Mr Johannson. We have a query here at the Brighton *Evening Chronicle* about Swedish family names."

"Really? Unusual for a provincial English newspaper."

"I won't bore you with the details, but I've got five names and I was wondering whether you might recognise any of them as Swedish."

"I'll try."

I reeled off the names. Johannson asked me to repeat them. I did so.

There was a silence while he thought about it.

"I've never heard of four of them, but one is used as a Swedish name."

"Which one?"

"Muppen. But I've never come across it as a family name. It's used occasionally as a boy's given name."

"But that wouldn't mean it couldn't be a family name. For example, in English, boys' names such as James, Anthony and Samuel all turn up as family names. There are plenty of other examples."

"It's possible," he said. "But I've never met a Muppen."

"I hope I may be able to change that for you. And thank you for your help."

I slammed the receiver back in the cradle. I was tense with excitement. My nerves felt like they were plugged into the National Grid.

Selina Muppen.

Could she be the woman Archie knew held the secret of his alibi?

And if she was, could I find her – and persuade her to speak?

Chapter 21

I hurried out of the newsroom and headed for Marcello's.

I'd said I'd ring Shirley and Tammy when I had news, but I decided it would be better to tell them the next step face-to-face. They weren't going to like it.

Besides, after Figgis's bombshell, I'd had enough of the newsroom. Yesterday, I'd thought there was nowhere else on earth I'd rather be. Now, I wasn't so sure. In my tenure as crime correspondent, I'd landed the paper some of its greatest front-page splashes. Now, I was being treated like an errant cub reporter who'd dropped a comma. If they were going to kick me out, perhaps there was life after the *Chronicle*. If so, I'd find it.

But not before I'd used every last second of the time remaining to save Archie's life.

I pushed through the door into Marcello's. After the chill of the street, it felt stuffy inside. The windows ran with condensation. A haze laced with cigarette smoke and fried bacon fumes hung in the air like a November fog.

Shirley and Tammy had taken a table near the back. Tammy was stirring a cup of coffee. Shirley was munching a large iced bun.

They both looked up with tense faces as I approached.

"Any news?" Tammy asked.

"We have a name. We're looking for a Selina Muppen. If we're right, she's Swedish. And I'm assuming from Archie's sketchbook that she lives in Brighton – or nearby. But we don't know where."

"Is there any way we can check?" Shirley asked.

"I had a quick look in the telephone directory before I left. No Muppens. I've asked Henrietta to check the morgue, in case the paper has written about her in the past. But I don't think she'll find anything. The only other possibility is the electoral register. It's very unlikely she's included if she's a Swedish national. But

Sally Martin is organising a team to run through the register street by street. That could take hours – and they probably won't find anything. But we have to try."

"So it's hopeless," Tammy said.

"I don't think so. Remember that Archie's pictures told us a lot about Selina's life. She worked as a cancan dancer at the Moulin Rouge, got into trouble, served a spell in prison, came to England and, for a time, was a stripper."

"But ended as a prostitute," Shirley said.

"Yes. That's the last occupation Archie's drawing suggests. I've discounted the gas-fitting pipers because they were men. And I don't think Selina would have been a drummer at the funeral. Although I think that if we knew the identity of the body in the coffin, we'd be a long way to solving this mystery. If Selina is still working in the oldest profession, I may be able to track her through one of Brighton's brothels."

Shirley's eyes turned into saucers. "Brighton has brothels!" she said.

"Brighton has brothels like rats have fleas," I said.

"Don't the police do anything about them?" Shirley asked.

"The police are running some of them. Or at least taking a hefty rake-off from the profits. I'm going to make the rounds to see if anyone has ever known Selina and can tell us where she lives."

Shirley tossed the remains of her bun onto a plate. "I'm coming with you."

"No. Strange to say, a brothel is no place for a lady. Especially a gorgeous one who's got a dab of icing on the corner of her mouth."

Shirley opened a paper napkin and wiped it off.

I said: "The best thing you and Tammy can do is to go back to your flat and rest. If I find Selina, I'm going to need both of you to help me persuade her to talk. You'll have to be at the top of your game."

Shirley nodded reluctantly. She gave me one of her laser-beam stares. "But make sure you confine yourself to making enquiries."

I grinned. "Don't worry about that. I won't be buying."

A few months earlier, the *News of the World* – a scandal sheet that specialised in sordid tales about vicars and choirboys – had offered me a fat fee for a freelance assignment. It appeared that the vicars had been behaving themselves and so the paper needed a fresh angle to fill its sex-fuelled columns. It was the summer – the silly season for journalists – and there was a shortage of news. Especially the scandalous type. So the editor decided to make his own. His idea was to run a series called a *Bit on the Seaside*. As he explained it to me, the aim was to show the seamy side of Britain's coastal resorts. (It actually only showed the seamy side of his mind.)

He wanted me to go undercover and act as a client visiting Brighton brothels. My mission was to find out what went on there and to try to catch a couple of prominent locals the paper could expose in its columns. At the appropriate moment in each of my visits – hopefully, while I still had my trousers on – I'd bail out before the serious business started with any of the girls.

Then I'd be able to write in my piece – as many had done before. Something like: 'At this point Charlotte (or Amanda or Veronica or whoever) offered me a sexual service. I made an excuse and left.' I guess the hacks who did this kind of work saw a fearless investigative journalist when they looked in the mirror. But I knew I'd just see a sleazeball who'd ruined a working girl's day just so he could write a few trite column inches.

So I turned the job down.

And then events took an unexpected turn.

Through the grapevine I heard about the reporter who'd taken the job on. His name was Mike Harris. He specialised in pulling sting operations for the fish-and-chip end of Fleet Street. With a difference. If he thought he could extract a bigger pay-off from the victim by canning the story, he'd do it. He'd walk off with a big bundle of fivers and tell his commissioning editor that he'd probed the story but there was nothing doing. If the victim didn't pay up, they'd see themselves splashed over next week's paper.

I thought I could turn Harris's visit to the fleshpots of Brighton into a sting operation of my own. It took a bit of setting up. But with a couple of colleagues we fed Harris information about a joy house in Kemp Town. In reality, it was a studio occupied by two artists' models. They'd agreed to play along with the scheme – partly for the fun of it and partly for as much Babycham as they could drink if the wheeze worked.

For three evenings Freddie Barkworth and I lurked in the girls' back room waiting for the fateful knock. It came on the fourth night. The girls played a blinder. Freddie got a great snap of Harris with his trousers around his ankles while the primly dressed girls looked shocked. The *Chronicle* ran the picture on its front page under the headline: Sex Reporter Overexposed.

The story was picked up by other newspapers – and Harris was last heard of selling papers from a stand outside Wapping underground station in London. The *Chronicle*'s sting also ended the *News of the World*'s 'Bit on the Seaside' series before it reached Brighton.

And, unexpectedly, I became a hero to Brighton's madams. If I'd accepted all their offers of freebies, I'd have been walking around the town bow-legged. There were a few pursed lips and some tut-tutting from the primmer elements at the *Chronicle*. But – what the hell? – it's nice to be appreciated.

I'd never cashed in my favours with Brighton's madams, but now it was time to start a run on that particular bank.

Chloe Cuddles – Ethel Sproggett to her mother and father – was the fourth madam I visited.

My credit at the bank of madams' favours had evidently been

holding up well. At each I'd been offered a 'quickie on the house'. (I'd used the excuse of an old rugby injury to decline without giving offence.) But when I asked about Selina Muppen, they'd looked vague, eased the elastic in their corsets and shaken their heads.

But not Chloe. The best word to describe her would be imposing. She was about four foot eight – in most directions. She had a round moon-face that was always laughing and lots of blonde hair in curls. She was laced into a black bustier apparently manufactured from super-strength elastic and reinforced steel. Her enormous breasts jutted forward like the twin prows of a pair of battlecruisers. She was wearing a lacy peignoir over the whole ensemble. She looked like a female wrestler having a night off.

Chloe's scarlet lips split, like a gash in a watermelon, into a welcome grin. "Mr Crampton, how good to see you. Come round because that nice Australian girlfriend of yours can't keep up with your pace?"

I smiled. "This is business, not pleasure, Chloe."

"Pity. You still haven't taken up our offer of a quickie on the house. You'd like our Sophia, a genuine Italian beauty from Grimsby. Granted she's not Australian, but she knows all about down under, if you know what I mean."

I said: "It's a Selina rather than Sophia I'm looking for. Specifically, Selina Muppen. Do you know her?"

"Knew, more like."

I felt my heart pound faster in a new rhythm. Full of zip and bounce.

Like it was dancing the quickstep on a trampoline.

So Selina Muppen really existed.

I tried to keep calm and organise the questions I wanted to ask into a logical order.

"She worked here?" I said.

"For a couple of years. She was a good girl."

"By which you mean a bad girl."

Chloe grinned. "Depends which way you look at it."

"What do you know about her?" I asked.

Chloe gave me a searching look. "Is she in trouble?"

"No. But she could help a man who is."

Chloe shrugged. "Men, trouble. They go together. At least, they do here."

"How well did you know Selina?" I asked.

"She talked a bit. More than most of them, if I'm honest. I think it was because she'd had no one to talk to for so long. At least, no one who'd lend a sympathetic ear. I think she looked on me as a kind of honorary mother."

"When did she come here?"

Chloe scratched her ear while she thought about that. "It would be two years come next February. Told me she'd been a stripper in London. I sussed her straight away. She was already a working girl. And running away from something. But they all are. Anyway, I took her on. She was a looker – a Swedish blonde with her figure is like a top-of-the-range Bentley in this game."

"More of a Volvo, I'd say."

"Don't know what you're talking about. Whatever, she soon proved popular with the punters. And over the months she began to open up. Not all at once, you understand. Little snippets here and there. It turned out that she'd come from Gothenburg in Sweden. Been a good pupil at school, but fell in with the wrong crowd. Her parents were both regulars at some strait-laced church. You know the kind. Act like an angel or burn in hell. Anyway, they didn't approve of the company she was keeping. There was a row and she left home."

"And went to Paris, I believe."

"Yes, she told me something about that. Looked like she'd make it as a dancer at one stage."

"But that didn't work out," I said.

"More trouble. That Selina seems to be a magnet for bad men.

Some girls are. She got mixed up with a gang dealing drugs in Montmartre. They used her. Made her the gang's runner. Then a rival dealer shopped her to the cops and she spent eighteen months inside. She laughed it off when she told me. But I could see that it had scarred her."

"Didn't she put that behind her when she came to Britain?"

"I think she tried. She got hired as a stripper in a Soho club. But then the old bad-man magnet switched on. And this time it was really bad. A sleazeball called Doug Tupper latched on to her. Gave her plenty of the smooth chat. She was better than stripping in a basement club, he said. They should be together, he said. She could entertain gentleman privately in a Mayfair apartment. Just for a few months. She'd become rich and live her dream to travel the world, he said."

"And she fell for it?"

"They always do, darling. She'd already been knocked about by life. She was still a vulnerable kid at heart. She soon found that Tupper's promise of a luxury flat to entertain gentlemen – company directors, peers of the realm, bankers – were lies."

"The bankers turned out to be bonkers?"

"If you want to put it like that. Punters, I'd call them. Selina called them worse. She tried to leave, but Tupper beat her up. He wasn't going to lose his best-earning girl. She said she didn't want to do it any more. But he said she had to. He moved her into a basement flat in St Pancras. Locked her in during the day. And when she still threatened to leave, he took away her shoes. And her clothes. Said she didn't need them in her work, anyway. But she did get away. One night when Tupper was drunk and had fallen asleep. She stole his keys and all the money on him, retrieved her clothes and fled with just what she was wearing."

"And came to you?"

"Eventually. When the money ran out. She was desperate. She had nowhere to go and she couldn't stay in London because she knew Tupper would find her there. She hated the thought of the beating he'd dole out to her. And for a few months she was safe."

"And then he found her again."

"Yes."

"When?"

"It was just before Christmas last year. He'd come down to Brighton for the day and spotted her strolling along the Esplanade. I don't know what happened, but I can imagine. Men like that are cunning bastards. He'd have made more smooth promises, but with some even nastier threats behind them. But I don't know for sure. It's just what I think."

"How do you know she went off with him?"

"Because he came here to let me know that if I tried to get her back, he'd see to me. I believed him, too. He showed me a nasty little revolver. Said he'd used it for target practice on people who'd crossed him. I've seen some low life in my time, but Tupper is pure evil."

"Did he take her back to London?"

Chloe shrugged. "Your guess is as good as mine, darling. Perhaps. But perhaps he kept her down in Brighton. Could be he was expanding."

"So you don't know where she is?"

"She'll be in a grotty flat somewhere with a sagging bed and stained sheets."

"Did she make friends among any of the other girls? Perhaps they could help me," I said.

Chloe shot me a sly grin. "All the girls here could help you, darling. But not with gen about Selina."

I punched my thighs in frustration. So this had turned out to be a knocking shop in a cul-de-sac.

Chloe said: "There is just one other thing; although I don't suppose it will be much help. A couple of months after Selina had disappeared, another girl came in here. About Selina's age, but brunette. And British. At least, her accent was. Wanted to know whether Selina was still working here. I was suspicious at first.

The local cops have been known to hire attractive women as narks to catch us out. Anyway, after a bit of a chat I thought she was genuine enough and told her the story. I left out some of the nastier bits. Turns out her name was Barbara.

"She'd been meeting Selina every few days until the girl fell under Tupper's influence. They'd go for coffee or a bag of chips. Cinema a few times. She was upset by the news that Selina had gone, but left me her address on a piece of paper. Asked me to get in touch if I heard from her."

"And you've still got the paper?" I asked.

"No. Lost it weeks ago."

I buried my head in my hands.

"But I remember the address," Chloe said. "It stuck in my mind: sixty-nine Congress Road."

I grinned. "I can see why you'd remember that."

Chloe laughed. "Are you sure you wouldn't like a quickie before you go?"

I shook my head. And then I had an idea.

"But there is something you might be able to help me with," I said.

It was close to midnight when I reached Congress Road. Late enough to hope that Barbara would be at home. But, perhaps, too late to persuade her to answer the door to a stranger.

Number sixty-nine turned out to be a smart Edwardian-style semi in a suburban street not far from Preston Park. There was a small front garden, smartly kept. Curtains were drawn in all the rooms, but a light showed through the stained glass window in the front door.

I marched up the garden path and rang the doorbell. I heard some ding-dongs chiming faintly far away in the house. A door opened and some sharp heels clacked their way up a tiled hallway. The shadow of a woman appeared behind the stained glass.

She opened the door and – if this were Barbara – I knew immediately why Selina would have befriended her.

The woman was wearing a tight-fitting black dress, which ended halfway down her thighs. She had fishnet tights and stiletto heels. She was about thirty but the heavy make-up – face powder, thick red lipstick and blue eyeshadow – made her look older. She was a working girl ready for action.

I said: "Are you Barbara?"

She smiled, revealing a set of teeth any dentist would have been proud to own.

"I can be anyone you want, handsome."

I said: "Is Selina here?"

The smile vanished. She scowled at me and moved to close the door. With a speed that wouldn't have disgraced a door-to-door salesman, I shoved my foot in the jamb. Winced as the door crashed onto it.

I said: "I'm here to help her."

"You've been sent by Tupper."

"No. Chloe Cuddles has told me about Tupper."

The door opened again.

"You know Chloe?"

"Well enough for her to offer me a freebie with any of her girls."

Barbara screwed her mouth in disgust. "She should never give it away. That's like communism."

"Working girls of the world unite. You have nothing to lose but your knickers."

"It's no joking matter."

"Neither is what's going to happen to Selina if you don't talk to me."

"Who are you, anyway?"

I rummaged in my jacket pocket for my press card. Yanked it out. Flashed it in Barbara's face. "Colin Crampton. *Evening Chronicle.*"

Barbara's face relaxed. "Journalists. They're lower down the social scale than we are. Only just above estate agents. You'd better come in."

I stepped into a small hall and Barbara closed the door behind me.

She led the way into a comfortable sitting room. It was furnished with a couple of easy chairs covered in red velvet. A standard lamp and a couple of wall lights bathed the room in a soothing pink glow. There was a carved wooden fireplace and a mantelpiece with various knick-knacks arranged along it.

In as few words as I could, I explained why I'd come.

While I spoke, Barbara peeled the cellophane off a new packet of panatellas, selected one and lit up. She blew a long stream of smoke across the room.

"That's why I must find Selina," I said. I glanced at my watch. "And I now have less than nine hours to do it."

Barbara leaned back in her chair. Puffed on her panatella.

"Selina came here last night," she said. "It was the first time I'd seen her since she left Chloe's."

"Does that mean she'd got away from Tupper?"

"Run away, more like. And she'll regret it if he finds her."

"But I don't understand, why now?"

Selina flicked the ash from her panatella into the fireplace.

"I don't know all of it myself. When Selina arrived last night she was exhausted, poor kid. She told me she couldn't stay with Tupper any longer. She'd rather die than remain there. You see, she's beside herself that Archie Flowerdew is going to hang. Blames herself. Says she should have spoken up earlier."

My eyes widened at that news.

"Did Selina know Archie in a professional capacity?"

"She didn't tell me everything. Just that she knew for a fact that Archie didn't kill that other artist."

"Percy Despart."

"Yes. But she couldn't say why she knew."

"For heaven's sake, why not?"

"I don't know. All she would say is that what would happen to her would be worse than anything Tupper could do."

"Where is Selina now?"

Barbara took a final drag from her panatella and flung the dog-end into the fireplace.

"I don't know. She left this morning. I wanted her to stay, but she said it would be hard on me if Tupper found her here. I tried to tell her we'd deal with him together, but she wouldn't hear of it."

"And you've no idea where Selina is now?"

"Sleeping rough in a shop doorway, maybe. She's nowhere to go. Tupper always made sure she had no spare cash."

I leaned back in the chair. Tried to imagine what a poor hounded girl, with a monster on her trail, would do. She'd run, certainly. But where to?

Barbara said: "I want to go to bed. To sleep, in case you have any ideas."

"My only idea is to find Selina. Let me ask you one last question. When you used to meet Selina in the days when she was with Chloe, what did you do?"

"This and that," Barbara said.

"But there must have been something Selina liked to do."

"She liked to get away from people. Especially men. Sometimes in the summer, we'd take the open-top bus up to Devil's Dyke. In the winter, when the summer crowds had gone, we'd walk on the West Pier. I remember she'd stand on the end of the pier for ages just staring at the sea. I asked her once whether she was thinking of jumping in. But she said she just liked to watch the movement of the waves. Said it relaxed her. Poor kid, nothing much else did. She loved the pier. Used to buy postcards of it when she had a few coppers."

Barbara yawned. "It's surprising how tired you get when your work involves spending the day in bed," she said.

I stood up and made my way into the hall. Barbara followed me. I turned at the front door. "Lock your door securely tonight," I said.

Barbara managed a grim little smile. "Always do, ducks. And, listen, you won't mention me in your paper, will you?"

I stepped through the door and closed it behind me.

Chapter 22

I left Barbara's house, climbed into the MGB and sat staring through the windscreen at the street.

I felt tired. More tired than I could ever remember being in my life. My eyes ached. But I knew I couldn't sleep.

I wondered whether Archie had managed to sleep on what would be the last night of his life. I didn't think so. He would sit up counting off the hours. In his life, an hour would become like a minute. A minute would seem like a second. Time would accelerate. He'd want to think about things that were important to him. To dwell on the happy moments in his life. To force the darker thoughts from his mind. But fleeting time would make that impossible.

Besides, the creeping fear that had lurked inside him would now bubble to the surface like a foul effluent. Archie was a man with artistic imagination. And now that gift would become a curse. Because his mind would conjure up the feel of the noose, the sensation of it tightening around his neck, the churning of his insides as the trapdoor opened. He would try to push the thoughts to the back of his mind, but they would flash back. Again and again. In widescreen and technicolour. He would become a slave to his nightmares.

And then he would shake with fear.

With difficulty, I pushed the thought from my mind.

I had seven hours before that trapdoor opened and I would use every minute to try to save him. Even though my brain felt like an engine running on empty. Even though my body had all the zip of a clockwork toy whose spring had snapped.

But I needed a plan. I had to make each minute count as two. What Barbara had said convinced me that Selina was the key to the mystery. She'd felt mounting distress in the past few days as Archie's hanging approached. Archie had claimed as long ago as his trial that he had an alibi witness. He'd said that she was a woman. Now I knew it was Selina.

Could Archie have been unwilling to name Selina because he'd been using her professional services? It was something he'd surely be ashamed of if it became known. He'd be embarrassed. But a red face is better than a broken neck.

Barbara had told me that Selina felt responsibility for Archie's predicament. That she knew for certain Archie hadn't killed Despart. So why hadn't she come forward? Perhaps it was impossible with Tupper keeping her a prisoner. But she'd escaped. She could have gone straight to the police and told her story. Instead, she'd flown to her friend – and then disappeared.

But had she vanished beyond my reach? Brighton was a big town and she could be anywhere. Barbara had suggested she might sleep in a shop doorway. It was possible, but I didn't think likely. The uniformed plods who patrolled the streets at night liked nothing better than arresting doorway dossers. It gave them an excuse to get back to the warmth and comfort of the cop shop, where they could have a nice cup of cocoa while they checked the poor sap into the cells.

Selina was a deeply disturbed woman and she would avoid more trouble. Besides, what had Barbara said? She liked to get away from people. Sometimes by bus rides up to Devil's Dyke. Sometimes with walks on the West Pier – to gaze at the sea because it helped her find peace.

No buses ran at night to Devil's Dyke and it would be too far to walk. But West Pier was close to the centre of town. It was closed at night. But people could climb over the turnstiles when no one was looking. I'd done it myself.

I fired up the MGB and drove to the nearest telephone box. I called Shirley's flat.

She seized the receiver after the first ring and said: "What's happening, Colin? Tammy is beside herself here."

In a few words, I told Shirley about my meetings with Chloe

and Barbara. "I think Selina may be on the West Pier. If she's there, I'm going to find her."

"There's more, isn't there?"

"What do you mean?"

"It's your voice. I've never heard it so tense. What is it, Colin? I have to know."

I said: "Her pimp is looking for her. A vicious thug called Tupper. If he gets to her first he could kill her. He's armed with a revolver."

"I'm coming, too."

"No, it's too dangerous. Besides, Tammy needs your support."

But Shirley had already slammed down the receiver.

I pulled the MGB into the kerb beside West Pier five minutes later and climbed out. It was those wee small hours when the world sleeps. So the seafront was deserted. No cars. No people. There'd been a stiff wind earlier and big waves were breaking on the beach. The roar of pebbles being dragged by the undertow of the waves filled the air. I looked out to sea. A full moon emerged from behind a cloud. It threw a pencil of yellow light across the water. The moonbeam cast West Pier into a ghostly patchwork of light and shadow.

I hurried to the seaward side of the prom and stared out to sea. Moonlight glinted on the dome of the theatre at the end of the pier. I strained my eyes, searching for movement. I thought I saw a figure dash down one of the colonnades. But the flickering shadows teased my eyes.

I couldn't see Selina. I'd felt so certain she'd be here. Now I was not so sure.

I walked swiftly over to the turnstiles. I glanced left and right to make sure the coast was clear. I flexed my left leg for a jump. Grabbed the turnstile's top rail for leverage. And swung my right leg to lift it over the gate.

And I was on the pier.

There was no turning back now.

I crept slowly towards the sea end of the pier, keeping to the shadows of the colonnades and pavilions.

My footsteps on the boards clumped like muffled drumbeats.

I approached the theatre not knowing what I would find.

Back towards the landward end of the pier the roar of a motorcycle in Kings Road broke the silence. For a moment I stopped. Looked back at the road. But I saw nobody.

I moved on. I turned the corner behind the theatre and trudged into the promenade area at the far end of the pier. In daytime, it would be crowded with fishermen hopefully casting lines out to sea.

Instead, a lone figure leant on the rails.

Selina was gazing at the waves. Just as Barbara said she did.

She must have been absorbed deep in her thoughts. She didn't hear me as I walked towards her.

I said: "Selina."

She swung round and I saw a pale face with large eyes and a sensual mouth that had dropped open with shock. Her long blonde hair gusted in the wind. She brushed it from her face. She had a kind of ravaged beauty. Fine features but haunted eyes. Skin drawn just a little too tight over her cheeks. She was dressed in a thin coat that ended just above her knees. She wore no gloves and her hands were crabbed with the cold.

She grabbed the rails as though they offered some kind of protection and screamed: "Don't come near me."

I said: "I'm not Tupper. I'm a friend."

"Tupper sent you."

"Barbara told me you liked to come here."

"You know Barbara?"

"I met her an hour ago. She told me you'd been with her. She told me a lot about you. I know how hard it's been. I want to help."

"I don't believe you. Those are just the kind of lies Tupper's thugs would tell."

I spread my arms like a supplicant priest before the altar. "Look at me, Selina. I'm Colin Crampton. Do I look like one of Tupper's thugs?"

Her right hand let go of the railings. She moved half a step towards me. "I haven't seen you before. Tupper is cunning."

"What are you doing here, Selina?"

With the agility of an acrobat, she swung her legs over the railings and clung to them precariously. One tiny slip and she would fall. The sea surged and boiled around the pier's pilings twenty feet below.

"I'm going to kill myself," she screamed.

I moved towards her.

"Don't come any closer," she yelled. "I'll let go if you do."

"Can we just talk?" I asked.

"What's to talk about now?"

"How we can save Archie Flowerdew."

"You know Archie?"

"No. I've never met Archie. But I'm friends with his niece, Tammy. She wants to save her uncle. I'm helping her."

"No one can save Archie now."

I glanced at my watch – three o'clock. "We still have six hours," I said.

"How can we save Archie in six hours?"

"We can find the truth. I believe you know the truth."

"The truth won't save Archie," she said. "And I can't think of any lies that will help him. That's why I'm going to kill myself on the same day he dies."

"Did you love Archie?" I asked.

"Love? It doesn't exist. There are just men and women – strong and weak. I should know. I'm weak. That's why Tupper says it's right he should beat me."

"Women don't have to be weak. You should meet my girlfriend, Shirley."

"She'd never survive Tupper."

"I wouldn't bet on that."

"Nobody could put Tupper down."

"If I know Shirley, she'd do it."

"I won't live to see it."

She loosed one hand from the railings. Her body swung out over the sea.

"Don't let go," I shouted. My voice echoed off the wall of the theatre.

She swung back. Grabbed the railings with both hands.

"I want to ask you about Archie."

"What about Archie?" she said.

"How did you come to know him?"

"He came to the house after Tupper moved the man in upstairs. In the flat above me."

"Who was the man?"

Selina thought about that. Looked down at the sea. "Just some man Tupper knew. He called him Bert. He'd just got out of prison. Tupper thought Bert would keep watch on me when he wasn't there. The man was a beast. As bad as Tupper."

"When was this?"

"In January. Just after the new year."

"I don't understand. Why did Archie come to the house after Bert moved in?"

"Because Bert was his brother."

The news hit me like a steam hammer. My mind buzzed into overdrive. The facts lined up in my mind.

Of course, Gilbert. Or Bert, for short.

Archie's adoptive brother.

And Tammy's father.

He'd been sentenced to prison years earlier for a long stretch. Tammy had told Shirley and me after I'd rescued her from the Royal Pavilion. But she'd never told us that he'd been released. Perhaps she didn't know. Or perhaps it was one more fact she'd kept from us.

I moved closer and said: "If Archie came to call on Bert, how was it you came to know him?"

"The first time Archie came Bert was out. He usually was – getting drunk in some boozer. Then coming back and expecting me to lie on my back and pretend I was enjoying it. I met Archie in the hallway. It didn't take long for us to realise we both hated Bert. Both of us wanted him out of our lives."

"If Archie hated Bert, why had he come to see him?"

"He told me the second – no, the third – time he came. Bert had come to Brighton to find Tammy. She was living in the town and Archie was keeping an eye on her. Bert wanted to know where she was. Wouldn't give up. Archie was trying to persuade Bert to go elsewhere. Convince him that Tammy didn't want him in her life any more. He gave Bert money to go away. But the bastard just took Archie's money and spent it on beer. We both wanted rid of Bert."

"Archie was with you the evening Percy Despart was killed," I said.

Selina gave a solitary nod. "Yes."

"So you're his alibi?"

"Yes."

"Even at this late hour, you could save him from the hangman's noose."

"I can't."

I slapped my thigh in frustration. "Why not?"

A man's voice said: "Because I'm going to stop her."

I swung round. A broad-shouldered man with a head of greasy hair combed back from his forehead was standing by the theatre. He had a fleshy face and a nose that looked as though it had been broken not long in the past. His eyes didn't blink. They were as hard as marbles. He was dressed in black motorcycle leathers. And I realised that the motorcycle I'd heard earlier must have been his.

He looked beyond me to Selina and his lips twisted into an ingratiating smile. The kind that offers salvation but hides the damnation that's its true promise. And I could see how he used it to dominate women.

"Now now, my little trollop," he said. "You don't want to stay out there. You might fall in and get wet."

He had a deep voice, which could have been impressive if he'd worked on it. Instead, it came out somewhere between a brusque command and a wheedling whine.

"Go away," she screamed. "I don't want you here."

Tupper moved towards me but kept his gaze on Selina. "If you didn't want me here, you wouldn't have pinned up all those nice postcards of West Pier by your bed, now would you?"

"Keep away from me or I'll jump," Selina shrieked.

"You know you don't mean it. Not on Christmas Eve. I've got a surprise for you."

"I don't want any of your surprises," Selina yelled.

Tupper moved closer towards her.

I stepped in front of him.

I said: "Selina's taking some time off from work."

Tupper curled his lip. "Really? How much time?"

"The rest of her life," I said.

"I'll decide how much time she takes off. As her business manager."

He leered at me and I caught the smell of whisky on his breath.

I said: "Consider me her union rep. Here's my first offer."

I took a swing at him with my right fist – a haymaker of a punch that should have put him on his back. But he dodged it and laughed. He reached into his pocket and pulled out a long black chain. He'd welded sharp bolts to one end of it.

He laughed again, this time a throaty chuckle loaded with menace.

"Here's my counter-offer." He swung the chain at me.

I leapt backwards. The chain flashed inches from my nose. I heard its sibilant whistle as it whisked through the cold night air.

Tupper advanced and swung again.

This time I was ready and moved back further.

But Tupper had the determined look of a man who knows he'll eventually land a blow.

On the far side of the pier, I glimpsed Selina climb back over the railings and rush towards Tupper.

"Leave him alone," she screamed.

"You keep out of this, whore. I'll deal with you later."

Tupper rushed towards me. He swung the chain like a flail. But I caught his arm and yanked him sideways. I kicked his legs from under him. He crashed onto the boards. I moved forward to kick him in the ribs, but he rolled away and scrambled back on to his feet.

But he'd dropped the chain.

"It's a fair fight now," I said.

Tupper grinned. "Sure. A fair fight."

He reached inside his leather jacket and pulled out a snub-nosed revolver.

"He's going to shoot us," Selina yelled.

"Not you, tart," Tupper leered. "Dead meat's no use to me. I need fresh flesh to keep my punters happy." He swung round and levelled the gun at me. "One shot on the pier at this time of night. Nobody will hear it."

"Don't be so sure of that," I said.

I began to back away.

"Think you can run faster than a bullet?" Tupper jeered.

"We're just about to find out," I said.

Ted Wilson had once told me handguns were remarkably inaccurate even at short range. Only one in two bullets fired found its target. I hoped he was right. If I ran now I'd have an evens chance.

But as I backed away, Tupper moved closer. A grey tongue

flicked his lips. His hand was tense on the trigger. His eyes were alive with fire. They were burning into me. He was enjoying the moment.

And then he fired.

I heard a crack as the bullet flew past my ear. Then a ping as it ricocheted off railings on the far side of the pier.

If Wilson was right, that was the one that missed. The next would find its mark.

I decided to rush Tupper and go down fighting.

But then his gaze flicked to something behind me. He looked confused. Bemused even. His gun hand dropped.

I spun round.

Shirley was standing on the far side of the pier. She was waving something in her hand.

She shouted with a long, ululating cry, which rose into the air. It was like no sound I'd heard before. Not from Shirley. Not from anyone. It was like a call to battle. Like a war whoop from an army of ghosts.

Shirley's arm shot into the air. It waved in a circle. Her wrist gyrated like it was double-jointed. And then she released the thing she'd been holding in her hand.

It flew into the air, twisting and gyrating like a drunken bat. The moonlight caught its edges, which sparkled like they were encrusted with diamonds.

And I knew that Shirley – my Shirley, my super sheila from the Outback – had thrown a boomerang.

The strange shape whirled in a curving arc over the sea, like a shooting star that had lost its way.

I forced my gaze back to Tupper. A grin – no, it was more of a rictus – of disbelief had appeared on his face. Yet he could not drag his eyes from the boomerang.

It turned in the sky as though ordered by an invisible air controller. I heard a chopping sound as it curved back towards the pier.

And at that moment a light flashed in my brain. Like doors had been opened on to a blazing sun. It was that moment when an insight that was previously way beyond your comprehension becomes clear – translucent with its own logic. And here it was reaching down the millennia in front of me. The simplest of artefacts handed down from prehistory was harnessing laws of physics – of aerodynamics, of gravity – that must have been unknowable to those who had devised it. And so it seemed like a miracle – as much to we who watched it now as those who'd marvelled at the dawn of time. And that was why we stood transfixed in wonder, unable to tear our eyes away.

And then the light in my brain went dark. And I realised vital seconds before Tupper what would happen next.

I ducked.

I felt strange pulses in the air as the boomerang passed over my head.

And then I heard the crunch of hard wood against bone as it hit Tupper full in the forehead. I turned towards him. His eyes had swivelled upwards in their sockets. Blood trickled from his temple where the sharp end of the weapon had cut into his skin.

His legs crumpled underneath him and his body thumped on to the pier's boards.

The boomerang landed with a clatter. Did a dervish dance across the boards. And skittered into the sea.

Shirley and Selina raced towards me. I reached down and removed the revolver from Tupper's grip.

Shirley collapsed into my arms. Tears had welled in her eyes. She sobbed on my shoulder.

I held her tight and stroked her hair.

"It's all right," I said. "I'm still in the land of the living."

In a tear-stained voice, Shirley said: "That's not why I'm crying, you mad bastard."

"Then why?"

"It was the boomerang. It was going to be your Christmas

present. Now I've got nothing to give you."

I hugged her tighter. "I'd just be happy to be with my very own Christmas fairy," I said.

She looked at me through her tears and smiled.

"And, anyway, how did you learn to throw a boomerang like that?"

"My uncle Barwon taught me."

"You've never mentioned him before."

"He wasn't a blood uncle. He was an aborigine. He used to come to our house to work in the garden when I was a kid. At least, that's what he was supposed to be doing. Most of the time he was teaching the finer arts of slinging the 'rang."

"Thank heavens he taught you well. If Ted's statistics on firing handguns are right, you saved my life."

I put my arms around Shirley, drew her close and kissed her.

Selina said: "What are we going to do with him?" She pointed at Tupper's body.

I reached down and felt for a pulse.

"Is he dead?" she asked.

"No, just unconscious."

"Pity." She drew her cheeks together and then spat a huge gob of spittle on his face.

"That's not nice," I said.

"He's not a nice man," she said.

From the landward end of the pier, I could hear the shrill ringing of a police car's bell.

"It looks as though Tupper was wrong about no one hearing a gunshot on the pier," I said.

Chapter 23

Detective Chief Superintendent Alec Tomkins glared at me through eyes still half asleep.

He said: "Mrs Tomkins doesn't take kindly to me climbing over her at five o'clock in the morning. It gives her dangerous ideas."

I said: "Then get out of bed on your side."

"It's pushed up against the wall. We've got a very small bedroom. We don't all live in luxury flats on the seafront."

Only a copper like Tomkins who'd spent much of his working life divorced from truth could have made Mrs Gribble's tenement sound like a Park Lane pad.

We were in an interview room at the police station.

Earlier, the police had arrived at West Pier in a blur of movement. Blue lights flashed. Whistles blew. Feet pounded. Voices shouted. But by the time they'd reached the end of the pier, the action was over.

Shirley, Selina and I had been hustled in cop cars to the station. We'd been kept apart and held in separate interview rooms. Tupper had been whisked under police guard by ambulance to the Royal Sussex County Hospital to have his boomerang bruises X-rayed and dressed. And a cosy cell at the cop shop was waiting for him. His pimping days in Brighton were over.

The handle on the interview-room door rattled. The door opened and a uniformed toady stuck his head round.

He said: "It's seven o'clock and the canteen's just opened. Do you want me to get you a bacon sarnie, guv?"

Tomkins said: "Plenty of brown sauce."

I said: "While you're ordering bacon sandwiches an innocent man is probably throwing up his hearty breakfast, just two hours before he's due to hang."

Tomkins shrugged. "Let's go over it again."

I said: "We've already been over it three times. The only pertinent point you need to keep in mind at the moment is that Selina Muppen can provide Archie Flowerdew with a cast-iron alibi. He no more killed Percy Despart than you did."

"Don't get snippy with me. I arrested Flowerdew. Never liked the cut of his jib."

"This may come as news to you, Tomkins, but we don't hang people in England because you don't like the cut of their jib. You need to contact the Home Office duty officer immediately and tell him that fresh evidence proves Archie is innocent."

"All in good time."

"We don't have good time. The only time we have is short time. And that's running out. While you're waffling about your bedtime acrobatics with Mrs Tomkins and how you like your bacon sandwiches, a man's life is dribbling away minute by minute."

"I'm not convinced we've got enough evidence to warrant stopping the execution. I think I was right about Flowerdew's guilt all along."

I thumped the table. "This is not about you. It's about Flowerdew. And justice."

Tomkins smirked. "We don't see a lot of justice in here. It's mostly crooks and con men on the make."

I said: "What more do you need to call the Home Office and tell them about the new evidence?"

"I need to interview Miss Muppen myself."

"Then get on and do it."

"I must conclude my interview with you first. So let's go over it again."

I stood up.

"Sit down," Tomkins snapped.

"No. I'm leaving."

"You'll leave when I say so."

"I'm here voluntarily as a witness." I moved towards the door. "But I've had enough. If you won't call the Home Office, I will. I'm going back to the *Chronicle* to do it now."

I reached for the door handle, but before I could turn it the door flew open. The toady stood there holding out a plate with the bacon sandwich.

I grabbed the sandwich as I went through the door. "Thank you," I said. "I haven't had breakfast, either."

Shirley was sitting on a chair in the corridor outside the interview room. She jumped up when I appeared and raced towards me. We embraced awkwardly. (Shirley would have given me hell if brown sauce from the sarnie had dripped on her jumper.)

She ran her hand over the bristles on my chin and said: "You look terrible."

I stood back and looked into her eyes. They were tired but sparked with fight.

I said: "You look terrific."

"I've given a statement."

"Who took it?"

"Your mate."

"Ted Wilson?"

"Didn't seem like a bad cobber."

"Unlike my own interlocutor. Tomkins. The man is delaying his interview with Selina so he can claim he didn't have first-hand evidence that she could alibi Archie. That way he doesn't have to call the Home Office and demand they delay the hanging."

"The bastard."

I said: "Granted, but let's deal with Tomkins later. I'm going to call the Home Office myself. Perhaps I can persuade someone to contact Brighton police direct to find out what's going on."

"I'll come with you."

"I think you should go back to your flat and stay with Tammy.

The poor kid must be at the end of her tether."

Shirley nodded. "Sure. It's going to be bad for her when nine o'clock comes." She paused. "And me."

I put my arms around Shirley and hugged her close. Too close, it turned out. She snatched the sandwich.

But she whispered in my ear: "If you've ever been brilliant, Colin Crampton, be brilliant now."

The clock on the newsroom wall pointed at quarter to eight when I burst through the swing doors.

It was Christmas Eve. But the place radiated all the fun of a funeral parlour. Phil Bailey pounded his typewriter like he wanted to kill it. Sally Martin chewed the end of her pencil and stared at her new year's calendar. Susan Wheatcroft took a mince pie out of a paper bag, looked at it like it was radioactive and put it back. Around the room, reporters prodded pencils at notebooks, mumbled desultory questions into telephones or flipped the pages of their diaries as if looking for something better on another day.

Frank Figgis stomped out of his office and came up to me.

He said: "After your adventures on the pier, you have a front-page lead to write."

I said: "There's a bigger story." I told how Tomkins had refused to call the Home Office about Selina's alibi evidence. "I'm going to call the Home Office duty officer now. I hope to persuade him to pass a message to Henry Brooke, the Home Secretary, to order a delay in the hanging."

Figgis shook his head. "Good luck with that. You know what the BBC TV's programme *That Was The Week That Was* said about Brooke."

"He was 'the most hated man in Britain'."

"And they added that, because he turned down valid pleas for clemency, he could 'get away with murder'."

"I know he's allowed hangings to go ahead, but public mood

is changing. Besides, if it's later proved Archie was innocent, Brooke will be hated even more than he is now."

Figgis patted me on the shoulder. "If your golden tongue can't save Flowerdew, no one can."

I hurried over to my desk. Rummaged in my contacts book for the Home Office number. Seized the telephone receiver and dialled.

But when I was finally put through to the duty officer, it turned out that my golden tongue had turned to lead. The duty officer – a man called Snetherton – adamantly refused to pass a message to the Home Secretary. He insisted only the police could ask the Home Secretary to consider a reprieve. I slammed down the receiver so hard I cracked the telephone cradle. What did I care? After today I wouldn't even be using the damned thing.

Figgis hurried up to my desk, looked at my face and said: "I don't have to ask how that went."

I glanced at the clock – ten past eight.

I said: "There's still fifty minutes. I'm going to call Brooke direct. Do you have a number for him?"

"Not his private line."

"I'll blag it from directory enquiries."

"No you won't."

"Why not? It's never bothered you in the past."

"Brooke is not some bent local councillor who nobody cares about. He's head of law enforcement in the whole country. Try to get his personal phone number and we'll have the security services crawling all over the office."

I slumped back in my chair. "So that's the end of the line."

Figgis pulled a packet of Woodbines out of his pocket, shook one out and lit up. "Not necessarily," he said after his first drag. "His Holiness will have Brooke's number. He was at Marlborough with Brooke. Those old-school-tie types stay in touch until they drop into the grave."

"Pope won't give me Brooke's private phone number. He's

sacked me."

Figgis grinned. "His Holiness never comes into the office on Christmas Eve."

"That figures."

"He keeps his private contact book in the top right-hand drawer of his desk."

"How do you know that?"

Figgis tapped the side of his nose. "Ask no questions and I'll tell you no lies."

"But Joan guards His Holiness's office like a dragon."

Joan Fotheringay was Pope's private secretary. She was a withered relic of the paper's pre-war days. She had a thin face, mean eyes and tut-tutting lips.

Figgis said: "I'll call Joan down to the newsroom on some pretext. That should give you a couple of minutes to nip into His Holiness's office and look up the number."

Figgis headed back to his office to organise the distraction.

I fidgeted at my desk, counting the seconds away. Joan stomped into the newsroom two minutes later. She had her arms crossed defiantly across her chest and a scowl on her face that made an Easter Island basilisk look like Crusty the Clown.

She barged into Figgis's office without knocking. I'd have enjoyed watching the verbal fisticuffs as Figgis deflated her balloon. But I had urgent work to do.

Heads turned as I raced across the newsroom. I took the stairs to the third floor two at a time. I was panting like a bookie's runner as I burst into Pope's outer office. I swiftly crossed the room and opened the door to his inner sanctum. I'd been in there only once before under circumstances I won't go into now.

The room had a thick Persian carpet, red flock wallpaper and heavy damask curtains with those fancy cord tie-backs you only ever see in *Homes & Gardens* magazine. The room radiated the kind of arrogance you get from snobs who drive their Rolls-Royces through puddles to splash bus queues. It was dominated by a huge desk made out of some opulent wood. Possibly walnut. Or it could have been oak. It certainly wasn't driftwood. The desk had red leather laid into the top. The leather had been hand-tooled with gold edging, probably by gnomes working by candle-light. There were fancy brass handles on the desk drawers. I moved across and tugged the handle on the top drawer. It slid open and I peered inside.

There were a couple of Manila files, which I hefted out. Underneath was a thick book bound in padded brown leather. I lifted it out and flipped the pages. It was Pope's contacts book. The edges of the pages had been cut away to provide an alphabet index down the side.

I opened the book at the Bs. There were three pages of names, addresses and telephone numbers, all carefully entered in His Holiness's spidery handwriting. I ran my finger down the list: Ballard, Best, Betteridge, Billmore, Bollington-Fyfe … Only one Brook. A Stephen Brook. Residing at The Mendicant's Rest, Stow-on-the-Wold. Not Henry. And not Brook with an -e on the end.

Perhaps His Holiness no longer hobnobbed with his old school pal. In which case, I was sunk. And Archie was dead.

But, wait. If Brooke and Pope were old school chums, perhaps he was listed under H for Henry.

I flipped over the pages. Found the Hs.

Haltemprice, Hamper-Smith, Hendricks, Henry …

Henry. I checked the full entry. Yes, Henry Brooke. A Hampstead private address. It had to be the one. Swiftly, I copied down the telephone number. Replaced the book in the drawer. Put the files back on top. Slammed the drawer shut with much less care than the craftsman who'd made it.

I'd left the inner sanctum and crossed the outer office when Joan stomped into the room.

Her eyes popped when she saw me.

She said in a voice that could have frozen a Christmas pudding: "What are you doing here?"

"Just called in to say goodbye to my editor."

"Mr Pope is not in the office today."

"Pity, I'd have liked to shake on leaving."

"You will have to shake Mr Pope's hand some other time."

"Who said anything about his hand? I was thinking his throat."

I went through the door before she could reply.

I was back at my desk within seconds.

Edition time was approaching, but the newsroom had become silent. Everyone knew what was happening.

No typewriters clacked. No telephones rang.

For five seconds I sat staring at my telephone. I was afraid to pick up the receiver. There had been so many last chances to save Archie's life.

But deep in my heart I knew that this was the last of the last chances.

And then I wondered how I could get Brooke to speak to me.

I had his private telephone number, but that didn't mean he would answer the phone.

What kind of house did he run? Was there a butler who'd give me the bum's rush? Would his wife pick up the phone and tell me to get off the line?

I reached out for the receiver. Withdrew my hand. It was shaking.

This was no good. Telephones magnify nerves. People can always tell.

I leaned back. Closed my eyes. Took a deep breath. I pictured Archie sitting in his cell. Probably shaking more than me. About to die. For a crime he didn't commit.

I felt anger surge deep inside my guts. My hand became steady.

Now I was ready.

I seized the receiver and dialled the number.

The phone rang four times before it was answered.

A young woman's voice, heavily accented, said: "'ampstead nine eight three four. 'Oo is speakings, *s'il vous plaît*?"

An au pair.

I said: "Snetherton, Home Office duty officer."

Yes, it was a lie. But, then, Brooke had told more than a few porkies in his political career. And, unlike most of his, my lie served a noble end.

"'Oo you want to speaks with?"

"The Home Secretary. It's an urgent matter."

"You holds the line. I see whether the 'ome Secretaries speaks with you."

I heard the receiver clumped down on the table. Dainty feet tripped off across a wooden floor.

I waited.

Heavier feet approached.

"Brooke speaking. What is it, Snetherton?"

"Actually, it's Crampton. Snetherton suggested I called you direct."

Not entirely true. But not entirely false.

"Crampton? Do I know you?"

"No. But you know my boss, Mr Pope."

"Pope? Do I know a Pope?"

"Gerald Pope. You were at Marlborough together."

"That Pope. Old stingy Pope. Knew the fellow slightly. He was my fag for a couple of terms. Hopeless. Couldn't fry a sausage to save his life."

"It's about saving a life that I'm calling."

"Whose life?"

"Archie Flowerdew's"

"Not a name I'm familiar with."

"He's the man whose plea for clemency you rejected last week."

"Oh, that man."

"He's the man who's going to hang in Wandsworth Prison in …" I glanced at the newsroom clock: "… fourteen minutes."

"That matter is closed," Brooke snapped.

"Fresh evidence has just opened it."

"What evidence? Nobody's told me about it."

"An alibi witness has come forward who swears Flowerdew was with her during the evening Percy Despart was murdered."

"I've not had any official notification of this."

"You wouldn't have. That's because the police officer who arrested Flowerdew is holding the witness at Brighton police station and is refusing to interview her formally until after Archie is hanged."

"What do you want me to do about it?"

"I want to you to order a temporary reprieve for Flowerdew until this evidence can be properly evaluated."

"That would be highly irregular. It would cause a lot of people a lot of inconvenience."

"Being hung for a crime he didn't commit would cause Archie a certain amount of inconvenience, too, Home Secretary."

"That's as maybe. But there's nothing I can do."

I was losing him. Perhaps I'd already lost him. I felt tired. I could feel something churning in my guts. I wasn't sure what it was. It wouldn't have been breakfast. Shirley had scoffed my bacon sandwich. Perhaps it was revulsion at this whole sordid business.

I said bluntly: "You can't enjoy being called 'the most hated man in Britain'."

"Politicians learn to grow a thick skin."

I said: "Sometimes people need a thick skin because they've got a closed mind."

"I don't follow."

"You attract criticism because you don't listen to other people's ideas."

"I considered the file on the Flowerdew case very carefully."

"But not all of the facts. Because now there are new ones."

Brooke harrumphed down the phone. "I can't be responsible for not considering facts that weren't placed before me."

"But you must give us a chance to place them."

"Time has run out."

"There are still twelve minutes to make the phone call."

"It's out of my hands."

"Make the call and give people a reason to think something different about you."

"The public has made up its mind about me. And I've made up my mind about them. In politics, sometimes you win and sometimes you lose."

I felt a cold fury rising inside me. I'd had enough of officials – police, judges, politicians – playing games of chance with a man's life.

I snapped: "Then, Mr Brooke, you're a fool – as well as an object of hatred."

"How dare you speak to me like that."

"Then show some compassion. Isn't Christmas the best time to do that?"

"Journalists like you will always give politicians like me a kicking."

"Then give us a reason not to. Show some mercy towards Archie Flowerdew. 'Blessed are the merciful: because they shall obtain mercy.' "

Brooke sighed. "If only that were true."

I said: "At least delay the hanging until you've received a report from Brighton police."

"Yes, if what you tell me about their delay is true, that would be worrying. Perhaps more questions in the House."

"And hostile editorials. If Archie hangs at nine o'clock, I can guarantee that at one minute past, I shall call Albert Petrie, the news editor of the *Daily Mirror*. By five past, he will have called Harold Wilson, the Leader of the Opposition. And by half past nine, radio will be carrying Mr Wilson's denunciations of a Home Secretary who let an innocent man hang. By ten o'clock, the political row will have reached such proportions that you will have received your instructions to report to the Prime Minister in Downing Street. And by quarter past you'll be walking down the street because you no longer have a ministerial car and chauffeur. Now do I have your attention?"

"You are a very impertinent young man, Mr Crampton. If you are wrong about this, I shall send the forces of law and order for you."

"But if I'm right?"

"That is the contingency that does now concern me. Very well, I will make the phone call."

I glanced again at the clock.

"You have five minutes. Thank you, Home Secretary."

I replaced the receiver.

I slumped in my chair not knowing whether to collapse or cheer. Around me the newsroom came to life again. I felt my back being patted. Fellow reporters crowded round to offer congratulations.

When Brooke considered all the evidence, he would have to release Archie.

If only I'd known the most crucial evidence was still to come.

Chapter 24

The call that changed everything came half an hour after I'd put the phone down on Henry Brooke.

It had been half an hour where the newsroom had moved into overdrive. Suddenly, everyone wanted a part of the story. Frank Figgis toured the room briefing the sidebars that always go to support a big splash. Phil Bailey was writing a piece on other prisoners who'd been reprieved at the last minute. Sally Martin was turning out a story on the softer side of a hated Home Secretary.

My first task had been to call Shirley and give her the news. She'd whooped so loud down the phone, the rest of the newsroom thought the fire alarm had gone off.

She said: "Got to go. Tammy's just burst into tears and I've got a feeling this is going to be a job for a whole box of tissues."

Then I'd hammered out the splash – the article that would appear under the main headline on the front page: Archie Flowerdew Freed.

I'd just rolled the last folios out of my old Remington and handed them to Cedric, when my telephone rang.

I seized the receiver and a worried voice said: "We need to speak. It's urgent."

It was a long time since I'd heard Ted Wilson's voice so tense.

I said: "How urgent?"

He said: "Life-or-death urgent. With the emphasis on death."

"Usual place, then."

"It won't be open yet."

"Then use the staff door at the side."

"Prinny's Pleasure doesn't have any staff."

"The door they'd use if it did."

I replaced the receiver.

Ted was hammering on the side door when I arrived.

From inside, we heard Jeff shouting: "If this is a police raid, let me get my socks on."

He opened the door. He was wearing a pair of long johns and two odd socks.

He said: "Can't you wait until opening time like my other customers?"

I said: "You haven't got any other customers. Go back to bed. We'll serve ourselves and leave the money on the counter."

"Mind you do." Jeff slouched up the stairs.

Ted and I hurried through to the bar, helped ourselves to drinks and took the corner table at the back.

I said: "You look like a man who's just been told he's got a week to live."

"I'm not the one who should be worried about living."

"Who's the unlucky devil?"

"Archie Flowerdew."

I nearly swallowed the lemon in my gin and tonic.

"Selina's evidence puts him with her the whole evening of the killing," I said.

"It does that, but it was why he was with her," Ted said. "When Tomkins finally got round to interviewing the girl the whole story came out. Tomkins insisted I sit in on the interview. You know we've always wondered why Flowerdew never used his alibi."

"Yes, I've been puzzling over that. It's one of the unanswered questions."

"Not any more," Ted said. "He couldn't use his alibi."

"Why?"

"Because his alibi was that he was at Selina's flat murdering the man upstairs. Gilbert Flowerdew, his brother."

I put down my glass so heavily the drink slopped on the table.

"Adoptive brother," I said mechanically.

I couldn't take it in. Archie Flowerdew was nearly hanged for a murder he didn't commit – but escaped punishment for one that he did. It was a travesty of justice.

No, a double travesty.

"But this means Archie could be charged with a new murder," I said.

"Will be," Ted said. "Tomkins is on his way to Wandsworth Prison now. He plans to arrest Flowerdew in the prison before he's released and bring him to Brighton for questioning about the new murder."

"How did this happen?" I asked.

"Tomkins teased it out of Selina over a couple of hours. You know what he's like. Nice cop offering tea and sympathy one minute, banging the table demanding answers the next."

"Selina would have been no match for him."

"It seems that when Gilbert was released from prison, he wanted to find Tammy. He had a score to settle because of the evidence she'd given against him at his trial."

"He bore a grudge against his own daughter?"

"Against everyone. Tammy was in lodgings in Brighton. She'd cut herself off from her father, so when he came out, he had no idea where she lived. But he did track down Archie. So he leaned on the poor bloke to tell him where Tammy was. Hand over Tammy's address or else. But Archie was stubborn."

"And some."

"He refused to let Gilbert know where Tammy was living. But he knew that eventually Gilbert would find out – and then he'd make the girl's life hell. As he had before. Gilbert had known that piece of lowlife Tupper inside. When he was out, Tupper gave Gilbert the use of the flat upstairs from Selina. No doubt he thought Gilbert could keep an eye on her when he was off running his other tarts.

"Anyway, one evening Archie called to plead with Gilbert to leave Tammy alone. The man was out. He usually was propping up the bar somewhere. But Archie met Selina."

"Selina had told me the same. They got talking and it turned out they both hated Gilbert for different reasons. They both wanted him out of their lives."

Ted nodded. "But she didn't tell you the next bit."

"I think she was about to on West Pier. But Tupper turned up."

"Well, I can fill that in. It seems that over the weeks Archie and Selina hatched a plan. Gilbert always left his door key on the top of the architrave above the door to his flat when he went out. Archie borrowed it one night and searched his room. The whole place was a slum. But Archie noticed that there was a loose joint on the gas pipe leading from the meter to a fire. The pipe had rusted badly.

"A few nights later, while Gilbert was out getting drunk, Archie entered his room again. He tied a piece of string around the rusty pipe and loosened the joint so it would pull out easily. He threaded the string through a nearby airbrick in the wall into the garden below. He hid in the garden waiting for Gilbert to roll back from the pub. When Gilbert had fallen into a drunken stupor, Archie tugged on the string. It dislodged the loosened joint in the pipe and gas poured into the room. Archie pulled the string off the end of the broken pipe and through the airbrick. What with the pipe already being rusty, the whole thing looked like an accident."

"The perfect closed-room crime," I said.

And, I realised, it explained the last two pictures in Archie's sketchbook. The eleven pipers – the gas fitters – were repairing the pipes in Gilbert's room. The drummers were beating out a death march at Gilbert's funeral.

It could also explain why Stella Maplethorpe had seen Archie dressed as a woman twice that evening – once on the seafront and once turning into New Steine. He'd have been heading for Gilbert's flat. He'd reckon his female rig would be the perfect disguise in case anyone noticed him in the area.

Ted said: "Next morning, Tupper discovered Gilbert dead in bed. Apparently, he moved Selina out of the place that instant. She didn't even get the chance to pack the few clothes she owned. There was no way Tupper wanted one of his girls, and himself, mixed up in an unexplained death. Selina moved on – free from Gilbert but not Tupper – and Archie thought he'd solved Tammy's problem forever."

"Until he needed an alibi for killing Despart," I said.

"That's it," said Ted. "Selina is being charged as an accomplice. And it looks as though Archie will hang, after all."

I hurried back to the *Chronicle* with my mind like a riot.

It was a though there were voices in my head shouting slogans at one another:

Archie is innocent.

Archie is guilty.

Archie must walk free.

Archie must hang.

'How many people have to die before this all ends?' the voices asked. Percy Despart, Toby Kingswell, Richard Stubbs, Gilbert Flowerdew.

Outside the Chapel Royal, the Salvation Army band was playing 'In the Bleak Midwinter'. It couldn't have chosen better. I knew a couple of souls who could do with a bit of salvation. Archie and Selina. In fact, I wouldn't mind a drop myself. And it wouldn't surprise me to find Shirley and Tammy in the queue.

A pert young Sally Army collector, with blonde hair peeping out from under her bonnet, shook a collecting tin in front of me.

She said: "Merry Christmas."

I fumbled in my pocket. Found sixpence. Slipped it in the tin.

"Merry Christmas," I said.

"Your soul will be saved," she said.

"If I give you a quid, could you save a job lot?" I said.

She laughed.

I tramped on towards the *Chronicl*e deep in thought.

My first worry was how I was going to tell Tammy. She thought her uncle Archie had been snatched from the gallows at the last moment. She'd be looking forward to welcoming him home for Christmas. She'd be writing a Christmas card, buying him a gift, hanging out a 'Welcome Home' banner. Far from bringing seasonal glad tidings, I'd be bearing news that the nightmare was about to start all over again.

My second concern was how all this would play out on the paper. I'd pushed hard to put the *Chronicle* behind the campaign that had cleared Archie of killing Despart. But how would the readers react when they discovered Archie really was a murderer? Would they switch to the rival paper? Would circulation plummet? And would I be lined up as the fall guy?

But I was forgetting. I'd already been sacked. In barely twelve hours, I would no longer be the *Chronicle*'s crime correspondent.

That didn't mean I wouldn't act like a professional in the meantime. Ted had given me an exclusive – and the *Chronicle* should be the first to carry it. But I needed to know more.

When I arrived back at the *Chronicle* I went straight to the morgue.

As I pushed through the door, I heard Henrietta say: "I couldn't manage another one."

I crossed to her desk and said: "Another what?"

Henrietta burped softly and said: "Mince pie. Last night was the mayor's annual competition."

"And I won," cried Mabel.

I turned towards the clippings table. The three Cousins were each sitting in front of large plates of mince pies.

"I won, too," said Elsie.

"And me," added Freda.

Henrietta explained: "For the first time in seventy-three years of the competition, the mayor decided there was nothing to choose between the top three entrants. So he's awarded the cup to be shared between the three."

Freda picked up the cup. "This will look good on my mantel-piece."

Elsie said: "And mine."

Mabel said: "Share and share alike, that's always been our motto."

The three started to argue about who should keep the cup first.

"Curious that all three should work in the same place," I said.

Henrietta looked embarrassed. She fiddled with the top button on her cardigan.

I said: "I know that look. You're hiding something."

Henrietta whispered: "Come into the filing stacks and I'll tell you."

We walked into the back room where the filing stacks ran from floor to ceiling. I sneezed as the musty air tickled my nose.

Henrietta said: "I knew that if one of them won, the other two would become impossible. Besides, they've all been cheating."

"How do you cheat with a mince pie?"

"You steal someone else's recipe. They knew I'd won the competition a couple of times in the past. Each of them is as sneaky as a snake. They each tried to tease my recipe out of me."

"And you gave the same recipe to each of them."

"Without the others knowing." Henrietta grinned. "So instead of pie war, peace has broken out."

"I wouldn't rely on that," I said. "But I'm not here to discuss mince pies. I urgently need a cutting. Do we have anything on Gilbert Flowerdew in here?"

"We certainly have Archie Flowerdew, but I don't know about Gilbert."

We traipsed through the narrow corridors to the filing cabinets with the letter Fs.

Henrietta pulled out a drawer. Rummaged through the files.

"Yes, there's a thin file." She handed it to me.

I took a quick look. There was one small cutting inside.

"I'll take this back to my desk," I said.

I sat at my desk and took the cutting out of the file.

It was a one-paragraph piece, probably from a news-in-brief column. It was headed: Man Died from Gas.

It read:

> Brighton coroner Sidney Walton returned a verdict of misadventure on Gilbert Flowerdew, who was found dead in bed in his Kemp Town flat from gas poisoning. The court heard that Mr Flowerdew had a dangerously high level of alcohol in his bloodstream.

That told me nothing I didn't already know. It was consistent with what Ted had told me in Prinny's Pleasure about Selina's confession. But if I was going to write a story about it, I needed more hard facts.

I lifted the phone and dialled a number at Brighton Town Hall. I asked to be put through to the coroner's office.

"There's no one in the office today," I was told. "Don't you know it's Christmas Eve?"

I thumped the receiver back in the cradle.

I'd hoped to get hold of a copy of the transcript of Gilbert's inquest. That would have told me more about what the police had discovered when they'd entered his room and found him dead.

The *Chronicle* nib didn't have a byline. Few news-in-brief items did. But the lumbering twenty-six word opening sentence carried the fingerprints of Jamie Hayes, the paper's court reporter. If Jamie still had his shorthand notes for the inquest, perhaps he could tell me more.

But Jamie wasn't at his desk. And Susan Wheatcroft, who sat at the next desk along, told me he'd gone out for a bevvy with some of the other reporters.

"Don't you know it's Christmas Eve, honeybunch?"

"Do you know where they're drinking?"

"Could be anywhere." Susan gave me one of her saucy winks. "But, hey, do you want to see what I've got in my Christmas stocking?"

I grinned. "Perhaps later."

I headed back to my desk not sure what to do next. I couldn't decide whether to write a story about Archie's re-arrest on the basis of what Ted had told me. Or to find out more first. On an evening paper with short edition deadlines, there's never any doubt about the answer to that question. You write what you know, before the competition scoops you.

But this could be the last story I'd ever write for the *Chronicle* and I wanted to get it right. I didn't want to leave the paper with angry critics chasing me down the street because I'd called it wrong. So I decided to wait until I could track down Jamie. No doubt he would appear after the pubs had closed at the end of their lunchtime session.

And then the telephone rang.

I lifted the receiver and Shirley said: "I thought you'd gone walkabout. Why haven't you been in touch? Tammy's been going mental here wondering why she hasn't heard that Archie's been released."

I said: "Is Tammy with you now?"

"No. I've told the kid to take a kip."

That, at least, was a mercy. I told Shirley what was happening. How Archie had been arrested for Gilbert's murder.

"I don't think Tammy can take another setback." Shirley's voice quavered with emotion. "I don't think I can take it."

I said: "Best not to say anything to Tammy just yet. I'm trying to get more details of Gilbert's inquest. That may give us a clearer idea of what happened."

"That's best," Shirley said.

"Try to get some rest yourself. I'll be in touch as soon as I have any news."

She hung up.

I sat back and surveyed the room.

A few of my fellow journos were still hammering on their typewriters. But the place had a sense of winding down for Christmas.

Like my career. In a few hours I'd be out of work.

While I was waiting for Jamie to lurch back from his lunchtime boozing, I wondered whether to clear out my desk. I decided I couldn't be bothered. The drawers were stuffed with my old notebooks, discarded story folios and used carbon paper. Whoever took over the desk could throw them out.

But wait a minute. Used carbon paper – that struck a memory.

When I'd typed out the story about Harold Beecher – the drunk who'd climbed a lamp post and been given a caution, not a cushion, by Abercrombie – I'd run out of new carbon paper and borrowed a sheet from Phil Bailey's desk.

A new carbon would bear a clear imprint of everything typed on it. It was only when a carbon had been used many times that the individual words became overtyped and illegible. If the new carbon hadn't been used since, it would prove that I'd typed 'caution' and not 'cushion'.

I closed my eyes and thought hard. What had I done with the carbon? Now I remembered! After I'd written the story, I'd given the folios and the carbon to Cedric. I'd asked him to replace the carbon in Phil's desk drawer. But which drawer had he put it in?

I stood up and hurried across to Phil's desk, yanked open the top drawer. There was a box of new carbons, from which I'd snitched one. No sign of the returned sheet, though. I tried the middle drawer. It was stuffed with Phil's old notebooks. No carbon.

The bottom drawer. A heap of old paper. I rummaged through it. And there was my original carbon. I held it up to the light. It had been used only once. And the imprint of my original copy was clear. And it read caution not cushion.

At least I could prove the mistake in the published story wasn't down to me. But that wouldn't stop Abercrombie's contempt-of-court case or change the fact that I'd been arrested and spent time in the police cells. It wouldn't save my job, but it would redeem my honour.

I hurried to Figgis's office to show him the evidence.

Jamie Hayes lurched into the office at twenty to four.

He swayed a bit as he crossed the office to his desk.

I hurried over to him and said: "Good lunch?"

"Great. All eight pints of it. Merry Christmas."

"Let's save the seasonal greetings for later. I'm on a big story and I need your help."

Jamie giggled. "You need my help? Do you think they'll give me your job when you've gone?"

"I shouldn't think they'll give you any job unless you sober up a bit."

"Don't you know it's Christmas Eve?"

"You're the third person today who's asked me that."

"Great minds think alike."

"No, great minds think differently. It's dim minds that think alike. Which brings me to a piece you wrote back in the early spring. An inquest at the coroner's court into the death of one Gilbert Flowerdew. Ring any bells?"

Jamie burped and slipped sideways on his chair. I put out a hand to steady him.

"Coroner's court. Always dead boring. Geddit? Dead boring."

"Yes, hilarious. Save it for the Christmas crackers. Have you still got your notes of the Flowerdew inquest?"

"As it's you and you soon won't be here, I'll take a look."

Jamie pulled the drawer with his old shorthand notebooks so hard it flew out and fell on the floor. The notebooks skittered in all directions on the cracked lino.

We knelt down and started to collect them. I found the one with the notes of the inquest before he did. Which wasn't surprising, as he'd now decided to crawl around pretending to be a dog.

I said: "I'll borrow this for a while. But you'll have it back before I'm kicked out on the streets."

Jamie's face had turned a dark shade of green.

He said: "I'm going to be sick." And he grabbed the empty drawer and chundered into it.

Jamie Hayes was a buffoon who wrote overlong sentences and threw up into drawers.

But he wrote a neat shorthand note.

I sat at my desk, flipped the pages of his notebook and deciphered his clear Pitman's.

Jamie had done a good job. He had recorded all the essential evidence. I finished and closed the notebook.

My mouth was as dry as Jamie's had just become. And my heart was thumping like a big bass drum. The inquest's finding could not be wrong. It had examined all the evidence, but in the absence of Archie or Selina.

Then I thought about what Ted had told me.

I thought about the big flaw in Selina's confession to Tomkins.

And about Archie's curious foible that Tammy had mentioned.

And about what a drunken man might do on a cold night.

And, at last – at long, long last – I was convinced I knew what had really happened that night in Gilbert's lodgings.

It was incredible, but it had to be true.

And I would write it for the *Chronicle*. As my last ever front-page splash.

I seized my phone and dialled a number at Brighton Police Station.

Chapter 25

"Archie Flowerdew never killed his brother, Gilbert," I said.

Ted Wilson took a generous swig of his scotch and said: "We have a witness in Selina Muppen who says otherwise."

"No. You have a witness who says she saw Archie plan to kill Gilbert."

"Same thing," Ted said.

We were sitting at the corner table at Prinny's Pleasure. It was just after five o'clock on Christmas Eve. Jeff was behind the bar wearing a Father Christmas hat and a sulky frown. He was annoyed we'd refused the turkey sandwiches he had in a glass cabinet on the bar.

"It's not the same thing at all," I said. "I planned to continue my career at the *Evening Chronicle*, but it's not going to happen because of circumstances beyond my control."

Ted's mouth twisted into a regretful moue. "Yes. Heard about that. Really sorry. But I don't see how it affects Archie. As soon as Tomkins got him back to the station from Wandsworth, he had him in an interview room for questioning. I gather that Archie's confirmed Selina's statement. He's admitted he killed Gilbert. It pains me to say it, but Tomkins has a confession."

"Tomkins's confession will become stale faster than those turkey sandwiches," I said. "The man has been so eager to fit Archie up for a second murder he didn't do, that he's forgotten the most basic police work."

Ted looked worried. "What do you mean?"

"He hasn't looked at the transcript of Gilbert's inquest. All he had to do was walk along the corridor to the coroner's office and retrieve it."

"And you have looked at the transcript?"

"No, but I have read the shorthand notes of the *Chronicle* reporter who covered the inquest. The verdict was misadventure."

"Could have been wrong. It's been known," Ted said.

"Not this time. The detailed evidence proves it. Selina told you that Archie planned to gas Gilbert by breaking the junction on a piece of dodgy pipe."

"That's what both Selina and Archie now admit happened."

"Wrong again. It's what they think happened. Neither of them was in the room when the pipe is said to have broken. Of course, Archie thought the pipe had broken because he pulled the tied end of the string through the hole in the airbrick just as he'd planned. And as if to confirm it, Gilbert was dead on the bed in the morning. Official cause of death: gas poisoning."

"So case closed," Ted said.

"And it would have been if the *Chronicle* had run a fuller story of the inquest rather than just a nib. Then both Archie and Selina could have read the whole truth."

"Which was?"

"That the pipe didn't break, even though Archie tugged on the string. What broke was the knot that he'd tied around the pipe."

"You're saying the knot unravelled?"

"It came back to me in the newsroom half an hour ago. I remembered that when Tammy had been telling us about Archie she mentioned that he was hopeless at some simple things – like tying his shoelaces when he was a kid. They always came undone because he had a blind spot with tying knots. The inquest confirmed that the gas pipes in the room were still intact."

"So how did it happen, then? Someone must have gassed Gilbert."

"Someone did. He gassed himself. Selina told me he often returned from his drinking sessions incapable. The inquest heard that the gas tap on his ancient fire had been turned on. The meter in Gilbert's room had been emptied earlier in the day, while he was out, the coroner's court was told. But there was a shilling in it. That could only have been inserted by Gilbert after he returned. According to my colleague's shorthand note, the inquest reasoned Gilbert must have turned on the gas but forgotten to light it."

"And do you buy that?"

"I think it happened a different way because of the evidence of the shilling in the meter. I can see Gilbert stumbling back into his room on a cold night. He lights the gas fire, but there was little credit left in the meter and the fire dies. He fails to turn off the fire's gas tap – an elementary safety precaution – before putting more money in the meter. He finds a shilling and shoves it in. The gas starts to flow. But before he can relight the fire he collapses on his bed in a drunken stupor. The gas from the unlit fire fills the room. The shilling's worth was enough to kill him."

Ted grinned. "Don't you know it's Christmas Eve?"

"Why does everyone keeping saying that?"

"Because it's true. And I'll take what you've just given me as a Christmas present. I know the chief constable has been getting a bit annoyed about Tomkins's high-handed ways. When this breaks, it's just what I need to take Tomkins down a peg or two."

I raised my gin and tonic. "I'll drink to that. Merry Christmas."

Ted raised his glass and drank. "Merry Christmas." He reached inside his pocket and pulled out a folded sheet of paper. "I've appreciated the help you've pushed my way this year. I thought this might help you. Don't know whether it'll be enough to save your job at the *Chronicle,* though."

"What is it?"

"It's a copy of the postcard Percy Despart was drawing in his studio the night he was murdered. It never got introduced into evidence at Archie's trial. When you take a look you'll understand why." He stood up and headed for the door. He turned back and said: "By the way, happy new year."

I unfolded the paper and gaped.

And then I laughed. Not a tiny hole-in-the-corner snigger. But a full-throated belly laugh.

I could feel my heart pounding hard.

Boom-ditty-boom-ditty-boom.

It was the second time in the day my heart had thumped like a bass drum.

But this time it was beating to a cha-cha rhythm.

Sir Randolph Abercrombie had a look on his face like a child who's just been told Father Christmas is going to snatch away all his toys.

He was slumped in a high-backed chair upholstered in red leather. He sat behind a huge desk with a silver inkstand. I perched on an upright wooden chair on the other side of the desk. But I felt like I was sitting on the throne of England.

We were in Abercrombie's office at Brighton magistrates' court.

He was staring at the sheet of paper I'd placed on the desk in front of him. His thick eyebrows were drawn together in a frown. His eyes bulged behind his rimless specs. His lips compressed in a scowl. And he had started to sweat. A sheen glimmered on his high domed forehead.

He said: "What is this?"

I said: "You know perfectly well what it is. It's the comic postcard Percy Despart had been drawing at the very moment he was murdered in his studio."

I glanced again at the drawing of the sexy woman lawyer and the leering magistrate.

Abercrombie's face had become crimson. "It's a disgrace," he spluttered.

"What's a bigger disgrace is withholding evidence," I said.

"I don't know what you mean."

"You were chairman of the bench at the committal proceedings when Archie Flowerdew was sent for trial. I recall the prosecution saying they didn't propose to submit certain papers in evidence. This drawing would have been one of them. Now why should the prosecution suddenly decide to withdraw papers it had previously included in the case?"

"You'd have to ask Truscott Bonner, the prosecuting counsel."

"I may just do that. But it's not hard to work out what happened. You knew this drawing would be made public and you had a quiet word with Bonner to remove it. I suspect you tipped him the wink that the committal would go without a hitch if he did. In fact, the prosecution evidence was thin enough for you to have rejected the case during the committal proceedings. If you'd have been acting like a fair-minded magistrate rather than watching your own back, you'd have done that. Archie Flowerdew would have been spared the agony of a trial, conviction and the nerve-shredding prospect of being hanged. And the town would have been spared the costs of it all."

Abercrombie ran a trembling hand over his sweating brow. "You can't prove any of that."

"You think not. In time, I think I can. I have the drawing. And I still need to speak to Bonner. Besides, I wonder what people will say when they see this drawing in print. I guess many will start to wonder what goes on in your courtroom – and out of it."

Abercrombie's face had turned crimson with rage. Above his wing collar, a vein in his neck pulsed.

"The *Evening Chronicle* will never print that. No newspaper in Britain will risk a libel writ."

"I know one that will."

"You're bluffing."

"Not this time. Have you ever heard of *Private Eye*?"

"You mean that London scandal sheet? Even they won't touch this."

"We'll see. The editor, Richard Ingrams, hates miscarriages of justice and will do anything to expose them."

Abercrombie drummed his fingers on the desk. "This is all about the contempt-of-court proceedings I've started against the

Chronicle, isn't it?"

I gave him my look of injured innocence. I leaned forward. Summoned up my most winning smile.

"Don't you know it's Christmas Eve?" I said.

"Of course. What's that got to do with anything?"

"Christmas is a time for forgiveness, I've been told."

"You mean I should forgive the *Chronicle* for its insolent misprint?"

"An honest error. And one that was swiftly corrected. Unlike withholding evidence at the committal proceedings."

An ingratiating smile appeared on Abercrombie's lips. "Forgiveness. Very commendable. Perhaps we should forgive. And forget?"

I grinned. "With a little mutual forgiveness, I think you can take it that any drawing you may have found offensive will be filed away from prying eyes forever."

"I have your word on that?"

"As one of Her Majesty's journalists and member of the fourth estate."

"I suppose that means yes," Abercrombie grumbled. "I'll tell my clerk to cancel the contempt proceedings."

I stood up and moved towards the door. I turned and faced Abercrombie. "Merry Christmas," I said.

"Is it?" he said.

I called Figgis from the phone box outside the court building.

I knew he'd still be in the office. He stayed as late as possible on Christmas Eve in case Mrs Figgis had her relatives round.

I said: "I bring good tidings of great joy to you and all mankind."

He said: "You're drunk."

"As sober as a judge – or, to be more accurate, the magistrate I've just seen."

"What are you up to now – creeping around the magistrates'

court?"

"You can take it that Abercrombie is dropping his contempt-of-court proceedings."

"How do you know that?"

"I've just seen him. He told me."

"Now why would he do that, I wonder?"

"Just put it down to my legendary powers of persuasion."

"You've got something on him, haven't you?"

"Not the kind of Christmas present he was hoping for. I'll tell you more back at the office. In the meantime, you'll pass the news to His Holiness. Do you think he'll rescind my sacking now?"

Figgis cleared his throat noisily. "It doesn't seem to be that easy."

"Why not?"

"He turned up at the office half an hour ago. Never known that on Christmas Eve before. But he seemed adamant about you. He wants you off the premises by midnight. He agrees the misprint wasn't your fault, and now you seem to have warned off Abercrombie. But that still leaves your arrest. That's Pope's sticking point. And there's nothing you or I can do about it."

"But the fact there'll be no contempt charge will change his mind, surely?"

"Pope changes his mind about as often as Mrs Figgis changes her hairstyle."

"When did she last do that?"

"It was 1953 – Coronation Day."

When I'd stepped into the phone box, I'd felt certain my news about the contempt proceedings would keep me on the paper. Now I felt like a party popper that had popped. There was nothing left.

I said: "I'll come back to the office and clear my desk."

Figgis started to say something, but the pips went. I didn't want to waste another four pence, so I put the phone down.

I'd run out of time in more ways than one.

Chapter 26

I trudged slowly back to the office through streets crowded with happy people.

A knot of office types surged out of The Cricketers singing 'I Want to Hold Your Hand'. The Beatles single was the Christmas number one. The merrymakers waved balloons at me and shouted happy Christmas. Across the street a young couple swapped stolen kisses in a shop doorway. A pair of drunks swigged from beer bottles as they staggered by.

Christmas was coming and, frankly, I couldn't care whether the goose was getting fat. One thing was for certain: when I lost my job I'd be scratching around even for a penny to put in the old man's hat.

It was past seven when I arrived back at the *Chronicle*.

The lights in the front office had been turned off. I doubted there'd be anyone in the newsroom. On Christmas Eve, they headed for the pubs early. So there'd be nobody to say goodbye to before I packed my few belongings and, like Dick Whittington, left to seek my fame and fortune elsewhere. The only bright point I could think of was that at least I wouldn't have to take a cat with me.

I dragged myself up the stairs and pushed through the swing doors into the newsroom.

And stopped in my tracks.

My eyebrows sprang north.

My jaw dropped south.

The newsroom was packed. Not a desk empty. Even Dickie Waterford, the paper's parliamentary reporter, was leaning against the bookshelf. It was said he hadn't been in the place since Clement Attlee was prime minister.

Sally Martin saw me first.

She shouted out: "He's here."

A ragged kind of cheer went up.

I said: "What's going on?"

She said: "We're having a sit-in."

"And we're not moving until Mr Pope reinstates you," Phil Bailey said.

"And if His Holiness tries to move me, honeybunch, I'll sit on him," Susan Wheatcroft said. She cuddled up to my side and kissed me on the cheek.

Then everyone in the room started talking at once.

Sally Martin climbed on a chair and shouted: "Quiet, you riff-raff. Someone's got to take charge."

Voices around the room: "Let's take a vote on it."

"Speak up, Sally."

"Who's got the beer?"

"Be quiet and listen."

Sally held up her hands for silence. The hubbub died down.

"A lot of you have been on the paper longer than me," she said.

"Like old Dickie Waterford."

"Oh, shut up, whoever said that."

"Yes, like dear Dickie," Sally continued. "And the fact he's here tonight of all nights when he could be spending it with his …"

"Bottles of vintage claret." Laughter.

"… with his family in Alfriston tells us how he feels. How we all feel. Colin has been on the paper for only two years."

"Feels like two hundred."

"More than that, surely?"

"Belt up and listen to Sally."

"In those two years, he's landed the paper some great stories. Stories that other papers didn't have – and wouldn't have found. Stories that needed to be told for all kinds of reasons. Sometimes because they righted a wrong. Sometimes because they fought for justice. Sometimes because they exposed bad people. And you can't find those kinds of stories without making mistakes. But if you're not prepared to take risks, the wrongs won't be righted, the injustices will fester and the bad people will walk free. I write for the women's page. Sometimes I'm writing about how to make an apron out of scrap material. Sometimes about how to bake scones. You won't catch many bad people when it comes to baking scones."

"You haven't tried my mum's scones." More laughter.

"As I was saying, you don't get to right many wrongs on the women's page. But I want to work for a paper that stands up for the decent values we hold dear. A paper that fights for justice for everyone – whoever they are and wherever they live. A paper that's not afraid to take risks to fight for the little people trampled on by the big battalions. Because that makes me feel proud when I walk into the newsroom in the morning. And when people ask me what I do, I can stand tall and say, 'I work for the *Evening Chronicle*. We're the paper that campaigned to save an innocent man from the gallows.'

"And we did. Or, rather, Colin did. That's why we need great reporters like Colin on this paper. Because his greatness rubs off on all of us. The victories he wins are victories we all share. The pride we get for working for this paper envelops us all. And that's why we're having a Christmas sit-in. And it's why we're not going to leave until we know Colin is going to remain a valued member of this newsroom."

Sally jumped down from the chair.

There was a moment's silence.

And then the cheering started.

The newsroom exploded into a ballyhoo of hurrahs and whoops.

They shouted. They yelled. They rolled sheets of copy paper into balls and tossed them in the air. They hugged each other. They slapped me on the back.

My throat felt tight. My eyes felt hot. My mouth was dry. My brain felt it was doing somersaults and swinging from a high trapeze at the same time.

I put my hand on my cheek and it was wet. And I didn't know whether I was crying for myself. Or for Archie. Or Tammy. Or everyone.

But it didn't seem to matter.

Because everyone was hugging me and crying, too.

And then the room went silent. Suddenly. Like a giant switch had been thrown and the world had been plunged into eternal darkness.

I swivelled round.

Frank Figgis was standing in the doorway. His mouth was set. The furrows in his brow seemed deeper than ever. He held a sheet of paper in his hands.

I pointed at it. "Have you come to give me my cards?"

He said: "I've just come from a meeting with the editor of this paper, Mr Gerald Pope."

"A prayer meeting was it?"

Figgis ignored the interruption. "I have some bad news for you all. Mr Pope believes that every aspect of the extraordinary stories of Archie Flowerdew and Selina Muppen should be told in detail in our newspaper. I have forcefully made the point that if the paper is to muster all the facts about these stories, it needs its full complement of editorial staff. I stress full complement.

"Mr Pope has decided that the paper will produce a Boxing Day edition for the first time in its history. And he has asked me to relay to you the unfortunate consequences of this decision. So the bad news I bring is that some of us, including myself, will have to work on Christmas Day."

Figgis grinned. "It is a matter of deep regret to me that I shall not be at home to sample Mrs Figgis's roast turkey alongside her sister, two aunts, an aged great-uncle and four cousins – one once removed and one who definitely should be. However, I swallow that disappointment with more relish than Mrs Figgis's chestnut stuffing. This paper I am holding contains a list of the names of those staff who will be required to work late tonight and those who are needed in the newsroom tomorrow. I shall pin it on the noticeboard outside my office. That's all."

He headed off to his office. Turned back. "By the way, you might be interested to know there will be an empty desk in the subs room in the new year. Mr Silas Burrage has decided to take early retirement."

A cheer went up.

I walked straight to my desk to start work. I knew my name would be on the list. I knew why Figgis had been in Pope's office. He'd been battling for my career on the *Chronicle*. I imagine he'd agreed to muster staff for a Boxing Day paper in return for me keeping my job. His downbeat performance in the newsroom had been his way of letting me know he didn't want any effusive thanks from me for fighting my corner with His Holiness. When it came to doing good deeds, Figgis was a man embarrassed by gratitude.

I sat at my desk, pulled the old Remington towards me and started typing the story that would lead the front page.

An hour later, I was rolling the last folio out of my typewriter, when Freddie Barkworth appeared at the side of my desk.

He handed me a photo in a small frame, winked and said: "Merry Christmas." He skipped off towards his darkroom.

I was about to take a look at the photo, when the telephone rang. I slipped the photo into my jacket pocket and lifted the receiver.

Ted Wilson said: "This you will not believe."

"If it involves more work, keep it to yourself."

"You'd rather I rang Jim Houghton on the *The Argus*?"

I sighed. "You already know the answer to that question."

Ted said: "After we'd arrested Florian Le Grande and Gideon

Burke as part of that painting scam, we searched his place in Lewes. We found another copy of that *Avenging Angel* painting among a job lot stacked against his studio wall."

"By a pupil of Raphael," I said. I'd kept shtum about the fact I knew the original was by Raphael – and that Camilla Fogg had scarpered abroad with it. If Tomkins knew I'd been involved in her escape – even though I couldn't do anything about it – there'd have been more trouble than even I could handle. And I couldn't tell Ted in case he felt duty-bound to pass the information on.

Ted said: "We assumed the painting we found was the original – the one that had been hanging in St Rita's – and Le Grande had been the person chosen to hide it. Anyway, we sent it to the art and antiques section at Scotland Yard and they had the country's top Raphael expert at the National Gallery look at it. You'll never guess what he's discovered."

"That it's not by a pupil of Raphael but the golden boy himself."

"How did you know?"

"Because someone with Le Grande's experience would have spotted that, even if Kingswell and Burke didn't realise. When you question him again, I expect you'll get him to admit that he made two copies of the original – one was hung in St Rita's and the other was given to Kingswell to sell as the original *Avenging Angel* by a pupil of Raphael. No doubt he planned to keep the real Raphael and disappear abroad and sell it himself, before Kingswell and Burke discovered he'd duped them."

"You might have told me you'd already worked it out."

"I only had suspicions, but what you just told me about the painting being a genuine Raphael confirmed them."

"I guess the other copy must have burnt to a cinder in the wreck of Kingswell's car," Ted said.

"I guess that must be right," I said. I felt a bit of a heel not telling Ted that I knew it hadn't.

So Camilla didn't know as much about Raphael as she thought

she did. She wasn't going to live off the proceeds of a Le Grande forgery until her dotage. I'd like to have been around when she realised that. Perhaps she'd turn up one day, poorer and wiser, and tell her side of the story, but I didn't think it likely. After all, she'd be facing a murder rap.

"There's more," Ted said. "Tomkins has just come out of his office like someone's shoved a lighted Christmas pud up his bum. It seems we've been ordered to release Archie Flowerdew on bail pending his appeal and commutation of sentence."

"That's great – in time for Christmas."

"But not good for Tomkins, according to the whispers. Apparently, the order came direct from the Home Office."

"Henry Brooke himself?" I said. "Seems 'the most hated man in Britain' is trying to redeem his reputation during the season of goodwill."

"Tomkins has also been ordered to drop the charges against Tammy. He's been told it wouldn't be good public relations for the copper who arrested the wrong killer to be prosecuting the woman whose campaign saved him from the noose."

"Any news about Selina Muppen?" I asked.

"She's made a statement about Tupper. She's given us enough to make sure we can put him away for years. I think Archie and Tammy are going to take Selina in until she can sort out her life. I believe there's some talk of her going back to Sweden."

I thought of Archie's sketch of the turtle doves' cracked egg in the crib – and the beginning of Selina's unhappy life. Perhaps Archie would one day be able to draw a thirteenth picture to round off the story on a happier note.

I wished Ted a merry Christmas and replaced the receiver.

But the damned instrument rang again.

I seized the phone and said: "Father Christmas speaking. Don't you realise I'm busy with the elves? Any more interruptions and the kiddies won't get their presents tonight."

Mrs Gribble said: "What's worrying me is that I might get an unwelcome present from that Mr Evans, the butcher. Such as his stuffing."

"I'm sure he's busy trussing his turkeys or whatever butchers do on Christmas Eve."

"Then there's my sister-in-law round at the Norfolk Hotel flirting with the men. Or so Mrs Hardcastle, who manages the dining room round there, tells me. I just feel I want both of them out of my hair over Christmas, so I can settle down with a bottle of cream sherry and listen to the Queen's speech on the radio. I thought you were going to solve this problem for me, but you've just made it worse."

A sex-mad butcher and a flirty sister-in-law. I had an idea.

"Leave this with me," I said. "Break out the sherry and have a merry Christmas, Mrs Gribble."

I replaced the receiver, jiggled the broken cradle to get a new line and asked for telegrams.

I dictated a top-priority telegram to be sent to Gwilym Evans and gave his address:

MEET ME AT NORFOLK HOTEL TONIGHT STOP LOOK FORWARD TO CHRISTMAS STUFFING STOP GRIBBLE

Evans wouldn't know the telegram had come from the Widow's sister-in-law until he reached the hotel. Both would be in for a surprise. Perhaps it would work out.

Why not? On Christmas Eve anything can happen.

A distant church clock was chiming midnight when I finally reached Shirley's flat.

It was Christmas Day.

I'd called Shirley earlier from the office to tell her the good news that I was still on the paper. But I hadn't mentioned that because we were producing a Boxing Day edition, I was rostered to work on Christmas morning. She wasn't going to be pleased. I was puzzling over how I could break the unwelcome news.

I rang the bell.

Shirley opened the door holding a wand with a silver star on the end. She was wearing a circlet of tinsel looped around her hair.

And nothing else.

I said: "It's a good job I'm not the milkman. You'd have blown the cream off his gold top."

I stepped rapidly inside and closed the door behind me.

She said: "When I lost the boomerang I'd bought for your gift, you said you'd be just as happy to make do with your Christmas fairy. So here I am."

"And is the fairy going to grant my wish?"

"Depends what it is. As if I didn't know."

Shirley put her arms around my neck and kissed me gently. I closed my eyes and it felt like all my dreams had come true.

We broke apart. I reached into my pocket and pulled out the framed photo Freddie had given me in the newsroom.

I said: "I only got this tonight, so haven't had time to wrap it. It's not really a proper present, but I thought you'd like it."

Shirley took the frame. Looked at the picture. Her lips curved into a big smile – and then she started to shake with laughter.

The picture showed Kristopher Pickles, the slimy photographer who'd tried to get Shirley to pose nude, wearing a tinsel crown and holding a fairy wand. He was stark bollock naked.

"It's great," she chuckled. "But however did you get him to do that?"

"I had help from Chloe Cuddles, the madam who put me on to Selina. She got one of her girls – Sophia, a genuine Italian beauty from Grimsby – to answer Pickles' ad for models. Sophia called him on the phone and hinted that she'd be more uninhibited if the photo shoot could take place in her flat where she had a comfy double bed. Pickles took the bait and turned up with his gear.

"He used the same Christmas-fairy ploy on Sophia he'd tried on you. But she said she was a bit shy, so could he show her what to do. It took a bit of persuading, but Sophia is the kind of girl who gets men to do her bidding. And within a few minutes she had Pickles in his birthday suit with tinsel in his hair.

"And that's when Freddie burst in. He'd been hiding in the next room. The upshot is that Pickles has been warned that if he continues to exploit young women for his sleazy modelling scam, his own picture will appear in print."

"I love it," Shirley said. "And now we can enjoy Christmas without worrying about innocent men hanging, or hiding naughty nieces, or being raided by the cops."

"Yes. There's a problem, though."

"What's that?"

"We've been so busy, we haven't got a turkey," I said.

Shirley nodded thoughtfully. "That's true. Or a plum pudding."

"Or any crackers."

"Or a Christmas tree."

"We could buy them tomorrow," I said.

"It's Christmas Day. The shops are shut."

"Not all of them," I said. "Sally Martin on the paper made a list of shops staying open. We were going to publish it, but it got bounced out by the Archie coverage."

"So we don't know where they are?" Shirley said.

"I could call into the office tomorrow and pick up the list."

Shirley fixed me with her laser-beam stare. "Colin Crampton, you're up to something."

"Well," I said. "It's like this …"

Read more *Crampton of the Chronicle* stories free at:

www.colincrampton.com

About Peter Bartram

Peter Bartram brings years of experience as a journalist to his *Crampton of the Chronicle* crime mystery series. Peter began his career as a reporter on a local newspaper, before working as journalist and editor in London and, finally, becoming freelance. He has done most things in journalism from doorstepping for quotes to writing serious editorials. He's pursued stories in locations as diverse as seven hundred feet down a coal mine and a courtier's chambers in Buckingham Palace. Peter wrote twenty-one non-fiction books, including five ghostwritten, before turning to crime with the *Crampton of the Chronicle* mysteries.

Follow Peter Bartram on Facebook at:

www.facebook.com/peterbartramauthor

A Message from Peter Bartram

Thank you for reading *Front Page Murder.* I hope you have enjoyed reading it as much as I enjoyed writing it. If you have a few moments to add a short review on your favourite online book website, I would be very grateful. Reviews are important feedback for authors and I truly appreciate every one. If you would like news of further *Crampton of the Chronicle* stories, please visit my website – the address is at the top of this page.

Acknowledgements

This is the third full-length novel in the *Crampton of the Chronicle* series and many people have helped to bring it to publication.

First, there is the great team at Roundfire Books. Special mention must go to publishing manager Dominic James as well as Catherine Harris, Maria Moloney, Mary Flatt, Nick Welch, Stuart Davies, Krystina Kellingley and Maria Barry.

Barney Skinner is the web genius behind the Colin Crampton website at www.colincrampton.com. The brilliant Frank Duffy created the caricatures of Colin Crampton and his colleagues, including the redoubtable Shirley Goldsmith, on the website, in the books and on my Facebook page.

I must thank the members of the Crampton of the Chronicle Advanced Team in the United Kingdom, United States and Canada, who read the draft manuscript of the book, made many proofing corrections and provided helpful comments. So thanks to (in alphabetical order) Nancy Ashby, Jaquie Fallon, Andrew Grand, Jenny Jones, Doc Kelley, Andy Mayes, Amanda Perrott, Mark Rewhorn, Christopher Roden and Gregg Wynia. Thanks to other members of the Advanced Group – Susie Alexander-Devers, Amy Bates, Lee Carson, Sue Gascoyne and Chris Youett – for their help and encouragement in the project. It goes without saying that any errors or failings in the book are mine and mine alone.

A very special thank you and congratulations to Chava Hoffman, who won the competition in my monthly newsletter to be a character in *Front Page Murder*. I hope she's enjoyed being a reporter in the *Evening Chronicle*'s newsroom!

Then there are the book bloggers in the United Kingdom and the United States, who have featured Crampton on their blogs. (Just Google 'Crampton of the Chronicle' and your search results will light up with their contributions.) Their help in spreading the word is invaluable for a crime series and I greatly appreciate it.

Finally, and most important of all, as with all my books, my family has been a constant source of love and encouragement during the long hours it takes to write a book.

Earlier books in the *Crampton of the Chronicle* series ...

Headline Murder

A *Crampton of the Chronicle* mystery

AUGUST 1962 and Colin Crampton, the Brighton *Evening Chronicle*'s crime reporter, is suffering the curse of the 'silly season' - no hard news.

HIS ONLY TIP-OFF: the disappearance of the seafront's crazy-golf proprietor, Arnold Trumper. Colin thinks the story is about as useful as a set of concrete water wings.

UNSOLVED MURDER: when Colin learns Trumper's vanishing act is linked to one, he immediately senses a scoop.

POWERFUL PEOPLE are determined Colin should not discover the truth. So he must use every newspaper scam in the book to land his exclusive.

THERE'S TROUBLE when Colin's Aussie girlfriend, feisty Shirley Goldsmith, ends up on the sticky end when the scams backfire.

COLIN OVERCOMES DANGERS they never mentioned at journalism school before he writes his story. *Headline Murder* is a racy romp through seedy Brighton, where there's a bad guy around every corner.

Available in paperback and ebook format.

Stop Press Murder
A *Crampton of the Chronicle* mystery

FIRST, the saucy film of a nude woman bathing is stolen from a What the Butler Saw machine on Brighton's Palace Pier.

NEXT, the pier's nightwatchman is murdered – his body found in the coconut shy.

COLIN CRAMPTON, ace reporter on the *Evening Chronicle,* senses a scoop when he's the only journalist to discover a link between the two crimes.

HE UNCOVERS a 50-year feud between twin sisters – one a screen siren from the days of silent movies, the other the haughty wife of an aristocrat.

BUT COLIN'S investigation spirals out of control – as he *risks his life* to land the biggest story of his career.

STOP PRESS MURDER, a Swinging Sixties mystery, has more twists and turns than a country lane. It will keep you guessing – and laughing – right to the last page.

Available in paperback and ebook format.

Roundfire

FICTION

Put simply, we publish great stories. Whether it's literary or popular, a gentle tale or a pulsating thriller, the connecting theme in all Roundfire fiction titles is that once you pick them up you won't want to put them down.
If you have enjoyed this book, why not tell other readers by posting a review on your preferred book site. Recent bestsellers from Roundfire are:

The Bookseller's Sonnets
Andi Rosenthal

The Bookseller's Sonnets intertwines three love stories with a tale of religious identity and mystery spanning five hundred years and three countries.
Paperback: 978-1-84694-342-3 ebook: 978-184694-626-4

Birds of the Nile
An Egyptian Adventure
N.E. David

Ex-diplomat Michael Blake wanted a quiet birding trip up the Nile – he wasn't expecting a revolution.
Paperback: 978-1-78279-158-4 ebook: 978-1-78279-157-7

Blood Profit$

The Lithium Conspiracy

J. Victor Tomaszek, James N. Patrick, Sr.

The blood of the many for the profits of the few... *Blood Profit$* will take you into the cigar-smoke-filled room where American policy and laws are really made.

Paperback: 978-1-78279-483-7 ebook: 978-1-78279-277-2

The Burden

A Family Saga

N.E. David

Frank will do anything to keep his mother and father apart. But he's carrying baggage – and it might just weigh him down ...

Paperback: 978-1-78279-936-8 ebook: 978-1-78279-937-5

The Cause

Roderick Vincent

The second American Revolution will be a fire lit from an internal spark.

Paperback: 978-1-78279-763-0 ebook: 978-1-78279-762-3

Don't Drink and Fly

The Story of Bernice O'Hanlon: Part One

Cathie Devitt

Bernice is a witch living in Glasgow. She loses her way in her life and wanders off the beaten track looking for the garden of enlightenment.

Paperback: 978-1-78279-016-7 ebook: 978-1-78279-015-0

Gag
Melissa Unger

One rainy afternoon in a Brooklyn diner, Peter Howland punctures an egg with his fork. Repulsed, Peter pushes the plate away and never eats again.
Paperback: 978-1-78279-564-3 ebook: 978-1-78279-563-6

The Master Yeshua
The Undiscovered Gospel of Joseph
Joyce Luck

Jesus is not who you think he is. The year is 75 CE. Joseph ben Jude is frail and ailing, but he has a prophecy to fulfil …
Paperback: 978-1-78279-974-0 ebook: 978-1-78279-975-7

Readers of ebooks can buy or view any of these bestsellers by clicking on the live link in the title. Most titles are published in paperback and as an ebook. Paperbacks are available in traditional bookshops. Both print and ebook formats are available online.

Find more titles and sign up to our readers' newsletter at http://www.johnhuntpublishing.com/fiction

Follow us on Facebook at https://www.facebook.com/JHPfiction
and Twitter at https://twitter.com/JHPFiction